ABOUT THE AUTHOR

Denise Deegan lives in Dublin with her family where she regularly dreams of sunshine, a life without cooking and her novels being made into movies. She has a Masters in Public Relations and has been a college lecturer, nurse, china restorer, pharmaceutical sales rep, public relations executive and entrepreneur. Denise's books have been published by Penguin, Random House, Hachette and Lake Union Publishing. Denise writes contemporary family dramas under the pen name Aimee Alexander. They have become international best-sellers on Kindle.

through the barricades

DENISE DEEGAN

ISBN-10: 1540695662
ISBN-13: 978-1540695666

Through the Barricades

To my very great friend, Maruja Bogaard,
with love, laughter and lilies

Prologue

1906

Maggie woke coughing. It was dark but there was something other than darkness in the air, something that climbed into her mouth, scratched at her throat and stole her breath. It made her eyes sting and tear. And it made her heart stall. Flames burst through the doorway like dragon breath. Maggie tried to scream but more coughs came, one after the other, after the other. She backed up in the bed, eyes wide, as the blaze began to engulf the room. She thought of her family, asleep in their beds. She had to waken them – with something other than her voice.

She hurried from her bed, peering through flame-lit smoke in search of her jug and washbasin. Reaching them, she flung water in the direction of the fire and began to slam enamel against enamel, fast and loud. She had to back away as flames lapped and roared and licked at her. But she kept on slamming.

Her arms grew tired. Her breath began to fail her. And she felt the heavy pull of sleep. She might have given in had she been alone in the house. But there was her father. There was her mother. There was Tom. And there was David. She could not give up.

Then like a miracle of black shadow, her father burst through the flames, his head tossing and turning. His frenzied gaze met hers.

'Maggie!'

She began to cry with relief but relief changed to guilt as she realised that she had only drawn him further into the fire.

'No! You were meant to take the stairs. You were meant to-'

'It's all right, Maggie Mae. It's all right,' he said, hurrying to her. He scooped her up and held her tight as he carried her away from a heat that burned without touching.

She felt cool air on her back as he opened the window. Wind rushed in, blowing the drapes aside. The flames roared louder, rose higher. But her father only looked out at the night sky. And down.

'Missus O'Neill! I'm dropping Maggie down to you!' he called. 'Catch her now, mind. Catch my little girl.' Then he looked deep into Maggie's eyes. 'Missus O'Neill is down below with her arms out for you. I'm going to drop you down to her.'

'Will she catch you too?'

But he just smiled and kissed her forehead. 'Make a difference in the world, Maggie.'

The sadness in his eyes filled her with a new terror. 'But you're coming too?'

He smiled once more. 'I am, as soon as I get the others out. Now keep your eyes on mine, Maggie Mae. Keep your eyes on mine all the way down.'

part one

one

Daniel
October 1913

Daniel's back stung from the rake of a rugby boot. What bothered him, though, as he cycled home, was how he had played. If he did not improve, he would lose his position on the team.

'It's too peaceful out here by far,' said his friend, Michael, beside him. 'You'd hardly know there was rioting in the city.'

'Will we cycle in and have a look?'

'I value my life too much,' Michael said.

'Is it that bad?'

'I was referring to my father. He'd kill me if he found me anywhere near the trouble. He was clocked on the head with a rock last night while trying to control the mob.'

'Is he all right?'

'Ah. It'd take more than a rock to bring him down.'

Daniel knew little about these riots – apart from the fact that strikers had started them. 'Why-' he began but was cut off by Michael, calling out.

'Behold! A damsel in distress!'

On the pavement, a girl was pushing her bicycle towards the city, bent forward as if in battle with life. Her front tyre was flat.

Daniel smiled at Michael's transformation into a gallant

knight. If he'd had a cape he'd have thrown it over a puddle – had there been a puddle. Instead, he flung his leg over his saddle and glided on one pedal to a halt beside her. Daniel had a feeling this would not end well.

'I'm not in distress; I simply need a bicycle pump,' the girl said. Wisps of black hair escaped her hat. Green eyes flashed impatience. She'd stopped but wouldn't remain so for long.

Michael turned to him. 'Daniel, a pump?' Three words demoted him to able assistant.

'A pump may not do it,' Daniel said, promoting himself to bicycle expert. 'How fast did the air go out?' he asked the girl while fetching the pump from his schoolbag.

She put out her hand for it.

'I'm already dirty,' he said, holding on to it.

'I'm not afraid of dirt.'

He felt suddenly that there was nothing this girl *was* afraid of. 'Still. I could do with the exercise.'

Michael rolled his eyes.

The girl raised a cynical eyebrow.

Daniel ignored them both, taking the bicycle, propping it up against a lamppost and attaching the tube.

'Allow me to introduce myself,' Michael said to the girl with a flamboyant wave of his arm.

'Must I?' she asked.

Daniel smiled as he began to pump.

But Michael seemed encouraged. 'So, where are you off to, anyway, in such a hurry?'

'I have business to attend to in the city.' She looked at Daniel impatiently.

'*Business,* no less.' Michael sounded amused. 'Why don't you take the tram? Here's one now.'

It was rounding a corner, flanked by six large policemen, all dressed in black, glancing around as if looking for trouble, encouraging it, almost.

'I'm boycotting the trams in sympathy with Dublin's strikers,' she declared with sudden passion.

Daniel looked up.

'You're on the side of the *strikers*?' Michael exclaimed as if he'd been prodded in the eye by a hot poker.

'Why does that surprise you – because I attend a posh school like yours?' She eyed his uniform with disdain.

'*Because* they're turning the city upside down!' he insisted.

'I'm sorry that, in demanding fairness, they are *inconveniencing* you.' She sounded the opposite.

'My father is with the police, so yes, it *is* an inconvenience, knowing that he has to face rioting thugs on a daily basis.'

'It's the police who are the thugs!'

Michael's voice rose. 'They are upholding law and order. The strikers are a mob of hooligans, too lazy to work.'

'*Lazy?* They've been *locked out* by their employers!'

'As they deserve to be, following that rabble-rouser, James Larkin, like clueless sheep.'

She moved like some kind of beautiful lightning, rising up into the air, her fist connecting with Michael's chin, knocking him off balance and onto the ground. Her hat fell back.

She was a vision.

He was Daniel's best friend.

'I'm fine,' Michael barked when Daniel went to help him up.

Daniel turned. Already, she was releasing the pump. She slammed it into his palm and mounted her bicycle. She took off like an angry wind.

'Lunatic!' Michael called after her, dusting himself off.

Daniel watched her disappear. It was like witnessing a flame go out. He had never met anyone more alive. She was fire and rage and passion and earnestness. No one he knew paid any attention to the strikers bar Michael whose father was involved. No one cared. And then this fireball arrives, taking their side, discarding gentility in favour of passion – passion for strangers and politics and *fairness*. She left him breathless.

He and Michael mounted their bicycles and resumed their journey in silence. But Daniel's mind was full of her.

'She'd a great face, though, all the same, hadn't she?' Michael said.

Daniel smiled. In fairness to his friend, he always bounced back.

'I wouldn't mind seeing that black hair of hers falling down over her shoulders,' he continued.

'Give over,' Daniel said, though he knew that she would neither want nor need him to jump to her defence. 'Who is this James Larkin chap anyway?' he asked casually. Now, more than ever, he wanted an education on the strikers.

'Ah God, Danny. You *must* know-'

'Just tell me.'

'James Larkin brought unions to Dublin. Without him workers would never have thought to band together and strike for better conditions.'

'Perhaps they need better conditions,' Daniel suggested, unable to clear his mind of her.

Michael gave him a withering look. 'Tosh.'

Daniel said nothing.

'The strikes have brought nothing but the Lockout,' Michael continued.

'Does it not seem a little harsh, though, locking them out of work? How can they earn a living?'

'Whose side are you on – some pretty, violent girl?'

Maybe, Daniel thought.

'Look, the employers only did what the strikers did, banded together. They took no nonsense. You have to be tough. It's the only thing these people understand.'

Daniel detected a direct quote from Michael's father. 'So what will happen to the strikers?' he asked.

'Oh they'll go back to work eventually,' Michael said with certainty. 'What choice do they have?'

Later, Daniel sat conjugating verbs at the drawing room table – or at least he should have been. He was looking at his father ensconced in his wing-backed chair by the fire, reading *The Irish Times* and puffing on his pipe. Normally, both these activities soothed Daniel. Not this evening.

'Have any lawyers gone out on strike, Father?'

He lowered his newspaper and laughed. 'The very idea! Strikes are a tool of the working classes, Daniel. Nothing whatsoever to do with us.' He returned to the newspaper.

'What are their conditions like, Father, the working classes?'

Down came *The Irish Times,* once more. His father frowned. 'Have you finished your studies, Daniel?'

'Yes, Father.'

Mister Healy folded his paper. He puffed on his pipe as if trying to decide where best to start.

'Their conditions are no more or no less than they deserve. What you must understand is that we are a nation of uneducated. We lack a skilled workforce. And what we lack in skills, we make up for in drink. Mark my words. There is nothing like alcohol to take the drive from a man.'

'Why do the workers not become skilled, Father?'

Mister Healy pointed his pipe at his son. 'Now, *there*, is a question. Why, indeed?' He seemed delighted with himself.

There had to be more to it than that, Daniel thought. The girl had spoken – so passionately – of unfairness. What did she know that Daniel's father did not? Was her own father a striker? Daniel doubted it, though, given that her uniform was from one of the most expensive secondary schools in the country. What was her motivation, then, this – pretty, violent – girl he couldn't get out of his head? And what was his own? For it was more than curiosity that had him dreaming that, one day, he would walk with her to the end of the pier at Kingstown, take her in his arms and kiss her.

two

Maggie
The Following Day

It was the worst day of the year. Maggie's father's anniversary never got easier. Her mother cooked his favourite meal, bacon and cabbage. And they sat down to dinner.

'Bless us oh Lord and these, thy gifts, which of thy bounty we are about to receive through Christ our Lord, Amen,' her mother prayed.

Maggie and her brothers, Tom and David, joined in on the 'Amen.'

'We'll take a moment of silence to remember Father, each of us in our own way.'

Maggie, fearing that there would not be time to say to her father all that she needed to, began in a rush inside her head. 'Father, I know what you asked and I'm doing all I can to make a difference but I'm only me. None of the girls at school care. They just think me odd. They don't believe me that people are starving. They just think the strikes a nuisance. I know I shouldn't have punched that boy but sometimes I get so *frustrated*. If it's any comfort, I crucified my hand....'

A throat cleared.

'Tom!' their mother admonished.

Maggie opened her eyes.

They were waiting for her.

'I'm sorry.'

'It's all right, love,' her mother said.

'It isn't as if we're hungry.' Tom loved his sarcasm.

'Leave her be,' David said to his older brother.

Maggie lifted her knife and fork so that they could start. Then, she simply moved the food around on her plate. How could she eat his favourite meal without him? How could she eat at all when on this day seven years ago, she had jumped and left him behind. It was so silent without him. More than that, it was as if there was a hole where he should have been, a hole she wanted nothing else to fill. She knew that the others felt the same no matter how hungry they pretended to be. Their silence was proof of it.

She looked at her little family. Her mother, though delicate in appearance, was the rock that had kept them going, moving forward when it seemed that their world had stopped. She had returned to teaching, managed a home without servants and still found time to help others. But it was her love of her children, her understanding of each of their needs that Maggie appreciated most. She was the one who quelled Tom's rage, who answered all their 'whys', who hid her own grief – for them.

Beside her, Tom, at eighteen, resembled a man. As restless as a wind, he longed to be out bringing in a wage and righting every injustice in the world. If Tom had been an emotion it would have been rage. David, on the other hand, would have been love. He was the type of person that would make a flower grow just because the flower wanted to please him. He was like the sun, warming everyone with his gaze. He helped their mother most, and studied hardest, wanting to do what their father had asked – to get a good education.

Maggie wished that she was more like David but knew herself to be more like Tom. She too wanted a good education and worked hard for it but it was her need to right the injustices she saw *everywhere* that drove her. She *would* make a difference. Most days it felt possible. Today, she just felt tired. She wanted the hole gone, just for this one meal, to have him at the table, raging about Ireland's history then softening into a story about boys becoming swans. He was a lot to miss.

Tom dropped his cutlery onto his plate with a clatter and turned to his mother. 'You should have let me go in after him! *Why did you hold me back? Why?*'

'You were eleven years old!'

'I'd have saved him!'

'Or died trying! I couldn't let you do that! It's the very last thing he would have wanted!'

'Then why didn't *you* go in?' he demanded accusingly.

'Stop!' David shouted. 'Stop it!'

But their mother faced Tom. 'Because I was willing him to walk through that door any minute and I had to keep you all safe until he did.' She bowed her head. 'But he didn't walk through.' She rose quickly and hurried from the room.

David, quiet placid David, slammed his palm on the table. 'Why did you do that? Can't you see that she misses him as much as us, feels as much guilt as the rest of us? For Christ sake Tom, we've all lost him.'

Maggie hated that she was crying. Weak people changed nothing.

Tom stood. 'All right! All right! Jesus. I'll apologise.'

Then he, too, was gone.

'It's all right, Maggie Mae,' David said.

She nodded – for him. She tried to stop crying – for him. But how could it be all right with a great big hole sitting beside them, with their mother upset and their brother a ball of rage? And how could it be all right when she couldn't make a difference, not really?

'Remember the time you started school and you thought that there was only one school and we'd all be together?' David asked her.

She nodded, aware that he was trying to distract her but liking the memory all the same.

'And remember how you refused to go back the next day because you missed Da's stories?'

She smiled. 'No one told stories like him.'

'No.'

She remembered that day like it was yesterday, how her father told her that it was the law to go to school and that the police would come for him if she didn't go.

'One day, Maggie, you'll understand that education will save this country,' he'd said.

'From what?'

He'd ruffled her hair. 'From bad stories.'

She'd sighed, long and deep, wholly unsatisfied.

'In the meantime, what would you say to a story?' he'd asked.

She'd folded her arms in silent rebellion.

'I'm thinking *The Salmon of Knowledge*?'

It had always been her favourite. And he knew it. She'd sighed again. 'You may as well go ahead so if I *have* to go to school anyway.'

He'd winked at her and smiled. 'That's my girl.'

'I'm going to check on Mam,' she said now.

David nodded. 'I'll clear up.'

'I'll help in a minute.'

'I'd like to have a go at it alone.'

She knew that he was lying and hugged him for it. He was smaller than Tom but still towered over her. At fifteen, she thought she'd have been taller by now.

'Tom's just upset,' David said.

'Still.' Not for the first time, Maggie wondered how different they all might have been had their father lived. Then she shook the useless thought away and went in search of her mother.

She knocked on the door to her bedroom, quietly so that she wouldn't have to answer if she didn't wish to.

'Come in, Maggie.' She always – magically – knew which of them it was.

Maggie found her sitting on the edge of the bed, eyes and nose red.

'Are you all right?' she asked.

'I am, pet. Are you?'

She sighed deeply. 'I miss him,' she whispered. It was good to say it aloud. She rarely did for fear of upsetting everyone.

'Me too.' Her mother smiled and patted the bed. 'Come sit with me.'

Maggie went to her gladly.

'Tom feels things intensely,' she explained as she put an arm around Maggie.

'I know.'

'He didn't mean to upset me.'

Maggie looked at her. 'Did he say sorry?'

'He did.'

Maggie sighed deep and long. Then she eyed her mother earnestly. 'You did the right thing, Mam. You did what Da would have wanted you to do. You must see that.'

'I do, Maggie. I do.' But her eyes welled.

Maggie leaned in to her and squeezed her tight.

Next day, Maggie, Tom and David cycled to school together as always, though Tom, looking like a man in a child's uniform, cycled ahead. Maggie doubted that he even noticed he had left them behind. Like their father had, he raged but unlike him he never softened. Maggie kept pace with David, allowing herself to see the world as he did, to notice the cloud formations, the birds, the butterflies.

Too soon, they were approaching Maggie's school.

David looked across at her. 'Tell me, sis,' he said softly. 'Have you made any friends in that school yet?'

She smiled brightly. 'Why would I need friends when I have you?'

He frowned.

'Anyway, I'm too busy for friends.' She would have to learn to lie to him. He was far too innocent for the world. She'd never have friends in that school now. It was too late for that. They thought her entirely queer. It wasn't simply that she had arrived there by scholarship and had none of their luxuries. She had none of their interests. She did not wish to sit quietly and listen while someone tinkled on a piano. She did not wish to tinkle. She did not wish to excel at needlepoint, plan social events or arrange flowers. How could she care, as they did, about turning herself into a fine marital prospect when there was so much to *do*? She knew that she was too intense, worked too hard, cared too much for things they did not understand, did not *wish* to. It had been a mistake to ever think that they might. She had only ostracized herself further. Not that she ultimately cared what they thought. They were idiots.

Reaching the school gates, though, her stomach clenched. She smiled widely at David and waved. Even Tom remembered to turn around.

'Stay out of trouble,' he said.

She rolled her eyes.

David smiled.

Maggie took a deep breath and turned into the school.

Locking her bicycle in the shed, Maggie heard giggling behind her. Instinct told her whom it was and she did not turn.

'How's the tyre pressure, Maggie?' Polly asked.

There was an explosion of laughter.

Maggie finished locking her bicycle, breathed deeply and straightened. Then she turned to face Polly and her gang of three. They were the prettiest and, at the same time, ugliest girls that Maggie had ever met. And now they were proving her right; it *was* they who had let the air from her tyre.

'My tyre pressure is grand altogether, Polly, ever since two handsome boys came to my rescue.' Maggie smiled brightly. 'Perhaps you should let the air out of your own tyre and see if it brings you the husband you so desperately seek.' She grimaced. 'Of course, he'd have to have a terrible sense of smell to spend any time in your company.' Then, holding her nose, Maggie walked straight through her tormentors, forcing them apart.

three

Daniel

Michael and Daniel looked out at the thunderstorm. Rugby had been cancelled. Michael would have missed it anyway having received detention for his latest prank.

'Wait till it's over,' he said, 'and we can cycle home together.'

But Daniel felt restless. 'I feel like adventure,' he said, mildly baffling himself.

Michael laughed. 'Well, if getting drenched is the adventure you're after, then off you go.'

Daniel picked up his schoolbag, the edginess like an itch now.

Five minutes later, he was soaked to the skin and shivering. Thunder growled and lightening illuminated a charcoal sky. And yet he did not go home.

He came to a halt outside her school, no idea why he was there.

The bell sounded signaling the end of the day.

But no one emerged.

At last, the door opened and a girl burst out, head down, alone and running. There was no mistaking her. It was the determination with which she moved. He found himself smiling.

She disappeared into a bicycle shed. The school door opened again and a few girls emerged tentatively under great black umbrellas. Motorcars began to arrive and collect their precious cargo.

Then she shot from the shed on her bicycle. Out through the gates she darted, passing him without seeing him, heading for the city. Whatever her 'business' there, it would not be put off by a thunderstorm. So curious was he that he considered following her. It seemed extreme. But then it *was* adventure. And he couldn't get any wetter than he already was. She made him feel as if he had been asleep. And he wanted more than anything to awaken.

So up he got onto his saddle and turned his bicycle around.

She was fast, hunched over and flying.

He felt like laughing. This was madness. And she'd *kill* him if she discovered him. He hoped that if he stayed far enough back, the downpour would shield him from view. He doubted, though, that she would look back, so intent was she on going forward.

He noticed very little around him, peering through the rain to keep her in sight. Such was his focus on her that they reached the quays before he realised that they were even in the city.

She came to a halt outside a building. He stopped immediately and waited. Only then did he notice the queue on the pavement. Women and children in dark, worn clothes stood in line in the rain, carrying mugs, bowls, tins, kettles, jam jars. She hurried past them and down into the basement of the building.

'What are *you* gawking at?'

Daniel turned to see that a shawled woman was addressing him, her chin jutting out aggressively.

'Come to see how the other half lives, have ya?' she demanded.

So appalled was he by her accusation that he struggled to find words.

Others glared at him, now, as if *he* were the aggressor.

'This is what the likes of you have reduced us to – handouts,' another woman said. 'Our men wanted fairness. You have given them hunger.'

'I'm sorry,' he mumbled, mortified. By his very presence, he had become a symbol of his class. He mounted his bicycle and began the journey home. Now he understood her passion. Now he understood her intensity. Now he understood why she had punched his friend. These people were starving.

That evening, Daniel read to his brother, Niall, bedtime stories about swallows and princes. Then he sat by the fire with a book, waiting for his parents to return from the theatre. He could not concentrate on the pages open in front of him. All he could think of were the chances of his plan working.

At last, they were home. They were, as he had hoped, in good spirits, his mother all agog about the play.

He got up from the chair and waited for them to settle. Then he made his move.

'Father,' he said, cheerfully. 'I have a suggestion.'

Mister Healy turned to him in surprise. Suggestions were new.

'Let us attend an earlier Mass this Sunday so that you can take us all for a spin in your new motorcar before luncheon.'

His father raised his eyebrows. 'Hmm. Not a bad idea.'

'The servants,' Daniel's mother said in a concerned voice. 'They have their routine.'

'It would only mean moving breakfast forward one hour,' Daniel said hopefully.

She looked at her husband.

'The boy's right,' he said. 'I run my house, not the servants. They can rise early this once. Let us go for a proper jaunt, out to Kingstown where we can take in the sea air.'

Daniel's mother frowned. 'Are you certain the motor will take us that far?'

'Don't encourage me or I'll have us all down in Wexford!' He laughed at his wife's appalled face then turned to his son. 'Excellent idea, Daniel! You are becoming a thinking man, it seems.'

He had, it was true, been doing a lot of thinking on this.

Sunday seemed to take an age to arrive. But arrive it did, and with it second thoughts. Why did he think that she would be at this Mass simply because her school was nearby and she was forever in a hurry? Even if she was there, how had he ever imagined that he could approach her?

His mother fussed over her choice of hat, making them – frustratingly – late.

Entering the church at last, they found a pew close to the back.

Daniel's eyes immediately set about looking for her.

To and fro the prayers went, the priest's solitary voice, the congregation responding in solemn Latin as Daniel switched from haphazard checking to methodically going from head to head.

He had done an entire half of the church when his system was thrown into chaos as people began to leave their seats and file up the aisle to the altar to receive Holy Communion. He gave up, partly in relief, mostly in disappointment.

There was something about the line. It reminded him of the food kitchen. There was one important difference. Here in the church everyone was equal. Rich and poor queued together for the Body of Christ.

Suddenly, he was jolted into a state of panic. There she was, returning from the altar. Walking slowly, she had her eyes cast down and hands joined in prayer. She was smaller than he remembered – like a miniature saint. How had she managed to knock Michael over? Perhaps it was all the passion she had packed into that punch. Watching her retake her seat, his heart began to pound for he knew suddenly that, whatever happened, he *was* going to speak to her.

He waited for the priest to utter his final blessing, then he took off, hurrying out of the church. He had no idea what he would say to her. All he knew was, he had to say it today. Another week and it would appear strange to approach her.

Standing in the sun, he watched the congregation spill out, faces smiling, duty done. She appeared, then, with her family – a mother and two brothers. Reaching the bottom step, her mother became engaged in conversation with another woman. Her brothers found friends. She was alone. Now was his moment. Why couldn't he move? He watched her drum gloved fingers against her frock coat then begin to untie her hat as though eager to be rid of it.

Then his legs were moving, carrying him to her.

'Good day!' he said, as though surprised to find himself beside her. He was, indeed, surprised, given the state of his nerves. 'That was quite the punch,' he said in desperation.

Her eyes narrowed. 'Are you saying that girls shouldn't fight? Is that it?'

'No. That's not it at all.'

She folded her arms. 'This may come as a surprise to you but girls are capable of more than people give us credit for.'

'I don't doubt it.'

She squinted at him. 'What do you want anyway?'

'Want? Nothing! I found myself beside you–'

'In that case–' She started to walk away.

'Wait! No! I do want something! I want to know about the strikers.'

'The strikers?'

'Do you think that they'll get what they want – ultimately?'

She looked at him as if he were an unusual stain – curious but ultimately disappointing. 'What do *you* care? The Lockout to people like you is a mere inconvenience. You care *nothing* for the workers.'

'People like me? Am I not like you? You attend a school like mine.'

'On scholarship.' She looked him up and down slowly. 'I imagine your father is... a lawyer.'

How did she know?

'You have a telephone.'

His father's pride and joy.

'A motorcar.'

Why did he feel guilty?

She squinted at him. 'How many servants do you have?'

'What does it matter?' he asked, defensively.

She sighed wearily and began to leave.

'How many do *you* have?' he countered.

She turned and raised her chin. 'Not a single one,' she said as though it was a matter of pride.

She was the first person he had ever met without servants. More importantly, he had no idea what they were arguing about.

'You know nothing of the life of the strikers.'

Ah. There it was. 'And you *do*?' he challenged.

'I know that their children starve. I know that they attend a food kitchen to stay alive. I know that it's not enough. I know that two tenement buildings collapsed, killing seven people. I know that more babies die in Dublin than any other city in Europe. I know that the police killed two men in the riots, cracked their heads open like eggs. I know what hunger looks like, and shame. I've seen people faint from weakness as they queue for food....'

'You volunteer at a food kitchen?' Of course she did. It made absolute sense now.

'I do. And if you cared, you would too.'

'Then I will.'

'You'll last a day.'

'How sure you are of me.'

'People, I find, are predictable,' she said as if she meant predictably disappointing.

'When are we going?'

'Well, I'*m* going tomorrow, after school.'

He hesitated. He never missed rugby. And yet.... 'I'll meet you outside your school.'

She shrugged as though expecting him to be as predictably disappointing as everyone else.

He stuck out his hand. 'Daniel Healy.'

She hesitated, taken aback. Then shook his hand quickly, neglecting to offer her own name in return.

He had never met anyone so dismissive, argumentative, so downright infuriating. Neither had he met anyone so intriguing.

'Maggie! Let's go.' The brothers were back.

Maggie. All his wondering was over. It was as if Daniel had been given a gift.

The bigger of the two brothers gave him a look that said, 'Stay away from my sister.' Daniel had no doubt that punching ran in the family.

And then she was gone, linking arms with the younger brother.

So perhaps there is one person in the world she tolerates, Daniel thought.

His own brother, Niall, hurried up to him. At eight, he looked two years younger.

'Where did you go to?' he asked Daniel.

'To get some air.'

'Why didn't you wait for us? The Mass was over.'

Daniel smiled. 'I knew you'd find me.'

Niall stood beside Daniel, hands in his pockets like a little man. An easy silence fell between them as they waited for their parents.

'Why can't Mass be-' Niall stopped mid-sentence.

Daniel looked at him.

He'd dropped his gaze to the ground. His shoulders drooped.

Daniel looked to see what had caused his distress. It was a boy, bigger and bulkier than Niall, who did not appear to have noticed him at all.

'Who's that?' Daniel asked.

Niall looked up cautiously. 'A new boy in my school,' he mumbled.

'Is he giving you a hard time?'

Niall's eyes welled with sudden tears. 'No one's minded my leg before.'

Infantile paralysis, at the age of six, had left Niall's right leg shorter than the left and he wore a shoe with an elevated sole to correct the imbalance. The disability was so familiar to family and friends that they had stopped noticing it.

Daniel tried to contain his anger. 'What's his name?'

'Jimmy Lyons.'

Daniel turned to his brother, put both hands on his shoulders and looked him in the eye. 'You stand tall and know who you are, Niall Healy.'

Niall looked confused.

'Does anyone else worry about your leg?'

'No.'

'That's because there's so much more to you than your leg. You are clever and kind and funny.'

Niall did not look convinced.

'How many friends do you have?'

Niall counted in his head. 'Six?'

'Well, that's six more than Jimmy Lyons. I can tell you that. You stand together all six of you. Understand?'

Niall nodded.

Daniel raised his eyebrows. 'I bet *Jimmy Lyons* doesn't have a motorcar.'

Niall smiled.

'Let's go sit in Father's,' Daniel added. 'And you can have a go at the wheel.'

Niall took off. And as Daniel followed, he recalled 'Maggie's' curt dismissal of the motorcar. She was simply wrong. It remained, in his mind, the greatest invention of their time. No horse to ready or tire, no man needed to guide the horse, greater distances to be covered in less time.... The motorcar would change the world. Of that he was certain.

Niall climbed up behind the wheel, Jimmy Lyons forgotten. Daniel winked at him. Fighting was rarely the answer. Daniel tried to avoid it whenever possible.

'Who was that girl you were talking to?' Daniel's father asked, glancing at him in the rear view mirror.

Niall looked at Daniel curiously.

'Just someone I helped with a flat tyre,' Daniel replied for he knew what was coming.

'Don't go getting distracted now.'

They were the exact words Daniel had predicted. To his father, girls were a danger to be avoided at all cost. Daniel did not point out the flaw in his argument. As a happily married man, he had clearly let himself get distracted somewhere along the line and the world had not ended.

four

Daniel

'I'm going to crucify you on the pitch today,' Michael said as he threw his games bag over his shoulder.

'That'll be hard given that I won't be on the pitch.'

'You're not *playing*?' he asked as if he meant 'breathing'.

Daniel had been debating all day whether or not to tell his friend. He did not want the strikers to come between them. And yet he could not lie. 'I'm going to meet that girl.'

Michael looked baffled. 'What girl?'

'The one that punched you.'

Michael squinted. 'You're going to meet her?'

Daniel attempted a casual shrug. 'I bumped into her after Mass, yesterday. She helps at a food kitchen. I said I'd go along and roll up my sleeves.'

'You met her yesterday and you're going to a food kitchen with her today? Are you telling me a girl like that just *invited* you along?'

'Well, it was more of a dare than an invitation. She is convinced that I will not show up.'

Michael laughed. 'Ah, that's more like it. But you are *going*?'

'The people are in dire need.'

Michael raised an eyebrow. 'So the black hair and green eyes have nothing to do with it?'

'In all honesty, I find her infuriating. And rude.'

Michael laughed again. 'You have it bad, Healy. Hopefully, she'll punch some sense into you.'

Daniel smiled, relieved that Michael had not made the connection between the food kitchen and striking workers. 'I'll see you tomorrow so.'

'Not if I see you first.'

Daniel laughed and punched him affectionately on the shoulder. 'Never change, Hegarty.'

She shot through the school gates as if her bicycle was a chariot. She looked neither left nor right and flew straight past him.

'Hello,' he called and raised an arm.

'Oh!' She braked in surprise, looked back and waited for him. 'You're coming after all.'

'I was always coming.'

'Keep up,' she said and took off again.

He knew not to make small talk. So he admired the view – a pair of swans wagging their tails on the canal, street vendors selling flowers on St Stephen's Green, a man wearing a sandwich-board advertising soap on Grafton Street. Late September and the trees were turning. He filled his lungs with air.

Reaching the quays, it was as if a grey cloud had blown over the city. Women and children in dark, worn clothes converged in grim silence from all directions, carrying anything at all that would hold food. Outside the building stood another weary queue. Heads bowed, women and children shuffled slowly forward. The ground shone from a recent downpour. Steam rose from damp shawls stretched tight across bony shoulders. Daniel had not known that you could see hunger. You could, he realised now, in the eyes of children.

He followed Maggie down to the basement. The air was laden with steam and the mingled smells of food and grime. Coughs, sniffles and occasional weeping were like the saddest music. Daniel passed a boy that so resembled Niall that he stopped and stared. Catching Daniel's eye, the boy shot out an upturned hand. Daniel fished in his pockets and gave him what he had. A woman snatched the coins from the boy, then dragged him away looking at Daniel as if to say, 'Judge me when you've nothing'. Horrified, Daniel turned and followed Maggie who had all but lost him.

He caught up with her as she neared a gathering of volunteers, most of them women. Their work, he noticed, was divided. Some collected tickets from those in the queue and went to fetch rations. Others stood at boilers, cooking. More peeled vegetables and chopped meat. The only man amongst them moved from boiler to boiler stoking the fires beneath. A lady in an enormous feathered hat snapped a cigarette from her mouth to deliver instructions.

'Who's that?' he asked Maggie. He had never seen a woman smoke.

He was rewarded with a rare smile. 'That is the Countess Markievicz.'

'A *countess*?'

'A countess that does not care for titles.' Maggie gestured to a group of girls sitting on stools around a heap of vegetables. 'How good are you at peeling potatoes?'

He had never peeled a potato in his life. 'Excellent!'

She raised an eyebrow. It was a stunning eyebrow. He raised both of his in response. He'd show her that he was more than she thought of him – much more.

Daniel approached the animated group. One of the girls saw him coming and nudged another. All eyes turned to him. Silence fell.

'Good day, ladies,' he said cheerfully, pulling up a stool.

'I think you are mistaken,' said a girl with the strong, unwavering gaze of a leader.

'Mistaken?'

'People like you don't do the peeling. You do the cooking and the serving. *We* do the peeling.'

Noticing then their worn shawls, faded dresses, grubby aprons, he was disappointed to find that, even here of all places, class divided the work. 'Well, I happen to like peeling.'

One giggled.

The leader extended a hand. 'Niamh Lynch.'

'Daniel Healy,' he said, shaking it.

'Lorraine Murphy,' the girl who'd giggled announced.

'Nora O'Driscoll,' a third volunteered.

The other girls remained silent. Niamh handed Daniel a knife and a cloth for across his lap. He watched them work for a moment. Then began. He was fingers and thumbs and losing too much potato with every cut but, with concentrated effort, he began, finally, to master it.

He looked up and noticed their silence. His presence had halted their conversation.

So he asked, 'Did you come directly from school?'

They looked at each other.

'We don't have the luxury of school,' Niamh explained.

He considered school many things, none of them a luxury. He looked at her questioningly.

'We work in factories,' she explained.

'Factories?' She was no more than fifteen, the others younger still.

'When there *is* work,' Lorraine countered.

'And we're not locked out,' Nora added.

The conversation was running away from him. 'But the strike is a good thing, is it not? If you stand together...'

'What choice do we have? Cross a picket and you're a scab. I've seen a man crippled for less.'

Daniel realised that he had stopped peeling.

Niamh looked at him in sympathy. 'So! What do you learn in secondary school?' she asked brightly.

He couldn't think. 'Latin,' he said vaguely.

'That'll be handy.'

He laughed with them.

'For when you're a man of the cloth,' Nora teased.

'Ah, God, don't become a priest! 'Twould be an awful waste,' Lorraine said.

'At least you can understand the Mass,' Nora offered in his favour.

'Oh, I *like* not knowing,' Lorraine said dreamily. 'It sounds so foreign and romantic.'

She got a slap of a cloth for that. 'You big eejit.' Niamh laughed.

Daniel smiled, glad that Maggie had sent him here, whatever her reason.

'Here's Madame!' whispered one of the formerly silent girls.

'And her cigarette,' Lorraine said.

Daniel coughed to hide a laugh as the countess approached – not alone with her cigarette but with a tiny dog that seemed to follow her everywhere.

'Ladies! Who are you hiding over here?' she asked as if Daniel was a man of intrigue.

He wiped his hands and rose. 'Daniel Healy.'

'And how do you come to be here, peeling potatoes, Daniel Healy?'

'I came to the food kitchen with... a friend.' He hesitated at the exaggeration.

The countess glanced at the girls. 'And who might that be?'

'Maggie Gilligan.'

Madame looked at him with growing interest, then at Maggie in the middle distance, stirring away at a boiler, sleeves rolled up, face flushed from steam, hair curling damp about her face. She was a renaissance painting from Daniel's history book. He could not remember the artist.

'I *see*,' Madame said. The implication was clear.

'I've come to lend a hand,' he clarified.

She reached out, took hold of his hands and turned them over. They were red and raw. 'Well, I imagine you've done enough peeling for today. Follow me, Daniel Healy. Ladies,' she said as a goodbye, then turned and marched off, fully expecting Daniel to follow.

He looked each of the girls in the eye. 'It has been a pleasure.'

'The pleasure was all ours,' Lorraine said with a spark in her eye.

Niamh shook her head, sadly.

Daniel smiled. These girls had more life in them than any of his friends at school – bar Michael, who had too much life. He turned to follow the countess.

Seconds later, he glanced back to the sound of their laughter. At what point exactly had this become the most curious day of his life?

Madame put Daniel at the boiler beside Maggie, gave him a few cursory instructions then marched off to her next task, her tiny dog in tow.

'I see that you tired of peeling,' Maggie said without looking at him.

'Actually, I was quite enjoying it. It was Madame's idea to put me here. It seems that there is a class divide even here in the food kitchen.'

Her mouth opened and closed like a fish.

'Now stop distracting me. I've work to do.' The girls seemed to have emboldened him.

'You tell her,' said the man stoking the fire beneath the boiler.

Daniel looked down at him. 'She can't resist me.'

There was a loud, indignant, snort to his right.

'I better get out of here before there's a murder.' The man gathered his things then scurried off to the next boiler, chuckling.

After a long silence, Maggie demanded. 'What makes you think you're so irresistible?'

'I've never understood it.' The effort not to laugh was immense.

She frowned. Then she nodded to herself as if taking an oath not to speak to him.

All afternoon, they stirred and scooped. It was hot work. Twice, Daniel burned himself. He reeked of stew but the company was good, though it was attempting not to be. That she wished him to give up only encouraged him not to.

Mid-afternoon, Maggie's mother arrived in haste. She rolled up her sleeves and took up position at a nearby boiler, replacing a woman who had to leave. She was small like Maggie and had a fading almost Spanish-like beauty. In her face he saw grief and determination. He liked her immediately. And wondered about Maggie's father.

Once she had settled into a routine, she looked up. Seeing Daniel, she smiled, stopped stirring and came over to shake his hand.

'I'm Mary Gilligan. It's lovely to meet you.'

Daniel smiled. 'Daniel Healy.'

'You've met my daughter, Maggie?'

He fought a smile. 'I have indeed.'

'Well, welcome to the food kitchen. It's good to have a boy amongst us. Most are too busy for work like this.' She turned to Maggie. 'How was school?'

'Delightfully challenging as always.'

Maggie grew more talkative than she'd been all afternoon.

Daniel did not mind. Better for her to be annoyed with him than immune to him.

When the food kitchen was finally closing, she was leaving without goodbye when her mother exclaimed, 'Maggie Gilligan where are your manners? You've been cooking beside Daniel all afternoon.'

'I'm sorry. Goodbye, Daniel Healy.' She blushed over her already rosy cheeks.

He smiled. 'Goodbye, Maggie Gilligan.'

He said her name in his head. It sounded like tinkling water. And it suited her.

Watching them go, he felt as though the room was growing dimmer, losing energy.

'Feisty little thing,' came a voice behind him.

He turned. Madame pointed a cigarette at him. 'A girl like that needs a boy like you.'

He cleared his throat in embarrassment.

'A calming influence,' she added.

Daniel stared at the countess. She was quite simply wrong. Maggie Gilligan's passion was the best thing about her.

There was so much to think about. First, though, as his father reminded him, there were his studies. Daniel joined Niall at the drawing room table.

'How was school?' he asked his brother as he opened his books.

'Good,' he said simply, his eyes glued to the masterpiece he was drawing.

'No more trouble?'

Niall looked up. 'No!' he said almost in surprise. 'Your plan worked, Danny.'

'Good! Stick to it.'

'We will. We've made a pact.'

Daniel looked at his brother and was reminded of the little boy in the food kitchen. He had never before considered himself lucky. He had never considered luck at all. Now, he understood why Maggie resented his father's motorcar, telephone, servants, *life*. He had all these things while others had nothing. The upper classes stayed upper while the lower classes stayed lower. And Daniel was – unmistakably – upper class. At least now, he understood her anger at him. Or at least he hoped he did. It could, of course, have been personal.

Later, with Niall in bed and his studies complete, Daniel sat gazing at the drapes, thick and luxurious; the rugs, soft and quiet underfoot; the wallpaper of the latest design, shipped in from... God knew where. Lamps, here and there, emitted cosy pools of light. The clock on the mantelpiece was a gift from a friend of his father's. How easily wealth was shared amongst the wealthy. The mantelpiece, itself, was ornate. Daniel had never doubted the blazing hearth or the servants that kept it so. The paintings of yachts at Kingstown Harbour displayed his father's taste and wealth. This may or may not have been deliberate.

Daniel watched his father puff on his pipe and gaze into the fire.

'How is it that we have so much, Father?'

He turned. 'How do you mean?'

Daniel gestured to the room.

His father's face took on a look of pride. 'Hard graft, Daniel. Hard graft.' He pointed at him with the mouthpiece of his pipe. 'Remember that.'

'Why is there such poverty in the city, Father, such…inequality?'

'Where has all this come from suddenly?' his father asked, frowning.

One mention of the food kitchen and Daniel would be forbidden from visiting again. 'We were having a discussion in school, a political debate.'

His father nodded. 'And did you not get to the root of the problem?'

'No, Father.'

'It's as I said, Daniel. We lack a skilled workforce.'

Daniel thought of Niamh and her friends and finally understood why. The poor did not have the luxury of skills; they had to go out to work. Poverty bred poverty.

Missus Healy, entering the drawing room, smiled as though encouraged to see that they were in discussion. 'What's this?'

'Political discourse,' his father said cheerfully.

'Perhaps I should get on with this.' Daniel looked down at his books not wishing the poor to become a source of entertainment.

His mother took a seat by the fire and opened her copy of *The Lady of The House*.

Silence returned.

———
40

At length, she put aside her magazine. She glanced at Daniel to ensure that he was occupied with his work. Then she spoke quietly to her husband. 'I don't know what to do with Mary.'

'Mary? The scullery maid?' his father confirmed in hushed tones.

'Cook saw her walking out with a man,' she whispered.

'Did you not explain to her the No Followers rule?'

'Most clearly but a girl can fall in love, James.'

'Has she been lying to you about where she's been going on her days off?'

Daniel's mother was reluctant.

'Well?'

'It would appear so.'

'Then it is very clear what you must do. Dismiss her without character.'

'She would be unable to find another position!'

'She should have thought of that...'

'She's a good girl, James, hard-working.'

'A rule is a rule, Elizabeth.'

Daniel looked up. 'There's no work out there, Father. People are starving.'

His parents turned in surprise.

His father frowned. 'Daniel, this matter does not concern you.'

Feeling the spirit of a green-eyed girl in him, he turned to his mother. 'Is Mary to be denied love simply because she's a *maid*? Could you not *reason* with her parents?'

'Daniel!' his father snapped. 'You do *not* question my authority.' He looked at his wife. 'The girl goes,' he said then snapped his newspaper open.

Silence returned.

Daniel's mother sneaked a glance at him, then returned her eyes to her magazine. His father began to turn the pages with impatience as though every news report suddenly displeased him. At last, he rose, wound the clock on the mantelpiece and placed the guard in front of the fire. He looked at his wife expectantly.

She smiled calmly. 'I will be up presently, James. I'm enjoying this article.'

'Daniel. Have you not yet finished that work?'

'Almost, Father.'

'I hope that you're not turning into a dreamer.'

'No, Father.'

'Make sure of it.'

They watched him go.

Daniel's mother turned to him, then. 'Is it true, Danny? Are people *starving*?'

'Yes, Mother. They are.'

'From the Lockout?'

He nodded.

'Then we must help.'

He suggested a charitable donation. Ladies such as his mother did not roll up their sleeves.

'Very good!' she said. 'It will be done tomorrow.'

'What'll become of Mary?'

'I will write to her parents. That rule was put in place when she came to us at fifteen. Mary is a woman now.'

'But what of Father?'

She waved a dismissive hand. 'Don't you worry about your father. I have ways of getting around him.' She looked at her son for the longest time. 'You know Daniel, for a boy of your age, you surprise me with your insight.'

It horrified him how little he had had only twenty-four hours earlier. How a day – and a girl – could change a person.

In the schoolyard, the following morning, Michael tossed a rugby ball to Daniel.

'*Today*, I'm going to crucify you,' he said.

'Not today.'

'Ah, Danny. You don't mean it. Not two days *in a row*?' He fired the rugby ball at him with force.

Daniel caught it and held on to it.

'Do you want to be dropped from the team?' Michael demanded moodily. 'Because that's what will happen if you keep gallivanting about the place.'

'I know. I know.' Rugby was Daniel's life. But: 'I can't unsee what I've seen.' And he could not be the person Maggie Gilligan had accused him of being. Neither could he ignore her existence. It was too late for that.

'That girl is trouble, Danny.'

'Most likely.'

'She doesn't care a toss for you.'

He laughed. 'Now, *there's* an understatement.'

five

Maggie

When he wasn't waiting outside her school, the following day, Maggie knew that her first instincts about Daniel Healy had been right. He had not come to the food kitchen to help. He had come as a dare or out of curiosity or because he had thought himself 'irresistible' to her. She had put him peeling potatoes to test him. And he had surprised her. Nothing had seemed to put him off – even her frostiness. Was he *always* so cheerful? She did not know whether she found it annoying or refreshing. It no longer mattered. He'd made his choice, the very choice she had expected him to make in the first place. Her only surprise was the disappointment she felt. Perhaps, she'd hoped that he would be the exception. After all, he *had* pointed out a class divide in the very place that struggled against it. She sighed. Even he had proven predictable after all.

Arriving outside Liberty Hall, Maggie glanced at the queue. One face stood out amongst all others. It was a little girl. No more than five, she had hair of pale sunshine and the face of an angel. Her dress was grubby and threadbare and she lacked a shawl. Maggie looked for a mother but there was no mother. How far had she come? And how far must she return with a pint of stew and a loaf of bread in a city with too many starving people for her to be left alone? Maggie had barely the thought out when a man sidled up to the child and began to whisper to her. His cap pulled down over his face, he seemed up to no good. The girl turned from him but he persisted.

Then Maggie was beside him. 'Can I *help* you?' she demanded.

He straightened and produced a rat-like smile. 'You could mind your business. *That* would help.'

Maggie gave him a look of absolute disdain, turned her back on him and stooped down to the child. 'Hello, sweetheart, is this man bothering you?'

She nodded.

'Then come away with me into the food kitchen.' Maggie held out her hand and the girl took it.

'Maggie!'

She turned. It was Daniel Healy, arriving on his bicycle.

Her stomach knotted with guilt. She had misjudged him.

'Is everything all right?' he called as though he had witnessed it all.

Maggie glared at the man. 'This gentleman was just leaving.'

Daniel faced him. 'Make sure that you do or I'll call the police.'

'On what charge?' he sneered.

'Go – and stay gone. I'm warning you.'

'Come along, pet,' Maggie said to the little girl. Her smile of thanks to Daniel was also an apology. Then she hurried the child inside.

In the basement, Maggie sat her at a table. 'Are you all right?'

'I must join the queue,' she said urgently, looking at it as if the food was about to run out.

'No queuing for you, today. I'll collect your ration. Have you got your ticket?' she asked to reassure her. Handing over a ticket issued to strikers meant the receipt of food.

The little girl immediately produced it.

'What did that man want, anyway?' Maggie asked as though he no longer mattered.

'For me to go with him but I'm only to go to the food kitchen and directly home.'

'Good girl,' Maggie said, taking the ticket.

Daniel arrived in, looking pale. 'He's gone.'

'Sit a moment,' Maggie said to him, guilt mixed with gratitude.

The child's eyes widened. 'I must collect my ration!'

Maggie rose. 'I'm on my way.'

'You stay, Maggie. I'll go.' Daniel put his hand out for the ticket.

Maggie smiled, glad not to have to leave the girl. 'Thank you.'

'I won't be long.'

Maggie looked at the angel child and wondered how to put her at ease. She remembered the one thing that had always worked when she was little. 'Do you like stories?'

She nodded.

'And pirates?'

Her eyes widened and her nod became ferocious.

Maggie smiled. Then, with only words, she whisked the little girl away to a far off land of tattooed men and mischievous fairies and a man with a hook for a hand.

She listened, wide-eyed and silent.

And then, just as Maggie finished, Daniel returned with the ration. He was also carrying a bowl of stew, which he placed in front of the child. 'I thought you might be hungry.'

'Thank you,' she said. And ate as though it was her last meal.

Maggie and Daniel sat with her, watching in humbled silence.

'I'm Maggie and this is Daniel. What's your name?'

'Lily,' she said, all caution forgotten now.

'That's a lovely name.'

'It's after the lily of the valley, me mam's favourite flower.'

Daniel and Maggie exchanged a relieved glance. So there *was* a mother.

Maggie helped Lily up onto the saddle of her bicycle. She put the billycan on the handlebar and the loaf in the basket.

'And we're off!' she said and began to push.

'Maggie!' came Daniel's voice behind them.

Turning, she saw, following closely, the man that had been bothering Lily. Maggie froze. As did the man. Daniel came running past him, holding up her coat.

'You forgot this!'

Maggie glared at the man but knew it would take more than a glare.

'Sure, I may as well come with you,' Daniel was saying. 'If we put Lily up on my crossbar, we can cycle.'

The man was on foot. Here, suddenly, was the solution.

Maggie smiled at Lily. 'You're going to get a spin!'

They transferred her onto Daniel's crossbar.

'Hold on tight,' he said.

Up along the quay they went, the pale sun sparking off the Liffey. They turned right, down Sackville Street, passing Nelson's Pillar and the tram terminus where women were selling flowers. Lily directed them down unfamiliar streets that narrowed and darkened. Here and there, women begged while children in rags played with hoops. A rat ran along a broken path and disappeared into a cellar. It seemed to get colder, damper, darker as they went. Clothing hanging from windows looked like they would never dry. A man emerged from a backyard of pigs.

Approaching a row of once grand, now dilapidated, three-storey, redbrick houses, Lily began to climb down.

'Wait 'til I stop, Lily!' Daniel said, easing on the brakes.

Coming to a halt, Maggie scanned the street.

'He's long gone,' Daniel said.

'You *knew*?'

'Of course I knew. Why else am I here?'

'The coat...'

'...was an excuse.'

How she had *underestimated* him. 'Thank you,' she said, awkwardly.

'Not that you needed me. I've seen you punch.'

She laughed.

'I'll carry the ration,' Lily said, reaching up.

Maggie handed it to her. Lily took off, marching purposefully towards the first building. They followed with their bicycles.

Maggie looked at Daniel and whispered, 'He'll be back, won't he, to the food kitchen?'

He grimaced. 'Well, punching didn't seem to deter him.'

'You *punched* him?'

Another grimace, as though it pained him to hurt another.

She remembered how pale he'd looked when he came in. 'Well, you're full of surprises.'

'For the record, I'm a pacifist.'

'I don't doubt it.'

'He got aggressive, Maggie. There didn't seem to be an option.'

She looked into his eyes. 'Sometimes there isn't one.'

They carried their bicycles up the steps of the house.

Daniel's face brightened. 'I know! I'll ask Michael's father to scare him off!'

'Since when do the Dublin Metropolitan Police help the poor?' Maggie raged suddenly.

'They're here for everyone, Maggie.'

'Tell *that* to the strikers whose homes they've smashed up. Did you *know* that they've been going house to house, breaking every last bit of their furniture to intimidate them out of striking?'

'Where did you hear that?'

'Where I hear everything, in the food kitchen.'

'If the police are committing these acts, then none of them is Michael's father. I've known him all my life. He's a good man.'

Maggie raised an eyebrow but said no more.

They followed Lily through a faded, peeling door on the ground floor. Her home was just one room. There were no drapes, no carpets, no lamps. The furniture consisted of a metal bed in the corner, a plain wooden table and one chair. Paint peeled from the cornice on the ceiling, evidence of former grandeur. The original marble fireplace had been torn out and replaced with a wooden alternative. The floorboards were rotting in places. It was colder in than out. The hearth was empty.

Lily hurried to the bed. Only then did Maggie see the woman lying in it. Eyes closed, she didn't move. She was so thin and pale that Maggie stared at her chest, praying for a breath. A harsh, bubbly cough racked her skeletal body, waking her.

"'Tis all right, Mam,' Lily said, patting a pale limp hand.

The woman raised her head and smiled weakly. 'Lily, love, have you eaten?'

'I have.' She broke a tiny piece off the loaf and put it into her mother's hand.

When she placed it to her parched lips, Maggie knew that it was to reassure her little girl. Their mutual concern moved her more than anything she had ever seen. And she had seen much.

She held back the tears. Trampled down her anger.

Back out on the street, though, she raged. 'She's a little girl, not a mother, not a nurse!'

'We must help,' Daniel said.

'We?' She looked at him in his posh uniform.

'Yes, we. You do not have a monopoly on caring, Maggie Gilligan. I know you don't think much of me but you look at all the wrong things. My father is who he is. He has what he has. But I am who I am. And I want to help.' Gone was his usual cheer, his usual jollity.

She blushed. 'I'm sorry. It's just that people like you…the girls at school….'

'I'm *not* the girls at school.'

They looked at each other for the longest moment.

'You think me queer, don't you?' she asked quietly. If he didn't, he soon would, as everyone did – eventually.

'Yes,' he said. 'I *do* think you queer... and like you all the better for it.'

She looked at him in surprise. 'No one has ever said a kinder thing.'

'It's not kindness, Maggie, but a fact.'

She lowered her gaze. 'Thank you.'

'Don't thank me. Just let me help.'

She nodded. 'We must go to Madame right away. Madame will know what to do.'

But when they returned to the food kitchen, the man was back, bothering another little girl, older than Lily, but also alone.

'Watch him while I get Madame,' Maggie said to Daniel. 'If he touches her, punch him – again.' She smiled and ran inside.

'I have *heard* of that trouble maker!' Madame exclaimed. 'All right. Time to end this. Wait here, Maggie.'

The countess ran up the stairs into Liberty Hall.

She returned in minutes with two men. One was James Larkin! The other was a small, stocky man with a thick black moustache. Neither looked in the mood for nonsense. Madame marched over to Maggie.

'Point this man out to us,' she instructed.

Maggie nodded then hurried outside. The man was taking the girl's hand. Daniel was approaching him, his face bleached of colour. Something inside Maggie melted at the sight of him.

'That's him!' She pointed at the man.

'Halt!' Larkin's colleague called out in a Scottish accent.

The man turned. His eyes widened on seeing Larkin and he dropped the girl's hand.

Madame hurried to her, said a few words, then picked her up and carried her inside.

Maggie joined Daniel. They watched – as did everyone in

the queue – while Larkin and his companion backed the man up against a wall. She could not hear what they said to him but it was clear from their stance and his fearful gaze that it was a threat. At last, head down, he scurried away.

The men began to make their way back to Liberty Hall.

'That's the last we'll see of him,' Larkin was saying as he passed Maggie and Daniel.

The other man stopped walking. '*This* is what we should be offering the strikers – protection.'

'You'd need an army,' Larkin said.

'Then we'll *build* one – an army of citizens to protect their own.'

They looked at each other and smiled. Then they carried on into Liberty Hall.

Maggie turned to Daniel, her eyes alight. 'Do you *know* who that tall man was?'

'Larkin?' he guessed uncertainly.

'Big Jim Larkin, the man who'll change the plight of the poor.'

In the basement of Liberty Hall, Madame had reunited the little girl with her weeping mother and was having what looked like a welcome cigarette. Maggie and Daniel approached.

'This country of ours,' the countess said then blew smoke up into the air.

'Madame, we need your help,' Maggie said.

'*Again?*' she demanded but with a smile.

Maggie told her about Lily's situation.

The countess listened with a growing frown, then dropped her cigarette and stubbed it out with a boot.

'Maggie, collect up two food rations. Daniel, help me gather fuel and blankets.'

'We'll need a doctor, too, Madame!' Maggie said.

'Let me see the lie of the land first, Maggie, but if a doctor is required, a doctor we shall get.'

six

Maggie

Maggie and Daniel stood in the dark hallway. In the distance, from behind a closed door, came the sound of a baby crying but from Lily's door there came no sound. Maggie turned to Daniel.

'The doctor said days. We have days.' It was herself she was trying to reassure.

Daniel knocked again.

A woman dressed in black answered the door, surrounded by four children, none of them Lily.

Maggie turned to Daniel, eyes wide. Were they too late?

'You must be Maggie,' the woman said.

Maggie remembered her manners. 'I am. And this is Daniel.'

'I'm Missus O'Brien, from next door. Come in. Please.'

Maggie hurried inside. Her gaze fell immediately on the bed. There, to her horror, Lily's mother had been laid out. Lily was lying asleep beside her, an arm across her body.

'I hadn't the heart to part them,' Missus O'Brien whispered. Then she bowed her head and blessed herself.

Automatically, Maggie and Daniel did the same. Maggie felt her throat burn and her eyes well. She longed to scoop Lily up and save her. She waited for Missus O'Brien to finish praying then turned to her. 'Does Lily have family?' she whispered.

Missus O'Brien shook her head. 'Her mother asked me to take her in – and I will – but I don't know how we'll manage. There isn't enough for my own.'

Back at the food kitchen, Maggie followed her mother to and fro, from the queue to the boilers and back again.

'She has no family! She's alone in the world!'

'Maggie, this is no place to discuss this,' she whispered, looking around.

'She could end up on the street! In the workhouse!'

Her mother stopped, a billycan of stew in her hand. 'We'll discuss this *at home*,' she said firmly.

'Then let us go!'

'Maggie, we have commitments *here*.'

'God Almighty!'

'Maggie Gilligan, do *not* take the name of the Lord in vain.' Her mother took a ticket from a woman who looked on the verge of exhaustion.

It took all of Maggie's strength to walk away. She positioned herself at a boiler. And stirred with a ferocity that did nothing to help. Minutes passed like hours.

'Maggie, it's a lot to ask, taking in a child,' Daniel said as though preparing her for the worst.

'She has *no one*,' Maggie insisted. 'Only us.'

'She has Missus O'Brien.'

'Who doesn't have enough for her own. You heard her.'

'Perhaps we can help Missus O'Brien.'

Maggie felt like hitting him. *And* screaming. People were being too calm about this altogether.

'Good luck,' Daniel whispered when it was time to go.

Maggie looked at him and saw then that he was only trying to help. 'I'm sorry. Only this is the *one time* I can make a difference. The *one* time.'

'Every day you make a difference, Maggie Gilligan.'

How she *wished* it were that simple. 'Wish me luck – again.'

He smiled. 'Good luck – again.'

It was dark when Maggie and her mother emerged from Liberty Hall. The street lamps dimmed in the wind. All across the city, church bells called rich and poor to pray the Angelus. Mother and daughter paused, blessed themselves and bowed their heads. Maggie thought that they'd never get home.

And yet they did.

Maggie closed the front door behind them. 'Mam?'

Her mother turned, taking the pin from her hat and resting it on the dresser.

'We're home,' Maggie said expectantly.

'Can we at least eat before we have this discussion?'

'No! It's too urgent!'

Her mother sighed and removed her coat.

'She'd be no trouble. She's the sweetest thing. You should *see* how she cared for her mother – like she was the mother.'

'Maggie, you're asking me to take in a child, to care for her for the rest of her life. That is a tremendous responsibility.'

'I'd mind her, Mam. I swear. You wouldn't have to do anything.'

'We barely get by on my income.'

Then Maggie hit upon it, the winning argument. 'She's receiving no education whatsoever.'

Her mother looked at her and for the first time hesitated. Education was her solution to everything.

'Missus O'Brien is only taking Lily in because she promised. There's not enough food to go round.'

'Maggie,' her mother said, gently now. 'You must understand that before we can help Lily, we must first see how best *to* help.'

She brightened. 'So we *are* helping?'

'Of course but Lily may wish to stay with the people she knows, the place she knows, the life she knows…'

Maggie reached for her coat. 'Let us find out!'

'I have a family to feed.'

David stuck his head out from the drawing room. 'You go on,' he said. 'I'll put on a few spuds.'

Maggie beamed at him. He was so easy to love.

'Will you boil a bit of ham as well, pet?' their mother asked him. 'You know how Tom likes his meat when he gets in.'

David nodded. He reached for his mother's coat and held it out for her.

She put it on, shaking her head at herself. 'I'm soft. That's what I am.'

Maggie looked at her. 'How can it be soft to make a difference?'

There were tears in Maggie's mother's eyes as she looked at Lily, still lying with her mother.

'There'll be a wake,' Missus O'Brien was whispering, 'then a pauper's grave. God rest her soul; she was little more than a child herself.' Her sigh seemed to slide to the floor under the weight of the world.

Maggie's mother straightened to her full height. 'She'll have a proper burial. Of that you can be sure.'

'Oh, bless you, Missus,' Missus O'Brien said as if a proper burial was more important than food, fuel, life itself.

Lily awoke. At the sight of her mother's motionless face, she began to cry. Maggie went to her, squatting down beside the bed so that, at least, Lily would know she was not alone.

Then Lily turned to her, eyes wide and asked, 'Who'll I mind now?'

Maggie had to run to keep pace with her mother as she dashed down the steps to the street.

'Where will we find money for a burial?' Maggie worried aloud.

Her mother stopped and looked at her, eyes blazing. 'I may

not be a woman of means but I'm a woman with friends. Lily's mother will have a proper burial and Missus O'Brien and her children will be looked after.'

'And Lily?'

'I'll speak with Missus O'Brien – and Lily – after the funeral.'

'So we *might* take her?' Maggie dared.

'If that is what she and Missus O'Brien want…but *only* if it's what they want.'

Maggie threw her arms around her. 'Oh thank you, Mam. You won't be sorry! I'll-'

'Maggie. It's still only a possibility. I don't want you to get your hopes up.'

'I know. But I never thought you'd take her!'

'Neither did I until I saw that poor little angel all alone in the world.' She kissed the top of Maggie's head. 'Your father would be proud Maggie Mae, so very proud of how you've turned out.'

Maggie bowed her head. A day didn't go by when she didn't think of him, miss him, and try to do what he'd asked of her. She understood what Lily was feeling, the longing, the ache, and she wanted so much to make her world better.

Maggie awoke, gasping for breath and calling out. She felt a cool, soothing hand on her forehead.

'You've not had that dream in a long time,' her mother said, sitting by her side.

Maggie sat up, her heart still racing. 'How did you know it was the same one?'

She cleared a tear from Maggie's cheek. 'You always call out for him.'

The ache in her heart was so fresh. It was as if she had lost him all over again. 'Poor Lily. She has no one now. At least I had you and David and Tom.'

Her mother took her hand. 'Come on, Maggie. Up you get. We have work to do.'

Maggie rubbed her eyes. 'What time is it?'

'Two in the morning.'

Maggie smiled and got up.

Down in the cellar, they collected carpets, rugs, drapes and clothing.

Together, they carried a rolled up rug up the narrow steps. Nearing the top, Maggie screamed and dropped it.

'Jesus!' uttered the figure at the top of the stairs. 'What are the two of you up to, down there? You frightened the life out of me.' Tom lowered the hurley stick he had raised over his head.

Maggie laughed. She could not imagine her brother being afraid of anyone.

'Help us up and we'll tell you what we're about,' their mother said.

Soon she was explaining the possibility of a child coming to live with them.

Maggie expected Tom to explode; it seemed to be his reaction to everything nowadays. But he didn't explode. He volunteered to help. And so, he and Maggie followed their mother as she strode around the house, picking up one beautiful thing after another to be given away.

'But Mam, these were gifts from your friends!' Maggie pointed out.

'Friends who would understand.'

At the front door, a pile grew. And at sunrise, Madame arrived in her motorcar. They had to squeeze everything in amongst fuel and food. Then the countess and Maggie's mother were away.

To Maggie's great regret, she had to attend school as usual. While she sat at her desk wondering what was happening with Lily, her teacher handed back essays. Sister Grace swished from desk to desk, slapping the sheets down, giving each one a pat and saying things like, 'Good girl,' or, 'Not up to your usual standard.' Maggie was beginning to wonder where hers was. She had never worked as hard on an essay and remembered it word for word:

My heroine is the daughter of an arctic explorer. She married a count from Poland. She is an artist, an actress and a poet. She was born wealthy but has given much of that wealth to those in need. She feeds the women and children in the food kitchen at Liberty Hall. She is a countess but without airs and graces. She is unafraid of work. She knows that questions will turn people away, so she feeds and helps and asks no questions. Her dedication to others has lost her her family. Her husband has returned to Poland.

Maggie especially loved that Madame wore trousers and smoked cigarettes because it meant that she did not give a toss for society. She did not include that in her essay, however, for fear that Sister Grace might be scandalised. The nun was walking between the desks towards Maggie now. Only one essay remained in her hand. As she approached, her face grew darker. Her brow creased into a frown. Maggie wondered what she had done wrong. She had been so careful. She could not think. Her heart thudded as Sister Grace, arriving at Maggie's desk, held up her essay, looked into her eyes and ripped it in two.

Maggie felt her face redden. Everyone was staring. Polly smiled.

'I will *not* have that name mentioned in this classroom!' Sister Grace bellowed, her face turning purple, her neck resembling a plucked chicken. 'That woman is no heroine. She's nothing but a socialist. And socialism, Maggie Gilligan, goes against the teachings of the Catholic Church. Or didn't you know that?'

'No, Sister,' she said quietly. All she understood of socialism was that it meant equal rights for all. Was there something more sinister that she'd not heard? Sister Grace made it sound like the greatest sin on earth.

'Well, you are better off not knowing,' Maggie's favourite teacher said, softening. 'Of that I can assure you.'

Maggie burst through the front door. She heard Tom and David in the dining room.

'Where's Mam?' she demanded. 'She wasn't at the food kitchen.'

'Out helping that girl,' David said.

'Lily,' Tom corrected.

'I need to know about socialism.'

Tom looked at her in surprise. 'You know about socialism.'

'Not why it's against the Catholic Church.'

'Who said it was?' Tom asked.

'Sister Grace.'

He threw down his fork. 'I've heard it all now.'

'She doesn't lie; she's a nun.'

'Then she's wrong.'

'So it's *not* against the Catholic Church?' she asked hopefully.

'Why would sharing power be against the Church?' He stopped and frowned. 'Unless, of course, the Church fears *losing* power! That would make such sense! At last, a reason why priests have not spoken out for the workers!' He looked like he was having an epiphany.

'Tom, that's sacrilegious talk,' David said as if fearing eternal damnation for his brother.

Tom looked at him with pity.

'Whatever about socialism,' Maggie said, '*Madame* wouldn't tear up a person's essay in front of them.'

'Sister Grace tore up your essay?' Tom demanded.

Maggie worried that he might go down to the school and make things worse than they already were. 'It's all right. I'll be more careful in future.'

'I've a good mind to-'

'Well, don't!' she said firmly. 'It's my school. I'll handle it.'

He pushed his plate away and raised his hands. Then he left the room, carrying his anger in his shoulders.

'Maggie, do you want me to speak to Sister Grace?' David asked.

She shook her head. 'Next time I'll pick Joan of Arc like everyone else.'

He smiled. 'Or a saint.'

seven

Maggie

Lily arrived with a luggage of sadness. She did not speak. She did not eat. She reversed into corners, wrapping her arms about herself. A worry grew in Maggie's stomach and spread throughout her body. She knew – because she had lost her father – not to crowd Lily, not to try to make her happy. But she did not know what she *could* do. She wished the house quieter, her brothers smaller, especially Tom who was practically a giant. At least he was out most of the time with his scouting.

'How's Lily?' Daniel asked, when they met at the food kitchen.

'Lost.'

'Have you tried one of your stories?'

Maggie looked at him in surprise. 'Why didn't I think of that?' Now she couldn't wait to get home.

When they finally emerged from the food kitchen, the rain was torrential. They stood in the doorway watching it.

'Maybe it'll stop,' Daniel said hopefully.

Madame arrived beside them and peered out.

'Daniel, help me strap your bicycles to the back of my motorcar. I'm bringing you home.' She took off then, out into the rain, she who never expected an argument.

Daniel shrugged at Maggie then took off after her.

Maggie ran to help.

'What are you doing?' he shouted over the rain.

'What does it look like? We're friends, Daniel Healy. One of us doesn't stand by while the other gets drenched.'

He stopped what he was doing and looked at her, rain dripping from his soaked hair onto his face. 'We're friends?'

She hesitated. Polly had once been a friend. Friends turned. Friends did not last. And so she shrugged, wishing the words back in her mouth.

Suddenly, he beamed. 'Well, that's the best news I've had all day, Maggie Gilligan. The best news,' he said, shaking his head like he didn't believe it.

Relief flooded her. But she did not let on. 'We couldn't have got any wetter cycling.'

'I have never been happier to be wet.' Still smiling, he ran to open the door.

They jumped inside.

Happy was something Maggie had not felt for a very long time. She felt it now, though. It surprised and warmed her in equal measure.

Madame opened the front door and threw Poppet in. Then she hurried behind the wheel. Poppet shook the rain from his fur, drowning Madame further, if that was possible. She laughed.

My favourite socialist, Maggie thought.

Then the countess took off like a bullet, accelerating so fast that Maggie and Daniel were pressed into the seat. Maggie's stomach lurched.

'How's Lily?' Madame called back, as if the child was a problem solved.

'Still settling,' Maggie said, wanting to sound grateful.

'Your mother is an incredible woman,' she said, looking back while travelling forward.

Maggie wanted to tell her to keep her eyes on the road.

They were speeding through Rathmines when Madame tut-tutted.

'I will forget my head someday. Any objections if I pop home for a moment?'

'No!' Maggie rushed – anything to get her to face forward again.

Soon they came to an – abrupt – stop outside a grand house on Leinster Road. Madame hurried inside with Poppet.

Maggie turned to Daniel, eyebrows raised. 'This is Surrey House!'

He looked at her blankly.

'Where Madame hid Jim Larkin from the police that time he was ordered not to speak publicly but did anyway! Let's have a look inside.'

'We can't just *go in.*'

'We're not *going* in.' She leapt from the car. At least the rain had stopped.

She hurried to the bay window, cupped her hands and peered inside, longing to see for herself where one of her heroes had hidden another. In the drawing room, the carpets had been rolled back, ornaments had been taken down and a great fire blazed. Furniture had been pushed aside and a swarm of boys wearing the same scouting uniform as Tom's were busy with what seemed like first aid. Some wore slings while others fixed them into position. Older boys walked amongst them, inspecting their work.

'What's your business here?' a voice demanded.

Maggie turned to see a uniformed boy emerge from the shadows where he must have been keeping watch. He was taller than Daniel and so dark in contrast.

'Well?' he demanded.

Maggie raised her chin. 'I'm Maggie Gilligan. I help Madame at the food kitchen. This is Daniel Healy. What are Na Fianna boys doing in Surrey House?'

He regarded her with interest. 'You've heard of Na Fianna?'

'Of course I have. It's a scouting group.'

He scoffed. 'We're far more than scouts.'

'What, then?' she asked longing to know what her brother got up to.

'We're modern day warriors, fighting for the defence of Ireland.'

'Are we under attack?' she asked, amused.

'We've been under attack for hundreds of years, Maggie Gilligan.'

She peered back into the room, scanning it for Tom. 'Can we come in?'

He pointed to Daniel. '*He* can. *You,* I'm afraid, cannot.'

'Why?'

'Na Fianna's for boys only.'

'That's ridiculous. Why halve your numbers?'

He sighed as if he was talking to an oaf. 'Girls don't fight now do they?'

'Some do,' she said though, outside of herself, she'd never met one that did.

'There's a separate scouting organisation for girls,' the modern day warrior said helpfully.

'I can only imagine what *they* do,' Maggie muttered. Sewing came to mind. 'So you ban girls while using a woman's house for your activities?'

'Madame helped to found Na Fianna; that's the only reason.'

'And yet she is undeniably female.'

'What's so great about what *you're* doing?' he demanded. 'You think that a few scraps of food thrown in the direction of the poor will change their plight? Nothing will improve in this country as long as it's under British rule.'

He had the same anger as Tom. Did *her brother* believe this too? 'I suppose you know Tom Gilligan?'

He looked at her with curiosity. 'I do but Tom's not with us any more.'

'Tom would never leave Na Fianna.'

'He's gone to join the Irish Volunteers.'

'Who?' She'd never heard of them.

'They're rebels like us, only men, and not half as good.'

She had a rebel for a brother, now? Maggie wished she had some influence over him. But then no one did. There was nothing she could do except keep the news from her mother; it would kill her.

Madame burst out of the house, carrying something wrapped up in a blanket. Poppet trotted along behind her.

'There you are!' she exclaimed happily. 'Oh and you've met Patrick! Excellent.' She approached. 'So, what do you think of my boys?' she asked, glancing in the window proudly, as though they were her sons.

'Maggie, here, wished to know why we have no girls,' Patrick said to her.

The countess looked at her with interest. 'They even tried to push *me* out. But I have the funding!' She laughed. 'I'll be back shortly, Patrick. Must dash.' Already, she was striding towards the car.

Daniel and Maggie followed.

'Did you see him in his *skirt*?' Maggie scoffed.

Daniel smiled. 'The skirt is a kilt and you know it.'

'He's not as great as he thinks he is. That's what I know.' She did *not* need to be told that she wasn't making a difference. She did not need that news.

Madame stopped abruptly outside Maggie's home, jolting them forward.

'I'll get out here too,' Daniel said and, when the countess began to protest, added, 'I need to speak with Maggie anyway. Thank you for the lift.' He jumped from the motorcar.

Maggie helped him with their bicycles. 'What did you want to speak to me about?'

He seemed surprised by the question. 'Oh. Nothing. I simply value my life.'

Maggie laughed.

They carried their bicycles to the pavement where they waved the countess off.

Maggie looked up at her bedroom window. The curtains were closed. Lily could *not* be in bed already, not without goodnight.

'I'll let you go on in to Lily,' Daniel said.

She looked at him in surprise. He understood her like no one else. If this friendship ever turned the way others had, she did not know what she would do.

'It'll be grand,' he said as he mounted his bicycle.

She felt suddenly that it would. She had an overwhelming urge to hug him but simply waved.

He smiled in return and then was gone, his whistling in the dark night air lifting her heart.

She found her mother and David in the drawing room.

'Where's Lily?' she asked.

'Gone up to bed.'

'Ah, Mam. You could have waited till I got home.'

'She was exhausted. Anyway, she's only just gone up.'

Upstairs, Maggie knocked gently on the door of her own room.

'Come in,' said a tiny voice.

Maggie's heart melted at the sight of Lily, kneeling on the floor in an old nightgown of Maggie's. Hands joined and head bowed, her lips moved in silent prayer. Then she blessed herself again and climbed into bed. Watching her, and remembering how she used to live, it occurred to Maggie that perhaps there was too much space for her here with everything spread out.

'Lily, would you like your bed in the corner?' she asked.

Lily raised her head from the pillow in surprise. She nodded. Then started to get out of the bed.

'Stay there! I'll give you a ride.'

So Maggie moved the bed with Lily in it, making the sound of Madame's motorcar as she did so. 'Will I push mine up to yours?' she asked, as an afterthought.

Again Lily nodded.

So Maggie positioned the beds so that they were touching.

Then her heart sank as Lily turned in silence towards the wall to sleep.

'Would you like a story?' she asked.

Lily turned around and nodded.

Maggie smiled in relief. 'Good because I've a great one,' she said, flinging off her coat and climbing up onto her bed. 'All right, here we go.' She took a deep breath. 'Long ago, in Ancient Ireland, there lived a warrior named Oisín. He was brave and handsome and, as often happens brave and handsome men, he fell in love. She was a beautiful girl with golden hair. Her name was Niamh. So *besotted* were they with each other that Oisín travelled with Niamh on her magical white mare across the sea to live with her in Tír na nÓg, the land where people never grow old, where happiness reigns and neither hunger nor thirst exist.'

Lily raised herself onto an elbow, her eyes fixed on Maggie.

'Years passed and Oisín grew homesick for Ireland. Niamh said that he could return for a visit but that he was, *under no circumstances,* to get off the white mare because if his feet touched the ground, he would age as if he had never left Ireland.'

Lily sat up.

'Off he went but when he got to Ireland, he learned that three hundred years had passed. Everyone was a stranger to him. He was riding sadly along when he saw some men struggling to lift a rock. He leaned over to help but his saddle snapped and he fell to the ground. *Immediately,* he grew old.' Maggie stopped as she remembered the ending.

'Did Oisín *die*?'

Maggie hesitated.

'*Did* he?'

At last, she grimaced and nodded.

'But I wanted him to return to *Niamh*! Why didn't you tell me a *happy* story?'

'I'm sorry. I wasn't thinking of the ending at the beginning. Let me tell you another. Do you know how Cú Chulainn got his name?'

'Is it a sad story?'

'No. It's a story of bravery.'

Lily nodded.

Maggie took her time and let the story find its own course. At length, she arrived at the end: 'And Cú Chulainn became the greatest warrior in all of Ireland!'

There was silence. Lily looked at her with the widest of eyes. 'But he killed the dog!'

'Well.' Maggie paused. 'Yes.'

'The dog was only doing his job, Maggie. He was a guard dog.'

'I know.'

'Have you any happy stories *at all*?'

Maggie searched her mind, discarding story after story until, at last, she found a happy one.

'There's the tale of how Saint Patrick rid Ireland of snakes! That's a good one.'

Lily eyed her suspiciously. 'Did he kill them?'

'*No!* He chased them into the sea!'

Lily frowned. 'Can snakes swim?'

Maggie grimaced. 'I don't think so.'

'So he drownded them?'

There was no denying it. 'I suppose he did, all right.'

Lily fell back on the pillow and groaned.

Which made Maggie laugh.

Lily smiled. 'What?'

'You're very dramatic, aren't you?'

She sat up again, encouraged. 'Am I?'

'You certainly are.'

'Is that good?' she asked hopefully.

'Oh. That's better than good. That's *wonderful*.' It was only then that she realised – Lily was talking! For the first time since she'd arrived, she was talking.

Lily looked thoughtful. 'Maggie?'

'Yes, Lily?'

'Do I have to call your mam "Mam"?'

Maggie looked at her and understood. 'Not if you don't want to.'

'She wouldn't be upset?'

'Of course not.'

'I could call her Mammy,' she suggested hopefully.

'That would be perfect.'

Lily looked as though a weight had been lifted. 'Can I have a happy story tomorrow?'

Maggie smiled. 'I will find you a happy story even if I have to make one up myself.'

The following Saturday, David took out his paints.

'Would you like a picture, Lily?'

She nodded shyly.

He painted puppies, rabbits and people with funny faces. Lily may as well have been watching a magic show such was her fascination. And when he finally handed the pictures to her, she threw her arms around him in delight.

Tom, encouraged, swept Lily up onto his great shoulders and galloped around the house with her, neighing like a horse. Lily's laughter was like music. Maggie and David exchanged a surprised glance; this was not the Tom they knew.

He fashioned a swing for her from an old tyre and a piece of rope.

Lily preferred to push. So Maggie humoured her. 'Come on, Lily, put your back into it,' she called from inside the barely moving tyre.

There was a pause.

'All right!' Lily said with great determination.

Then Maggie was flying, propelled forward by an almighty push.

She turned in time to see Tom dart behind the tree.

Lily was doubled over, laughing.

'Watch out, Lily. I'm coming back!'

Lily jumped out of the way, still laughing.

With every passing day, Lily settled more. She stopped hoarding food at mealtimes for fear of it running out. She moved through the house at ease with the space now. Through her, Maggie began to appreciate simple things like taking a bath in hot water or having cake melt in your mouth.

Then talk of starting school began.

'No, Mam!' Maggie insisted. 'She's not ready.' In school, they'd kill her.

'Lack of schooling is Lily's worst enemy, Maggie. She has missed so much already.'

'But I'm teaching her lots of things.'

'Lily needs a formal education. In any case, it's the law.'

Didn't she know it?

'In any case, I must return to work,' her mother said. 'They were good enough to offer me leave while Lily settled in.'

Maggie sighed. 'Just when we'd made so much progress.'

Her mother winked. 'We'll make more progress.' Then she kissed the top of her head. 'I'm proud of you, Maggie Mae.'

It was no comfort. Maggie rushed home from the food kitchen the following day, praying that Lily had survived. But she had forgotten one thing, Lily was used to doing things alone. Lily was a survivor.

'I like school!' she announced.

She liked all that Maggie hated – the structure, the rules, the boundaries. Maggie couldn't understand it – until it occurred to her that all those things meant certainty and security.

In the evenings, along with her stories of Ireland, Maggie helped Lily with reading and mathematics. Lily was bright and learned quickly and when Maggie marvelled at how clever she was Lily seemed to grow. So Maggie made a habit of it.

By Christmas, Lily walked taller. Her skin and hair glowed. Her laughter was no longer a surprise. But as she thrived, the rest of Dublin's poor did not. Those arriving at the food kitchen were thinner, sicker and more despondent than ever.

It was Tom, in January, who brought news that the strikes had ended in defeat.

Maggie stood up from the table. 'It can't be over. They wouldn't give up.'

'Their backs have been broken, Maggie.'

'Has there been no improvement *at all* in their conditions?' She needed something, some result from their suffering.

'None.'

'Jesus.'

'Maggie!' her mother said.

But Maggie didn't hear. 'It's all been for nothing.'

'It's worse than that, Maggie,' Tom said. 'Some men will never work again. They've been branded troublemakers and blacklisted.'

Maggie held her head. Then she looked up with sudden hope. 'What about Larkin?'

Tom's face grew even darker. 'Larkin! Larkin has fecked off to America, left them all to rot!'

'Language, Tom, *please*,' their mother said, glancing at Lily.

'To hell with language,' he countered.

David looked at Lily. 'Don't worry, Lil. Tom's not angry at you but at the world.'

Lily eyed Tom gravely. 'Poor Tom.' She reached out and gave his hand a little pat.

He looked at her in surprise and then rubbed the top of her head. Strands of fine hair remained standing. The sight of that seemed to magically calm him. He sat at the table.

His mother placed his dinner in front of him. He looked at it, then at Maggie. 'They'll be closing the food kitchen of course.'

'What of the blacklisted families?' she demanded. 'How will they live?'

'I don't know.' He pushed his plate away. 'The strike is over. There is no union to fund the food kitchen.'

Silence spread out like spilled water.

Maggie broke it. 'Mam, what's a good charity?'

'The St Vincent de Paul never forget the poor, Maggie,' she said.

'Grand. I'm joining.'

Then something entirely different occurred to Maggie. With the food kitchen closed, would she ever see Daniel again?

part two

eight

Maggie
July 1914

'Why would I need a head start?' Maggie asked then sped away, feet pumping the pedals.

'God knows!' Daniel called after her.

She laughed as they tore along the quays. She could feel him behind her, already closing the gap. She hadn't a hope against him. He had too much muscle.

'To the next lamppost!' she called, a short race her only hope.

She turned to see how close he was. It was the end of her. One look at his determined face and she exploded into laughter. He shot by her and, seconds later, reaching the lamppost he raised both arms in the air and kept them there as he glided forward.

'Show off!'

He slowed so that she could catch him.

'You made me laugh,' she accused.

'And what was it the last time – and the time before that?'

'Someday, I'll get you Daniel Healy. I might have to cheat...'

'You *might* have to cheat?'

They were laughing when they first heard the yelling. They turned to look up the quay towards O'Connell Bridge. A battalion of British Army soldiers was marching onto Bachelor's Walk, pursued by a large crowd of civilians who seemed to be jeering them. Someone fired a stone.

Maggie and Daniel turned to each other in surprise. No one ever bothered the army.

'What's going on?' Maggie asked curiously.

'We need to move back,' Daniel said. The soldiers – and the mob – were getting closer. A tension cut the air. 'There's going to be trouble.'

The words 'Irish Volunteers' sailed to them on the summer breeze.

'Tom's with the Volunteers!' Maggie exclaimed.

'We need to go now, Maggie.'

She glanced about. 'We'd be fine on the Ha'penny Bridge – out of the way and still able to see.'

'No. I've a bad feeling about this. We should leave altogether.'

'I need to find out about Tom!'

He sighed. 'All right. Hurry then.'

They had only taken up position on the bridge when another mob swelled onto the quay from a side street, firing rocks now. Three men grabbed a soldier and began to drag him away. A handful of his battalion charged to his rescue, bayonets fixed. An officer called upon the crowd to disperse. A stone hit him on the chin. Another got his ear. A glass bottle exploded into the face of another soldier. An officer ordered a line of men onto one knee, another line to stand behind them. They aimed at the crowd.

'It's just a warning,' Maggie said. 'To get them to disperse.'

Then she heard shots and echoes of those shots. Men and women crumpled to the ground. Maggie threw her bicycle down but Daniel grabbed her before she could run to help. She struggled against him but he held her fast and turned her away. But she heard the sound of bayonets being plunged into people. She heard the screams of men and women, citizens of Dublin who had dared to tackle the British Army.

Only when the soldiers began to march away did Daniel finally release her.

She ran. They both did.

On the ground, people lay bleeding. Others were trying to help. Children looked on, pale and stunned.

Maggie fell to her knees beside an injured woman but did not know how to stop the tide of blood. The woman stared up at her, eyes wide like a startled horse. There was a terrifying gurgling sound.

'It'll be all right. It'll be all right,' Maggie repeated, over and over. But she knew that it wouldn't.

The woman gasped and grew heavier in her arms as the life left her eyes.

Maggie looked up at Daniel. 'Oh Jesus, Danny. Oh no.'

He dropped to his knees beside her, took the weight of the woman from her and laid her down. He closed over the lifeless eyes. He and Maggie blessed themselves and prayed for her soul. Then he took Maggie's hand and helped her up. Her knees were shaking. Her entire body was. She fought tears.

'I didn't know what to do! I couldn't save her!'

'No one could have, Maggie. She was too far-gone.'

Maggie stared in disbelief at the sight before them. It was as if they had tumbled into a nightmare. People lay bleeding and groaning in pain. And Maggie hadn't the first idea how to help them.

'Are you all right to cycle?' Daniel asked.

She stared at him. 'I'm not *leaving!*'

'To get help, Maggie. There's no one faster on a bicycle than you.'

'There's *you*.'

'And I'll be right beside you. As always.'

'Let's go.'

Standing watching ambulances race from the hospital, Daniel put an arm about Maggie.

'You're shaking,' he said.

It was true. Every part of her was trembling. Try as she might, she couldn't stop it. She would never forget that woman's face. She would never forget the blood. Or the screams. Or the eerie silence before the shots. And she would never forget how she had trusted the British Army not to shoot. How could she have been so ignorant? She knew Ireland's history. She knew what the British Army was like. Hadn't her own father told her often enough?

'Let's go,' Daniel said.

Maggie didn't know where she wanted to go but she wanted to be moving. And so she went.

It was her mother who opened the door.

'Lord God Almighty! What happened?'

Maggie looked down and saw that she was covered in blood. Then, she spied Lily, standing with a hand clamped over her mouth. It hit Maggie with such force then. If they hadn't taken Lily in, she might have been there. She might have been killed.

'I'm all right,' Maggie reassured. 'I'm not hurt. We came upon...an accident,' she said to protect Lily.

Her mother ushered them inside and shoved a chair under Maggie so hard that she landed into it.

'Are you certain you're not hurt?' she asked, checking her daughter over from head to toe.

Nodding, Maggie closed her eyes. But behind her lids, she relived it all, every detail. She shivered.

Lily hurried a glass of water into her hand. Maggie had not seen her leave to fetch it.

'How are you, Lily?' she heard Daniel ask.

'I'm very well thank you,' Lily said.

Maggie had an overwhelming urge to hug her but she would only cover her in blood.

'How are you, Daniel?' Maggie's mother asked. She loved him, loved that her daughter had a friend at last, not that Maggie had ever admitted she had been without one. Most mothers – along with society – would have frowned upon a male companion.

Maggie's mam was simply grateful.

'If you're all right, Maggie, I'll leave you all in peace,' he said, looking at her little family, not wanting to intrude. 'I'll see you tomorrow?'

'You will,' she said firmly. She would *not* be stopped by the British Army.

Maggie bathed and went to bed early. Later, though, she woke to the sound of raised voices. She lay very still and listened. It was Tom and their mother. Maggie crept from her room and down the stairs.

'Don't try to hide it, Tom. I know where you were. News travels fast in this city, especially news of this magnitude. You are to finish with Na Fianna!'

'I have finished with Na Fianna,' he said calmly. 'I'm with the Irish Volunteers now.'

'Sweet mother of Jesus! People were murdered! You might have been killed!'

'I was never in danger. Didn't you know? The British Army only fires upon the unarmed.'

'The deaths of those people are on your hands.'

'No, they're on the hands of The British Army.'

'You were running guns. *Guns,* Tom. You antagonized them.'

'And because they were angry with us, they fired upon civilians. *That* is the respect for life in this country. And *that* is why we need them out.'

'It is education and dialogue that will change this country. We are *so close* to Home Rule.'

'Home Rule be damned!'

'Don't scoff at a peaceful solution.'

'It wouldn't *be* a solution. We'd never be completely free of England. Politicians are full of hot air.'

'I forbid you to be in a rebel organisation.'

'I'm nineteen, a man, now. And I've been the man of the house a lot longer.'

'And *as* the man of the house you have a responsibility to stay safe for us,' she said desperately.

'I have a greater responsibility to my country,' he said, quieter now.

'Untrue.'

'You've always said that the problems of others are our problem. Ireland's upper classes blindly accept British rule because it suits them. No one cares for the poor, only those prepared to fight.'

'Remember our history, Tom. *Every* rebellion ended in failure.'

'Because the rebels had no military training. Now it's different.'

'Fighting is not the answer.'

'Well *striking* certainly isn't. Ask Larkin – if you can find him. As for *jeering...*'

'Ireland is a piece of *land* like any other piece of land!'

'It's not *about* land. It's about *people*. It's about a better life for all, especially those like Lily and her poor mother. Who do they have to stand up for them? You can't adopt everyone.'

Maggie touched her heart. *Now* she knew why he loved Lily so much; she represented all that he cared for. Now she understood his anger. And she loved him for it. Everything he said made sense. Why had she not seen it?

'Education-'

'Is the privilege of the upper classes. It won't change a thing. You have your ideals, Mam, and I respect them but you must respect mine. That is how you've raised us, to respect the ideals of others whether or not we share them. I'm staying with the Volunteers and if I must disobey you to do so, then so be it. I'm sorry. I'll leave home if you want. I'll still give you most of my income.' Tom had left school now and, having failed to secure a university scholarship, worked as a clerk.

'You're going nowhere. You're staying right here with us.'
There was a pause. 'Your heart is too big, Tom Gilligan.'

'At least it beats. And it loves you to pieces, Mam.'

Maggie's eyes welled with emotion. Then she bounded upstairs as the door opened.

nine

Maggie

Maggie paced her bedroom. Nothing she had done had made a difference because none of it had addressed the root of injustice in the country: British rule. It was the British who had, through their Penal Laws, deliberately set out to make the Irish poor, uneducated and powerless so that they would be easier to control. It was the British who were responsible for the tenements, the endless cycle of poverty and the hopelessness of the people. Tom was right, the boy keeping watch outside Madame's, too. Striking was not the solution. As for Home Rule? Only a fool would trust the British. There was only one way to make a difference.

Maggie would join a rebel organisation. And not one for girls.

She went to her dresser and fumbled in the drawer for a pair of scissors. Then she sat in front of the mirror. She lifted a strand of hair, then cut it off, an inch from her head. She snipped off another strand. And another. The clumps piled high as Maggie began to resemble a boy, a boy with a terrible hair cut. Clumps stuck out in all directions. She tried to achieve balance by cutting further into it. At last, she admitted defeat.

She looked at the stranger in the mirror, horrified that she could be so upset by such a superficial thing as her appearance.

She would go to bed. Things were always better in the morning.

She was pulling the covers up when a gentle knock came to door. She blew out the candle, slipped her head under a pillow and closed her eyes. She heard the door creak open.

'Maggie?' her mother whispered.

She breathed deeply like Lily. Her mother would be more able for this in the morning.

'Maggie,' she said, coming closer. 'We need to talk about what happened today.'

Maggie breathed deeper still.

'That was no accident you witnessed, was it?'

Maggie groaned in her pretend sleep.

At last, with a sigh, her mother left.

In the morning, her hair seemed worse than ever. It was as if she had been attacked as she slept, for what person would deliberately do that to herself?

'Oh, Maggie,' Lily said sadly. 'Do you have nits?'

Maggie laughed. 'No, Lily. I have clarity.'

'Good, because nits are *awful*.'

The bedroom door opened and her mother peered in as if their laughter was music. On seeing Maggie, she clasped her hands over her mouth. When she recovered her powers of speech it was to exclaim, 'Your hair! Your beautiful hair! What have you *done*?'

'I'm selling it for charity.' At least there was that.

Her mam tried to be calm. 'What in God's name, possessed you?'

There was no easy way to tell her. 'I'm joining Na Fianna.'

'Na Fianna is for boys.'

'Thus the hair.'

Her mother looked like she had been slapped. She turned to Lily. 'Go downstairs, Lily. I'll be down in a minute.' This was not a voice to be argued with.

Head down, Lily left in silence.

'You were there, on the quays. You witnessed what happened.' It was more a statement than a question.

Maggie nodded.

'I'm sorry, pet. That must have been so difficult. But you must understand *why* it happened. Na Fianna – and others – were running guns. Out in broad daylight. They antagonized the army. They caused the deaths of those people.'

'I saw them fall, Mam, normal people like you and me. I could do nothing to help. At least with Na Fianna, I'd learn first aid.'

'You'd also bear arms and that I cannot allow.'

'You allowed it with Tom.'

'When I thought he was simply scouting.'

'You're allowing it now with the Volunteers.'

Her mother stared at her. 'What can I do to stop him? He's nineteen years of age.'

'I won't bear arms, Mam.'

'You won't because you're not joining.'

'You can't stop me! I have to make a difference in the world! I have to! And everything Tom said is right. Someone must act.'

'Not you! Not the both of you! From the day your father died, I have *dreaded* that I'd let him down in the rearing of you.'

'And *I* have dreaded that *I'd* let him down. If I can't make a difference in the world, I may as well have died in that fire along with him.' Her eyes filled with tears.

'Don't say that, Maggie. Never say that.' She turned away. With jerky, distressed movements, she began to gather up the severed hair on the dresser.

Maggie went to her, took the hair from her hands. 'Mam, you reared us to care. How can that be letting him down? I would rather be who I am and dead...' Her mother flinched. '...than the girls at school who have never lived – and never will.'

Her mother pulled away. 'If you join, I'll go to them! I'll tell them you're a girl!'

'No you won't,' Maggie said calmly because she knew her mother; and she'd never do that.

'Why are you so *willful*?'

'Do you think Father would want me any other way? Honestly, Mam. Do you?'

Her mother closed her eyes and sighed deeply. 'I'm too soft. Too soft by far.'

Maggie threw her arms around her. 'I'll be all right, Mam. I'll stay out of trouble. I'll only help the wounded. I'll be grand. You'll see.'

Maggie examined her reflection. Her thin frame coupled with her cropped hair and David's hand-me-down cap, trousers, shirt and jacket rendered her a convincing boy. She looked at him in the mirror and tried out different names. Ruairí, she decided at last and pulled the peaked cap down over her face.

She sought out the opinion of the family rebel.

Tom looked at her as though seeing her for the first time. 'I'm proud of you, Maggie.'

'I've done nothing yet.'

'You've stepped up.'

'Not to fight, though. Only to help.' She had to be straight about that.

'I know. We'll need all the help we can get when the time comes.' He ripped her cap from her head and held it out of reach as if she had, in fact, become a brother.

She jumped for it. Never had she felt closer to him. They would make a difference – together.

And yet Maggie hated going against her mother's wishes. She put the clothes away and tried to be the daughter her mam wanted her to be. She sat with Lily, struggling to draw a boy with a swan's wing. Every so often, she glanced over at her mother who was at her bureau, working as always, though the schools were closed for the summer.

'How about a story while we draw?' Lily asked.

Maggie looked at her. A story of Irish heroics was out of the question. So Maggie fell back on Joan of Arc.

'Sorry about the ending,' she said, grimacing.

'I like that she wore her hair short and dressed as a man,' Lily said cheerfully.

Maggie's mother threw her pen down. 'It got her killed! Did you tell her that, Maggie?'

The girls went quiet as she hurried from the room, muttering, 'I'm sorry,' as she disappeared.

Lily stared after her. 'What's the matter with Mammy?'

Maggie hesitated. 'I've upset her, Lily.'

'You should say sorry, Maggie.'

Maggie rubbed the top of Lily's head. Strands of hair remained standing. Maggie eased them down again. Lily was not a rebel; her hair ought to know that.

'Should we see if she's all right?' Lily asked.

'She is. She's only getting used to an idea of mine.'

'What idea?'

Maggie sighed. 'The idea of me growing up.'

'We all have to grow up, Maggie,' she said wisely.

Maggie smiled then. 'How about another story?'

'Have you got one about Na Fianna?'

'Well there's the one about Oisín and....'

'The other Fianna. Your Fianna.' She nibbled the end of her pencil.

'It's not my Fianna yet. They might not let me in. Anyway, it's not half as interesting as the ancient warrior troop.'

'Tell me anyway.'

'Another day. Now let's see who can draw the best Joan of Arc.'

Lily, the superior artist, brightened. 'Is there a prize?'

'Of course there's a prize.'

The following day, Daniel was waiting for her at the end of her road as arranged. Head high, she cycled past him. When he failed to recognise her, she laughed, stopped and cycled back removing the cap as she did so and waving it over her head.

He stared at her. 'Is it *you*?'

'Who else?' If she could fool Daniel, she could fool anyone!

But as he stared at her hair, she realised that he hated it. And she *hated* that she cared.

'What happened?' he asked.

She raised her chin. 'Na Fianna happened. I'm joining.'

'What?' he whispered.

'Nothing's going to change in this country until we get Britain out.'

'Maggie, this is a reaction-'

'Perhaps, but it's the right one.'

'How do you know? You must allow yourself time to recover before you commit to anything.'

'I've committed my hair.'

'Hair will grow.'

'Things must change, Danny,' she said quietly. Her mind was made up.

'How can a bunch of boy scouts change anything?'

'A bunch of boy scouts is a start. There are other rebel organisations-'

'You want to fight *the British Army*?'

'No but I'll do First Aid, run errands, act as a lookout.'

'You'll still be in danger!'

'Opening your mouth in this country is a danger!'

He looked at her for the longest time, then sighed deeply. 'Maggie.' It was just one word but it seemed to contain so much emotion.

She felt the same emotion welling up inside her. 'I don't expect you to join,' she said hoarsely.

Time seemed to slow. And yet life carried on around them. In the park beside them, a nanny pushed a perambulator, cooing at the baby inside. A little girl chased a hoop. A boy struggled with a kite. She looked at Daniel and her heart ached. How had he come to mean so much to her?

'I'll join,' he said.

Relief flooded her but then she imagined him facing fire as those people had on the quay.

'No. It wouldn't be right. You're a pacifist. This is my battle.' Then she had to ask. 'We can stay friends outside of Na Fianna. Can't we?' Suddenly, she feared the answer.

'If you join, I join and that's that. We belong together, Maggie. You and I.'

She bowed her head. She felt it too. 'We do.' She looked up again. 'But promise you'll stay out of trouble. I couldn't bear it if anything happened to you because of me.'

'I'll promise if you do.'

She smiled. 'He cares,' she joked.

He looked into her eyes. 'He does.'

Had she known that friendship would be like this, she might have tried harder with the girls at school. But then trying with people who don't want you only makes them not want you more.

Arriving home, Maggie entered the drawing room. David, Lily and her mother were playing a backgammon tournament. She brightened at the sight.

Everyone looked up and smiled – apart from her mother, who kept her eyes on the board. It felt like a stab to the heart.

'We're playing backgammon!' Lily said. 'It's great fun. I'm winning. See?'

Maggie came around and rested her hands on Lily's shoulders. She looked at the board.

'So you are.' Maggie glanced at her mother. 'That's only because Mam's hopeless,' she teased.

Still she did not raise her eyes. It was as if she had decided to concentrate her attention on Lily and David, as if she had already lost Maggie.

'You haven't lost me,' she wanted to say. But maybe it was better this way because if they *did* lose her, it wouldn't hurt so much. Maybe that was what their mother was doing, preparing herself and everyone else. 'I'm only joking,' Maggie said to Lily, bending down to kiss the top of her head. 'You're winning because you're clever.'

'I know!'

Maggie and David shared a smile. Maggie glanced at the picture he was drawing while awaiting his turn. Didn't he *know* that the rose was the symbol of England? But when she looked at his face, she forgave him. He was a dreamer. And dreamers could be forgiven anything.

'Do you want to play, Maggie?' Lily asked.

'Lily, take your turn,' their mother said.

'It's fine, Lil,' Maggie said quietly. 'I'm tired. I'm going to sit by the fire for a while.'

'I'll be over to you when I'm finished,' Lily said.

Maggie sat by the fire and looked into the flames. Make a difference, he'd said. He hadn't asked her to make her mother happy; he hadn't asked her to do what she was told. He'd asked her to *make a difference in the world* because he knew that he would never get the chance to. He knew that when he turned to face the fire it would be the last difference he would attempt to make. His request to her had been monumental. She had felt it at the time. She felt it now.

Soon Lily was climbing up onto her lap. She took Maggie's face between her hands and looked into her eyes. 'Are you all right, Maggie?'

Maggie smiled. Then she widened her eyes and said in a sinister voice, 'I'm all the better for seeing you, my dear.' She bared her teeth and took bites of air.

Lily screamed and leapt from her lap. 'Save me, Mammy!'

Maggie made clawing movements.

Lily screamed.

And then, like a new day dawning, their mother smiled.

The following evening, Maggie put on David's old coat and pulled his cap down over her eyes. She did not want to upset her mother by appearing dressed as she was but she knew she would upset her more by not saying goodbye. She opened the door to the drawing room.

Lily jumped to her feet and ran to her. 'You're a lovely boy, Maggie!'

She smiled. 'Thanks, Lil.'

'You're going to have to sound a lot gruffer than that,' Tom said.

'I'm not planning on saying a word.'

'Good.'

'Maggie, could you not join an organisation of girls?' her mother tried.

Maggie glanced at her brothers as she replied, 'Because in my experience, boys are far and away more decent than girls. Don't worry, Mam. Daniel will be with me.'

'Daniel?' Tom asked warily.

'My friend.'

'You've a friend that's a boy?'

'If you spent more time at home you might know this,' Maggie said.

Tom looked at their mother. 'How can you allow this?'

She raised an eyebrow. 'Do you think, Tom Gilligan, that having a friend who's a boy is more dangerous than joining a rebel organisation?'

'A rebel organisation of *boys*,' David pointed out helpfully.

'I'd trust Danny with my life,' Maggie said.

'You may have to,' her mother countered bitterly.

'About this boy-' Tom began as though he'd transformed into a parent.

'*This boy* will protect her from other boys.' Maggie's mother turned to her. 'Go on. Off with you now. And be careful.'

Her blessing meant the world. 'I love you, Mam.'

She raised her eyebrows. 'Because you got your way.'

'No. Because I love you.'

ten

Daniel

With her shorn head, Maggie looked more beautiful than ever to Daniel. But it was about more than her beauty. Or even her passion. Somehow, she had become the most important thing in his life. He would do anything to protect her, even join a rebel force. It would not come to a fight, he was certain, but it could come between him and his father – if he were ever to find out.

As they approached Surrey House, Daniel turned to Maggie. 'If Madame comes anywhere near us keep your head down and leave the talking to me.'

'Have you *no* faith in me?'

'I've too much. That's the problem.'

She smiled. 'Impossible.'

The front door was wide open so they walked in, Daniel leading the way.

The drawing room was mobbed with boys, eagerly chatting in small groups. Daniel and Maggie moved to the back in silence. As they waited for the meeting to start, he glanced briefly at her to see how she was doing. He had to hurry the back of his hand to his mouth to stifle a laugh. She was standing with her legs spread, hands on her hips and chin raised.

'Very convincing,' he whispered.

Encouraged, she proceeded to scratch herself in a place that only a boy would scratch himself.

Part mortified, part hysterical, he exploded into a fit of coughing.

'God, the freedom of being a boy,' she whispered.

'Don't get carried away,' he managed. Life was never tedious with Maggie.

At last, there was a hush as Madame arrived at the top of the room. She clapped her hands with authority. Silence fell. Then, looking from boy to boy, she began to speak. 'It is *heartening* to see so many of you here today wishing to join Na Fianna. We are about to change this country, boys. Change this country. And why, you might ask, does it need to be changed?' She let her gaze wander the room. 'Because!' She paused for effect. 'Ireland is a country where people go hungry, where workers have no say and where the police are in the pockets of the rich. Let me ask you a question. Why do one third of Dubliners live in tenements?' Again she scanned the room. 'Why are they forced to pay rents that in other countries would buy a house? Why *is* that, boys? Why?'

There was an uncertain silence. Boys exchanged glances unsure as to whether or not to reply.

'Do you know your history, lads?'

They shifted from foot to foot.

'Do wish to *hear* your history?'

A timid cheer rose up.

'Then let me introduce you to Con Colbert. Con?'

A man-boy in full uniform joined Madame. He thanked her then turned to the assembly.

'The British,' he began. 'You know who they are, don't you?'

The boys laughed.

'Well, in 1695, they introduced the Penal Laws to this little country of ours. For almost a hundred years, we Catholics could not own land. We could not become lawyers or doctors or have any profession or trade whatsoever. We could not vote. We could not practise our religion or educate our children. We could not speak our own language.' He stopped.

No one moved. There wasn't a sound.

'And so, you see, they used the law to make us ignorant, poor and useless. Then came the famine to break us even more, to send the starving piling into the cities, into the tenements – those that didn't die, that is. Is it any wonder that this country is in the state it's in? No. It is not. *But!* There *is* hope. There is *one thing* the Brits have *never* been able to take from us.' He paused. 'Our spirit. We've *kept* our religion. We've *kept* our education. We've *kept* our music *and* our stories. We've passed them down from generation to generation behind their miserable British backs. The one thing they'll *never* be able to take from us is our spirit. Our spirit will forever be ours.'

There was no doubt in their cheer now. But while they erupted into applause, Daniel stood stunned. He had never heard of the Penal Laws. Could they really have existed without him knowing of them? He learned history at school. His father was a lawyer. One question followed the next in Daniel's mind. He felt like he had that first day in the food kitchen. Lost.

'A time has come for Ireland to say, "no more,"' Con Colbert continued. 'A time has come for Ireland to be free of British rule, to stand tall and proud and rule herself, to face the poverty and solve it. A time has come for Na Fianna Éireann. A time has come to take back this grand little country of ours.'

The applause rose, loud and proud. Then Con Colbert raised his arm. 'Patrick, would you come up here and explain to these fine young lads what exactly they're signing up for today?'

The boy who arrived beside Con Colbert was the one who had been keeping watch outside Surrey House. Colbert slapped him on the back then stood aside. Patrick looked from boy to boy, taking his own sweet time.

'You might have heard that we in Na Fianna are boy scouts,' he said, then paused. 'Well, you heard *wrong!*' he shouted. 'We are soldiers! Fighting for the defence of Ireland!'

A great, united roar rose up.

'No other rebel organisation in this country is as well trained as Na Fianna. That I promise you. With us, you'll learn to shoot and care for a weapon like a beloved pet. You'll learn to signal and track. You'll go on drills and route marches in the Dublin Mountains. You'll study our city till you know every back alley, every dead-end, every escape route there is. You'll learn how to fight the British Army by studying its weaknesses.' He smiled. 'And there are many. You'll learn street fighting, boys. And you'll learn to defend your country.' He looked around. 'Does that sound like something you might be interested in?'

Another roar, louder than ever. Daniel felt the excitement in the room like it was a living thing.

'Well, that answers my question.' Patrick grinned. 'Let us begin, then, with musketry training.'

Daniel looked at Maggie. They hadn't even signed up and they were about to handle guns?

''Twould be no harm to know what to *do* with a gun, I suppose,' she whispered.

They were ordered down to the basement, where Madame stood at the head of the room with a revolver. She held it with reverence. Once everyone had settled into stillness, she spoke.

'Now pay attention. The gun is a powerful weapon. You must, at all times, respect it. Failure to do so will result in immediate expulsion from Na Fianna. Do I make myself clear?'

'Yes, Madame.'

'Louder, boys.'

'Yes, Madame,' they shouted.

'That's more like it. Now, let us begin.'

She showed them the best stance to take and how to aim. Then she herself took aim and fired. She hit the centre of the target, turned and looked at them.

'That is the accuracy you will learn in Na Fianna.'

'Isn't she fierce?' whispered the boy beside Daniel.

That is exactly what she was.

'She learned to shoot growing up on her father's estate in Sligo,' the boy said knowledgeably.

Everyone seemed to know something about Madame. She seemed to Daniel to be an almost mythical creature so wild were the stories.

'All right, I would like you all to form a line,' she ordered now.

Automatically, Daniel and Maggie made for the back. Before they reached it though, Daniel heard his name.

'Daniel Healy?'

He stopped and turned.

Madame was approaching at a clip. 'It *is* you! What a wonderful surprise! And who do we have here?'

He cleared his throat. 'Eh, this is my brother, Ruairí.'

Maggie tipped her head down.

'Timid little chap. Well, let's see what he's made of.' With a hand to each of their backs, Madame steered them to the front of the line.

She placed the revolver, cold and heavy, into Daniel's hand.

'Off you go,' she said cheerfully.

He wished for time to slow, rewind even, so that he could take stock.

Madame began to tap her foot.

Daniel faced the target. He tried to remember all that she had said about firing. He took aim. Then he cast aside the instructions and simply squeezed the trigger.

Madame laughed. 'That was your *first time* firing a weapon?'

He nodded, stunned.

'Take another shot,' she ordered, eyes fixed on the target as if she expected another direct hit.

It was what she got.

Maggie stared at him.

He shrugged.

'Bravo!' Madame exclaimed, taking the gun from him and handing it to his timid brother. 'Let's hope it runs in the family.'

Maggie took up position, spread her legs, took aim. And fired.

Madame shook her head and lit a cigarette. 'Incredible.'

Maggie had hit the centre of the target.

'It's always the quiet ones,' the countess said when Maggie's second shot also found its mark. She put her hand out for the gun.

Walking to the back of the line, Maggie nudged Daniel with an elbow. He nudged her back. He could not believe it. Perhaps shooting was easy. Perhaps everyone else would have equal success.

Patrick arrived beside them. 'Not bad for a pair of toffs.'

Daniel met his eye. 'You must be in awe of Madame then, a toff *and* a woman.'

He laughed in surprise. 'Well. Madame *is* exceptional.' Had any of the other boys said it, it would have been a compliment.

'By the way, that girl you were with, last time, Tom Gilligan's sister? The *mouth* on her.'

'Lippy enough, all right,' Daniel said, trying not to smile. 'But she has her own unique charm.'

'She kept it well hidden, I can tell you.'

'Lippy, am I?' Maggie said as soon as they'd left the building – but she was smiling.

'Maybe not *that* lippy– you managed to stay quiet.'

'I *managed* to not kill him.'

He smiled. 'An achievement given what a good shot you are.'

'Must have been luck.'

'You were incredible.'

'Well then, so were you.'

'We were both incredible.'

They laughed, in bafflement. Then Daniel grew serious. 'Had *you* heard of the Penal Laws?'

She nodded. 'But not through school where they teach British history. My brothers go to St Enda's where they learn everything Irish – the history, the language, the music. David fills me in.'

'It's hard to believe.'

'Not when you consider how they still treat us.'

'Well, how they treat *the poor*.'

'And those who buck against them.'

'As we'll be doing. Are you certain you want to join, Maggie? You could still change your mind.'

She raised an eyebrow and mounted her bicycle.

They cycled in silence for a while. He thought about his father. 'Any bright ideas what I'll tell my parents I'm doing in the evenings?'

'The truth?'

He laughed. 'You don't know my father.'

'I'd like to.'

'That would *not* be a good idea.'

'Why not?'

'For one thing, he believes girls to be a distraction.'

'Ah, but I'm a boy.'

He smiled. 'There's something else. You *were* right about him. He *is* a lawyer.'

She laughed. 'Honestly?'

'Honestly. So, as I say, I'll need an excuse. A good one.'

She frowned as she cycled. Then she turned to him. 'The Gaelic League!'

He looked at her blankly.

'Do you know *nothing* of your country?'

'It seems not.' What else was he ignorant of? He needed to know. He did not wish to walk the earth a fool.

'The Gaelic League is an organisation that teaches all things Irish – language, history, music.'

'Is it legal?'

She laughed. 'It is. It's educational.'

'He still may not agree to it.'

'Just inform him that you're doing it.'

It was his turn to laugh. 'Is that your approach?'

'It is. Try it. He might surprise you.'

'All right. I'll try,' he said, though his father was not a man for surprises.

Maggie looked thoughtful. 'If you're in the Gaelic League, you'd better know a few stories.'

'Stories?'

'Legends – like how Cú Chulainn got his name.'

'Who?'

'Jesus, Mary and Joseph.'

He laughed. And so all the way home, he learned of a boy who killed a hound, brothers who were turned into swans by their evil stepmother and a student who received all the wisdom of the world from a salmon. The more he heard, the more he wanted to know. He had always considered himself Irish. Only now was he beginning to learn what that meant.

His father was in the drawing room, reading, as usual. Normally, Daniel would have chosen his moment. Now, he couldn't wait. He took a deep breath – and Maggie's advice.

'Father, I've joined the Gaelic League.'

He looked up from *The Irish Times*. 'Pardon?'

'I've joined the Gaelic League.'

'What on earth for?'

'We *are* Irish, Father,' Daniel said, surprised by how irritated he felt.

The man looked genuinely confused. 'I hope you're not becoming a republican,' he joked.

Daniel decided against asking about the Penal Laws. He took his history book from out of his schoolbag and began to flick through it. How had he never noticed? There was no Irish history. None. It was the history of the British Empire. But then, until he had met Maggie, he had, like his father, blindly accepted that he was part of that empire.

He thought about everything that had been said at the meeting. His reality had not been *the* reality. To him, poverty had simply existed. Instead, it had been manufactured to control a people. The thought horrified and infuriated him in equal measure. It made him want something he had never considered until now – Ireland's freedom from British rule. It did not, however, make him want to take up arms. He had joined Na Fianna for Maggie. Not to fight.

'Father, may I read the newspaper when you have finished?' He needed suddenly, to know the world.

His father looked pleasantly surprised. 'You can read it now if you have finished your studies.'

Daniel went to retrieve the newspaper, hoping that, in its pages, he would discover a peaceful path to freedom, if such a thing existed.

Days later, at a dance organised by Na Fianna to raise funds for The Defence of Ireland Fund, Daniel, Patrick and Maggie stood side by side, watching the dance floor, catching their breath after five in a row.

'Two o'clock,' Patrick said.

Daniel turned to locate the latest girl Patrick had selected for praise. He did it to humour him. In reality, Daniel had eyes for one girl only and she was standing right beside him in trousers and cap. And she was not happy. Arms folded, she was looking dead ahead, ignoring Patrick's commentary.

'Ruairí,' Patrick called over the music. 'I think you've an admirer.' He nodded to a girl opposite who immediately looked away. 'Why don't you go on over?'

'Why don't *you* go if you're so keen?' Maggie snapped.

'Sure, why don't I call her over, altogether?'

Daniel laughed.

Maggie stared at him, then stomped from the hall.

'He's a shy little bastard, all the same,' Patrick said.

Daniel went after her. He had no idea what had her so vexed but he shouldn't have laughed all the same.

He found her outside, down the side of the building, facing into the wall. Her shoulders were shaking. Was she *crying*?

He went to her. 'Maggie, are you all right?'

'Go away,' she said without turning.

'What is it?' he asked, gently.

'Leave me alone.'

'I'm sorry I laughed. I-'

Then she was flying past him. 'I'm going home.'

'Wait! I'll go with you.'

'I don't want you to.'

'And *I* don't want you to go alone.'

'Tough bloody luck.' She grabbed her bicycle and was away.

She had forgotten her jacket, he realised. With a sigh, he went back inside to get it for her.

eleven

Maggie

They had only just joined Na Fianna and already they were up in the Dublin Mountains with them. After a day of drills, target practice and manoeuvres, Maggie and Daniel were sent to fetch wood for a campfire.

Maggie kicked at the undergrowth. She did not know what was annoying her. It seemed to be her permanent state lately – infuriation – mostly at Daniel, though he'd done nothing wrong. Even now, he was doing all the work, his arms filling with sticks.

'What's the matter?' he asked.

'Nothing.'

'Then give me a hand, you slacker,' he joked.

'I'm *not* your little brother.' She turned from him and hurried to collect kindle. What was *wrong* with her? She couldn't understand it.

From all about them came the patter of raindrops.

Maggie looked up through the trees. 'Oh for crying out loud!'

'What?' he asked.

'I left my *bloody* coat back at the camp.'

He smiled. 'You'd think it was the end of the world.'

'Stop laughing at me.'

'I'm not laughing at you, Maggie. I'm baffled by you.'

He came to her then, removing his coat and settling it over her shoulders. She felt the warmth of his body from it. She looked up at him. Then she was saying it.

'Why do you always treat me like a boy?'

'You know why.'

'You think I'm boyish, don't you?'

'Isn't that what you're aiming for?'

'That's not what I meant.'

'Then what *did* you mean?'

'You don't see me as a girl, at all, do you?' She turned from him as sudden, infuriating tears ambushed her. She busied herself with a desperate search for decent wood not those annoying twigs that seemed to be everywhere.

There was a long silence.

At last, she could bear it no longer and turned to see what he was doing.

He was standing very still, watching her. 'Come here,' he said, his voice soft, different.

She didn't budge.

'Come here.'

'No.'

'Maggie.'

'What?' she demanded.

They stood, eyes locked. He let the sticks fall. Then he was walking towards her, his eyes holding hers. Her heart raced. And there he was, before her, so close that she took a step back. He took another forward.

'Of course I see you as a girl,' he said huskily. 'Despite this silly hat.' He reached out and removed it. He settled her hair back in place, his touch making her shiver and gasp. 'You've girl hair – despite hacking it to bits.' His voice was hoarse. 'And girl eyebrows.' He ran his thumbs slowly along them. 'And a girl mouth.' He touched her lips so lightly it tickled. Her whole body ached for him, Daniel, her best friend. What was happening?

He answered with a kiss.

But his kiss was a question too.

And her answer was another kiss.

His hands were in her hair, then cupping her face then wrapping around her and pulling her close. He whispered her name. And she closed her eyes. So *this* was what was wrong with her; *this* was what she'd been longing for without even knowing it.

He pulled back, gazed down at her and smiled. 'Do you know how long I've wanted to do that?' he asked, voice deeper than she had ever heard it. Gravelly.

She shook her head, in absolute shock.

'Since you punched Michael.'

She could not believe it. 'Honestly?'

'Honestly.'

'I wish I'd been nicer to you.'

'That would only have made you like everyone else.' He held her to him and rested his chin on her head.

Her heart soared. She had never been happier, all those minutes, hours, days, months, years she had been alive. She gazed up at him. 'When you told me you liked me all the more for being queer, that was the sweetest thing anyone has ever said to me.'

He bent down and kissed her. 'You make me happy, Maggie Gilligan.'

'You make me happier, Daniel Healy.'

'Is it a competition?' He smiled.

'Of course.'

'Then I suppose we should see who's best.' He kissed her again, slowly, his tongue parting her lips. She pressed herself to him and, as the rain splattered about them, they could barely contain themselves.

A sudden rustling, a snapped twig and they jumped apart. Here, they were brothers.

They turned to the sound.

'It's a deer!' Maggie laughed in relief.

Daniel continued to look around. 'We'd better get back before they send out a search party.'

'Let them find us. I don't care.'

He smiled. 'Here, put back on your silly hat,' he said, putting it back himself and stealing another kiss.

She wanted to stay in the woods forever. Kissing him. And getting used to this new place they had arrived at together. She could not believe it. Did she know nothing of herself? Of him? Of the world?

Walking back, she longed for his touch. She made do with gazing up at his face, her favourite in the world. How she wanted to stroke his cheek, pull his head down and feel his mouth again. She shook her head. It was incredible; despite her shorn hair, Daniel liked her as a girl. He had wanted to kiss her since they'd first met! She hadn't been ready until... the night of the dance, she realised. She'd have welcomed a kiss that night. The thought astounded her.

As they approached the camp, they moved apart. She dropped the wood by the campfire and wiped her hands on her trousers.

'Is that all ye have?' Patrick said. 'I thought ye'd have collected a forest by now. I was about to come looking for ye.'

'We can go back for more,' she said. She looked at Daniel, longing for him.

'Ah, you're grand. I was only pulling your leg.'

They sat across the campfire from each other. She forced her eyes to stay on the flames, watching them spark up into the sky. But they returned to him all by themselves. And when she found him looking at her, it was as though a missing piece of her life had slotted into place. She had been lonely and had not known it. His smile seemed different now, as if for her alone. And as they all sang *A Nation Once Again*, her voice soared like a bird's up into the starry sky.

After they had eaten, one by one, they recounted their favourite rebel tales. Maggie told of Red Hugh O'Donnell's escape from captivity in Dublin Castle and how he battled the elements in the Wicklow Mountains and had to have half his foot sawn off on account of frostbite. She finished to applause.

Only Daniel wasn't clapping. He was frowning. She could

not understand why but it bothered her more than it ever would have before.

Later, they shared a tent with four others. As the lantern was dimmed, he seemed preoccupied. Did he regret the kiss? Was he worried that everything would change between them now? *She* was. She valued his friendship more than anything in the world. Had she lost it? Should she talk to him about it? Could she? She had always been so sure of herself with him. Was this, too, going to change?

She tossed and turned and, at length, slept.

He woke her just before dawn and they stole into the woods. They reached for each other and pressed together, bodies, mouths, skin, breaths. It had only been hours, but it felt like they had been a lifetime apart. She needed this like air. She would give up anything for it, yes, even their friendship. No. No, not that. She pulled back.

'Danny. We can still be friends, can't we?'

He brushed back her hair and looked into her eyes. 'Maggie Gilligan, we will always be friends.'

She felt her body deflate in relief.

He led her further into the trees. On a fallen, moss-covered trunk, he sat her down. He took her hand in his and rubbed his thumb over her palm. All she wanted to do was kiss him but there was so much to say.

'Danny. I'm so sorry for how I was with you at first. My expectations were low – to protect myself. I thought you'd let me down.' She looked up at him. 'But you never have.'

'I never will, Maggie.' He said it like an oath.

They gazed into each other's eyes.

'This is more than kissing,' he said.

'What is it?' she whispered. But she knew.

He laughed. 'You had to ask.' He kissed the tip of her nose. 'It's love,' he said softly, like a breath. 'And I've felt it since the day I met you. Is that possible?'

She bit her lip. 'You're not talking to an expert, here.' Heart soaring, she rested her cheek against his chest. In one way, it felt like she had known him all her life. In another, it felt as if she had not known him at all, not *appreciated* him. She looked up at him. 'Did I do something to upset you, last night, at the campfire?'

He looked baffled. 'No.'

'When I was telling my story, you were frowning.'

'Oh.' He sighed deeply. 'It's only that, sometimes, I worry that you've started to believe all they say, that dying for your country is romantic and worthy, that martyrdom is the ultimate glory.'

'I'm no fool, Daniel. But I *am* grateful to those who have sacrificed their lives, fighting for our freedom.'

'There's talk of Home Rule – freedom without a fight.'

'Home Rule wouldn't change a thing!'

'We'd rule our own country!'

'No. Britain would still control the army *and* our dealings with other nations. We need a republic, Danny, nothing less.'

'Where did you learn that?'

'From Patrick.' Of all the boys in Na Fianna, he was the one most itching for action and, despite what she thought of him, Maggie admired him for that.

'Perhaps he's wrong.'

'No. I asked Tom. Anyway, Home Rule would lead to civil war.'

'*Civil war?*'

She nodded. 'The Unionists, up North, fear that it would give the power to us Catholics. They're already armed. They'd fight Home Rule with force. Home Rule is the *last* thing we want.'

'The last thing I want is for you to get hurt. You're the most important thing in my life, Maggie Gilligan.' He swallowed visibly.

She looked into his eyes.

How she could climb into them and swim around in there. How she could creep up under his shirt and burrow into the heat of his skin. How she could lose herself in him. 'Why are we even discussing this when we could be doing this?'

She cupped his face in her hands and brought it down to

hers, brought his mouth to hers. Then she closed her eyes and lost herself in him.

Too soon, they had to return home to Dublin. Separating from him was the greatest wrench. But Maggie had the memory of how her world had changed to colour.

In the drawing room, she gazed at the hearth and brought herself back to the campfire and Daniel's eyes on the other side of it. She sighed.

'So it's finally happened.'

She turned and frowned at David. 'What's finally happened?'

'Your friend has become more than a friend.'

Maggie stared at him as colour shot to her cheeks. 'What?'

'It was only a matter of time. Love conquers all, Maggie Mae,' the poet of the family said knowledgably.

'You read too much.'

He chuckled. 'That may be. But I also notice things. You've been giving out an awful lot about Daniel Healy, lately. An awful lot.'

'Only to you. And he *was* annoying me.'

'So he's not an eejit after all, then?'

She smiled, wide and dreamy. 'No. He's not an eejit.' *She* had been the eejit. Now she imagined his face, his blue eyes speckled with gold, his generous mouth, his ready smile, the most special smile in the world. She could float up into the sky at the thought of it. She sighed again.

'God, you have it bad.'

She came to her senses. 'Don't tell Mam!'

'Mam'll be blind if she doesn't see it.'

'See what?'

'You're positively floating, Maggie.'

'Am I?' She smiled.

'And you'll have to stop all that smiling. God Almighty. You're as transparent as water.'

She bit her lip and smiled again. There was every reason in the world to. Every reason.

twelve

Daniel

On a rug in the Phoenix Park, she lay with her head on his lap. He stroked her hair, still not believing that the dreams he had long ago shelved had somehow come true. Maggie loved him in return. He'd thought, up on the mountain, that he was losing her. The truth was more than he'd ever hoped for. After that first kiss he could hardly contain himself. This new vulnerability in Maggie set him on fire. He was grateful of that deer disturbing them. And yet he wasn't. Part of him wanted to slip over that waterfall with her.

'You've never asked about my father,' she said now, waking him from his thoughts. 'Did you never wonder?'

'I knew you'd tell me when you were ready.'

She sat up and kissed him. 'You're so patient with me, Danny.'

'You have no idea!' He laughed and kissed her forehead.

'I do. You had to wait a year for me to realise that I loved you.'

'I never expected it, Maggie. Friendship was enough.' He looked at her then to see if she thought less of him.

'*Was* it?' she asked in surprise.

'No.' He laughed. 'I'd just convinced myself it was.'

She took his hand in hers, brought it to her lips and kissed it. But her smile was sad. 'I don't talk about him to anyone. Ever.'

'You don't have to, now.'

'I want to.' She picked a shamrock and began to pull the leaves from it. 'He died in a fire, Danny. He saved me and went back for the others.'

'God, I'm sorry, Maggie.'

She looked up into his eyes, as though willing him to understand. 'His last words to me were, "Make a difference in the world, Maggie."' Her eyes filled with tears.

And, *finally*, he understood. Everything. He wondered if the man knew the full extent of what he was asking at the time. 'What age were you?' He was almost afraid to ask.

'Eight.'

He could have cried. Instead he pulled her to him and kissed the top of her head. He wanted more than ever to protect her from the world.

Daniel and Michael walked off the cricket pitch, Michael tossing the ball in the air and catching it.

Daniel looked down at his whites. 'God, if Maggie saw me in this get up.'

'Maggie,' Michael said moodily.

Daniel looked at him. He debated. Then finally, out of loyalty to both Maggie and Michael, he said it. 'I love her.'

Michael's head swiveled. 'Ah no, Danny!'

'Ah yes.' He smiled. Nothing could spoil his mood.

'You're doomed!'

'It feels like a nice place to be.'

'You know that girl is nothing but trouble.'

Michael didn't know the half of it. Daniel had kept Na Fianna from him. With his father in the police, he had had to. About Maggie, though, he wanted to be honest. 'She is the most important thing in my life.'

'Ah, Jesus.'

Daniel could not stop smiling. 'I'm too far gone for prayers.'

'Jesus,' Michael repeated.

Daniel laughed. 'You do know that you two would love each other if only you'd agree to meet.'

'One of us under her spell is more than enough, thank you very much.'

thirteen

Maggie
August 1914

Maggie wore a pretty summer dress and matching bonnet. She had never tried harder to look like a girl. And had never been happier to be with a boy. She slipped her hand into his.

In the People's Park in Kingstown, he spread a rug on the grass and waved his arm ceremoniously.

'Maggie Gilligan,' he said with the formality of a butler. 'If you would be as good as to take your seat, the fine dining can begin.'

Laughing, she knelt down on the rug. 'You're an awful eejit.'

'Thank you, Ma'am.'

He opened a picnic basket.

Maggie stared. 'You prepared all this *yourself*?'

He looked guilty. 'Well, Cook....'

'Ooooh, *Cook*,' she teased, reaching for a cucumber sandwich

He snatched it from her hand. 'If you don't *want* it...'

She laughed and snatched it back. 'I want it.'

She gazed at him and sighed in satisfaction. Was this the most perfect day in her life? Or could any day match the one on the mountain when she discovered that she loved her best friend?

She tipped her head back. The trees were heavy with leaves. Here and there, the sun broke through in shafts.

'It doesn't seem right to be so happy when countries are declaring war on each other,' Daniel said.

Maggie sobered. 'I know.' In only days, Austria had declared war on Serbia. Germany had declared war on both Russia and France and had already begun to invade Belgium. 'Tom tried to explain it to me but I don't fully understand.'

'I don't either. It's all about agreements between nations. It makes no sense.'

'Do you think it will affect us?'

'I don't know, Maggie. We are part of the British Empire.'

She hated that thought. 'Let's talk of something else.'

'I have an admission to make,' he said brightly.

Maggie looked at him in surprise.

'Remember the day we met?'

'Of course I do.'

'Well, on that day I promised myself that I would, one day, bring you to Kingstown and kiss you.'

'Oh you *did*, did you?' she asked, delighted. 'How presumptuous.'

'And yet here we are.'

'But you haven't *had* that kiss,' she teased.

He turned his face to the side and ran a finger down it. 'With this profile? A matter of time. A matter of time.'

She laughed. She picked up his hand and kissed it. 'How's that?'

'Weak. Very weak.'

She laughed again. 'Where do you expect this kiss? We're in a public place, Daniel Healy. Are you trying to corrupt me?'

He puckered up his lips.

She felt that her entire body was a smile.

'Do you know that my father believes me to be sailing out of Kingstown today?' he asked.

'So you haven't told him about your new *friend*?' She was one to talk.

'I tell him nothing. Unlike your mother, he forbids things.'

'Only because you allow him to.'

'I'd like to see how *you'd* fare as his daughter for a week.'

'Don't worry. I'd break him.'

He laughed. 'I don't doubt it.'

It was great to be alone with him, no one to interrupt, no guns to clean or fire, no one listening in.

'You were right about him, by the way,' Daniel said. 'Not just that he's a lawyer but everything else. The telephone. The motorcar. The servants.'

'I know, you poshy.' She reached down and pulled a blade of grass. She made a slit in it with a fingernail and blew through it.

'There *is* someone I'd like you to meet, though,' he said.

'Do tell.'

'Michael.'

She groaned.

'You two got off on the wrong foot. And you're my favourite people in the world. So...'

'Is he as obnoxious as ever?'

He smiled. 'I think that what you hate about him is what I love. Like you, he pulses with life. No one makes me laugh like Michael.'

'Not even me?' She pretended to be wounded.

'You do other things to me.'

His gaze falling over her was certainly doing things to her. She had to kiss him now. Right out in the open. Their mouths met. Her eyes closed. Her toes curled. She never wanted to stop. But there was the issue of being in public. And so she dragged herself away from the most kissable boy in the world.

He smiled. 'You taste of grass.'

'What you're tasting, *Mister*, is a girl pulsing with life.'

He laughed.

'What's your favourite book?' She could never know enough about him.

'What's yours?' he asked, instead of answering.

'*Robinson Crusoe.*'

114

'Ah. Adventure on the high seas. I should have known.'

She shrugged. 'It has cannibals. And I asked you first.'

'*The Count of Monte Cristo*. It has revenge.'

She nodded sagely. 'Revenge is always good.'

'Favourite song?' he asked.

'*A Nation Once Again*, of course.'

He rolled his eyes. 'Maggie, have some imagination.'

'Tell me a better one.'

'*I Send My Heart Up To Thee*.'

'Oh, you old romantic.' But she *loved* that he was romantic.

He kissed her then. 'I don't deny it.'

After the picnic, they strolled the pier. Passing women with parasols, they watched yachts tilt as they sailed out of the harbour. Mariner terms blew over to them on the salty air like butterflies. Lee ho. Ready about. The world was, very suddenly, a better place. There was so much *beauty* in things Maggie had never noticed before, the pattern of clouds, a bird in flight and a boy who had loved her for almost a year.

Maggie floated home. She shut the front door behind her and leaned against it, sighing. Her mother came out of the drawing room, her face grave. Maggie wished, now, that she had told her how things were with Daniel. One thing was certain; they had been seen.

'England has declared war on Germany,' her mother said.

Maggie froze, remembering Daniel's words. 'What does this mean for Ireland?' She thought of Daniel. Was his father telling him the news right at this moment? She longed to speak to him, be with him.

'It means that any Irishman who has signed up to the British Army will be off to fight. God knows how many with all the recruiting that's been going on.'

The rebel in Maggie spoke. 'It's their own fault for siding with the British.'

Her mother frowned. 'I thought that you, of all people, would understand that soldiering is a paying job, a rare enough thing for those that were involved in the Lockout. Men have families to feed, Maggie.'

She blushed, remembering how life was in the tenements. It must have killed those men to sign up. 'You're right. I'm sorry. I didn't think.' She worried that she was becoming like Tom. The thought of Tom jolted her. He was nineteen. 'They won't force Irishmen to join the army, will they?'

'No. Thank the Lord. There's no conscription in Ireland.'

Maggie breathed out in relief. 'So the war will only affect those that volunteer?'

'It will affect all of us in some way, Maggie, you can be sure of it.'

It was only then Maggie noticed Lily standing small and pale outside the drawing room door, listening to everything they had been saying. Maggie smiled widely and reached out her hand.

'Come on, Lil. Let's play outside on the swing.'

Lily took her hand but asked, 'Can we play when the world is at war?'

'Lily, it is *especially* important to play when the world is at war.'

fourteen

Daniel

Suddenly, it was everywhere, the call to war. Recruiting sergeants walked the streets, promising glory and a wage. Posters sprang up like mushrooms overnight, appealing to Irishmen's sense of honour. From the pulpits, priests urged men to defend their country. It was that contradiction – a man of God calling on his congregation to break the fifth commandment – that woke Daniel up to the power of words. Defend your country. Answer the call. Defend our women.

Despite all of this, life continued as normal. At Na Fianna meetings, Maggie and Daniel studied first aid. They learned to signal, track and read code. They even learned the Irish sport of hurling, which was fast, furious and thrilling.

Then Daniel returned to school. And war was everywhere again. It was all that his classmates spoke of. They wished themselves older so they could join up. Daniel wondered if they would have felt so strongly if it were truly possible?

One afternoon, as he and Michael removed muddy rugby boots in a room full of rain-drenched, steaming boys, Michael turned to him.

'Let's sign up! Let's stop the tide of the Hun!'

The tide of the Hun? 'You've been reading too many posters, Hegarty.'

Michael abandoned his boots. 'Don't you wish to make your father proud?'

Daniel's father had already declared war to be a folly embraced by the working classes. It was as though he and Daniel were growing further and further apart and his father did not even know it.

'Our fathers are different, Michael.'

'He wouldn't be proud?' Michael looked appalled.

He shook his head, not willing to go into it. 'Make your father proud in other ways. Do well at school.'

'What good will school be if we're overrun by the Hun?'

Daniel, too, abandoned his boots. It wasn't often that Michael took life seriously. 'There's the issue of our age,' he said, to put an end to it. At eighteen, they were almost men. Daniel suspected that, for Michael, this was about becoming one.

'And you've never heard of a little white lie?' Michael countered.

Daniel looked at him in all his eagerness. Even if Daniel did share his hunger for war, there was one all-consuming reason why he'd never sign up. 'I'd never leave Maggie. That's the truth of it.'

'Always Maggie,' Michael said glumly.

It was true. She was his life now. She was only sixteen but he longed to marry her, spend every moment of his life with her. He would wait. A lifetime if he had to.

That Saturday, Na Fianna was ordered to march through the streets of Dublin in full uniform.

'Be a thorn in the side of the British Army, boys!' Madame declared cheerfully.

Daniel stared at her. It was one thing for an illegal organisation to march the streets in full uniform, quite another to bother the troops.

'This is madness,' he whispered to Maggie.

'Madame has her reasons. And we have our orders,' she whispered back.

'So you would blindly follow orders that might get you killed and, for what, *annoyance*? You saw those people gunned down.'

'And that is why I'm here, Danny, with Na Fianna.'

'To die the same way? This is just a game to her, entertainment. It's our *lives* she's playing with.'

'Fall in!' the order came.

Maggie did so.

Shaking his head, Daniel did too, not beside her – he was too angry for that – but near enough to come to her aid if needed. It was as if they were soldiers, obeying orders, no matter how ridiculous.

As they marched up Sackville Street, Daniel expected trouble at every moment. He noticed every man that moved, every leaf that fell. Every sound was a potential danger.

Then his mind began playing tricks on him. He imagined a bullet entering Maggie's head. He saw it explode and her brains splatter over the boy beside her. It was a flashback to all he had seen on the quays but with Maggie as the victim. He saw her crumple to the ground. He saw the life leave her eyes. He saw it all. He even saw Lily's face on hearing the news. It felt like a prophecy. And it made his legs weak. How could he have believed that they would never rise? How had he not seen that it would come to this? He had to do something. He couldn't stand by and let this continue. He had to persuade her to stop – somehow.

When they finally returned, without incident, Daniel looked at Maggie, cheering along with the rest of them, and felt his stomach contract further. He waited until they were outside, at their bicycles, before confronting her.

'That was madness. We must leave Na Fianna.'

'You know I can't do that.'

'We risked our lives for nothing!'

'Not nothing.'

He looked at her and knew that he could not fight a father's last request.

So he took a deep breath and prepared to face reality. 'I need to know if you plan to fight when the time comes.'

She looked at him for the longest time, and then bowed her head. 'I don't know.'

Gently he guided her chin back up so their eyes met.

'There are just so few of us and so many of them,' she said desperately. 'Look around you, Danny.' She looked at all the boys leaving the hall. 'These are our friends, our brothers. They expect me to fight alongside them. When they're coming under fire, how can I stand by? How can I just deal with wounds when it would be *their* wounds? How can I not pick up a gun and help *prevent* those wounds?'

He shook his head in sorrow.

'I'm sorry, Danny. I can't stand by. These are my people. I've never belonged anywhere before Na Fianna.'

'You belong with me.'

They stared at each other.

He could not give in. He would not. 'So you'd take a life?'

She closed her eyes. 'To save the life of a brother.'

'You would put Ireland before yourself?'

She nodded.

'Before us?'

She bit the back of her hand. Her eyes welled.

Then Patrick arrived beside them. 'That damned fool Redmond!'

They looked at him in confusion, as though woken from a dream.

'John Redmond, the politician,' Patrick clarified as if that was the source of their confusion. 'He's only gone and called on the Volunteers to join the British Army in return for Home Rule when the war is over.'

Daniel was lost.

'Well, no one will listen to him!' Maggie announced.

'That's where you're wrong, Ruairi. Already, they're

following his call in the thousands. If this keeps up, there'll be nothing left of the Volunteers.'

Maggie looked at Daniel as if to say, 'You see, now, why I must fight?'

He could only *see* that he must stop her. Somehow.

Patrick took off to spread the news.

Watching him go, Daniel saw it, suddenly, a way to keep her safe! If Ireland were granted Home Rule, most rebels would be satisfied. Some, like Maggie, would remain committed to a republic, but not in big enough numbers to rise. By joining the British Army, Daniel could stop her rising for her country! Everyone was saying that the war would be over by Christmas. He would keep his head low and give it three months of his life. Could he take a life, though? That was the problem.

Daniel arrived home, deep in thought. As he entered the drawing room, his father jumped to his feet, flinging his newspaper to the ground.

'There you are!' he bellowed.

Whatever trouble Daniel was in would be minor compared to the choice that he faced: to go to war or to let Maggie rise for Ireland.

'How long have you been involved with that idiot brigade?' his father raged.

So there it was.

'How long have you been going behind our backs now, Daniel? The Gaelic League how are you! Did you not *think* that, sooner or later, you would be *seen*? Dublin is a small place. Have you given any thought, *at all*, to how this would look for me, a man of the law, to have it known that *my son* is part of a rebel force?'

Daniel bowed his head. 'I'm sorry, Father.'

'Sorry won't do, Daniel. I cannot *comprehend*, after *all* that I've done for you, that you would treat me in such a manner, fraternising with a bunch of, of, *working class republicans!*'

Spittle flew from his mouth.

'The working class do not have a choice, Father,' he said quietly.

'*Riffraff*,' he spat.

And suddenly Daniel's hackles were up. 'Have you *ever* spoken to an ordinary worker? Have you ever visited a tenement? Have you ever seen the way your so-called riffraff lives?'

'I will have you know that the people you are so keen to defend occupy some of the finest properties in Dublin.'

Daniel scoffed. 'That is so far from the truth.'

'Excuse me! I own four of those properties myself, Daniel. They are prime Georgian buildings.'

There was no longer sufficient air in the room. 'You are a *landlord?*'

'Is that a crime?' he scoffed.

'Why did you never say?'

'I do not bring my *business* into my home, Daniel.'

'You are a landlord.' He still could not fathom it.

'Yes and you, my friend, have *no notion* what it is like trying to extract rents from those people. Blood from stone. Blood, from, stone.'

'Why do you imagine that is, Father?'

'Laziness, pure and simple, and let us not forget the demon drink.'

'Have you been to your properties, lately?'

His father stood taller. 'I do not need to. I grew up in one.'

'Then why are we not living there, still?'

'It is the fashion to live in the suburbs, Daniel, as you know. My properties remain sound. Many of my happiest years were spent there.'

'And were *you* crammed into that sound property with one hundred others?'

His father's face flared red like a beacon. 'If they choose not to work and to pile in together like rats, that is their business.'

Daniel could feel his own cheeks flame. 'They *choose* not to work? Have you *never* heard of the Lockout? Have you *never* heard of blacklisting?' He could hear his own voice rise. 'You spend too much time in your club, Father. How do you expect skills when children must leave school to support their families in order to pay your overinflated rents?'

His father strode towards him. Daniel sensed that he was about to be struck for the first time in his life. Instead, his father slammed both fists down on the drawing room table. He inhaled deeply, then lowered his voice. 'Who are you to complain? What do you think funds your education?'

Until now, it had been the law. 'If *that* is what funds my education, I want none of it.'

'Then, leave. Go and live in your precious tenements.'

Daniel looked at his father's face and imagined him wigged, gowned and resting his case. He had won his argument.

'Goodbye, Father.'

Daniel's eyes wandered about his bedroom like a final caress, alighting on his school scarf pinned to the wall, his uniform, discarded casually over the back of a chair, his rugby ball, grubby and worn, lying by the door as if fully expecting to be picked up again in the morning. He took a deep breath, then fetched his satchel. Tipping it upside down over the bed, he watched his schoolbooks slide out. It was like watching his childhood slip away.

He did not know what he would be required to bring with him to the army, perhaps nothing at all. He collected one of every item of clothing, three undergarments and five pairs of socks. He folded them all neatly, delaying his departure. At last, he could hold off no longer. He swung the bag over his shoulder.

Out on the landing, he stopped outside Niall's bedroom. He could not leave without goodbye.

Niall was on the verge of sleep, eyelids heavy, hair tossed. Daniel smiled. Niall's return smile was sleepy and innocent. Daniel's throat burned as he tried to commit to memory this little cherub face. He sat on the bed.

'Nially, I've come to say goodbye. I'm going away for a while.'

Niall sat up, suddenly awake. 'Where?'

'France most likely.'

'Where's France?'

'Not *too far* away.'

'But why?' he whined. He was tired.

'I'm going on an adventure.'

'Can I come?'

'No but I'll soon return.'

'When?'

'By Christmas, most likely.'

'That's *miles* away.'

'I'll write. I'll send you your very own letters.'

'Really?' Niall had never received a letter.

'How are things at school?' Daniel asked.

'Good.'

'And how is Jimmy Lyons?'

'He's my best friend now. Isn't that mad?'

'Who made that happen, only you?' Daniel ruffled his hair proudly. He was about to say, 'Fighting is never the solution,' when he remembered where he was headed. He stood. God, those little striped pyjamas of Niall's; he'd remember them forever.

'Must you go?'

Daniel nodded.

'But you'll write me my very own letters?' he confirmed.

'I will. And I'll see you at Christmas.'

'Are you leaving now?'

'I am.'

Niall bit his lip.

'I'll write to you, tomorrow. I promise.'

Niall nodded.

'But it will take a day or two to reach you,' he remembered to reassure. He glanced about the room, already looking forward to the day he would walk back in and be home. But could he come back? Could he ever come back now?

'Will you wait till I'm asleep to go?'

Daniel smiled and nodded, relieved at the reprieve. He sat down.

He stroked Niall's hair until at last he slept. Then he kissed his forehead.

He took a deep breath and stood.

On his way downstairs, he stopped to listen to the familiar chime of the grandfather clock in the hall. It had rung in every hour of his life.

Onward, he urged himself.

Passing the coat stand by the front door, he reached out and touched his mother's coat.

fifteen

Daniel

It was late when Daniel arrived at Maggie's house.

Her mother called through the door. 'Who is it?'

'It's Daniel, Missus Gilligan. I'm sorry for the late hour but I must see Maggie.'

The door opened and light spilled out.

'What is it, Daniel?'

He took a deep breath. 'I need to say goodbye. I'm going to war, Missus Gilligan.'

'Oh Lord.' It was as if the breath had left her body. 'Come in, come in.'

'I'm sorry.'

'No, no.' She ushered him into an empty drawing room, the fire on its last legs. 'I'll fetch her.' She hurried out.

He paced, trying to get the words. There were none.

She burst in, eyes wide, cheeks drained of colour, her dressing gown wrapped hurriedly about her.

They stood facing each other.

'You wouldn't,' she whispered.

'It'll be over by Christmas, Maggie.'

She stepped back as though he had hit her. 'Why would you do this?'

'To defend our country,' he lied.

'You are *betraying* it. What of the oath you took when you joined Na Fianna never to join the British Army?'

'An *Irish regiment* of the British Army.'

'Our oppressor for hundreds of years.'

'I do not do this easily. John Redmond said....'

'Do *not* mention Redmond, the man who wants a peaceful solution for Ireland by sending thousands to war.'

'Home Rule-'

'Home Rule! If you believe in Home Rule, let others fight for it. One person won't make a difference.'

'I could say the same to you about a republic.'

She bowed her head.

'I'll be home by Christmas,' he found himself repeating.

'Should you live that long! Don't go, Danny. Please. I beg you. I love you. That must count for something.'

'It counts for everything,' he whispered. And that was why he had to do this. 'But I must go.'

'So, there's nothing I can say?' There was a note of warning in her voice.

'There's something you could *do*.'

She looked at him hopefully, then all hope faded as though she knew what he was about to ask.

'Leave Na Fianna, Maggie. And I won't go.'

'You can't ask that of me!'

'And yet I am. I love you. I don't want to lose you.'

She began to pace, her distress clear.

He prayed like he had never prayed before. He would return home, grovel to his father if he had to. If only she would leave Na Fianna.

At last, she stopped, and turned to face him. And he knew.

'I have to make a difference! Don't you see? I can't stand by and let this continue! I couldn't live with myself!' She was crying.

He nodded and took a deep breath, accepting his fate; he had known it all along but he'd had to ask. His heart ached at the thought of leaving her. 'Do you have a photograph?' he choked.

She covered her mouth and ran from the room.

Minutes passed. She did not return.

Was this it? Was he to show himself out? He could not walk away from her, not like this.

And then she was back.

Relief almost floored him.

Without meeting his eyes, she held out a small photograph.

'Thank you,' he whispered, looking down upon the sepia face that he loved like no other. He could not believe that it had come to this. 'I'll treasure it,' he said, voice hoarse.

At last, her eyes met his. 'You had better.'

He took her in his arms and breathed her in. A photograph would not be enough to sustain him. 'Do you have a lock of hair?'

She laughed through tears. 'My best feature.'

'Long or short, it's my favourite hair in the world.'

She pressed her cheek to his chest, then slipped from his arms.

She fetched a pair of scissors from her mother's bureau and returned to him with it. 'You do it.'

He couldn't imagine not seeing her the following day. Or the next. Or the next. He swallowed.

'What is it?' she asked.

He shook his head. He took a deep breath and then turned Maggie around. He chose a lock low down where it would not be missed. The nape of her neck was elegant like the rest of her. He touched it with his fingertips. He bent to kiss it. Tears rushed to his eyes. He dashed them away. He placed his hands on her shoulders and turned her to face him.

'Promise me that you'll stay out of trouble till I return.'

Tears flooded her face now. 'You can't ask that of me, Danny. You're joining the enemy.'

He nodded, then prayed for the war to be over and Home Rule in place before the rebels could organise. What could they do in three months? Their numbers were being hammered.

'Do you have notepaper in that bag of yours?' she asked.

How could he have forgotten the most important thing?

She threw her eyes to heaven like a wife who loves her husband despite his frustrating ways. It made him smile. She returned to the bureau and collected notepaper and envelopes.

'I'll write every day,' he promised.

'No! If I missed one, I'd imagine the worst.' She gasped at the thought. 'Tell me you'll not go directly to war. Tell me there'll be training, at least.'

'They wouldn't send us off without it, Maggie.' *Would they?*

'How long for?'

'I don't know. But I'll write as soon as I do.'

She looked at him with sudden hope, 'Perhaps the war will be over before you've finished!'

He smiled. 'Wouldn't that be something?' They would have Home Rule without him ever having to raise a weapon.

Daniel stood on the street, his bag on his back. No recruitment office in the country would be open now.

Michael would have a piece of floor for him for the night.

The house was in darkness. Daniel went to the rear and began to lob pebbles at Michael's window. Presently, the drapes parted and he appeared, hair standing on end. He opened the window and smiled down at Daniel.

'What are you up to, you big eejit?'

'Let me in.'

Two minutes later, Daniel was following Michael up to his bedroom, where the dying embers of a fire glowed gently. Michael turned up the lamp. Warm, yellow light spread out like liquid. Daniel smiled at the state of the room.

'You're a great man for keeping the servants busy.'

'I try.' He smiled. 'To what do I owe the pleasure?'

'I'm going to sign up, Mick. I need you to put me up till the morning.'

Michael stared at him. 'What are you talking about? What about Maggie?'

'It's because of Maggie that I have to do this.'

'I don't understand.'

So Daniel explained.

Michael's face grew darker. 'How long have you been in a rebel organisation without telling me?'

Daniel sighed. 'I couldn't tell you without asking you to keep it from your father. And I know how you love him.'

He looked at Daniel for the longest time. At last, he nodded. 'I told you she'd be trouble.'

'I wouldn't be without her, Mick.'

'And yet, you're going to war.'

'I don't see that I have a choice.'

A silence fell.

'Tell me, was your father proud?'

'He doesn't know.'

Michael stared. 'You're going to war without as much as a goodbye?'

'I said goodbye to Niall.'

'In fairness, Danny, you ought to tell your parents.'

'I'll write to my mother when I've signed up.'

'And your father?'

Daniel shrugged.

'We have only the one, Daniel.'

Whenever Michael grew serious, everything seemed twice as grave. So Daniel told him what had happened between them.

'I'm sorry,' he said with such feeling.

'I'm not.'

'Ah, Danny. He's a good man beneath it all.'

Daniel thought of the tenements. His own education had relied on them.

'So you're going, honest to God?'

He put his hand on his chest and nodded.

'I'll never understand you, Danny.'

'I surprise myself, sometimes.' He smiled.

Michael twisted a button of his pyjamas, round and round.

'It'll come off,' Daniel warned.

Michael looked up. 'We'll sign with The Pals.'

'What?'

'You don't think I'd let you go off by yourself and have all the adventure?'

'Michael, it won't *be* adventure. You haven't seen people die. Nothing can prepare you for the horror of it.'

But he had leapt up and was now emptying out his satchel. He stopped and glanced at Daniel's. 'What have you got in yours? I've no idea what to bring.'

'Look, Mick,' he said softly. 'It would make all the difference in the world to have you along but I can't have you risk your life-'

'Must I open your bag myself?'

'Can you please discuss it with your parents before deciding.'

'Says he. I *have* decided. I'll tell them in the morning.' He grabbed Daniel's bag and started to rummage through it. He looked up. 'So what do you think? The Pals?'

'Who are they, Mick?'

Michael shook his head sadly. 'You, my friend, have been spending too much time in the company of boy scouts. The Pals are D Company of the 7th Royal Dublin Fusiliers, a special unit formed from members of the Irish Rugby and Football Union.'

'I *have* heard of them!' They had famously gathered on the pitch at Lansdowne Road then marched off to sign up together.

'They refused officerships so they could stay together as a unit. I'm telling you, Danny, it's The Pals for us.'

There was one issue. 'We're not members of the Irish Rugby and Football Union.'

'We play rugby and we're good. We'll play our way in. What do you say?'

'It's worth a try.'

He'd do anything for Michael now.

Michael's father swelled with pride. His mother was hysterical.

'If you go *near* a recruitment office, I'll be in after you telling them you're underage.'

'Ah, Nora, let the lad do what he must do.'

'He's only a boy, Denis. *My* boy. Let him finish out his schooling. Let me have him for another year.'

It pained Daniel to see her beg for her son. 'Stay, Mick. Finish school.'

'And miss the war? Not on your nelly.'

'Let him go, Nora, love. 'Tis what he wants.'

She covered her mouth and ran from the room.

Michael's father gripped his arm. 'I'm proud of you, son.'

Daniel swallowed.

Michael's mother returned.

There were tears and hurried wrapping of parcels. And, finally, embraces.

Out on the street, the air was lighter. Michael whistled and made a stab at a march. Daniel began to step in time. Michael looked at him and grinned.

'Our first time out of Ireland!'

'Making our own way in the world!'

'No parents to answer to!'

'No teachers!'

'No coaches!'

'We're freeeee,' Michael joked. 'Jesus this marching is surprisingly tiring.'

They passed children on their way to school. Daniel thought of Maggie. He was doing this for her – so why did he feel like he was betraying her? It would be over soon, he reminded himself. And they'd be together again.

sixteen

Daniel

Daniel ran clammy hands along his trouser legs and wished that moustaches could be grown overnight. At least he was tall for his age, he reassured himself as he came face-to-face with the recruiting officer. Seated at a table behind a mound of forms, the man looked bored.

Daniel stood tall. 'I wish to sign with The Pals Regiment.'

The officer sat up. 'The Pals?' he asked as though he'd never heard of them.

'D Company, 7th Royal Dublin Fusiliers.'

He peered at Daniel as if at a troublemaker. 'We're recruiting for the 6th Royal Dublin Fusiliers *not* the 7ths.'

Daniel thought about Michael, behind him. He owed it to him to persist. 'I was told that one could request to join the Pals.'

The officer's eyes narrowed. 'What is so great about the Pals regiment that you would chose it over the 6ths?'

'Rugby, sir.'

'Rugby?'

'We play it. It binds us.'

The officer sat back. 'Are you sure that it's not being a toff that binds you?' he asked with the resentment of a man who had risen through the ranks.

'I'm quite sure.'

'*Are* you a toff?'

'No, sir.'

'What is your name?'

'Daniel Healy.'

'And what do you do with yourself, Healy?'

'Study, sir.' He felt a slow poke in the back. 'At university.'

'Which one?'

'The Royal College of Surgeons.' Daniel had never told anyone – not even Maggie – that he dreamt of being a doctor for the poor – that *that* was how he'd like to do his bit for Ireland.

'You're studying medicine?' the officer asked with sudden interest.

Daniel realised the reason for this interest and panicked. 'First Year, sir.'

The officer toyed with his pen reminding Daniel of a cat with a mouse. 'You're a university student. Why have you not requested a commission?'

'I do not wish to be an officer, sir.'

The officer squinted. 'Why would any man refuse a commission?'

Daniel remembered what Michael had told him about the Pals. 'More important to me is to join the Pals with my friend, Michael.' He turned around. Michael raised an awkward hand.

'A word of advice, Healy,' the officer sneered. 'If you wish to survive the army, you'll put aside wishes and dwell on one thing only – orders.' He pushed a form across the desk and called, 'Next.'

It took a moment for Daniel to realise that he had passed the first hurdle. Now all he had to do was fill in the form and pass the medical examination.

'Here's *another one* that wants the Pals,' the officer announced to no one in particular as Michael stepped forward.

Thank God for the rugby, Daniel thought as he watched Michael stand erect before the officer. He had, at least, the body of a man. His face, though, could have done with a little hair. Daniel had to turn around to avoid a smile; Michael too was studying medicine.

Seconds later, they were reunited.

'The Royal College of Surgeons,' Michael whispered. 'You big eejit.'

Daniel smiled. 'You should have gone first. You're a better liar.'

'I won't argue with that.'

They completed the forms, ageing a year in the process, boys to men. Pens poised, ready to sign, they looked at each other.

'Ready?'

'Ready.'

They signed together.

They looked at the queue of men lined up to be poked, prodded, explored and questioned by a military doctor with a scar through his eyebrow.

'You go first,' Daniel said.

'No, you.'

Daniel shrugged, then obliged.

Stripped to his underwear, he coughed when asked to, raised his arms when asked to, and answered questions that intrigued him. At last, the doctor removed the cold metal disc of a stethoscope from Daniel's chest and the earpieces from his ears.

'If only they were all as fit as you,' he complained.

Michael, too, passed the medical. But it was only when they were handed tickets for a train to the Curragh Camp that Daniel and Michael truly realised that they had got their wish.

They were Pals.

Michael punched Daniel's arm in silent celebration. Daniel punched him back.

'No going back now,' said a man beside them.

They were sobering words. There could be no change of heart, no leaving now. To do so would be to desert. And to desert would mean court-martial and execution.

Daniel looked out at a steam-filled station. One by one, the doors of the train were banged shut. A whistle blew. Slowly, the train of new recruits began to move. Daniel and Michael exchanged a glance. All their lives, they had been assured of the familiarity of the next day. This was a train to the unknown. All about them, conversations were being struck up, introductions made, hands shaken, cigarettes passed around. Someone produced a hip flask. Out of nowhere, Daniel's father's words returned to him. 'Go live in your precious tenements.' His stomach churned. Turning to the window, he rubbed himself a circle out of newly formed condensation and watched a wet and rainy Dublin slip away.

The flat land of The Curragh made for the largest expanse of sky Daniel had ever seen. The clouds deserved their name. They were magnificent and monstrous, and as Daniel and the others approached the barracks on foot, they proved just how much rain they could hold.

Their first meal as Tommies was tea, bread and jam. Then their sergeant showed them to their quarters, a barrack room of sixteen narrow beds called biscuits, tightly packed together. With his bag, Michael claimed one by a wall. Daniel took the one next to it.

'Not a sound out of you lot after Lights Out,' the sergeant barked. 'Should you wish to relieve yourselves, use the piss pot.' He pointed to the centre of the room. Then he looked at a chap with an open and friendly face. 'What's your name, Private?'

'MacDonald, Sergeant.'

'Well, MacDonald, you can have the pleasure of emptying it tomorrow.'

MacDonald made his first military error. It was a grimace.

'Given your obvious delight at the task, MacDonald, not only will you empty said piss pot, but you will clean it with a toothbrush until it shines like a baby's bottom. Should it fail, on inspection, to shine like a baby's bottom, MacDonald, you will be on piss pot detail for a month. Do I make myself clear, Private?'

'Crystal, sir.'

They stood to attention as the sergeant left. Then they released a universal breath.

MacDonald collapsed onto his biscuit. 'Jesus, Mary and sweet Saint Joseph. What was that?'

'Your very own personal welcome to the British Army.'

'That was a rhetorical question, Wilkin,' MacDonald said miserably.

Washing in a room full of men who played sport at national and international level did nothing for Daniel's confidence. Rugby, at least, had given him muscle. Compared to these athletes, though, it was baby muscle. Daniel guessed that Michael was feeling equally as inadequate once he began to joke.

'Don't forget to take a leak, boys,' he called to the general assembly.

'You imagine that we *could*?' Wilkin asked.

They all looked at MacDonald.

'Got your toothbrush, MacDonald?' Michael asked.

'Feck off, Hegarty.'

With laughter came relief.

Maybe, Daniel thought, that was how they'd get through this. Laughter. Well, laughter and letters. Already he longed for one. And he had all of five minutes to write three. He'd promised Niall and Maggie but he owed his mother. And so he began with her.

Dear Mother

I am sorry for leaving without goodbye. I have joined the war effort. I am with the 7th Royal Dublin Fusiliers or The Pals, as we are known. It is a unit of rugby and football players so Michael and I feel at home. Yes, Michael is with me. Please do not worry. The war will be over by Christmas.

Your loving son, Daniel

He had not been able to admit to Niall that he was going to war. Now he must. Once his mother knew, it would be family news. Daniel tried his best to be gentle.

Dearest Niall

I am training to be a soldier. It's like school only with more rules! Michael is here with me, with his usual jokes, so all is well. I have always thought of you as a little man, never a boy. Take care of Mother for me. Some day, you might send me one of your drawings or a few words so that I know how you are getting along. I will write often. Look after yourself and stand tall, as always.

Your brother, Danny

And now the person he would find it hardest to be without:

My dearest Maggie

I am sorry for the shock. I hope you can forgive me. All is well. I'm a Private with the Pals, The 7th Royal Dublin Fusiliers. I have been sent to the Curragh Camp for training. Michael is here with me. I'm rushing this letter for it will be Lights Out in less than a minute and if I have learned anything today it is that orders must be obeyed. I hope that I will have time for a longer letter tomorrow. I long to hear from you.

Your dearest, darling, Danny

He worried that 'darling' was too much. He'd never used such words with her yet it was how he felt. Crossing it out would make it worse, as if he didn't think she was his darling after all. In any case, he had time left only to place the letter in an envelope and scribble the address. With seconds to spare, he took out her photograph. That is what he was looking at as the lights went out. He decided that, for as long as he was in the army, this is what he would do – look upon her face as he fell asleep.

seventeen

Maggie

Maggie beat her mother to the post. She rifled through it, then silently passed the bundle to her.

'Give him time,' her mother said gently.

'It's only that I need his postal address.'

Her mother cupped Maggie's face in her hands. 'Occupy yourself.'

'I know!' Lily said. 'Knit him something!'

Maggie eyed the little girl who had come to be better than Maggie at mostly everything. 'I'm hopeless at knitting.'

'I'll teach you,' Lily said immediately, grabbing her by the hand and dragging her into the drawing room.

Maggie looked at her in admiration. 'Perhaps I could manage a scarf, if you started me off.'

'A scarf would be simple.'

'Simple for you.'

'Practice makes perfect.'

Maggie smiled. 'Are you six or sixty, Lil?'

But Lily wasn't listening. She was on a mission. Rummaging through her knitting basket, she produced a pair of needles. She looked up. 'What colour wool do you want?'

Maggie thought about that. 'Do you have any green?'

'Green for Ireland?'

She nodded. 'So he doesn't forget.'

'How could he forget the country he's fighting for?'

'Hmm,' was all Maggie said. She sighed.

The knitting was impossible. The tension was, in places, too tight, in others too loose. Then there were the dropped stitches. Maggie threw it down in frustration.

'Give it here to me,' Lily said.

Maggie was humiliated. And relieved.

Lily started her off again. 'Now, watch.'

Maggie tried to concentrate but there were too many questions racing through her mind. Where was he? What was he doing? Had he, at least, a good rifle? Did he miss her?

Lily was handing the knitting back to her.

'Ah, knit me up a few lines, Lil, will you? So I'm certain.'

Lily gave her a look that began as bossy but softened on seeing the worry in Maggie's eyes. She put her hand out for the knitting. Then she was off again, flying.

At length, she stopped, looked up and held it out to Maggie. 'Now, you do some.'

'Aw, Lil.'

'*You're* the one knitting the scarf for Daniel. 'Tis *you* that should be pouring the love into it.'

Maggie took it back, grumbling, 'You should be a politician.'

'Maybe I will,' Lily challenged.

And there it was suddenly, all the possibility offered by a new republic.

A girl, like Lily, *could* become a politician, *could* have a say. *This* was why Maggie could never give up on her dream.

Arriving at Na Fianna, Maggie felt lost without Danny. She'd had to force herself to come. Looking around the hall, it was hard to miss the drop in numbers as more and more boys answered Redmond's call. Soon there would not be enough rebels to rise.

She shoved her hands into her pockets and kicked at a tiny pebble that must have come off someone's boot.

'Boys!' boomed Patrick's voice from the top of the room.

Maggie looked up.

'It is *good* to see you here, lads. You'll have heard, no doubt, that many of those *Volunteers*...' He said it as though it was a dirty word. '...have gone off to fight with the Brits. We've even lost a few of our own.' He paused. 'Do you think that that is going to *stop* us? Do you think that that is going to change a *thing*?' His voice rose.

The energy in the room lifted.

'No!' they called.

He put a hand to his ear. 'What? What did you say? I didn't *hear* you.'

'No!' they roared, smiling now and exchanging glances. This was what they had needed.

'Well, let me tell you something, boys. This *Great* War is *great* news for us, *great* news for *Na Fianna Éireann*. Why? Because it's going to keep the Brits well and truly occupied. That's why. They'll have their eyes on the Hun. They'll be looking east not west, lads. And they won't see us coming.' He raised his eyebrows.

The entire assembly cheered.

'England's difficulty is Ireland's *opportunity*!' Patrick shouted, raising a fist in the air.

They roared.

'While they are otherwise engaged, we'll be sharpening our tools. We'll be sharpening our *wits*. And we'll catch them with their pants down. What'll we do, lads?'

'Catch them with their pants down!' they yelled in delight.

'Boys, I give you Con Colbert.'

Con Colbert stirred things up even further until the boys were tripping over themselves to get to the basement.

Maggie followed, alone. The speeches had cheered her as much as anything could. The fact remained; her refusal to give up Na Fianna had sent Daniel to war.

'Where's Daniel tonight?'

She looked up to see Patrick. The words stuck in her throat.

'Daniel, your brother?' he teased.

She closed her eyes. 'He signed up.'

'Ah, feck.'

She bowed her head. 'I know.'

'Our best shooter.'

She looked up suddenly. 'That was *not* my first concern, Patrick.'

'I'm sorry.' He cleared his throat. 'What regiment did he join?'

'The Pals.'

'Of course. The toff.'

'Shut up.' She'd had enough of him, of everything. She just wanted to go home.

'Ah, Ruairí, sure, I didn't mean it.'

'One more remark like that and I'll clock you, Patrick Shanahan.'

He smiled as though admiring the fire in the tiny boy before him. 'If it's any comfort, you're not the only one. Hasn't me old man gone and joined the 2nds?'

She stared at him. 'Is he a Home Ruler?'

'He believes himself to be defending Ireland,' he said, shaking his head in disbelief.

'As does Danny.' Her every breath, now, seemed a sigh.

'It's hard to credit, isn't it?'

'Sometimes, I could *kill* him for going.'

'You may not have to,' he joked.

She took a swipe at him but he caught her fist. Smiling fondly, he let it go.

'Why am I even *talking* to you?' She marched off.

He came after her. 'I'm sorry, Ruairí. He'll be grand. They both will.'

She saw it, then, the worry. He was as bad as she was. The jokes were to get him through.

'They will,' she said but thought, *If only he'd write.*

Days passed. Maggie thought she would go out of her mind if she did not hear soon. Then two letters arrived together. She tore open the first. It was hurried and brief but contained the words, 'My Dearest Maggie' and 'Darling'. Eyes closed, she held it to her heart. Then, like a gift, she had a second. This she read very slowly, tracing a finger under each word.

Dearest Maggie

Finding time to write is harder than I ever imagined. They fill every minute, if not with drilling, then marching or learning. We must complete certificates of education – just when we thought we'd escaped school! Any spare moment is occupied with cleaning – our kit, our barracks, ourselves. That doesn't mean that you're not in my thoughts. Today, I was dreaming of you and missed a command. I was made to run around the drill square with a rifle over my head fifty times with full kit on. I was glad of the punishment, though, for it was time alone with you in my head. Your picture and lock of hair are no substitute for you.

Yesterday, as a punishment for failing to clean his weapon 'on-the-double', Michael was ordered to cut the grass with a pair of scissors. He has been trying to remove grass stains from his breeches ever since. If you have any advice on that front, do let us know!

There is nothing if not togetherness in The Pals, Maggie. A nicer bunch of Irishmen you could not meet.

With my fondest love, always, Danny

PS The first time you called me Danny my heart leapt with joy.

He was training! Not at war! He was still in Ireland and not that far from Dublin even! She hurried the letters upstairs where she read them over and over till she knew each word by heart. In that way, she could carry him with her wherever she went. She took out pen and paper and began to write.

Dearest Danny

I'm glad to be in your thoughts. You are constantly in mine. Patrick's father signed up with the 2nds and we moan about you, together! Why did you join, Danny? I will never understand it.

It's intolerable going to school with you preparing for war. You occupy an adult world now while I am still in childhood. It is as if we are building up to a great explosion in our lives. Do you feel it too? I am impatient, Danny. I want it all to be over and for you to be back safely with me.

All my love, Maggie

She ran downstairs, questioned her mother, then raced back up and added a postscript: *Mam says try vinegar on the stain – if you can get your hands on any.*

eighteen

Daniel
Curragh Camp

Daniel and Michael struggled. In drills, steeplechases and marches, they were invariably last and out of breath – at times, close to vomiting. Wilkin regularly dropped back to keep them company.

'Take it handy, boys. No prizes for coming first.'

Daniel smiled but wondered what kind of soldiers they'd make. They were getting fitter but remained boys in the company of men. And he wasn't alone in noticing.

'I'm thinking of growing a moustache,' Michael said, one evening, examining his reflection in the washroom mirror.

'A thick and luxurious moustache would be a sight to behold, all right,' Daniel agreed.

'That settles it.' Michael looked at his friend. 'How about you?'

'I'll see what I can produce.'

'We'll live in hope,' Michael said.

One week later, Michael was back at the mirror, fingering his upper lip in frustration. 'Is there anything at all that might stimulate hair growth?'

'If I knew I'd be using it myself,' Daniel said.

'I've heard that a few drops of urine applied twice a day will result in a fine moustache in weeks,' MacDonald volunteered. You could not have a conversation in the army without being overheard. 'Probably best to use your own.'

They laughed.

'It's only what I've heard,' he said in that innocent way of his. 'Here, sure, ask Gregor.'

They looked automatically to the chap with the blackest, thickest moustache known to man.

'Feck off,' Gregor said.

It was the banter that kept Daniel going in a life of orders, the banter and the letters – from Maggie, his mother and Niall. He tried not to think of his father.

Weeks passed with no talk of action. With their first pay came an air of celebration. As the men around them cheered and made plans, Daniel and Michael looked at each other in silent wonder. It was as if they had been handed their manhood.

'I'm keeping mine as a memento,' Walkey said with uncharacteristic gravity.

'I'm planning my first pint,' Michael said with pride.

'Your *first pint*?' MacDonald asked. 'Where have you been, Hegarty, in a seminary?'

'My first pint *as a soldier*,' he corrected.

Daniel knew how easy it was to let your guard slip amongst friends, to forget that you had arrived as a boy and remained so by age.

'What will you do with yours?' Walkey asked him now.

'I've been looking for something to send to... my girl,' Daniel said, awkwardly.

'Ah, the great letter writer,' Lecane confirmed.

Daniel smiled. He thanked God that she was.

'You are far and away too serious about that girl,' Michael said.

'She is my life, Mick. It's that simple.'

146

Michael sighed. 'I had better buy you a pint, so, when the time comes or I'll be drinking alone.'

'You never drink alone in the army,' Wilkin said.

Michael stroked his upper lip as if trying to encourage hair growth.

'He'll be talking to it next,' MacDonald said. 'Like a pet.'

'Why don't you grow one yourself, MacDonald, if it's that easy?' Michael snapped.

'I like the feel of the air on my skin,' he said fanning his face. He had the constant appearance of being on the verge of laughter. Daniel loved that about him.

'That's it! I'm getting rid of it.' Michael leapt from his biscuit.

'Ah, keep the little thing,' Walkey encouraged. 'Or we'll have nothing to tease you about.'

'I'm sure MacDonald will come up with something,' Michael said. 'He always does.'

'True enough,' MacDonald said. 'True enough.'

It was school all over again – but with men.

A fear began to grow at the Curragh Camp that the war would be over before they had completed their training. When, in November, they received their uniforms, they brightened, expecting that they would soon be off to the front. But no orders came. Snow covered the plain in a silent, white blanket. Musketry training was introduced.

'Where the blazes did you learn to shoot, Healy?' asked Lieutenant Julien.

'Beginner's luck, sir,' he said, then deliberately missed the next two shots.

Madame had taught him well, not only to shoot but also to care for his rifle. When his next pay was increased to reflect his ability, he ceased to miss shots.

Slowly, their training began to change. They were

introduced to trench warfare, learning to attack, defend, dig, reinforce and maintain trenches. They engaged in night manoeuvres, one attack involving some four thousand men, bringing with it the first real feeling of war. They were taught gas defence and to work with barbed wiring. There was, they heard, a whole new method of warfare being employed on the fields of France and Belgium, which meant that the war would not be over by Christmas nor any time soon. Both sides had dug in.

Men began to arrive at the Curragh who had seen service. They had been wounded and, now, following recovery had been sent to the camp to regain their fitness before returning to war. They were the quietest of men, older in appearance. Weary. They gravitated to one another or remained entirely alone. They looked upon the new recruits with a mixture of pity and annoyance. They were a different species of soldier.

One day, in the Mess, a young Private approached the veterans' table. He could not have been much older than Daniel himself.

'Tell us of the war.' He threw the question out like a novice fisherman casting a fly in the vague hope of a bite.

They eyed him as though he was indeed an annoying insect, then returned their eyes to the army fodder.

'We'll be over there soon enough,' the Private insisted. 'We must know how it'll be.'

There was silence in the Mess, all eyes on the war-weary soldiers because the lad had spoken for everyone.

One veteran looked up from his plate. There was strength in his face but humanity too. He looked into the boy's eyes as though stepping into his very soul.

'Nothing you do here will prepare you for what's to come – except perhaps prayer. That's all you can do, Private. Pray. Hard. For it is down to luck alone whoever makes it home in one piece.'

How could a silence have become more silent? And yet it had. Daniel pushed his plate away. Throughout the Mess, men rose and left.

In December, they were granted leave. Michael, whistling *Silent Night*, began to pack immediately. He paused and looked at Daniel.

'What are you waiting for, Healy? Let's go.'

'I'm grand here.'

'Are you out of your mind?'

'He never wrote, Mick,' he said quietly.

'Then you'll stay with me. They'll be delighted to have you, at home.'

Daniel smiled. 'I'm staying put.' It would most likely be Michael's last few days with his family before war. Daniel could not take that from him - or his parents. 'You don't think I'd miss British Army turkey?' He would request permission for a day visit to Dublin to see Maggie.

On Christmas Day there was a parade and, later, a concert. C Company played its pipes and drums, up and down in front of the barracks. There was a great snowball fight with the Munsters. Windows were broken and they joked of the Christmas miracle – no punishment administered.

On the final day of leave, Daniel was granted his wish - a day visit to Dublin.

As the train chugged its way to the capital, he could barely contain himself.

Daniel put a finger to his mouth when Maggie's mother answered the door. She smiled and nodded and led him to the drawing room in silence. She gestured that she would be in the dining room. He mouthed his thanks. Slowly, he opened the door. Maggie's image revealed itself inch by inch. Her short hair reminded him of all that she was - as if he could have forgotten. She was seated at the fire, head bent - *knitting*?

She frowned then and threw it down. 'Blasted thing.'

He laughed as he stepped into the room, closing the door behind him.

She swung around. 'Danny!' She jumped to her feet, raced to him and leapt into his arms. He laughed at the joy of it. 'What are you doing here? Why didn't you tell me you were coming?'

He drank her in, the curve of her lips, every inch of her face, each eyelash. At last, he lowered her to the floor.

She remembered her hair and attempted to flatten tufts of it.

He took her hands away. 'How I've missed this hair,' he said, running his fingers through it. 'And these eyebrows. And these cheekbones.' One by one, he kissed them. 'I have especially missed this mouth.' He closed his eyes as they kissed. He could have died at the softness of her lips. He held her to him. After months of only men, it was as though he'd been transported directly to heaven. 'Let's stay like this forever. Let's never move again.'

Her laughter was the most magical sound.

His eyes fell upon the tangled mess, discarded on the floor. He smiled. 'You're knitting?'

She rolled her eyes. 'A scarf for you. Any sign of the wretched war being over – so I can stop?'

He laughed but was greatly touched. 'You have my full permission to stop.'

'Not on your life.'

There was a moment of mutual horror.

She clung to him. 'I can't lose you, Danny. I can't.'

'You won't.'

She pulled back and looked into his eyes. 'Promise me.'

A lie was preferable to the truth. 'I promise.'

Tears threatening, she turned from him suddenly. 'Come sit by the fire,' she said, her voice high.

They sat on opposite sides of the hearth. To Daniel it seemed a great distance.

'How is your family?' she asked.

He looked into the fire. 'I've not seen them.'

'Ah, Danny.'

He shrugged. 'I'm not welcome.'

'I'm sure that your father is sorry.'

'Then why has he not written?'

'You should have met your mother and Niall, separately.'

He shook his head. 'I wouldn't ask it of them – to go behind his back.'

She nodded. 'I'm sorry that you didn't get to see them.'

'I sent Niall a letter with a shilling in it. I felt like Judas. I promised I'd be home for Christmas.' His voice cracked. 'And I promised you that the war would be over.'

She went to him and slipped onto his lap. She took his face in her hands and kissed him. Then she smiled bravely. 'So I don't get to see that famous moustache of yours?'

'What I grew wasn't worthy of the word moustache.'

She smiled.

'You should have seen it, Maggie. You'd have gone right off me.'

'It'd take more than a moustache.'

He stayed all day, then took the last train of already-homesick soldiers back to the Curragh Camp.

nineteen

Daniel
1915

In February, the Pals were transferred to The Royal Barracks in Dublin, a step closer to war. It was strange being so close to home and as distant as ever. They were trained in trench warfare in the Phoenix Park and musketry on Dollymount Strand. Then the rumours began. The first that Daniel heard was that they were 'off to France in ten days' time'. He began to write letters but then orders never followed and he recognised the rumour for what it was. After that, they were 'off to Egypt', 'off to France', then 'off to France' again. All in ten days' time!

Then in April, a rumour *was* followed by official notification. They were off to Basingstoke, England for further training, then on to war. There were whoops and cheers and caps in the air and, of course, more orders. Daniel had never witnessed so much scribbling in one barrack room.

Ten days later, he stood at the door of that same barrack room, empty now of soldiers, kit and sound. This had been his home for three months and the army his family for five months longer. He walked out, last to leave, tucking a final letter from Maggie safely into his breast pocket. As he followed the others down the echoing corridor, he was gripped with a sudden and terrifying fear that he would never see her again.

Relatives and friends crowded the square at the Royal Barracks. A photographer recorded soldiers holding up rations, tins of corned beef and canned peaches. Families arrived with gifts and embraces, laughter and tears. Daniel searched the crowd for Maggie.

'Daniel!'

He turned and laughed in delight. He had written to his mother to tell her that he was away. He had not expected her to come; such was her loyalty to her husband. But here she was with Niall, who ran to Daniel and threw his arms around him. Daniel lifted him into the air.

'How you've grown! Did you get my shilling?'

Niall nodded. 'I bought you Humbugs for the journey.' From his pocket, he fished a brown, creased paper bag.

'My favourite brother.'

They laughed at that. Then they stood, the three of them, with lumps in their cheeks, silent amongst the noisy crowd.

'We were gladdened to learn that you were with the Pals,' his mother said at last. 'Father knows Ernest Julian, a man of high character and much learning, a lawman too.'

'He is a Lieutenant.' And the kind of man that Daniel's father would have liked as a son.

'He's sorry, Danny,' she said quietly.

'Then where is he?' he asked, equally quietly.

'He's working. The courts don't stop for a man whose son is going to war.'

'Have another sweet,' Niall rushed as though to end the conversation.

Daniel's heart ached.

'Do you have an address in England?' his mother asked.

'No but I'll write to you with it.'

She rummaged in her handbag and produced a handkerchief.

As she dabbed her eyes, Niall put an arm around her. He looked at Daniel as if to say, 'See, I'm looking after her.'

It was too much to ask of him, Daniel realised. He was so

sorry for bringing the war to them. 'It may be over before we finish in Basingstoke,' he said.

She nodded.

Suddenly, and way too soon, it was time to leave.

Niall abandoned his mother, running to Daniel. 'Don't go!' he begged.

Daniel squatted down. 'I'll be back soon, Nially. I promise.'

Hurt filled his eyes. 'Like you promised to be home by Christmas?'

'I'm sorry about that. I thought-' Behind Daniel a whistle blew. 'I must fall in. I'm sorry.' He grabbed Niall and squeezed him tight. Then he hurriedly embraced his mother.

He left them then and fell into line beside Michael.

'This is it!' Michael said jovially. 'At long last.' But his eyes were red from crying.

The marching orders were given.

The Pals were off.

Niall ran alongside the formation. But at the gates of the barracks, his mother held him back, her hands on his shoulders, silent tears streaming down her face. Daniel kept his eyes on them until he could see them no longer. He had never felt as guilty.

Out along the quays, they marched, past pavements thronged with people cheering and waving handkerchiefs and hats. Up ahead, the army band played. Daniel felt as though he were underwater. Where was Maggie? Was he to leave without goodbye? Was she all right? He had no way of knowing.

They passed the Four Courts. Outside on the steps, a group of lawmen, finished for the day, had gathered. They cheered and called goodbyes to friends and colleagues. His father would be inside, reading over some paper, advising some client, his argument-filled life going on undisturbed. Daniel reminded himself that his mother had come. And Niall. He would never forget that.

He glanced at each privileged face. And then it was there, the one he had known all his life. His father was standing, chin raised, scanning the marching troops. His eyes worked methodically, searching line after line. Daniel knew when their eyes would meet and still it was a jolt. Time seemed to stand still. Then, slowly, his father raised an arm above his head. He held it there and kept his eyes on his son. Daniel remembered all the times those eyes had offered encouragement, support, affection. Despite their argument, despite even his beliefs, he remained Daniel's father and he loved him. Daniel longed to go to him, to tell him all of that and apologise for his part in the argument. Then he could see him no more.

twenty

Maggie

Maggie pushed her way through the crowds, scarf in hand, heart a flutter. Despite a note from her mother, her teacher had not allowed her to leave early. At last, Maggie had left of her own accord. She wished, now, that she had done so earlier.

She heard a band and pipers and knew that she was too late. They had left the barracks. All she could do now was wait where she was and hope that she could somehow get to him as they passed.

At length, they came into sight. Her heart began to hammer. In uniform and cap, they all looked the same. How would she pick him out?

All around her, people jostled for position. Maggie had to jump to see. Desperately she scanned each face. But none were his.

Then they turned right and began to cross the river. They would not pass her way! Perspiring and desperate, she took off after them.

Soon she was running with children, alongside the troops. Up Dame Street they went and still no sight of Daniel. At Trinity College, students in striped blazers had gathered, some clinging to the railings for a better view. On seeing the Pals, they cheered and threw their flat-topped, straw hats into the air. The Pals in return, let out a united roar.

Maggie nudged her way through the hordes and climbed up onto the railings. Her eyes scanned face after face. She could not cry. For then she would never see him.

At last, and with incomparable relief, she spied him, his own eyes scanning faces with a desperation that she understood.

'Daniel!' she called but her voice was lost amongst so many others. '*Daniel!* Daniel Healy!' She waved like a wild thing.

It was Michael who saw her. He elbowed Danny and pointed. *At last*, their eyes met, relief flooding his. He laughed and waved. She jumped from the railings and made her way to him. He hurried to the edge of his line, his friends moving quickly to fill the gap.

He held her to him so tightly that she laughed.

'I thought I wouldn't see you,' he said.

'I'm sorry. They wouldn't let me out, the old biddies.'

'You're here now.' He kissed her.

And then she was fumbling for the scarf and pressing it into his hands. 'Can you credit it? I actually finished the blasted thing in the end.'

He wrapped it around him immediately. 'I'll wear it always.'

'God, but you're gorgeous, Healy,' Michael said.

'Don't mind him.' Danny smiled.

'I never do,' she said directly to Michael.

'You haven't changed,' he replied.

'No, I punch as good as ever.'

He laughed.

An officer barked an order. They faced forward – all three of them.

'Should I go?' Maggie asked.

'If you go, I'll follow,' Daniel warned.

'Come on, then,' she dared.

'Do you want to be walking out with a deserter?'

'Is that what we're doing, walking out?' she teased.

He turned to her suddenly, his face alive. 'Marry me, Maggie. As soon as we're together again and you're old enough, will you marry me?' He stepped out of line, lowered himself onto one knee, held her hand and said, 'Maggie Gilligan, will you be my wife?'

She began to laugh and cry. 'I will. I will. Get up quick before they kill you.'

He grabbed her then and lifted her up. A great cheer rose from the Pals. He lowered her to his face and kissed her, carrying her forward to keep his place in line. She looked at the officer to see if Danny was in trouble. He winked at her. She remembered then that they were going to war. That changed everything.

At the train station, they clung to each other.

'I must go,' he said but made no effort to leave her.

'I know.' She didn't move either.

It took an order for them to pull themselves apart, their eyes still holding each other.

'Don't worry, I'll take care of him,' Michael promised gravely.

'Do.'

She kept her eyes on him as they boarded. She searched the windows, willing him to get to one. Then he appeared, waving. She waved with both arms, crazily until they were laughing. A whistle blew. The doors were slammed. And the train eased out of the station, taking him from her.

She stayed on the platform long after he'd gone. It did not matter what she did now for nothing would be the same without him. And yet she could breathe. She could walk. She could find her way home. It shouldn't be so.

'I'm engaged to be married,' Maggie announced at dinner. For that was how she was going to deal with this. She was going to think, only, of the happy future that they would have when they were back in each other's arms. For they would be. And that was that.

'Oh, Maggie,' her mother said sadly.

'Oh, Maggie!' Lily enthused at the same time, clapping her hands with ferocity. She jumped up, ran to her sister and threw her arms around her.

Maggie smiled and kissed the top of her head. 'You always make me feel better, Lil. Always.'

'Congratulations, Maggie!' David said. He raised his eyebrows. 'Of course, I predicted this.'

'Have you all lost your *minds*?' Tom demanded. 'You are sixteen years of age, Maggie Gilligan.'

She turned to him calmly. 'I said I was engaged, Tom. I didn't say I was getting married this very minute.' Though she would have given anything to do exactly that.

'You're too young by far to be even considering such things.' Tom glared at their mother as though she had single-handedly brought about the situation.

'I'm too young to be considering many things, Tom. That is the world we are living in. You of all people should know.'

'It's this Daniel fellow, isn't it?'

Maggie rolled her eyes. 'Yes, it is *this Daniel fellow*.'

'I must speak with him,' he said as though it was a matter of life or death.

'Well, that'll be tricky given that he's gone to war,' Maggie said merrily. He was only improving her mood with his melodrama.

'Are you *saying* that you are engaged to be married to a British Army soldier?'

'That's exactly what I'm saying.' She put her hands up. 'Shoot me.'

'Maggie!' her mother uttered in shock.

Maggie turned to her pleadingly. 'He's being ridiculous!'

Tom squinted at her. 'Are you still in Na Fianna?'

'Yes, Tom,' she said trying to be patient. 'I'm still in Na Fianna.'

'Then be very careful what you say to your British Army soldier.'

'Do you think I'm an utter idiot?'

'And be particularly careful what you write,' he continued. 'The army will be censoring all mail – especially from their Irish regiments. On that you can rely.'

'I know *that*,' she said though the thought had not occurred. He was, after all, far too bossy for a brother.

twenty-one

Maggie

Maggie avoided newspapers and all talk of war. She shared stories of happy princes, selfish giants and swallows. She waited for his words. Then came news that no one could escape, the sinking of the British ocean liner, the Lusitania, off the coast of Cork, torpedoed by a German U-boat with the death of almost one thousand two hundred men, women and children. Maggie saw them in her dreams, struggling in the water, children calling to mothers, then going under. The images haunted her. Sometimes, at night, she dreamt them there, Lily and herself, struggling to stay afloat. She could no longer keep the enemy clear in her mind. Perhaps there were two. Nothing was simple any more.

At last, an envelope arrived carrying the insignia of the Royal Dublin Fusiliers. Maggie ripped it open. Her eyes raced through his words, hungry for news of him, starving, but at the same time not wishing to reach the end, for the words to stop.

My dearest Maggie

There is talk of America joining the fight in the wake of the Lusitania. How could she not? God rest their souls, every last one.

I hope that I did not put you on the spot with my proposal. I was gripped by a moment of madness and you should feel no pressure whatsoever to stand by your answer. It was thoughtless of me to ask under such circumstances – but if you would still have me, I'd be the happiest man alive.

Good news. I have received a letter of apology from my father. How his words have lifted my heart.

Write soonest and let me know if you are still happy to, one day, be Missus Daniel Healy. I will understand...

Your dearest, darling Danny

Maggie snatched up pen and ink.

Dear Daniel, do you have <u>any idea</u> how many times I have written the words Missus Daniel Healy? Let me write them again: Missus Daniel Healy. <u>Of course</u> I will still have you. You have made me the happiest girl in Dublin.

I am so glad to hear of your father's letter. We only ever get one father – and not forever.

Life here carries on as normal, which does not feel right at all. I live for news of you. Tell me more of Basingstoke. You have begun to see the world!

Your beloved fiancée, The Future Missus Daniel Healy

She kissed the envelope and posted it immediately, not wishing him to be in limbo a moment longer. She needed his letters like air but the next one she needed even more for it would be confirmation that he had received hers and that their engagement continued uninterrupted.

Maggie felt as if she had, at last, taken a giant step towards adulthood. She longed to keep stepping in that direction, to let her hair grow, to let her body develop as was happening to some of the girls at school. For the first time in her life, she wished that she were just a normal girl with no expectations on her shoulders, no dead father whispering to her at night to make a difference. She wished she were free to just *live*.

His letter took days to arrive. When it finally did, Maggie accidentally tore it in two when ripping open the envelope. She hurried the halves together and devoured his words.

Dearest <u>Fiancée</u>!

Hurrah! It seems that we are the two happiest people on earth!

When I am out on a route march, my tongue parched from thirst, my feet aching to the point of pain and miles more to go, I repeat these words in my head with every step: Missus, Daniel, Healy. Missus, Daniel, Healy. Missus, Daniel, Healy. The thought of you would get me through hell.

We saw our first airplane, Maggie. All of us stopped what we were doing and stared up in wonder. It was a sight to behold, a miracle of engineering. Luckily, it was one of our own or I would not be penning this letter! It does not seem that America will be joining us after all. No matter. The war will soon be over, with or without them.

I miss your laugh. I miss your eyes. And the rest of you just as much.

Write soon,

Your loving <u>fiancé</u>, Daniel

PS I am one of twelve from the 7ths to have been selected as a sniper!

twenty-two

Maggie

The more Maggie longed to be a woman, the harder she had to try to remain a boy. She had begun to starve herself, having noticed that it was the heaviest of girls who developed first. Now, as she looked in the mirror, she knew that she would have to wear an extra vest – or two. She tried stooping her shoulders forward. It helped. But for how long?

Arriving at the hall, she was deep in thought – she could perhaps *bandage* her chest – when she noticed that the room was almost empty. Those present looked pale and shaken – except for Patrick who looked murderous.

'What is it?' she asked.

He looked at her in disbelief. 'Have you not heard of Ypres?'

'No.'

'Then you are alone.'

'Patrick, what is it?'

But at the top of the room, Con Colbert was already speaking. 'A moment's silence, please, for the brave Irishmen who have fallen at Ypres. To all the boys here tonight who have lost family or friends – you do them proud to turn out here this evening. To those that cannot be here, please pass on our deepest sympathies. There will be no drill tonight. Now, let us pray.'

Heads bowed, they blessed themselves and prayed in Irish. A sob broke through the unified voices, a pair of shoulders shook and a tearful boy raced out.

When the prayers ended, the young rebels began to leave in silence.

Maggie turned to Patrick. 'Tell me.'

'Thousands have been gassed to death, my father and two uncles included.'

She covered her mouth.

He spoke as though in a trance. 'The Germans sent poison out on the air to do their dirty work for them. My father didn't even go down fighting.'

She longed to hold him, comfort him but she was a boy. And he was Patrick. 'You're good to come out.'

Fury raged in his eyes. 'Na Fianna is the only way I have to avenge their deaths.'

She didn't understand. 'But we'll be fighting the *British* not the Germans.'

'Yes, the British who push the Irish troops up to the front-line before their own. Cannon fodder, that's what we are, over there. Cannon fodder.'

She held her head. She could not hear this.

'If I do nothing else in this world, I'll get revenge.' He turned and stormed out.

His horror was hers now. Jolted back in time, another enemy climbed into her lungs, stealing the air from them. She rushed to the window. Tearing at her collar, she sucked in great gulps of air. This is what he faced. And there was nothing she could do to stop it. Nothing.

Maggie's mother held her.

'Why didn't you *tell* me?' she demanded.

'Maggie, you asked us not to speak of the war.'

It was true.

Her mother rubbed her back. And Maggie wanted to be

comforted. But she also wanted to be alone. She didn't know what she wanted. She broke free and ran to her room.

Lying on her bed, she wept for all those who had been killed so horrifically, for all their loved ones, and for Daniel and the Pals who had marched, erect and proud towards war.

She ignored the weight on the bed as someone sat down. She ignored the hand that brushed her hair over and over. But she could not ignore the tiny voice that said, 'There, there.' Lily was mothering her as she'd done her own mother. Maggie cried harder, then, at the pain of the world.

'What you need is a story,' Lily said firmly, like a doctor prescribing a cure. 'A happy one. First, you must blow your nose.' She passed Maggie a handkerchief. And when Maggie did as she was told, Lily bossed, 'Now, sit up.'

Maggie smiled through tears and did as instructed. Lily brought the pillows from her bed and placed them on Maggie's. Then the two of them sat side by side.

'I'm going to have to make up my own story, Maggie,' she said with gravity. 'Yours are just too sad altogether.'

'Don't I know it?'

And so Lily invented a story of a lost dog that, after a series of terrifying adventures, returned safely home with a slight limp. When that made Maggie cry, Lily told the story of a little girl who had been lonely and lost but who found a family that told sad stories and made her happy.

Maggie enfolded her in a hug. She rested her chin on her tiny blonde head. 'What would I do without you, Lil?'

'You saved me, Maggie. I'm only saving you back.'

part three

twenty-three

Daniel
Summer 1915

At the end of June, the Pals received orders to ready themselves for Gallipoli, not France, after all. Daniel agonised over his letter to Maggie, rewriting it over and over. At last, he had to let it go. He placed it in an envelope for posting the following day.

In the early hours, he woke with, suddenly, so much he needed to say. By the light of the moon, he found his pen and paper and, at the window, he began again.

My dearest Maggie,

We are off. To Gallipoli, in the end. But do not fear. They say that the Turks are poor fighters!

I love you, Maggie, more than you love your country, more than Lily loves stories and your mother loves education, more than the sun, the moon and life itself. You are a fire that springs from an empty hearth. You are a bird that bursts from a tree and startles a horse into a gallop. You are the pulse in my veins, my reason for living. I will come home to you, Maggie Gilligan. I promise you.

With my fondest, fondest love always, your future husband, Danny

He read it over and wondered at himself. A fire that springs from an empty hearth! Was he losing the run of himself altogether? And yet that was what Maggie had brought to his life – fire. Until she had entered it, had he even been living?

'I wish I had a girl to write to.'

'Jesus, Michael!' He'd come out of nowhere.

'Sorry.'

Daniel moved to make space for his friend on the windowsill and they sat side by side.

Michael sighed. 'If I'd a girl to come home to, I imagine I'd try harder to stay alive.'

'You have a father who is proud of you,' Daniel said without envy.

Confidence drained from Michael's face. 'Are we doing the right thing, at all, Danny?'

'Damned if I know!'

They laughed because what else could they do?

Daniel prayed that Maggie's return letter would reach him before he left for Gallipoli. As the days passed, it became an omen. If he received it, he would survive the war.

To his immense relief, it arrived on his last day in Basingstoke. The paper was bumpy and some of the words blurred. He was sorry for causing her pain.

My darling Danny,

You have promised me that you will return. So you must. That's all there is to it.

And now for the advice (I have given this much thought): Never underestimate a man with a gun, Turk or no Turk. Stay close to Michael. Two pairs of eyes are better than one. Two pairs of arms, legs, two spirits. Two is better than one, Danny. This I have learned from you.

Forget what I said and write to me every day. I need to hear that you are well. You are in my prayers every night, every morning, every minute. Stay safe, stay safe, stay safe. Come home to me, Danny, so we can live happily ever after.

Maggie

He loved her for her practicality. He loved her for her concern. He loved her for her vulnerability. He loved her and he was leaving her.

twenty-four

Daniel

On July 10th, they left England under cover of darkness. The ship's captain was the same man who had been in command of the Carpathia when she rescued survivors from the Titanic; another omen, Daniel hoped.

Life was good as they inched towards war. The food was better than army fare and included oranges chilled by refrigerator and gin cocktails they called 'Gallipolis'. They swam and raced in saltwater baths and began each day with a run around the deck. Daniel learned poker and made a hesitant stab at bridge. He wrote to Maggie of sunsets like paintings and porpoises that seemed to guide them safely along.

They called to Gibraltar, Malta, Egypt.

'A bronzed Irishman is a fine-looking specimen,' MacDonald said as they sat on deck, one evening.

'Even Hegarty looks half-decent,' Wilkin teased.

Michael flung an orange at him.

In a flash, he raised an arm, snatching it out of the air.

'Jesus, where did you learn that trick?' Lecane asked.

'What trick?' he asked casually as he peeled and subsequently ate Michael's orange.

In Greece, they landed to await further orders. Out in the harbour, alongside colourful native boats, they watched minelayers, battleships and torpedo craft. And when Red Cross boats came ashore with hundreds of wounded from the very place they were headed, the rumours about Turks as fighters changed. All cockiness vanished.

MacDonald turned to Daniel.

'Have you ever wondered what it'll be like to take a life?' he asked quietly.

Daniel's smile was sad. 'Every day.'

Then, on August 6th, orders came that they were to set sail for Suvla Bay, two words that meant war. Daniel and his friends hugged, all manliness forgotten. As they boarded a barge, Daniel noticed bullet holes on the bridge and blood stains on the deck. No one said a word but many blessed themselves. Daniel silently prayed for all those who had died before him – and all those who would die beside him. He prayed that, if that were God's plan for him, death would be swift. He prayed too for forgiveness for whatever he would have to do in the name of war.

The quartermaster issued a ration of cigarettes donated by the 'Friends of Ireland.'

'Whoever they are, I fecking love them,' Michael said.

Then they were away, taking a westerly course to escape Turkish submarine and coastal observation. All day they sailed in increasing silence. Daniel thought of Maggie and his family. It comforted him that he had made up with his father. It was important, suddenly.

As night fell, all cigarettes and pipes were extinguished. Portholes were boarded up to contain light, creating a furnace below deck. The men slept under the sky, side by side like tinned sardines.

In the early hours, they were awakened by the sound of shelling. They rose in dreaded silence and stood in darkness watching the flash of guns and shells from Turkish positions, high up on a ridge. It was their first hint of the terrain – low-lying beaches backed by high ground. One did not need to be a war strategist to work out that they would be picked off as they tried to land.

In the darkness, all around them, bobbed the red and green lights of hospital ships. Moans came to them over the sea. Beside Daniel, a man thumbed a rosary beads. Daniel remembered the veteran at the Curragh Camp who had warned that prayer was the only preparation for what was to come. His stomach heaved.

Just before dawn, they waited to board motor lighters that would take them ashore. Stores, ammunition and cases of rations were loaded onto the first of the lighters. Then the troops received the order to board. More and more men were loaded on until there was standing room only. As the lighter took off, Daniel wished it Godspeed.

One by one the lighters left. Too soon, it was Daniel's turn to board. He and Michael exchanged a glance, an embrace and a clap on the back. He closed his eyes and took a deep breath. Then they dropped silently onboard.

Daniel's prayers started up again along with the engine. They tumbled out, one after the other: the Our Father, the Hail Mary, the Glory Be. The order did not matter. Daniel just kept them coming. If he died mid-prayer perhaps he would go straight up, cut out purgatory altogether and, Heaven-forbid, hell. Maybe he should pray to be killed before he himself took a life. But he wanted to live! He had so much to live for. He was eighteen! He turned in horror to the sound of shellfire. The first of the lighters was coming under fire. A voice in the darkness cursed 'Johnny Turk'.

Daniel's heart had never raced so fast. He needed to crap but that was clearly out of the question. And all the time they inched nearer and nearer to shore. Dawn broke quickly and, through a light mist, Daniel saw the beach and on it stretcher-bearers carrying wounded down to the sea. He had the strongest feeling that they were arriving at the gates of hell.

The lighter stopped close to shore. The gangplank went down.

They were ordered up. Michael was one of the first, Daniel directly behind him. Then somehow, in the swell to disembark, Daniel found himself six or so men behind. He pushed forward and was up at last. He had only taken two steps when he heard a shell come in. There was a great plume of water to his right and he was blown in the opposite direction into the sea. Cold, salt water swamped him, rushing into his eyes, ears, mouth. He gasped for air and tried to swim but his kit was dragging him down. He struggled to remain calm as he went under, reminding himself that they were close to shore; the seabed could not be far. But his kit unbalanced him, forcing him down, back first, so that his legs rose above him. His breath began to fail him. Sweet Mother of Jesus, was this how he would die, on his first day, without firing a single shot?

His kit made contact with the sea floor, giving him his bearings. He struggled onto hands and knees, got his feet under him and pushed up with all his might, kicking his legs as he had never kicked before. He broke the surface, grabbed a mouthful of air, tried to right himself into a swimming position but was dragged down again.

He hit the bottom and pushed up once more. Breaking the surface, he thought to remove his kit. He struggled to do so, weakening now and beginning to go down again. His face had just submerged when his descent stopped. Then someone was pulling him up out of the water by the collar of his jacket. Who could be that strong? He turned. And could not fathom what he saw. It was the recruiting officer from the 6ths! What was he doing here? It made no sense. And how could he be this tall?

'Ah, tis yourself,' he said to Daniel as though they were long-lost friends. Then he threw him over his great shoulder, kit and all.

Behind them, Daniel could see a great horde of Irishmen run along the gangplank. It was a cheering sight. Then bullets began to ping water that was now up to the officer's thighs.

'I'm grand now, sir,' he shouted, fearing a shot in the ass.

He was tossed abruptly forward and went under again. This

time, though, his boots struck ground and when he stood, he was waist deep. He turned to thank the officer but could not see him. He looked towards the beach and back again. Then there he was, face down in the water. He had not tossed Daniel deliberately. He had been hit.

The sea slowed Daniel's dash to a wade. Reaching the officer at last, he grabbed his shoulders and heaved him over. Bright red blood spurted up into Daniel's face. The man was bleeding from the neck. Daniel knew from first aid that if he did not stop the bleeding, death would follow in minutes. Putting one hand under his neck and pressing the other flat against the wound, Daniel waded backwards towards shore, the salt water working with him now, to support the officer's weight. And still the bullets came. He felt one enter his kit bag and closed his eyes, expecting the end. But it did not come. He felt nothing at all. Reaching shore at last, he heaved the giant up onto the sand, dropped to his knees and pressed both hands flat against the wound. Sniper fire peppered the sand around them as Daniel shouted for a stretcher-bearer.

'Fuck on off with you and that's an order,' the fallen man said but very weakly and with affection.

A stretcher-bearer was hurrying to them.

'He's bleeding from an artery,' Daniel shouted.

The stretcher-bearer dropped to his knees beside Daniel. 'Ah, sure, he's gone. Sorry, lad.' He clapped Daniel's shoulder.

Daniel stared down into eyes emptied of life. A great rage rose inside him. What kind of heathen would kill a man trying to save a life?

Then he was being hauled up.

'He's gone, Danny.'

Daniel looked up as if from a trance. Michael had come back for him.

'Come on quick before you get yourself killed.'

'He saved me, Mick.'

'Then he died a hero.' Michael picked up the dead man's rifle and held it out to Daniel.

But Daniel was a sniper; his weapon had been adjusted specially for him. He scanned the sand in desperation. Then he saw it. He crawl-raced to it, grabbed it and scrambled to his feet. Bent low, he and Michael stumbled forward, past stretcher-bearers, wounded, dying, dead, past groans and muttered prayers.

A shell came in, sending them diving to the ground.

'Are you all right?' they shouted together.

Then answered together. 'I'm all right.'

Ears ringing and mouths spitting sand, they were up again and running.

A mine exploded some poor unfortunate to pieces. Daniel stopped at the sight: a person, a life, *shattered*, *fractured*, *disintegrated*. Gone. In an instant.

'Healy!' Michael shouted.

He came to his senses. And followed.

Out of breath, they reached the base of the ridge, where they took shelter. Daniel looked back. At the water's edge, the sea lapped gently over the body. Minutes from landing and already Daniel had learned two lessons of war: The most unexpected of men can make heroes. And heroes can die. Bowing his head, he prayed for the man's soul.

Michael shoved a flask into his hand. 'Drink,' he instructed. 'And forget.'

Daniel drank the burning rum. Forgetting was another thing.

'See anything?' Michael asked, looking up the ridge.

Daniel squinted but could see nothing only sand, rock and scrub. 'No. You?'

'No.'

Daniel had always imagined the enemy as one man, faceless and contemptible. Now he knew otherwise. The enemy was terrain. It was unbearable heat, already at this hour. It was thirst. It was shells, machine gun fire and mines. *Plus* the faceless contemptible man, better armed, better positioned, better camouflaged and better motivated because he was a man defending his land.

As they awaited orders, other regiments joined them, the 5th and 6th Royal Irish Fusiliers and the 6th Inniskillings from the north of Ireland. *How strange the workings of the world,* Daniel thought. Had there been no war and Home Rule instead, he might have been fighting these very men in a civil war.

twenty-five

Maggie

In the Dublin Mountains, Maggie and Patrick stood side by side, each holding a rifle. Maggie had little respect for the Mauser, needing as it did to be reloaded after every shot and cast aside to cool after every three. It also produced a three-foot flame, turning the shooter into a target the minute the trigger was pulled. Still, a gun was a gun.

They took aim. On the count of three, they fired.

'You're losing your touch,' Patrick said triumphantly.

His smile was like a star appearing in the night sky. Since Ypres, he had barely spoken. The darkness of his hair and eyes seemed to spread beyond their edges and swamp him. He carried his anger with defiance. But there was more than anger; there was a sorrow so intense that it seemed to ooze through his very pores and into the air. The sudden smile gave Maggie an idea.

She missed the next shot altogether.

He looked at her. 'What was *that*?'

'You moved.'

'Don't blame *me*.' He was smiling again.

Her third shot wasn't a total disgrace or he might have copped on.

'All right,' he said. 'Stop.'

'Stop what?'

'Letting me win.'

'I'm *not*.'

He gave her a look. 'I'm *not* an eejit.'

'Well, you must be because I'm not letting you win.'

His face changed, the darkness returning. 'I don't need pitying, Ruairí, all right? I can still shoot.'

'I know you can.'

'Then stop.'

'I can't stop what I'm not doing.' But she did stop.

And when they resumed after the rifles cooled, he did win.

They passed the guns to the next two and made their way to a nearby stream to wash soot from their hands and faces. They took advantage of the warm August sun and sat on a boulder that formed part of a pathway across the stream. The gurgling water was peaceful and, for a moment, Maggie forgot all else. She threw a stick in and watched its bumpy journey.

'How's Daniel?' Patrick asked.

Her heart thudded. 'His last letter was from Egypt. He's on his way to Gallipoli, Patrick.' Only it didn't feel like he was on his way. It felt like he was there. She had awoken from a dream where she was not drowning in smoke but water. Ever since then she felt fear like she had never felt it before. She pressed her lips together. She could not cry. Not here. She picked up a stone and fired it downstream. It punctured the water with a plop that seemed too innocent for the times they lived in.

'I'm sorry, Ruairí.'

She just nodded.

'Does he write often?' he asked, a longing in his voice as if he'd give anything for one last letter from his father.

'Most days but they arrive haphazardly.'

He turned to her. 'God. You must be fierce close!'

She gazed down at her hands. 'He's my best friend in the world.'

'You're lucky. My brothers crucified me at your age.'

She had cut her hair, dressed as a boy and yet this was the first time that it felt like a lie. She considered telling him the truth. Then discarded the idea. Patrick Shanahan put Na Fianna Éireann before all else. He would have her dismissed.

twenty-six

Daniel

They had waited in the sweltering heat. They had advanced and then retreated under terrific fire. Now, as the Turks concentrated their efforts on the beach, they were ordered inland once more. The sun beat down. The air hummed with heat. Flies formed a welcoming party, feeding on their perspiration. Daniel tried to ignore the thirst; his ration had to last till sundown.

Up ahead, a mine exploded into the 5th Royal Irish Fusiliers.

'Jesus.'

'Fuck.'

'Christ.'

Without even knowing it, the Pals halted.

How quickly war took you into its jaws.

As they were ordered on, Daniel prayed for their souls. He prayed for his own. Every step, now, was a gamble, a game of life or death. At any moment, it could all be over. How great would the pain be? *Missus Daniel Healy. Missus Daniel Healy. Missus Daniel Healy*, he repeated to himself. As he passed their remains, he called to mind Maggie's face, every detail, the exact green of her eyes, the freckle on her lip, the most beautiful eyebrows in the world, black and arched and full of expression. She smiled at him then and whispered the words, 'You can do this'. He felt her strength in him and he began to believe those words.

Another mile in the hellish heat and they were ordered to remove their packs. They were leaving behind the weight but also their blankets, oil-sheets, clothing and washing materials. Daniel hurried two pairs of socks into his pocket and wrapped Maggie's scarf about his waist.

On they went, bayonets glinting in the sun. They reached a saltwater lake that had dried up from the heat. The sand glistened like diamonds as their boots disturbed it. Daniel tried not to think about what might be buried underneath. He tried not to think what might be hidden in the hills that surrounded them. Here, they were fully exposed to fire.

And it came, just as they reached dry, ploughed fields. Ahead of them, if they could only reach it, was the most basic of cover – small hillocks, rocks and brushwood. They broke into a run. Months of racing against each other paid off as they dived for cover. Then, from the sea, British Army naval guns opened fire on the hill.

The Pals dug in as best they could. Daniel could fight the thirst no longer. He took a swig of water, warm now. He swished it around in his mouth, making it last. Swallowing finally, he forced himself to cap his flask.

The bombardment lasted twenty minutes, leaving the top of the hill smoking like a volcano. Dusty and sweating, the troops were ordered on once more. As they advanced on the base of the hill, Daniel readied himself for the next onslaught. But when they arrived at a network of trenches they found them empty. They fell into them, grateful to be alive.

'What is that tied about your waist, Healy?' an officer asked.

Daniel's heart sank. 'It's a scarf, sir.'

'Give it here, like a good man.'

Daniel held it a moment before handing it over.

The officer picked up a stick and pushed it, in and out, through the scarf. 'Perfect,' he said and held it up.

Maggie's scarf had become an Irish flag. Daniel smiled. How she'd love that.

Too soon, they were ordered to ready themselves to move out. They fixed bayonets. Daniel fumbled for his photograph of Maggie. Fingers trembling, he gazed at it. Then he kissed and put it back in his breast pocket. All around him, men prepared themselves. Some were doing what he had done. Others bowed heads and blessed themselves. Michael took a swig of rum. Behind them someone retched. Then the Commanding Officer let out a mighty roar and was off, up out of the trench. They followed with the deafening cry of a Lansdowne Road rugby chant. It was as if craziness had entered their blood. But they needed that craziness.

Racing up the hill, they met the enemy face-to-face and screaming. They ran at each other in a frenzy of gun and bayonet. Run and fight, run and fight and try not to think, to see. All around, men met death, some with terrifying wails, others curses, and other still with a proud silence. Daniel would go screaming blue murder. And yet the force of his will to survive surprised him. He leapt and stumbled over bodies, over rocks and scrub that reached up to trip and scrape. Then a shell. Michael heard it come in and let out a roar. They hit the ground, the explosion deafening. Then blackness engulfed them like a blanket.

Daniel awoke, covered in debris. One by one, he tried his limbs. He lifted his head. Smoke obscured his view like a thick fog, climbing into his eyes and up his nostrils causing him to cough. It seemed too quiet for war. He raised himself onto hands and knees and searched for his gun. He found it, intact, in the scorched earth beside him. He searched for Michael. Crawling, he trawled the blackened ground, calling his name with growing desperation. Bodies lay strewn like dropped puppets. Daniel forced himself to check the face of every Pal. With each one, he died a little inside. Guilt flooded him, guilt at the relief that none of them was Michael.

He looked up the hill. There was only one answer. He must have advanced. This was war. There was no place for waiting for friends to regain consciousness.

Daniel had a sudden feeling of being left behind. Far off up the hill, his friends were fighting the enemy without him. He took off as fast as the terrain allowed, ever alert. Intermittently, smoke obscured his view. The ground was a carpet of bodies, dead and wounded. Men groaned and called out as he passed, tugging at his heart.

'The stretcher-bearers are coming,' he reassured. Orders were to fight and if everyone abandoned orders, there would be no order at all. That was how wars were lost.

And so he carried on. Passing wounded Turks, he feared a shot in the back. And when smoke blew into his face, he expected, at any moment, to be confronted by an enemy face or a silent bayonet in the gut.

Missus Daniel Healy. Missus Daniel Healy. Missus Daniel Healy.

A hand gripped his ankle. He whipped around, bayonet at the ready.

Ah, God, he thought. It was a Pal, the lad in the canteen who had asked of war. A shell had got him. It was a miracle that he was alive.

'Finish me off,' he begged.

Squatting down to him, Daniel scrambled for his ration of rum. Fingers shaking, he put it to the boy's lips. But he spluttered and choked and wasn't able for it.

'Shoot me, for pity's sake,' he said weakly. 'Put me out of my misery.'

Daniel's heart was tearing; he imagined he could feel it. 'Don't ask me that. Anything but that.'

'Don't leave me here to bleed to death. Release me.'

Daniel closed his eyes and asked the Lord for strength.

'Release me, Healy, old sport.'

Daniel opened his eyes, then looked at the boy and nodded.

His smile was beautiful. 'Tell them I fought like a hero, won't you?'

Daniel put a hand on his shoulder. 'I will.'

'I'm ready.'

Oh Jesus, Daniel thought. He told himself that if the roles were reversed and he had to die, he'd want it to be quick. It was what they all wanted. And so, he put the gun to the boy's head, turned away. And fired.

He had to make sure. And so he looked. A great sob gripped him. Never had he imagined – and he had done a lot of imagining – that he would ever take the life of one of his own. The relief on the boy's face did nothing for Daniel's pain.

twenty-seven

Daniel

The sounds of battle grew nearer. The smoke was everywhere, now. Daniel could not see, could barely breathe. And then he was falling, tumbling down into blackness. Landing on hands and knees, he saw that he had stumbled into a great smoldering crater. He picked himself up, found his gun and, bent low, hurried forward to the lip. He peered out. The smoke was clearing in patches. On and off, he had a view ahead. The sniper in him awoke. He removed his jacket, folded it and placed it on the ground before him. Then he lowered himself onto one knee and readied his rifle.

He watched for the flash of machine-gun fire. Slowly, patiently, he pinpointed the gunner. He took aim. His blackened, shaking fingers stilled. He breathed slowly, deeply, and then released a single shot.

The machine-gun fire stopped instantly.

There was no regret in taking this life. The pacifist in Daniel had died.

A burst of fire alerted him to the location of another gunner. Calmly, like before, he took him down. He waited, coldly, for someone to take over, for it to begin again. Behind him, a footstep!

He flung around. Out of the smoke, loomed the whites of two eyes, a face covered in soil.

Which side? Which fucking side?

'Healy, is that you?'

Daniel almost pissed himself in relief. 'Christ! Sergeant Miller! Sorry for cursing, sir.'

The sergeant looked like he was made of soil. He had lost his helmet and his jacket was ripped at the arm.

'Are you wounded?' Daniel asked.

'Only a graze.'

Daniel took off his helmet and passed it to his superior. Miller refused it, then simply bent down and picked one off the ground. Behind him, three men loomed into view. Daniel raised his gun.

'At ease, Private,' Miller said.

Daniel lowered his weapon.

'Picked these lads up along the way,' the sergeant said.

None of them were Pals.

'You haven't seen Hegarty, have you, Sarge? I've lost him.'

Miller shook his head. His eyes were sad but then his eyes were forever that way, beautifully sad. You'd nearly want to hug him.

'I imagine he's up ahead,' Miller said. 'Are we safe to advance, do you think?'

'Don't know, Sarge. I just took out two gunners. I was waiting to see if they'd be replaced.'

They took up positions at the lip of the crater, watched and waited.

'Do you have any water, Healy?'

'I'm drained, Sarge. The smoke.'

Miller grinned. 'And we thought Basingstoke was bad!'

'What I wouldn't give for an old English puddle.' On route marches they had drunk from them.

'Right oh,' Sergeant Miller said after five minutes had elapsed without fire. 'Ready to move out.'

They readied themselves and, at the order, climbed from the crater. They picked their way through bodies and scrub. Neither bullet nor shell came their way. The smoke was at its thickest now. The only sounds were the groaning of the wounded. Daniel tried not to think about what he had done to his dying comrade but knew that he would remember it for the rest of his life – however long that would be.

Nearing the top of the hill, they grew ever more cautious. They crouched low, expecting, at any moment, to come under the terrific fire of a last stand. Bayonets at the ready, they made their final approach. They exchanged one last glance, then ran and leapt into the air.

They landed in amongst their own men who immediately surrounded them, bayonets at their throats.

'At ease, boys,' Sergeant Miller ordered.

They obeyed in relief.

'Healy!'

Daniel turned. 'Walkey!'

They laughed and embraced while all about them, men collapsed into weary heaps. Those with water drained their bottles, one with his tongue out to catch the last drop. From down in the bay floated cheers from the men aboard the Royal Navy gunboat that had been guarding their left flank all the way up.

'We did it!' Walkey said. 'We took the hill!'

'Have you seen Hegarty?' Daniel asked.

He shook his head.

'Has *anyone* seen Hegarty?'

Crouched low for fear of snipers, he made his way through the trench. If he didn't find him, he'd go back down.

Then he was laughing. He and MacDonald clung to each other.

'You little fucker,' MacDonald said affectionately.

Tears sprang to Daniel's eyes. It felt as though they were holding each other up.

'We did it!' MacDonald exclaimed.

Daniel pulled back. 'I'm looking for Hegarty. Have you seen him?'

'No but I'll help you look. You go that way. I'll go this. Don't worry, we'll find him.'

Good old MacDonald.

Daniel passed men pushing the fly-infested bodies of dead Turks and the odd German officer up out of the trenches. He stepped over a body, then halted, his foot in mid-air. What heathens would have women at the front-line? Then he thought of Maggie, unstoppable in her quest to fight for her country. She could *not* end up like this. He would *not* let it happen. It was why he was here. All he had seen, all he had done, was for that reason. He was glad to be reminded of it, to find some sense in this.

Yards ahead and around a corner came the sound of someone dropping into the trench. Daniel raised his rifle on reflex. He approached, bayonet at the ready, praying he wouldn't have to use it, praying for the killing to be over, at least for today.

He rounded the corner.

Bent double, catching his breath, the soldier slowly turned. At the sight of Daniel, he smiled, exhausted. 'There you are, you old bastard.'

Daniel had to laugh to hide his tears. 'Where were you? I looked everywhere. I thought you'd advanced without me. I was about to go back down.'

'The shell threw me clear, knocked me out for I don't know how long. When I woke, I was alone. You'd all gone on.'

'But I looked everywhere!'

He shrugged. 'I was black as the ace of spades.' He examined himself then and laughed. 'Look at me, not a scratch.' He dusted himself down as if he could not believe his luck. Then his voice changed. 'Who's here?'

'MacDonald and Walkey! The two Gunnings. Sergeant Miller.'

'I'm almost certain I saw Lieutenant Julian go down.'

'Ah, no.' He thought of his father.

'I need a coffin nail.' Michael pulled a battered packet of cigarettes from his pocket.

Neither of them had smoked before the war but whatever one got in rations one gladly took. Daniel accepted a cigarette with thanks. They sat on the floor of the trench. Daniel removed his pith helmet and scratched his scalp. Immediately, he had to replace the helmet against a swarm of flies.

'Maybe the smoke will get rid of them,' Michael said hopefully.

'Nothing will, Mick. It's like they've been released from hell itself.'

But they ignored the flies, the bodies and the stench of already rotting corpses. For a few precious moments, they stole a slice of peace.

Darkness fell.

The groans coming from outside the trench grew louder, reminding Daniel of all the wounded he'd walked by. Soon, he could bear it no longer.

'I'm going out.'

'You are *not*.'

He began to climb the trench wall.

Michael pulled him back down.

'Just one, Mick. Just, for Christ's sake, one.'

'What if it's a Turk?'

'Then it's a Turk.'

'You're mad.'

'I'll *go* mad if I don't get him.'

It was one of the 6th Iniskillings, a lad no older than them, the shadow of a moustache barely forming. His bottle was dry and no one had any to share. There were no stretcher-bearers. Daniel doubted that they would have been of use. He removed his own blackened jacket, rolled it and tucked it under the boy's head. Michael covered him with his but it did not stop the shaking. It was with relief that they saw the padre coming along the trenches, placing his hand on a man here, another there, administering words of comfort and prayer.

Daniel raised an arm. 'Padre!'

He came immediately in that calm way of his. They moved aside as he knelt beside the lad. He tipped a little water into his mouth and whispered a few words. Daniel wondered if it mattered that the boy might not be Catholic.

He called for his mother as death took him.

Daniel shivered. It was the saddest, loneliest moment.

With the sun gone and the sky clear, another enemy arrived. Cold settled in on them. Daniel remembered Maggie's scarf. He would not survive the war without it. And that had nothing to do with insulation.

When he finally tracked it down, his heart sank. An officer had it wrapped around his neck. Daniel turned to walk away but an image of Maggie slaving over it for months had burned itself into his mind. He could not let it go. He approached the officer.

'Sir, the scarf, if you don't mind. It was a gift.'

The officer seemed more surprised than annoyed by the request but, with officers, you never knew what they were thinking until it was too late.

'I've grown quite attached to it, Private.'

'It's of great sentimental value, sir.'

'How's that?'

Daniel produced his picture of Maggie.

The officer peered at it by the light of the moon. 'Is that a boy or a girl, Healy?'

'Girl, sir.'

He looked up, surprised, as though he had decided otherwise. 'What happened to her hair?'

'Long story, sir.'

'I've all the time in the world, Healy.'

'She sold it to help the poor, sir.'

'She did, did she?' He sounded impressed.

'She did, sir.'

'Have you anything to trade me for the scarf, Private?'

Daniel thought. 'A fresh pair of socks, sir.' They would be invaluable after the day's marching but would they be as invaluable as a scarf on a freezing night? Perhaps he'd take the socks and hold on to the scarf.

'Well, why didn't you say so earlier?'

That's exactly what he was wondering. He pulled them from his pocket.

'I don't want your socks, Private.'

'No, sir?'

'I only wanted to see how important the scarf was to you.'

'Important, sir.'

'I can see that.' He took a drag on the cigarette. 'Private?'

'Yes, sir?'

'Your girl?'

'Yes, sir?'

'She's very beautiful. Despite the hair.'

He smiled. 'I know, sir.'

The officer unwrapped the scarf. It took a while. 'She made enough of it.'

'She did, sir.'

Daniel made his way back to Michael. He sat down and held the scarf to his face. What he wouldn't give to have her here with him, to watch her frown and fret and give out about Ireland's history. But then, he wouldn't bring her to a place like this. Not for one minute.

He and Michael received sentry duty together. For two hours, they stood on the fire-step, looking out into an alien wilderness. Daniel didn't know which was colder, his hands or his weapon. And yet, despite the cold, the thirst and constant fear of attack, his eyes began to close. He widened them. They closed again. He slapped his face to stay awake.

'Here, let me do that,' Michael offered.

'Feck off you mad bastard.' Daniel wondered how he'd have survived without him.

twenty-eight

Maggie

There began to appear on the streets of Dublin men with missing limbs, scarred faces, haunted eyes. They limped and hobbled as if from out of hell itself. People stared. Mothers turned their children in to their skirts. Maggie's nightmares became more frequent. In them, it was Daniel who faced the flames now and, instead of running from them, he was walking calmly towards them. When Maggie woke calling his name, Lily was always there. Maggie worried what it was doing to her.

'Tonight we are letting our hair down!' their mother announced. 'We are going to see Madame perform at the Abbey Theatre.'

Maggie smiled. She had always wanted to see Madame on stage.

They took the tram, all of them except Tom who, as usual, was busy.

As Lily chatted, Maggie's eyes returned, again and again, to a handsome couple talking quietly to one another, heads almost touching. She knew that they did not appreciate the easy togetherness they shared – a person could not truly appreciate such things until they lost them. But they climbed into her heart, proof that love could survive war.

They disembarked ahead of Maggie and her family. Arm in arm, they too seemed theatre-bound. She laughed at something he said and rested her head against his shoulder.

Ahead of them, the lights of the Abbey looked gay and inviting. A small cluster of women had gathered outside. In their hands, they held small tins.

'They must be collecting for the war effort,' Maggie's mother said and reached for her purse.

One of the women approached the young couple, blocking their way, forcing them to stop. From the tin, she took a white feather.

The young man stared at the symbol of cowardice that had somehow ended up between his finger and thumb, then hurried the shame into his pocket. The group of women shared triumphant glances. The couple rushed on, heads down.

Suddenly, Maggie was moving, propelled forward by a breathless need to tip the balance back in favour of love. She marched up to the woman, blocking *her* path. She held out an upturned hand as though asking for a feather but before the baffled woman could respond, she shot her hand forward under the tin and brought it swiftly up. It leapt into the air and then clattered to the ground. The wind whipped white feathers against the woman, covering her. One attached itself to her lip. She batted at it as though struck by a fatal disease.

'If you are so keen to get people to the front-line why don't you sign up yourself?'

She stared at Maggie as if she had lost her mind. 'I'm a *woman.*'

'Are you saying that war is not for women?'

'You know that it's not.'

'In that case, keep your nose out of it.'

Lily began to clap. David and their mother joined in. Then strangers.

The woman stared at Maggie's mother. 'What kind of children have you raised?'

'Children that I'm incredibly proud of,' she said, placing an arm behind them and guiding them forward into the theatre.

The play was a spectacle, Madame a sensation. Was there anything she could not do?

'Let us go backstage and tell her how wonderful she was!' Missus Gilligan enthused.

'Yes, let's!' Lily said.

'No!' Maggie blurted at the same time.

'Why not? She hasn't seen us since the food kitchen closed. She'd be delighted-'

'Mam, she's involved with Na Fianna. She sees me regularly – as a boy. I can't have her recognise me.' She touched her shorn hair.

Her mother frowned. 'What is Madame doing with Na Fianna?'

'She helped set it up,' Maggie said.

'Lord God. Is everyone in the world becoming a rebel? What is *wrong* with a peaceful solution?'

People turned at the sound of a raised voice.

The mood had changed. It was as if the evening had become tarnished. Maggie wished that she could make the war go away, the British go away, produce a pied piper who would simply attract them out of Ireland. If only life were as easy as stories.

twenty-nine

Daniel

It seemed a lifetime since they had taken the hill. It was days. The 6ths had fought fiercely to advance further inland but the Turks, heavily reinforced, had been ready for them. Now orders were to 'sit tight'. They crouched like animals in holes dug by the enemy, while heat, thirst and flies drained whatever strength they had left. They baked by day and froze by night. Lips cracked and blistered. Faces hollowed out. Eyes grew bloodshot and haunted.

In Basingstoke, Daniel had believed himself pushed to the limit of human endurance. He had had no notion of what that was. Time and again, the words of the war-weary soldier at the Curragh came back to haunt him. He had been right. Nothing could have prepared them for this. All the drills, all the marching seemed like a joke now when they couldn't even stretch their legs. All of those personal hygiene lessons had omitted one crucial fact: for a man to clean himself, he needs water. There was not enough to drink, never mind to work up a lather. Daniel had seen men rub sand onto their skin to rid themselves of grime. Leftover tea, a rare commodity, was used for washing but nothing could rid them of the stench of sweat, dirt, latrines and rotting flesh. Corpses bloated in the sun and burst open – they had not learned that at the Curragh.

Constant sniper fire kept heads low and prevented them from burying their dead. Now and again, a truce was agreed so that both sides could dig and fill graves, the most upsetting, stomach-churning work Daniel had ever known. They did it for their friends – their brothers, more like. They hoped that there would be someone to do it for them should their time come.

A roll call became a reminder of who had gone and that it made no difference whether a man was clever, brave, strong, fast, funny or kind. A machine gun was not discerning. Shrapnel was not choosy. A life could be snuffed out in a second. But that was not the end. No. There was the rotting, the slow decomposition of a body, helped along by flies and rats. The rodents gorged on the eyes first, then the liver, then the rest. It was no surprise to Daniel that men went doolally. He had witnessed it himself, a young Private wandering about aimless and babbling, his body contorted. Daniel wondered if it was a relief to give up the fight for sanity, to just let the mind slip away from the hell that they had been plunged into.

On a regular basis, the Turks sent over 'cricket balls', (as they called the grenades), to remind them that they were still there. The chief concern, though, was water. It occupied their every thought. Daniel had seen good men steal for it, lie for it, die for it. He had seen tongues go black for the want of it. The journey from the beach was so long and treacherous and the heat so intense that there was never enough. They rolled pebbles around in their mouths to generate saliva, blackening their teeth from the earth. There were wells up here but the Turks guarded them with snipers. Those that they had abandoned, they filled with dead bodies. The British Army had underestimated its enemy entirely.

Perhaps the best military weapon that the Turks had, though, was the purple and green Gallipoli fly, the hardiest in the world, persistent, determined, everywhere – like the Turks themselves. Great swarms lived off corpses, latrines and wounds then descended onto food like a black cloud before it could be eaten. The result was dysentery.

When stretcher-bearers could get up, they carried the men off – those that were willing to go. Most stayed until they could no longer shoot. Then, lying prostrate, they were labelled like parcels and stretchered off, pith helmets covering faces against the sun. The ship that had brought them from England had been refitted as a hospital ship, Daniel had heard, accommodating up to two thousand men. The stretcher-bearers risked death on their trips to and from the beach. Sometimes, Daniel would watch them and imagine that that was what he should have been doing. Then he'd remember the friends he had lost and the white-hot hatred he had for the enemy. He *wanted* to kill.

'I thought that a man had to die before going to hell, not the other way around,' Michael said, on his return from the latrine.

Daniel could only smile. If Gallipoli was hell, and it most certainly was, the latrine was the point where the hell fires burned hottest. You used it breathing through your mouth for the smell but with that mouth only open a slit because of the flies. And all the time you feared that a sniper would finish you off while you sat in the most undignified of positions. You dreaded and delayed nature's call. When you finally gave in, you joked that you were going to Brooklyn. Michael had started that one. MacDonald had been born there.

In amongst all of this, they had to eat.

'What I wouldn't give for a spud,' Lecane said.

'With a great dollop of axle-grease.' MacDonald loved his butter.

Daniel ground a rock-hard biscuit between two stones.

Michael dunked his in his tea. 'Wilkin, you owe me an orange.'

'Once we get out of here, I'll buy you a crate of them,' Wilkin promised, swatting at the flies.

'I'll hold you to it.'

Dreaming of roast lamb, Daniel's mouth watered. He would never underestimate Cook's food again.

Daniel tore up the letter he had been writing to Maggie. It had somehow become a list of all that Gallipoli had taught him about war – that the smallest of things (like lice) made a man feel small, that silence can be more terrifying than shelling and that Maggie was right – one person makes no difference to a war. Of course, he couldn't tell her any of this. How, he worried, would he ever be able to talk to her again, hold a conversation about the unimportant? But then, Maggie was never one for the unimportant.

He tried to imagine what she might be doing now. She'd be on holidays from school. He hoped that she was not out with Na Fianna, though in all likelihood she was. What was he doing all the way over here, stuck in a trench, baking alive? He wasn't helping her. He wasn't helping his country. He was fading fast, blending in with the dry, sandy soil. It was only a matter of time before he became it.

No. He must not let his spirits flag. He was there for a reason, the best reason in the world, a reason to live and die for.

A shot rang out.

'Good,' Walkey said. 'One less bullet for us.'

'Ever the optimist,' Michael remarked.

Daniel made another stab at the letter.

Michael, oiling his rifle, looked over. 'Maggie?'

Daniel nodded.

Michael looked about. 'What could you possibly be telling her?'

'Lies.'

He smiled. 'I'd like to hear them.'

'Well, I haven't written them yet but I'll be focusing on the scenery, the sunshine and the *marvellous* smell of thyme.'

Michael raised an eyebrow. 'You don't think she'll smell a rat instead?'

Daniel considered. 'I'll tell her that the flies are bothersome.'

He laughed. 'Bothersome.'

Thereafter, it became Michael's favourite word. He used it to describe everything. The darkness of Gallipoli brought out the

201

light in him, always on hand with a quip or an imagined game of rugby featuring Walkey, MacDonald, Lecane and Wilkin. MacDonald regularly dropped the ball. Daniel counted fifty-nine different jokes on flies alone, all of them amusing. And learned that if you could laugh at something it lessened the power of it. By popular demand, Michael's diary was passed around as a form of entertainment. Sometimes, he even read it aloud, as if on stage at the Abbey.

0700   *A quarter pint of neat rum, rationed out by the sergeant is for medicinal purposes, for surely it would kill anything that might be lurking in the intestines.*

0730   *Breakfast, the source of our best arguments. And biscuits that could break a man's teeth.*

0830   *Rifle inspection, an excuse for our beloved sergeant to make rude remarks about the state of man's best friend.*

0900   *Ah, the life of the sniper's assistant. With my trench periscope, I observe enemy movement enabling Healy to get a single well-aimed shot. At least, it gets us out of digging trenches. Keep up the good work, Healy.*

1130   *This would be the time to write to your girl – if you had a girl.*

1300   *Fly invasion caused by sumptuous dinner of rice, tea, biscuits and jam.*

1430   *The Gallipoli orchestra: Chip, chip, chip – the sound of picks and shovels taking our trenches closer to Johnny Turk.*

1457   *Dong, dong, dong, dong – four beats of a lead pipe warn us to take cover. Mmmmm – enemy plane overhead. Boom – explosion. Dong, dong – two beats of the lead pipe. Danger past. For now.*

1730   Magic show – making a meal from biscuits, fried beef, desiccated potato – and an onion if you're very lucky.

1930   My favourite words – Stand to arms! Sentries are doubled. No more than three hours sleep for a man. Sure, this is the life.

0330   Stand to arms! Instantly awake and shooting. The night explodes in fire. And dies as quickly. Unfix bayonets and back to sleep standing up.

Join the British Army! Travel the world!

Daniel had never loved or needed his friend more. The officers treated them as a pair, selecting them together for fatigues. Whether it was latrine duty, burying the dead or keeping watch, it had become either a habit or an accepted fact that they worked as a pair. It helped Daniel stay sane.

thirty

Maggie looked in the mirror then closed her eyes. Despite starving herself, her body had insisted on maturing. She'd have to strap herself down. Perhaps she could get some bandages at the first aid lesson. Hearing someone on the stairs, she buttoned up her shirt.

Lily burst in. 'What are you doing?'

'Getting on my uniform.'

Lily looked at her breeches admiringly. 'Could I join, one day?'

Maggie looked at her little sister. For the first time, she saw Na Fianna as her mother did – as a threat to the person she loved. She reminded herself that it would all be over long before Lily was old enough to do anything. She rubbed the top of her head and smiled.

'We'll see,' she said.

'We could fight together.'

Maggie squatted down. 'How about a quick story before I go?'

Lily jumped up on the bed in immediate readiness.

Maggie laughed and sat opposite. She took a deep breath then widened her eyes.

'You're a good storyteller, Maggie.'

'I am?'

She nodded enthusiastically.

'All good storytellers start with air.'

She sucked in a huge exaggerated breath and Lily laughed.

'Once upon a time, there was a salmon who ate nine hazelnuts that fell from nine trees that grew in a circle around a pond on the River Boyne. In doing so, he gained the wisdom of the world.'

Lily stared as though she could see actual words tumble from Maggie's mouth.

'The poet, Finnegas, sought out the salmon and its wisdom. It took him seven years and one almighty struggle before he finally caught that fish. Then, the old poet was tired and needed a rest. *So* he asked Fionn Mac Cuamhaill – the boy he was teaching about the world – to cook the fish but not, *under any circumstances*, to eat it.' Maggie stopped for effect.

'Go on,' Lily urged.

'*Well*, Fionn Mac Cuamhaill turned the fish over and over on the spit while the old man slept. At *long last*, it was cooked.'

'The blister,' Lily reminded her.

Maggie pointed at her. 'Good girl, the blister. There was a *blister* on the skin of the salmon. Fionn, who wanted the fish to be *perfect* for his master, burst the blister with his thumb. But the *oil* in the blister was *roasting hot*.' She opened her eyes wide, '...and *burned* poor Fionn Mac Cuamhaill. He put his thumb into his mouth to cool it down.' Maggie sucked her thumb to demonstrate. 'In an *instant*, Fionn gained the salmon's wisdom. Finnegas, when he awoke, saw the wisdom shining in Fionn's eyes. He was *furious* and asked Fionn if had he eaten the fish. Fionn explained what had happened. Finnegas's anger left him and he gave Fionn the rest of the fish so that he would gain the knowledge of the *entire world*. Throughout his life, whenever he needed guidance, Fionn MacCuamhaill could call on all this knowledge by sucking his thumb.'

'That's not the end.'

'It's not?'

'No. You left out the bit about Fionn MacCuamhaill growing up to become the leader of Na Fianna, the greatest warriors in the land of Ireland.'

'Someday, you'll taste salmon, Lily,' she said, secretly meaning Irish freedom.

'Today?'

'Probably not today. But soon.'

Lily clapped. Maggie gazed on her with such affection. Whenever she began to doubt her own actions with Na Fianna, all she had to do was look at her sister.

An hour later, Maggie and Patrick were combing the back alleys around Sackville Street, committing them to memory. If the revolution was to be fought in the city, they had to know every inch of it, where to attack, hide, escape. They needed to know Dublin better than themselves.

'God. I remember a fight we had down here,' Patrick said, smiling.

Maggie looked at him.

'We had to steal a Lee Enfield rifle from a Tommy so we started throwing punches at each other – real punches mind. He was glued to us. Next thing he knew, his precious weapon was gone. As were we. We got a lot of rifles that way.'

'The Lee Enfields are a hundred times better than the Mausers. Wish we had more.'

'Ah, they're impossible to get now. The feckers are on to us.'

Maggie marvelled at how at ease he was with her now, speaking so freely – for Patrick. The higher up he got in Na Fianna the more he seemed to take her under his wing. It was as if he believed that he was responsible for her, with Danny gone. What really baffled her, though, was that she had time for him. The first time she'd fired a gun, she had wanted to rip off her hat and shout at him, 'Can you believe it, a girl that can shoot?' But here they were now, so comfortable in each other's company. War did strange things to people. Sometimes it united them.

Maggie watched children play with hoops and skipping ropes.

'Sometimes I find it hard to imagine that there'll ever be a revolution,' she said.

'Well, you'd better start imagining it. If we don't rise soon, the war'll be over and we'll never get a chance like this again.'

She nodded. It was what he and Con Colbert continually said: England's misfortune would be Ireland's opportunity. But Maggie thought of Danny and her stomach turned. 'If your father was still out there, would you feel like you were betraying him by rising here?'

He stared at her. 'It is the exact opposite. What did I tell you about the Brits putting the Paddies at the front-line?'

'I wish you wouldn't say that,' she said quietly.

'I'm sorry, Ruairí, but I won't lie to you. It makes no difference to Danny what you do.'

She fought tears of bitterness and distress. Daniel's life was a trifle to them, to be tossed aside like a worn-out toy. How long could he last at the front?

Maggie could not sleep without writing to him.

My dearest Daniel,

You speak of war like it's grand. You forget that I see the men who return. I see their ruined bodies. I see their haunted eyes. It is not grand so stop pretending. We should be honest with each other, Danny. Share the war with me so that I can find words of comfort – if such things exist. Be safe, my darling, and come home to me.

All my love, Maggie

thirty-one

Daniel
August 15th, 1915

For two days, other divisions fought fiercely to take a ridge that dominated most of the surrounding plain. They had succeeded in part but with heavy losses. Now the Pals were being ordered up to try to take the remainder of the ridge. Victory was vital. As they readied themselves, Daniel remembered Maggie's words. 'Two pairs of eyes are better than one. Two pairs of arms, legs. Two spirits.' Daniel looked at Michael. 'Whatever happens, we stay together.'

'I've a bad feeling about this one, Danny. I don't know why.' He took a swig of Dido, accustomed to its bite by now. 'If I don't make it, can you give this to my father?'

'Together, we'll be all right,' Daniel assured him but he took Michael's letter. 'And if I go, will you look after Maggie for me?'

He nodded. Then joked, 'And if we both go?'

'Then, we're well and truly fucked.'

They laughed.

'Good luck, lads.' MacDonald's voice lacked its usual confidence.

'See you on the other side,' Daniel said cheerfully.

'You can count on it.' MacDonald smiled.

'Sorry for all the slagging, MacDonald,' Michael said.

'Did my fair share,' he replied. 'And Hegarty?'

'MacDonald?'

He winked. 'It wouldn't have been the same without you.'

'Likewise, you old bastard.'

The three of them embraced, patting each other's backs with force.

They all faced forward, waiting for the whistle.

Missus Daniel Healy, Daniel willed the words out into the universe so that, one day, they might come true. He thumbed the lock of hair that she had given him, searching for its softness, her softness. He put it to his nose but it had lost her scent a long time ago.

The shrill blast of a whistle and they were up, scrambling like rats from a hovel. But it was a relief to be out, moving, stretching and feeling that they were doing something at last. It was also terrifying.

They marched in the dark over treacherous terrain towards a silent, hidden enemy. All about them, stretcher-bearers worked feverishly to get the wounded down. Groans filled the night air. It went against every instinct to walk by the wounded. But orders were to press on.

When, at last, they reached the crest of the ridge, they were instructed to take up positions along it until light returned. There were no trenches, no proper cover and the ground was too rocky to dig in. The best that they could do was pile a few rocks in front of them and stay awake.

At 2200, Daniel was distracting himself from the cold by imagining how Niall might have grown, when the Turks piled over the ridge like a great swarm of Gallipoli flies.

'Holy Mother of Jesus!' Michael said fumbling with his gun.

The alarm was sounded. Then gunfire erupted like thunder, illuminating the enemy.

Daniel took aim, fired; took aim, fired. But he needn't have aimed at all there were so many of them, a great and endless wall of roaring shadow. Bullets pinged the ground around them, rising dust into their faces. Every second felt like Daniel's last. Sweat poured into his eyes and as he tried to clear it, his helmet fell off. He scrambled for it and fumbled it back into place. And all the time, he prayed for his comrades, wanting each and every one to stay alive. Curses, wails and screams confirmed the impossibility of his request.

'Fuck off back to your hovels, you *fuckers*,' Michael was roaring.

Daniel wondered which was more powerful, his stream of prayer or Michael's profanities.

Finally, unbelievably, the enemy retreated. The firing slowed then stopped altogether. Darkness returned.

Daniel and Michael lay flat on the stony ground, shattered.

'Fucking Turks,' Michael said quietly.

Despite everything, Daniel laughed. Then he closed his eyes and thanked God for their salvation.

'I need to know who's made it,' Michael said then.

It was like wondering which of your family had survived.

Moans, sobs and tearful prayers filled the night sky. Stretcher-bearers began to creep about. Daniel wondered when the war was over – if it ever were – would they continue to walk with a stoop as though expecting a bullet at any moment. He met the eyes of a stretcher-bearer, then. They were bloodshot, exhausted and melancholy.

'Up the Irish,' Daniel called.

The eyes smiled. Then they were gone.

Listening posts were set up. Daniel and Michael were positioned closest to the edge of the ridge. Lying in the dark on full alert, the hairs on the back of Daniel's neck stood on end.

'Do you still have that bad feeling?' he whispered to Michael, his breath fogging up in the cold night air.

'Worse than ever, old pal. Worse than ever.'

Daniel wished that he had left Maggie with a proper goodbye or, at least, a goodbye fitting a soldier that might not return. But then, a proper goodbye would have terrified her.

Just before dawn, stiff, frozen and dying for a piss, Daniel heard shells flying in overhead like a great flock of birds. Sounding the alarm, he stared at Michael. Never before had they experienced such a bombardment. Behind them, ground and men exploded. And still the shells kept coming, no stop, no break. The only sensible response was to reply with grenades. But after two days of fighting, supplies were exhausted.

As Daniel saw it, he had two choices, to lie waiting for the end or do what he had been trained to do. He turned to Michael and tapped his gun. 'Let's take out a few, so our men can advance.'

'Fuck,' was Michael's way of agreeing.

They blessed themselves and began to crawl forward. Daniel prayed that the Turks weren't advancing at the same time. At last, skin torn from scrub and rock, they peered over the edge.

They were everywhere, emerging time and again from behind rocks to lob over their grenades.

'Tell me when you've found a target and we'll fire together on three,' Daniel whispered.

They fired. Two men went down.

They looked at each other, nodded, and went again. With equal success.

Machine gun fire broke out. They clung to the ground.

'Awww *shite!*' Michael groaned.

Daniel turned. Michael's face was in the soil. His uniform had been torn to shreds where bullets had entered. 'Oh Christ,' Daniel uttered, dropping his gun and scrambling back to Michael's feet where he began tugging him out of range.

A shell went off beside them, blowing Daniel clear.

Dazed, he crawled back, ears ringing.

'It's all right. It's all right,' he said over and over.

But Michael wasn't responding, wasn't moving, eyes closed, face flat to the ground. Fumbling, Daniel checked his neck for a pulse and cursed in relief when he found one. It was weak, though. Almost gone. He looked towards the ridge. Orders were to fight not tend to the wounded. He looked down at his best friend. They'd shared so much: laughter, fear, thirst, life. Brotherhood. Michael would not be there if it weren't for him. He knew his duty. It was to his friend.

He grabbed Michael's arms and heaved him onto his back. As he turned down the hill, the sky lit up with an explosion. Like something out of a dream, he saw a Pal leap up into the air, arm outstretched.

'Oh Jesus,' Daniel whispered, realising that the Private was trying to catch an incoming grenade.

A split second of darkness, then the sky lit up again to reveal him snatching it from the sky, letting his arm arc back, under and forward again to release the 'cricket ball' back at the enemy.

'Another one for Ireland, if you don't mind,' he called.

Daniel wanted to scream. It was Wilkin! He remembered him laughing in the sun, snatching Michael's orange out of the air. Now he was catching death in his bare hand and firing it happily back as if he were on the cricket pitch on a sunny afternoon. If Daniel survived, *this* is what he would remember of heroes – his pal, Wilkin.

Wilkin was hurtling towards another cricket ball when they were plunged once more into darkness. Then bravery lit up the sky. Good old, fucking adorable Wilkin, blown into a million pieces. The scream in Daniel's head would not stop. He didn't want it to. Wilkin was gone. Wilkin who had all those times fallen back to tell them to 'take it handy.' There was no justice in the world.

In the rapidly breaking dawn, Daniel made out a company of Pals, led by Captain Hickman, running towards him in a bayonet charge. It was a heartening sight – until they too exploded, right before his eyes, so many of his beloved Pals – years and years of life and love perishing in a split and ugly second. A great numbness fell over him. He could feel nothing now, not even his legs. But they must have been moving still because he found himself at a wall, behind which was a makeshift trench. He climbed over and in. Hands reached up to take Michael. Daniel called for a stretcher-bearer. But there were none, just more men readying to go over the top. Desperately, he looked for something to bandage Michael with but there was nothing. He would die if Daniel didn't get him down to the beach. He looked at Major Harrison.

'Permission to bring Hegarty down, sir.'

The major paused. He looked at Daniel and then at Michael, the most inseparable of Pals.

'You are, of course, wounded yourself, aren't you, Healy?' he hinted.

'Yes, Major.'

The major winked. From his breast pocket, he produced a notebook and pencil. He scribbled a note, tore out a page and passed it to Daniel. 'You'll need this.'

'Thank you, sir.'

Harrison put a hand on Daniel's shoulder. 'You've done your bit, Private. Off you go.'

Daniel saluted. He watched as the major moved to the head of his men, then paused for a moment, head bowed. Daniel saw a number of men bless themselves. Then Harrison gave a sharp blast on his whistle and yelled, 'For Ireland!'

With a mighty roar, the Royal Dublin Fusiliers charged up into the breaking dawn.

Daniel, too, blessed himself. Then he heaved Michael onto his back.

He had no memory of how he got down all those miles alive but here he was, on the beach, carrying Michael into the field ambulance tent. They had to peel his friend off his back. They placed him on a stretcher bed and began immediately to attend to him. Daniel hovered.

'Let us do what we can,' the medical officer said, without looking up. It was a kind way of asking him to leave.

Outside the tent, all energy drained from him and, no longer able to stand, he sank to his knees, shaking all over.

His journey to the sea was on hands and knees. He crawled into the wash and lay in the ebb and flow letting the gentle surf lap over him like the stroke of a mother's hand. His eyes were closing, his body shutting down. She came to him then, Maggie, telling him to wake up, wake up and find a safe place to sleep. With all his might, he heaved himself onto his elbows and then used them to drag himself backwards away from the sea. Halfway up the beach, he collapsed onto the sand and let the blackness come.

He woke to a raging sun, feeling at the same time hot and cold. His head pounded with pain. His mouth did not have enough space for his tongue. Michael! He sat up and squinted in the blare of the sun. Down at the shore, a lighter was being loaded with wounded. Daniel stumbled towards the field ambulance tent. Outside it, now, lay row upon row of wounded and dying, carried down during the night. Weary orderlies tried to attend to them.

Inside the tent, chaos reigned, with doctors desperately trying to spread their care.

Daniel found Michael alone, unconscious, barely clinging to life. He knew only one thing. There were too few medics here with too many demands for Michael to survive. Daniel had to get him onto that lighter. He eased his arms under his friend's back and legs and lifted him. If anyone noticed, they did not stop him.

At the shoreline, casualties were lined up, awaiting evacuation. A quick glance told Daniel that he'd need a stretcher to get Michael onto a boat. He lowered him onto the sand and hurried back to the tent. The first man waiting outside was unconscious. Daniel lifted him from his stretcher and carried him inside to Michael's bed. It would be better for him in the shade and he'd receive medical attention quicker.

Daniel raced the stretcher to the shore. He was lifting Michael onto it when sniper fire broke out, lifting sand in spouts. A stretcher-bearer fell. Two others helped him to the tent. The casualties were abandoned on the beach. The engine started up on the lighter. Daniel raced to it, arms waving.

'Just one more! Please! Take one more!'

The Private looked at Daniel and seemed to take pity on him. 'Hurry then.'

Daniel ran to Michael and began to drag his stretcher over the sand.

The soldier jumped from the lighter to help.

'How quickly can you get him to a hospital ship?' Daniel asked as they carried him aboard.

'I'm sorry, lad. They're all full. All we can do is seek out trawlers that are headed for Mudros.'

Daniel panicked. Mudros had hospitals but would Michael survive the journey without medical attention – if indeed they found a trawler? It was a gamble, just as leaving Michael here was a gamble. Daniel looked back at the hospital tent. And decided.

'Take him. Please.' He put his hand on Michael's chalk-white forehead. 'Godspeed, my friend.'

Daniel jumped ashore and the boat departed in haste.

He sat at the water's edge watching the lighter till he could see it no longer. Then he stripped naked and walked into the sea. He dived down. Underwater, he was free from sound and sight. He emptied his mind of the horrors, concentrated only on the sensation of water on his skin, the weightless stretch in his limbs as he swam. Up ahead, something zipped through the water, a bullet, he realised, zooming down into the depths. After it, came another, then another.

'Fuckers,' he said, as Michael would have.

Then he dived down further.

A medical officer, out for a hastily smoked cigarette, found him unconscious on the sand, diagnosed him with exhaustion and ordered a week of rest. In reality, he was granting Daniel a week of life.

And so, for one week, Daniel lived.

He swam, slept, washed, ate and, when he had the energy, shaved every hair on his head. He treated himself and his uniform for lice. And he drank and treasured every bit of water that came his way. After three days regaining his energy, he started to make himself useful. He constructed shelters for those waiting on the sand. He used all he knew of first aid to help them as they waited to be seen. He shared cigarettes and water. The wounded shared their stories, stories that Daniel did not want to hear. Major Harrison had been killed in action, leading the Pals forward. Daniel's heart swelled with sadness, remembering the note that the major had written for him, the note that he hadn't needed after all. He took it out now and read it.

Private Healy is acting on my orders. Harrison (Major).

One of the last things he had ever done was save their lives.

He longed for news of Walkey and MacDonald. But there was none. Instead, he heard with growing frustration that his beloved unit was out of ammunition and water, still valiantly continuing to hold the ridge, throwing anything they could get – rocks, unexploded grenades – at the enemy and refusing to retreat until they received the order. *Where was the fucking order? What good were they doing up there? Get them bloody down!*

He smoked cigarette after cigarette, praying for the Pals on the ridge and praying for Michael. Had they found a trawler? Would Michael reach Mudros on time? Would he have had a better chance here? Or had Daniel made the biggest mistake of his life?

part four

thirty-two

Maggie
November 1915

Maggie had retired to her room when there was a call to the front door. She wondered who could possibly be calling at this hour. She thought of Danny and her heart went cold. She hurried out onto the landing, wrapping her dressing gown about her. If it were a telegram she would die.

'Who are you and what business do you have here?' she heard Tom demand.

Relief flooded her; it wasn't a telegram.

She wondered if it could be Patrick. But why would he be calling to the house – and so late?

Halfway down the stairs, she – and her heart – stopped. Light spilling onto the porch revealed a military uniform.

'Danny!' She began to run.

Tom stood aside but did not leave.

The soldier removed his cap.

She stopped dead. 'Michael!' She did not mean to sound so disappointed. He was – after all – alive. She turned to Tom. 'It's fine. Go back to bed.'

But he stood glaring at the enemy.

'Tom! I said it was fine. This is my friend.'

He raised an eyebrow. 'Another friend in the British Army?'

'Go!' She began to shoo him.

And finally, with a grunt, he went.

She turned back to Michael. 'Don't mind him. Come in! It's so good to see you. Danny has been so worried. We all have.'

He stepped into the light.

Maggie tried not to stare. His face. It was different, unbalanced. Unnatural. It was a mask, she realised. It covered the left side of his face, beginning at his eye and extending down to cover his cheek and half of his mouth, disappearing under his chin. She wondered if what was behind it could be any more grotesque than the mask itself. She tried to ignore it.

'I'm sorry for the late hour.' He touched his face. 'I don't venture out by day.'

'Do you think I care about the hour? You're alive!'

Maggie's heart ached for him as she showed him into the drawing room. She gestured to a seat by the fire. He limped to it with the aid of a cane and sat slowly as though it pained him to do so. He settled with one leg outstretched, the other bent. Maggie sat opposite. She held steady as his eyes rested on her for the longest time. It was as if he was trying to match the face before him with one from the past.

'That photograph of you was the most looked at in the whole of Gallipoli. He lives for you, Maggie.'

Tears welled; it no longer felt that way to her. 'His letters have changed, Michael. *He* has changed.'

'War does that to a man.' His voice was filled with regret.

'But your being alive will change everything! He is desperate for news of you! I have been scanning the casualty lists, daily, for him.' In truth, it was David who was doing the scanning while Maggie paced the room, unable to read name after name with the words, 'killed in action,' 'missing in action,' or 'died of wounds' beside them.

Have you written to him?'

He shook his head.

'Then you must!'

'I've tried, Maggie. I've been home two weeks now and I still can't find the words to tell him I won't be returning to fight alongside him.'

'Those words would be music to his ears, I can assure you. He would not want you back there.'

He smiled his half-smile. The mask took care of that.

'What do you think of it?' he asked.

'Of what?' she pretended.

'You can't take your eyes off it, Maggie. No one can.'

She struggled. 'It's good.'

'Good?'

'You'd hardly notice it,' she lied.

'Will I remove it?' he dared.

She held his eyes. 'If you wish.'

His voice lost its bitterness. 'It's all right. You don't want to see it.'

'I do, Michael.' For his sake.

'You may believe so.'

'I know so.' Whatever horror there was, she must not react.

With a scarred hand, he unhooked the mask from behind an ear. There was a fist-sized hole in his cheek as though a great metal claw had torn it away. Maggie could see the inner workings of his mouth, his teeth as though bared.

'You hide your horror well, Maggie.' He began to hook the mask into position.

'Is it painful?' she asked as if the look of it did not matter.

'Only in the way people react. Michael Hegarty no longer exists. There's not one person who treats me as they did.'

'I will.'

'Then punch me.'

She laughed but could as easily have cried. She rose and went to him. She took his scarred hand in hers. 'You're home, Michael. You're safe. That's all that matters.'

'Nothing matters.' His voice was dead.

'Your friendship with Danny matters. Write to him.'

'Sometimes, I wish he'd left me there on the ridge.' He took a deep breath. 'Anyway, I didn't come here to moan. I came to make things right. I've had time to think – a lot of time. I wasn't the best person when I had my face. I didn't treat you well, Maggie.'

'If I recall, it was *I* who punched you.'

'I tried to turn Daniel against you. I told him that you were trouble.'

'Perhaps I am.' She smiled.

'The truth is,' he determined. 'I was envious of what he had with you.'

'Michael, none of that matters now.'

'Should he get out of that hell alive, you must love him. I mean really fucking love him – I'm sorry, my language – but you must – no matter how many bits he's in.'

'I will.'

'Promise me. It's all I live for now – for him to return and find happiness in you.'

She was trying so hard not to cry. Michael had left Dublin a boy, a happy, carefree boy. 'You can be happy in yourself, Michael.'

'How, when I'll be forever alone?'

'Nonsense.'

'Who will love me with this face, this non-face?' He tapped out a hollow sound from the mask.

'It's not a face that a woman falls for but the spirit of a man.'

'Are you saying that Daniel's face means nothing to you?'

'It is the most special face in the world to me. But should he return with a different one, I won't love him less. I would just be so happy, so *relieved,* to have him back in my arms. You'll get your spirit back, Michael, and there'll be someone for you.'

'Someone blind.' He smiled.

'That's it! Don't you see? You'll make someone laugh and that'll be the start of it.'

'You think?' he asked doubtfully.

'I *know.* Wait and see.'

He seemed to brighten.

Then, she had to know. 'How bad is it?'

He looked at her as though struggling with what to say.

'The truth,' she prompted.

He closed his eyes. A vein in his temple began to throb. Perspiration broke out on a face drained suddenly of colour. He began to tremble all over. It was as though Gallipoli had crept into the room and up onto his shoulders, whispering in his ear, 'remember me.'

'Michael?'

He was no longer present. She didn't know how to rescue him, comfort him, if that was indeed possible.

'Michael!' she said, more urgently.

He seemed to wake from it then. He fumbled for his cigarettes, lit one and inhaled deeply, hands shaking. He looked at her with urgency. 'Write to him. *Assure* him of your love. It's all that keeps him going.'

'It was you that kept him going. And you will again once he knows that you're alive. Write to him. He's in Salonika now, in Greece.' She looked at him hopefully. 'Perhaps it's better there?'

'Perhaps,' he said without conviction. He looked at her. 'There's another reason I came.' His eyes beseeched her suddenly. 'Leave Na Fianna, Maggie.'

Her breath caught. 'He *told* you?'

He smiled. 'There are no secrets in the trenches, Maggie.'

She struggled with what to say. 'I know that you don't believe in the plight of-'

'It has nothing to do with my beliefs and everything to do with my experiences. I rushed to take up arms for this country. I was not prepared. No one can be. For the destruction. You cannot imagine it. Destruction that I try not to think of – every day, every night. Fighting is not the answer – to anything.'

'You don't understand!'

'It is you who doesn't understand. You haven't *seen* what I've seen.'

And because he was desperate and haunted and broken, she lied. 'I'll consider what you've said.'

He smiled. 'If you think I believe that, you don't know me at all, Maggie Gilligan.'

'It's too important, Michael,' she explained.

'Then I can only hope that a day will never come to make you realise your error, as I have done.'

She went to her mother's bureau. With a heavy heart, she wrote out Daniel's address for him.

He placed it in his top pocket then patted it. He rose. 'Let's have a race. Whoever writes to him last is a rotten egg.'

'Then you're the rotten egg for I'll have started before you reach home.'

'Send him socks.'

'You're only trying to slow me down.'

He smiled. 'All right, *I'll* send socks. You send cigarettes.' He grew serious. 'Allow me to tell him the news about myself, though, will you Maggie?'

'I would never take it from you.'

Sitting at her writing desk, words failed her. How confidently she had spoken of a man's spirit but what if that was what the war took first, a man's spirit, then his heart and soul? She imagined Danny cold and lonely and she could not help the bleakness that crept into her heart. Would he ever return? Would this war ever end? She needed him home, safely in her arms. She needed him to kiss her and talk of the children that they would have. She needed to stop crying.

She reminded herself of Michael's words. She must keep Danny going and get him home. What could she write that would be powerful enough? She rose and went to the window.

She gazed up at the stars, millions of them, twinkling away as though all was well with the world. Did Danny see the same ones? She imagined herself floating up to the brightest, then leaping from it to the next one east, then swinging to the next until she crossed over the Great War to where he was.

She imagined herself drifting down to him, holding out her hand and returning with him, star by star.

But when she opened her eyes, he was as far away as ever. So she closed them again.

'Dear God, keep him safe, just for tonight.' Tomorrow, she would pray for tomorrow and the next day, the next. That was not too much to ask of a God in such high demand, to keep one person alive for one more day?

Maggie had plans for Michael. He would not remain hidden in darkness. She would drag him out into the sun and walk beside him. After school, the following day, she called to his home.

His mother was so visibly grateful that someone would visit her son that Maggie's heart ached for her. It made her more determined than ever.

'Michael and I are going for a stroll,' she said as though it had been prearranged.

'Excellent,' his mother said with surprised delight.

Michael opened his mouth to argue but Maggie raised her eyebrows. 'I thought you said you wanted to make things right between us. This is the only way, Michael Hegarty.'

His mother left the room smiling.

'All right,' he said. 'A quick one.'

It wasn't lost on Maggie how he lowered his cap over his face. She was an expert at it herself.

Out on the street, a passing woman stared at the mask, making no attempt at subtlety. Maggie linked Michael's arm and stared back at the woman who blushed and lowered her gaze.

'So you wrote to Danny?' Maggie confirmed.

'I did.' He looked relieved. 'I'm glad you made me.'

'I didn't make you do anything.'

'All right, you encouraged me. And now I want an *immediate* reply.'

She smiled. 'Ah, so now you know my life – a constant state of eagerness.'

They entered a park and strolled to a bench. Sitting down – uncomfortably – Michael lit a cigarette. He closed his eyes as he inhaled. His whole body seemed to relax. Then he turned to her.

'Where are my manners?' He held out the packet to her.

'No bad habits,' she smiled.

'I can think of one.'

'Don't even *mention* Na Fianna.'

He looked at her boldly. 'What would you do, shoot me?'

'I might.'

'I wish you would.'

'Stop.' She put a hand on his arm.

They gazed at two children chasing each other around the park. Their shrieks were the most joyful, carefree sound.

'What will you do now?' she asked. 'Do you need to return to school in order to be accepted into university?'

He inhaled deeply on a cigarette and blew out a great plume of smoke. 'How could learning possibly matter when nothing at all does?' He forced a smile. 'I'm sorry for being so morbid.'

She shook her head. 'I'm sorry for asking. It was insensitive.' She knew now that he could never return to his old life. 'Do you hate the British for what they've done to you?'

'You mean the Turks?'

'No, the British Army for putting you on the front-line.'

He seemed confused. 'They put everyone on the front-line.'

'But the Irish more than any other.'

He frowned. 'Who told you that?'

'A friend.'

'Who was not at Gallipoli. We were all in it together – English, Irish, Welsh and, on other beaches, Australians, New Zealanders, French, even the Gurkhas from India, all fighting the same enemy, all of us only trying to live one more day.'

She stared at him. Could it be true? He had no reason to lie.

'It's not, and never will be, as simple as you say,' he continued. 'War has taught me one thing only: all that matters is getting along with your fellow man, living in peace. There *is* no other way.'

226

'There will be peace. When we get our country back.'

He sighed deeply. 'What must I *do*?'

'There's nothing you can do.' She grabbed his hand and dragged him up from the bench. 'Now, where is this girl who needs someone to make her laugh?'

thirty-three

Daniel

In his dugout, Daniel wrapped Maggie's scarf about his neck and face, then up under his helmet. He blew on his fingers and rubbed them together for all the difference it made. He wondered if he stopped blinking would his eyeballs freeze? His eyelashes were frozen along with the rest of him. It was as if the cold had climbed inside him and lived amongst his organs. Behind him a throat cleared.

'A letter, Sarge.'

He turned. The Private was skin and bone, unshaven and reeking of too many things. He stood to attention before Daniel, a reminder of how he himself was. But there was a letter. That was something.

'Thank you, Private.'

Alone again, he squinted in the candlelight at the scrawl on the envelope. He brought it suddenly to his eyes as he was transported back in time, back to school and the copybook of the boy beside him. He tore it open. And there it was, at the bottom of the page, proof that he wasn't dreaming. Sudden relieved tears blurred his vision. He dashed them aside; there was too much to know.

My dear friend,

Forgive the silence. I could not find the words to tell you that I'll no longer fight alongside you. There, I've said it. It wasn't so hard, after all. I have lost vision in one eye and have only partial in the remaining one. So that's the end of the rugby too! We'll say no more on it. How are you, my dearest friend? Tell me of Salonika. Is it the hell that Gallipoli was? Could it be? I will not ask after our old Pals for I do not wish to hear who is no longer beside you. Still, I long to know who is! You make a decision on it and keep that head of yours low.

I got my discharge but in my mind I'm still in the trenches. I doubt I'll ever leave. Nothing here seems to matter. I would go back in the morning – despite everything.

I was mistaken about Maggie, Danny, as I was about possibly everything. You have a great girl there, though, of course, you already know that. She will have you back, whatever shape you're in, however disfigured your face. I'm ruined, as it happens. No one will have me now. I must get used to that.

Come home to us, you old bastard, preferably in one piece, though I know that Maggie will have you no matter how many pieces you are in. She has told me so. How she loves you, Dan.

Your dearest friend in the world, Michael

Daniel kept the bottle of ink in his pocket to prevent it from freezing. In his hurry to open it, it fell. He scrambled to retrieve it, praying that it had not broken. He opened it in relief, dipped his pen in and was off, scratching as best he could with frozen, shaking fingers and the words blurring from tears he had been holding in too long.

Dearest Michael,

I am the happiest man alive to receive your letter and <u>delighted</u> that you will never again see war. You say that you do not know what to do with yourself. Here is what to do – look after Maggie for me, Mick – now and should I fail to return.

You saved our lives by getting wounded that night. Had we stayed up on that ridge, we would have been annihilated for certain. It was a bloodbath. You will be saddened to hear that we lost poor old MacDonald, killed in action the day after you were wounded. I'm not ashamed to say that I cried when I learned of his death. Gone too is Major Harrison, who gave me permission to run you down out of there. I will never forget his kindness. You ought to have seen Wilkin, Mick, what a stunt he pulled, grabbing cricket balls and throwing them back – until he exploded to kingdom come, God Bless his beautiful soul. I don't suppose you have news of Walkey? He came down with dysentery and was taken off.

You ask of Salonika. Well, someone up there is having a good laugh at our expense, I'll say that much. In Gallipoli, we baked to death. Here, we freeze. Men have died from exposure, no lie. Frostbite is our newest enemy. When we arrived, it was malaria – a different location, a different fly, equally eager to finish us off. Should I make it home, there will be diseases lining up for me to cure. I often consider that a better use of time for the human race would be finding cures rather than ways to kill. We are over here, helping Serbians fight Bulgarians, though it would appear we are too late for that. Who are these peoples anyway and why are they fighting and what has it got to do with us? What is this war about anyway? Has anyone stopped to ask?

Our dear Pals. We have been broken up. Leaving Gallipoli, they asked those of us that were left (79 out of the 239 we started out with) to become officers, as they were urgently needed. It was a wrench to disband but it was our duty and that was that. I am a sergeant now. It suits me fine since I find it hard to bond with all these rookies forever arriving only to be mowed down. I remind myself of that old sweat at the Curragh who warned us of war. Like him, I am happier in my own company. And yet, sadly, I find myself developing a fondness for my men, despite it all, each with his own habits, quirks, ways.

I am weary. Your letter, though, is the greatest boost. Thank you for the fags. They won't last long! I'm dreaming of leave like we dreamt of water in Gallipoli. I'm glad that you're out of it. Don't say a word to Maggie about what it's like out here. It wouldn't be fair on her. You know yourself. I made the mistake of sending her a letter or two when I was not in good spirits – losing MacDonald comes to mind. I did not whine or anything like it but my mood could not have been good. I ought to have waited. But she is keen for news. She worries.

I must stop talking of Maggie – I'll drive you insane.

Look at that! I have not written a letter this length in a very long time. It is good to have someone to write to who understands.

Take care of yourself, Michael,

Your old Pal, Danny

thirty-four

Maggie

Patrick, in full uniform, stood to attention before Maggie in the empty Na Fianna hall. He had called her here in advance of the usual meeting, without explanation.

'Remove your hat,' he ordered.

She hesitated. They were friends. He never pulled rank on her. But there was something in his tone that made her obey. Something ominous.

'You are being formally dismissed from Na Fianna Éireann.'

She stared at him. 'I don't understand.'

He looked at her with obvious disdain. 'Maggie, I'm told your name is,' he said as if they were strangers, as if they'd never shared all those conversations, never laughed together and almost, at times, cried.

'*Who* told you?'

'A letter arrived detailing your deception.'

'Deception?'

'What else would you call it?' His eyes were so cold.

'Who wrote the letter?' That was where the deception lay.

'It was anonymous. Your dismissal takes effect immediately.' He put out his hand.

Stunned, she reached out to shake it.

But he had not offered his hand. He simply wanted her hat.

She passed it to him as though it were her life.

'Now, leave.'

She swallowed and then turned in silence.

Her footsteps echoed through the empty hall. Her eyes soaked in every last inch of it. Who had done this to her? Who would? Reaching the door, fists clenched, she turned.

'Where was the letter posted?'

His expression changed then, softened, for he knew what she was asking. He opened his jacket and removed a folded envelope from his inside pocket. He looked at it, then at Maggie.

'Dublin.'

No one knew that she was in Na Fianna outside of her family, Danny and – now – Michael. She remembered his words: 'What must I *do*?'

Clearly, he had figured it out.

She marched to his home and hammered on the door.

Then, suddenly, she was facing a member of the Dublin Metropolitan Police. In her fury, she had forgotten about Michael's father. Now they faced each other, the policeman and the rebel. She could see him take in the detail, her uniform, her face. Then Michael's mother appeared behind him. Her face lit up and she clasped her hands together in delight.

'Maggie! Maggie! Come in. Come in.' She shooed her husband out of the way.

'I'm not staying, Missus Hegarty. I simply need to talk to Michael for a moment.'

'Of course. Let me fetch him.'

Maggie heard the cane before she saw him. It would *not* influence her.

Their eyes met. She read in his an admission.

He reached for his coat. 'Let us take a walk.'

She turned on her heels, storming to the gate, where she waited.

'*Why?*' she demanded when he reached her.

'Let's get a bit further from the house before you finish me off.'

She marched to the end of the street where she waited for him, folding her arms, turning one way, then the other.

At last he reached her.

'Do you have *any idea* what Na Fianna means to me? *Any* idea?' She didn't let him answer. 'Let me ask you this. What would you have done had someone informed the army you were underage?'

'I'd have loved them for it, Maggie. Not immediately. But now.' He said it earnestly. 'You haven't seen a man shot in the head. You haven't had a friend's brains blown into your mouth. You haven't heard a dying man call for his mother.'

'I have seen men die *and* women, innocent, unarmed civilians shot dead right in front of my eyes by the British Army. Do you imagine that I'm doing this for fun, for *amusement*? I'm doing this because I could not live with myself if I did not. You had no right to betray me like this. No right. You cannot decide other people's lives! You are *not* God!'

'No. But I've seen hell. And I won't have you in it. I promised Danny to keep you safe and I will do whatever it takes.'

She stopped breathing. 'Did *Daniel* put you up to this?' she asked slowly.

He calmly raised his eyebrows. 'Do you, honestly, believe that of him?'

She looked down in shame. Danny would never betray her, just as she would never have betrayed him when he was signing up. 'I don't know what to believe,' she said quietly. 'I'm unused to being deceived.' She looked up at Michael. 'You've taken something very precious from me. You must know that.'

'And I would apologise but I'm not sorry and if it means that we can never be friends then so be it. I don't regret it, nor will I, as long as you're safe.'

Her eyes fell on his weary, broken, half-face and she couldn't hate him. Neither could she forgive him.

'Then good luck.' She turned and walked away.

It was midnight when Tom finally crept in the back door. Maggie was sitting in darkness waiting for him. She stood up.

'Jesus, Mary and Joseph!' he said. 'You frightened the life out of me.'

She laughed at the sight of the hardened rebel gripping his heart.

'What are you doing up at this hour?' he asked, lighting a lamp and regaining his dignity.

'I've been dismissed from Na Fianna.' Maggie explained why.

'That little bollocks,' he said of Michael.

'What will I *do*, Tom? Would the Volunteers have me?'

He raised an eyebrow. 'You might have fooled Na Fianna, Maggie, but these are men.'

'Where would *you* go if you were me?'

He ran a hand over a grizzly chin.

She drummed her fingers on her trousers.

Then he looked at her from head to toe.

'What?' she asked.

He squinted. 'What age are you, again?'

'Jesus, Tom! Don't you know the age of your own sister?'

'Less of the language, Maggie.'

'Feck off.'

He laughed.

'I'm seventeen. A little subtraction would have got you there.'

'God, you're awful skinny for seventeen.'

'I can eat.' After all the starvation, she'd be glad to.

'All right, I have an idea.'

She sat up.

'The Citizen Army takes women. Women, mind, not girls.'

She could be a woman. She could use balled up stockings in crucial areas. And eat ferociously. Why wait? She reached for a banana.

'What do you know of The Irish Citizen Army, Maggie?' he asked, folding his arms.

'I know they're *rebels*.' That was it, though.

'The Citizen Army was set up to protect the striking workers during the Lockout.'

'That's who they are!' Maggie remembered Madame's friends at Liberty Hall who had spoken of protecting the workers. A bolt of excitement shot through her. This was where it had all started for her. Suddenly, the Citizen Army felt like her destiny.

'Handy for you is that they're all for equality – not just between rich and poor but between men and women.'

She nodded enthusiastically.

'It has grown into perhaps the most radical of the rebel organisations,' Tom continued.

'Then why are you not in it?'

'Ah, my friends from Na Fianna were joining the Volunteers.'

'Would it be hard for me to get in?'

He scratched his chin. 'Well, your friend, the countess, is high up in it.'

Maggie went pale. 'Madame! She's bloody everywhere!'

He laughed.

'It's not funny. She'd never let me in! Haven't I just been kicked out of Na Fianna for deception?'

'And would you let a little thing like that stop you, Maggie *Gilligan*?'

She smiled. In some ways, they were so alike.

The following day, Maggie stood outside the door of Surrey House, wearing a dress, a wig and crucially positioned stockings. She took a deep breath and knocked.

The countess herself swung the door open. For a moment, she looked at Maggie blankly. Then she squinted. 'Is that *Maggie Gilligan*?'

'It is, Madame.'

'My goodness, you have grown. You are a woman, Maggie.' She shook her head in disbelief. She opened the door wide. 'Come in.'

Despite the warm reception, Maggie remained wary as she stepped inside.

Madame showed her into the drawing room. 'How *long* is it since we have seen one another?'

'A week, Madame.'

The countess squinted at her. 'Maggie, I would have remembered.'

'So you do not *know* of Ruairí?'

'Ruairí?'

'From Na Fianna.'

'What of him?' she asked, concerned.

'*I* was Ruairí.'

'I beg your pardon?'

'I was playing a part, as you do on stage. I wanted to be in Na Fianna. I had to become a boy. There was no other way.'

Madame stared at her. 'Are you telling me that you and Ruairí are one and the same?'

'I am.'

She tipped her head back and laughed. 'I must be losing my eyesight!'

'No one else guessed,' Maggie reassured. 'But someone informed on me and I've been dismissed.'

'When did this happen?'

'Yesterday.'

'That is why I have not heard. I've been busy with the Citizen Army.'

'The Citizen Army is the reason for my visit.'

The countess frowned. 'Sit down, Maggie.'

While Maggie took a seat by the fire, Madame bent over a printing press. 'This infernal contraption,' she said, slapping it with a blackened hand.

'I wish to join, Madame.'

The countess looked up from the printer. 'Last week, you were a child. A boy-child.'

'I'm almost eighteen.' It was an exaggeration.

She shook her head in disbelief. 'Little Ruairí...'

'Little Ruairí was the best shot in Na Fianna. I'm sure you wouldn't wish to lose him entirely from the cause.'

Madame put her grubby hands on her hips and considered Maggie. 'Why the Citizen Army? There is an organisation called Cumann na mBan for women. They support the Volunteers.'

How well Tom had known not to suggest it. 'I don't want to *support* men. I wish to *fight alongside* them for a better Ireland, an equal Ireland. The Citizen Army is all for equality – between rich and poor, men and women. I was there when the very idea of it came about.' Maggie relayed the conversation she had overheard outside Liberty Hall.

'You, my friend, are full of surprises. All right. Let me have a word with James Connolly, the leader of the Citizen Army.' She slapped her hand down hard on the printing press as though it was a horse's hindquarters. It juddered into life. They looked at one another. Madame laughed.

'Maggie Gilligan, you are my lucky charm.'

Maggie prayed that James Connolly would feel the same.

thirty-five

Daniel

Daniel had hoped that he might get leave for Christmas but here he was. He closed his eyes. He pictured a windowsill with red and yellow candles. He pictured his mother carrying in the cake with snowy icing and Niall fashioning decorations from rings of paper. He brought to his tiny, freezing dugout the smell of roasting turkey, the taste of sugared fruit. He brought bright red berries of holly. He brought the white of mistletoe and a girl standing under it, smiling. He brought Maggie. With Adeste Fidelis, he drowned out the sounds of war.

He wished to send gifts to everyone. But he had nothing to send. The greatest gift, he knew, would be his survival. It struck him, then, in a sudden moment of clarity, that what he dreaded most about dying was the pain that it would cause those he loved. He was filled with a sudden urgency. He must write to them so that, should the worst happen, they would have, at least, a proper goodbye. The difficulty was: how to explain a letter that would arrive after his death. He must try.

Dear Niall

I'm writing this letter and putting it in a safe place so that, should my luck run out, someone will send it to you. I'm writing to say goodbye and to tell you that I have always loved you, from the very moment you came into my life, with your little baldy head and big blue eyes. I have always been proud to call you my brother. You are one of the strongest, kindest, smartest people I know. I want you to have my room and all my things. Keep the rugby ball for Michael. Though he's not playing, he might like it. I have a friend called Maggie who I hope you will meet. She has been a very special person in my life and I would like you to know each other. Mind mother for me. It's a lot to ask, I know, but you are the one man who can do it.

Until we meet in heaven, your loving brother, Daniel

Sealing the envelope, Daniel felt a great relief. He picked up his pen and gathered his thoughts. He would tell Maggie the truth, explain why he had signed up, so that there would remain no secret between them. And yet he could not do it. If he were to admit that he had gone to war to stop her rising for Ireland, guilt would be his legacy to her.

My dearest Maggie,

If you receive this, I will have failed to keep my promise. I'm sorry. You have been the very best thing in my life. How I would have enjoyed our future together. The Healys! I know I have no right to ask, but please, Maggie, put down your arms. If it comes to a fight, be somewhere else on that day. You can't ignore the last wishes of a man. I'm sorry that my final letter is one of requests but please be the friend to Michael that I can no longer be, call to see Niall (I know that you would love one another), be happy, be safe and, when you can, remember me.

All my love, Danny

He did not feel relief now, only a great ache at the thought of leaving her. He didn't want her to ever have to read this letter. He wanted to live. But the choice would not be his. He must face that. And continue his goodbyes.

Dearest Mother

Dying men call for their mothers at the time of death. That is how

important you are to us. Thank you for all that you have done for me.
Forgive me.
   Daniel

Michael, me old segotia!
   If you read this, I've gone and done it. Watch over Maggie for me.
Niall will be in need of a brother. He comes highly recommended. Thank
you for being the best friend a chap could have had. We'll meet again, in
heaven, I hope.
   Daniel

Daniel looked at the blank sheet. He felt that no matter what
he wrote to his father it would not be enough.

Dear Father
   We have had our differences. For that I am sorry. I would like to
have made you proud. Forgive me.
   Daniel

Outside, he heard the alarm sound. As always, even still, it
put the heart across him. He grabbed his rifle and ran.

thirty-six

Maggie

Facing the mirror, Maggie settled her skirt, jacket and wig. She straightened her Sam Browne belt and nodded. She was ready.

In the hallway, her mother was arranging flowers. She heard Maggie on the stairs and turned. She stopped humming.

'You said that you'd finished with Na Fianna!'

'I'm joining the Citizen Army, Mam.'

Her arms fell to her side, an ostrich plume still in one. 'Without consulting me?'

'It happened so fast…'

'Too fast to notice the word "army" in the title?'

Maggie pressed her lips together.

'You promised me that you would not use a weapon.'

'And I believed at the time that I wouldn't. But nothing will change without a fight, Mam!'

'It needn't be your fight!'

'I can't sit back and leave it to others! I simply can't!'

'You must! I cannot lose you, Maggie. I lost your father. That is more than enough for me to bear. Please. I'm begging you.' She was tearing at Maggie's heart. 'Can a woman not be a little selfish? Can I not keep you to myself?'

'There's too much to put right! I cannot turn the other cheek! It's not who I am.'

Her mother took a deep breath. 'Then the time has come for me to speak out. I wish I didn't have to. But here it is. You must ignore what Father asked of you. He did not understand the full extent-'

'No! You weren't there, Mam! You didn't see his face! You didn't hear his voice! Those were his last words to me. That was his last wish. He *knew* what he was asking. And he was *right* to ask it. What point was there in me surviving if not to make a difference in the world?'

'Your heart is too big. He forgot that.'

'My heart is there to beat, to feel, to guide me to do the right thing. I'm not afraid to do it, Mam. Don't be afraid for me.'

'I *am* afraid, Maggie. This country will take my children!'

'This *country* is already taking children through hunger, poverty, injustice-'

'And should I forbid you?'

'I would join anyway. I would *hate* to go against your wishes but I *would* do it. I'm sorry, Mam. But this is bigger than the both of us. It simply is.'

Her mother covered her mouth, turned and hurried away into the kitchen.

Sick with guilt, Maggie left for Liberty Hall. She told herself that she was not disobeying her mother for she had never actually forbidden Maggie from joining. The truth remained. Maggie was going against her wishes and causing her upset.

Arriving outside Liberty Hall, memories flooded her – the sights, sounds and smells of poverty, hunger and desperation. How clueless she had been then, believing herself to be making a difference.

Now she glanced at a blackboard propped up outside the building. She frowned and reread the words of chalk. Could it be true? Could the Citizen Army be surrounding Dublin Castle that very night? Could they honestly be attacking the seat of British rule in Ireland and, if so, was it *wise* to announce it for all to see?

Maggie hurried inside. She was immediately stopped and questioned, then directed to a long, dimly lit hall. Her heart began to race; there was no mistaking the preparation for revolution. Stacked against the walls were rifles, bandoliers and haversacks. Men and women sat in groups cleaning, polishing and repairing guns, sharpening bayonets and fashioning handmade grenades. Maggie was given a Mauser to clean. She dared not ask if she would be using it that very night. Instead, she sat at a table and got to work, deep in thought. If they were to rise tonight would it be with or without the other rebel forces? She tried to remember how Tom had been that day. The last time she saw him was at breakfast and he had seemed fine or at least as fine as Tom ever seemed. The door to the hall banged shut. Madame entered with a small, stocky, moustached man Maggie recognised from the days of the food kitchen. It was the person who had spoken with James Larkin about setting up an army of citizens to protect the strikers. It was James Connolly! A thrill of admiration ran through Maggie.

Deep in conversation, he and Madame were passing Maggie's table when the countess spotted her and stopped.

'Maggie! You're here! How wonderful!'

Maggie stood to attention.

'James, this is Maggie Gilligan, the girl I was telling you about – who was in Na Fianna.'

Maggie did not want him to think her underhand. 'I only ever wished to fight.'

He smiled and, in a warm Scottish accent said, 'Then you've come to the right place. No movement can be assured of success that has not women in it.'

Maggie liked him immediately.

'Sit for a moment, Maggie. There's something I must ask.'

All three of them sat.

'The question I'm about to put to you should not be considered an oath or in any way binding,' he said.

Maggie nodded eagerly.

He held her eyes. 'Do you promise on your word of honour that, should the Irish Citizen Army be required to fight alone in the coming revolution, you will take your place in the ranks?'

Her heart pounded with excitement. *This* was the right organisation for her. She ought to thank Michael for what he had done. 'I promise.'

'So you'll join us on our route march tonight?'

She could not help herself. 'Will we, truthfully, be surrounding Dublin Castle?'

James Connolly smiled. 'Ah, you saw our little blackboard? That's only to confuse the G-men, the Castle's secret police. Shout wolf enough times and they'll stop listening.'

She nodded at the wisdom of that.

'What's that you're cleaning?' He nodded to the weapon.

'A Mauser.'

'You do not think much of it?'

Surprised that he'd gathered that when she had been deliberately avoiding even a hint of it, she said, 'It's grand.' Then her curiosity got the better of her. 'Do we have any Lee Enfields?'

He laughed. 'You know your guns.'

'Maggie was one of the finest shots in Na Fianna,' Madame said.

'Well,' he smiled. 'Their loss is surely our gain. Welcome to the Irish Citizen Army, Maggie Gilligan.' His smile reminded her of her father.

Marching the lamp-lit, largely deserted streets alongside adults, Maggie felt as if she had, at last, shaken off the child's world that had been holding her captive. Being amongst men and women from mostly working class backgrounds reminded her of the Ireland they were fighting for – where everyone was equal. It was as though they were marching together towards a better future.

At Dublin Castle, Maggie held her breath. She felt that she could hear every individual footfall. She expected, at any moment, for a shot to ring out and a rebel to fall. But nothing moved –

except the Citizen Army. James Connolly truly had cried wolf.

They returned to Liberty Hall too soon for Maggie. Her veins pulsed with energy. She wished to march till dawn. And yet it was time to disperse.

There would be no tram for Maggie tonight. She would walk home and think about all that her new leader had said.

She strode over O'Connell Bridge, swinging her arms. All was quiet until she turned onto D'Olier Street. Up ahead, a group of Na Fianna boys poured out onto the street after a meeting. She slowed, a great loneliness growing in her chest. They had been her brothers. Did they all think her deceitful now? She caught her breath and stopped automatically as Patrick emerged directly in front of her, head down, deep in thought. She recognised, in the back of his dipped head, the loss of his father; he carried it still. Here was the one person she had shared a war with. Despite everything, she called out to him.

Turning, he seemed confused.

'It's Maggie.'

Coldness replaced confusion. 'What are *you* doing here?'

'Returning from a route march with the Irish Citizen Army. *They* take women.'

'Did you *lie* to get in there too?'

'I dressed as a boy, Patrick. It was the only way I could join. There's no need to make it personal to you.'

'I thought we were friends.'

'We were.'

'Friends don't lie.'

She stared at perhaps the toughest boy she knew. 'What would you have done had I told you the truth? What would it have been your duty to do?'

He considered that. At last he admitted, 'I'd have reported you.'

'And I thought we were friends.'

He smiled grudgingly. 'Why couldn't you simply have been a boy?'

'I've asked myself the same question many times.' And each time she had reminded herself of the best reason to be a girl: Daniel Healy. 'How are things?'

He shrugged moodily. 'You're missed.'

'Oh? By whom?'

He grew flustered. 'You were our best shot.'

'We *can* stay friends, Patrick. It *is* possible. Despite me being a *girl*.' She widened her eyes at the horror of it.

He made a face. 'Look at you. You have *hair*. You're *old*.'

She lifted the wig. A man walking his dog, stared in disbelief, and then tripped.

'I haven't changed, Patrick. I can still throw a punch and knock a can off a wall with a groany old Mauser.'

'That sounds more like you.' He shoved his hands into his pockets and looked down. 'So. What's the Citizen Army like?'

She brightened. 'They mean business, Patrick! You should join! You'll be too old for Na Fianna soon. And you don't want to be a Volunteer.'

'I don't?'

'The Citizen Army are ready to rise. They'd go out alone if they had to. I'm sure of it.'

His eyes narrowed. 'Was something said?'

She grew alert to him. She should have been more careful. 'It's only what I feel.'

'There *is* a concern that Connolly will go off half-cocked without the rest of us.' He sounded like someone high up, connected.

'The rest of who?'

'The other rebel groups. We must all rise together – *with* the Citizen Army. Only then will we have a hope.'

Maggie grew ever more cautious. 'I'm only new. Don't listen to me.' She began to rub arms that had grown increasingly cold the longer she'd stood still. 'I should go.'

'How are you getting home?'

'I had planned on walking but I might take the tram. It's getting cold.'

'I suppose you'll need seeing onto it so – now that you're a girl.'

'I need no such thing.'

He laughed. ''Tis on my way.'

They began to walk in silence.

Then he turned to her. 'I still can't believe you killed off Ruairí.'

'*You* killed off Ruairí.'

'What choice had I?'

'Silence?'

He looked surprised as if that option had never crossed his mind. 'Duty is duty,' he said at last.

A cab passed, horses' hooves clicking on cobblestone.

Patrick turned to her abruptly. 'Is Daniel even your *brother*?'

She had kept enough from him. 'We're engaged to be married, Patrick.'

He stopped, staring at her in disbelief. 'Since when?'

'Since before he left for Gallipoli.'

When he recovered it was to say, 'You two always were as thick as thieves.'

She remembered with sadness. 'We were, weren't we?' She reminded herself that Daniel's letters had brightened since he'd heard that Michael was alive. That was something to be happy about, at least.

Patrick's eyes softened. 'He'll be all right.'

She sighed and began to walk again.

'I imagine he's the best sniper they've got.'

She turned to him. 'For all the difference it'll make. You said yourself that the Irish are cannon fodder.'

'Sure don't be listening to me. I only get angry sometimes.'

'Are you saying they're *not* cannon fodder?'

'No more than anyone else.'

'Then why did you *say* it?'

'I was angry.'

'The worry you put on me.'

'I'm sorry.' He halted once more and then spoke to his shoes in a mumble. 'I needed my father's death to be the fault of the British Army. Otherwise, it would have been mine. I should have stopped him from joining. If I'd stopped him, he'd be alive.'

'He was your father. How could you have stopped him?'

'I could have tried.'

'Could *he* have stopped *you* from joining Na Fianna?'

He looked at her in surprise. 'I never thought of it like that.'

'Isn't it just as well you bumped into me so?'

He looked at her for a long time. 'Maybe it's not entirely bad that you're a girl.'

'Is that right?' She raised an eyebrow.

'No one ever suspects girls,' he rushed. 'And skirts are great places for hiding things.'

'Patrick Shanahan, you truly know how to flatter a girl.'

They laughed.

'So do you forgive me?' she asked.

He hesitated.

'It was never about you, Patrick. It was always about Ireland.'

He nodded.

'I want the same as you do,' she continued.

'I see that now,' he said with what sounded like regret.

They arrived at the terminus just as a tram was arriving.

'Well, good night, Patrick,' she said cheerfully.

'Good night.' He shook his head in disbelief. '*Maggie*.'

'You'll get used to it.'

He smiled then. 'I suspect I will.'

She boarded, found a seat and looked out.

He was still standing there, waiting for the tram to pull away.

Surprised, she waved.

He saluted.

And she was so glad not to have lost this gruff old friend.

Days later, Maggie attended a lecture on street fighting given by James Connolly. She loved how everyone shushed when he stood before them. She loved his voice. Most especially she loved his directness. There was no sugarcoating with James Connolly, no dreamy talk of a poet.

'When we rise for Ireland we will be outnumbered two thousand to one.' He paused to let that sink in. 'Our biggest weapon will be our wits. And we will use them.'

We had better, Maggie thought, reeling from the figures.

'The key will be to catch them unawares.' He looked around the room. 'And how do you think we will do that?'

'Street fighting,' someone volunteered.

'Aye, exactly. The British military receive no training in street fighting. Spring it on them and the result will be mass confusion. Now, what is the key to street fighting, comrades?'

'The element of surprise,' someone said.

'Aye, and?'

Silence as people thought.

'Cover,' James Connolly said. 'We will be hidden in the buildings. They will be out in the open. We will let them get close, very close, then we will let them have it.' He smiled. 'Anything else?'

'Ambush.'

As just described, Maggie thought. Some people simply wished to sound clever.

'Aim for the officers,' Connolly said. 'Properly covered, one rebel can upset an entire battalion by targeting those giving the orders. And, yes, we will ambush them right, left and centre.' He paused. 'And if *we're* surrounded?'

Another silence.

'We tunnel through walls,' Connolly said, 'the walls between houses. We move from house to house without ever going outside until we're away – away to fight again.'

Maggie wanted to cheer. He had thought of everything.

'And why will the people let us through their homes, breaking down their walls? The best reason in the world, comrades: to restore justice to this fine country. That is why.'

James Connolly did not look like Maggie's father. He did not rage like her father. And yet he reminded her very much of her father. It was his unshaken sense of justice, his desire for a better life for all and his willingness to sacrifice everything for it. He *would* make a difference.

thirty-seven

January 1st 1916
Daniel

Daniel opened his eyes. He was laying on his back, above him, his friends the stars. All was calm. A face looked down on him. He smiled at the padre, a great man for arriving with a fag or a swig of rum or a comforting word when you were at your lowest, a great man to have around, in general, with his soft, sad face and kind eyes. He was mumbling but Daniel could not make out the words over the ringing in his ears. It had the intonation of a prayer, a prayer that Daniel had heard many times. And then he had it. The padre was offering the Last Rights – to him!

'Is that how it is?' he asked. He felt no pain.

'You'll be grand. The prayer is only insurance.' But there was pity in his eyes and Daniel knew that he was done for.

He gazed beyond the priest. 'Look at those stars.'

The padre glanced briefly up, returning his eyes swiftly to Daniel's as if fearful he might slip away, alone.

'Was it a shell?' Daniel asked. A man should know what finished him off.

'It was a bombardment of them.'

He nodded and now pain shot every which way. 'I knew they'd get me in the end.' He smiled.

'You're not done for yet, Sergeant.'

The rank surprised him, still. 'My men?'

The priest lowered his gaze.

'*All* of them?'

He nodded slowly. 'I'm afraid so.'

Daniel dropped his head back.

'Here come the stretcher-bearers, now,' the padre said, looking up along the trench and raising an arm. 'Over here! Quick, boys.'

Daniel struggled to retrieve the photograph of Maggie from his pocket. Her face was the last thing he saw.

thirty-eight

Maggie

Maggie woke with a start. The room was in darkness. In the bed beside hers, Lily breathed softly. Maggie told herself that it was her imagination. Daniel was fine. But she knew otherwise. She felt it in every part of her being; he needed her.

And she couldn't help.

She paced the room, her arms wrapped about herself. She needed to be there, to hold him and tell him over and over that she loved him. She needed him to *feel* it. And so she sent the words to him, willing them through the night air so that he would hold on: for her.

The sun rose, unconcerned.

Maggie returned to bed not to sleep but to be with him in her mind – and to pray – all day – for one more day.

'You *do* feel feverish,' her mother said, resting the back of her hand against Maggie's forehead. 'And you do look pale. All right, stay in bed, pet.'

'I'm sick too, Mammy,' Lily said.

'What a coincidence.'

She closed her eyes dramatically. 'I'm *dying*, Mammy.'

She smiled. 'You've a very healthy colour for someone's who's dying.'

Lily groaned.

'All right,' she said. 'All right. I give up. You'll be the death of me, the lot of you.' But she said it affectionately, as if she was happy for them to have a break from the seriousness of life.

Lily waited until she was gone and then jumped from the bed. 'I'll mind you, Maggie.'

Maggie never uttered a word of her fears yet Lily seemed to understand. She fixed her hair and pulled the blankets up to her chin. Then she sat on the side of the bed and told Maggie a story – about a bird that flew beyond the stars.

The dreaded telegram did not come. Maggie dared to hope. Perhaps her prayers had worked. Perhaps her love was seeing him through.

Every day, she continued to send it.

After a visit from the doctor, her mother shooed her back to school, which seemed the most pointless place in the world.

Then it occurred to Maggie: Michael may have heard from him!

She called to his house only to discover that he was at school.

'School?' she asked in surprise.

His mother lowered her eyes. 'He did it for me, Maggie.' She looked up again, almost pleadingly. 'I only want him to have a normal life, to finish his education.'

Maggie smiled for her, knowing the sacrifice this would mean for Michael, facing hundreds of boys looking as he did. 'I'll find him, there. Thank you.'

She waited outside the school gates, ignoring the curious and often admiring looks of the uniformed boys that poured out. Though many were her age or older they seemed so young to her as they shoved each other about and acted the maggot.

At last, she saw him emerge alone, all around him a great gap of air. Behind him three boys were goading him. She understood only too well how he felt. She wanted to knock their heads together. And then, the leader was down. Michael had turned suddenly and flattened him with a punch. She smiled as his thuggish friends hurried to his aid.

Then Michael saw Maggie. He grimaced.

She smiled.

At last he reached her. 'It seems I may have picked up some of your bad habits.'

'You haven't joined a rebel organisation, have you?'

'Eh, no.' He looked at her sheepishly.

'Then you're probably safe enough.'

He smiled then.

'Can we walk for a bit?'

'As long as you don't mind keeping company with...' he widened his eyes, '...a Freak Of Nature.'

'I have a particular affection for freaks of nature.'

As they strolled away from the school, boys stared as if they could not believe that a girl like Maggie had time for Michael. So she ripped off her wig and glared at them. Unfortunately, her hair had begun to grow so the effect was not as dramatic as she'd hoped. Still, at least Michael laughed.

'I forgive you, by the way,' she said.

'That *is* welcome news.'

'You meant well, I suppose.'

'I did. Fighting's a messy business.'

'I've joined the Irish Citizen Army.'

'Ah, Maggie.'

'Don't you "Ah Maggie" me. You're lucky I didn't kill you, Michael Hegarty.'

He sighed wearily. 'Couldn't you be passionate about tapestry or flower arranging or something? Why does it have to be this country of ours?'

She stared at him. 'Tapestry or flowers before a *country*? Are you *insane*?'

He smiled then. 'I may have to imprison you, lock you up in a tower or something.'

'You could try.' She was smiling, too, now.

'I always said that you were trouble.'

'Being trouble is exactly what I wish to be.'

He looked at her wistfully. 'Will we be forever at each other's throats, do you think?'

She regarded him with a fondness she did not understand. 'I suppose we could *try* not to kill each other.'

'Only I'm running low on friends. I'm all aloooone. Nobody loooves me,' he said in a tiny voice.

'Aaaall right,' she said, trying not to smile. 'As long as you *know* that I'm driven by pity alone.'

He laughed.

And then she remembered why she was there. She turned to him. 'Michael, I'm worried about Danny. I haven't heard from him in three weeks. Have you heard anything?'

He looked at her in concern. 'No. Nothing. I thought you might have.'

'It's never been this long.'

He frowned. 'Well, he hasn't appeared in the casualty lists. Every day, I check for friends.'

She knew how hard that must be. 'Me too – or at least David, my brother, does.'

'Perhaps it's easily explained: a letter going astray, his regiment moving...'

'Thank God his name hasn't appeared.'

Michael nodded.

A silence fell between them, each lost in thought.

'Did he ever tell you?' he asked, suddenly. 'Your scarf was carried into battle as an Irish flag!'

'It was *not!*'

'It absolutely was.'

The thought of Irish patriotism in the British Army warmed Maggie's heart. She stopped walking and looked at him with such hope. 'He'll come back to us, Michael, won't he?'

'Perhaps if we will it hard enough. Two is better than one, as Danny used to say.'

She touched her heart. 'He *said* that?'

'All the time.'

Her eyes welled with tears. Then she linked her arm with his and leaned into him. 'Together we'll get him home.'

Days later, Maggie arrived at Liberty Hall to pandemonium.

'He went to lunch and never returned,' a young woman said of James Connolly. 'Madame is going out of her mind with worry. We all are.'

The countess was pacing the room, holding her head. When she saw Maggie, she stopped.

'Maggie Gilligan, come with me! We are going in search of him!'

Maggie nodded. She would rather do something practical than wait around worrying.

Reaching the motorcar, Madame turned to her. 'You're my lucky charm, Maggie. Don't let me down now.'

Maggie opened her mouth to speak but there was nothing at all she could say to that.

They drove all over Dublin to homes and places of business unfamiliar to Maggie. Everywhere they went Madame left worry and worked herself up into a further state. Maggie could not help but wish that it were the other way around – that Madame was missing and that Maggie and James Connolly were searching for her. He would be calm. And Maggie could think. Madame only induced panic.

The countess slowed as she drove past Dublin Castle. 'They have him! I am certain of it,' she insisted. 'If you want to stop an organisation, remove its leader.'

It made a terrifying sense.

'James would not simply disappear,' Madame continued.

It was true. He was too kind for that.

But Madame had a different interpretation. 'There is too much to do for that!'

That, too, was true, though.

'Is there anywhere else he could be?' Maggie tried. She could not bear the thought of him being held captive.

But Madame was so deep in her own thoughts she did not hear. 'We should storm the castle!'

Maggie stared. 'Just the two of us?'

'No, no, the entire Citizen Army.'

But when they returned to Liberty Hall, other leaders urged patience. 'We must not act until we know for certain where he is.'

It was late now and Maggie had to return home; her mother would be worried. As she was leaving, Patrick approached her. Already, to her great delight, he had joined the Citizen Army.

'Let me walk you to the tram,' he said.

She nodded, needing to hear his theory on where their leader might be.

'Are you all right, Maggie?' he asked when they got outside. 'You look wretched.'

'It's as if everyone has gone missing! I haven't heard from Danny in three weeks and now James Connolly vanishes!' She was close to tears. 'I'm sorry. It was a mistake to go with Madame. She has worked me up into a state.'

He looked thoughtful. For a long time, he did not speak. At last, he turned to her.

'Don't worry about Connolly. He's all right,' he said with such certainty that she frowned.

'How do you know?'

'I can't tell you, Maggie. And you can't tell anyone either that he's all right. If you do, I'll deny it.'

'What's going on, Patrick?'

'I'm not at liberty to say. I just want you to know that he's safe.'

'But how do you know when no one else does, not even Madame?'

'Madame will never know. She couldn't keep a secret if her life depended on it.'

She looked at him. 'You've never had time for her, have you?'

'She's like a butterfly, flitting from flower to flower. I doubt her solidity. There, I've said it.'

'I knew it anyway; you're not one to hide your feelings, Patrick Shanahan.'

He smiled. 'No.'

'But James Connolly is truly all right? You're certain?' How she needed to believe him.

'I'm certain. And Maggie? I told you as a friend and because you're worried about Danny but I wouldn't have said a thing if I didn't have faith in *your* solidity.'

She bowed her head. It meant so much. 'Thank you.'

'Now get on that tram and get home to your family.'

She smiled, grabbed a quick hug – she did not care what he thought – and ran to catch the tram.

Onboard, relief hit her like wave. It had been as if she had lost her father for a second time and she only realised that now.

Three days after James Connolly went missing, he reappeared, simply walked back into their lives. He would not say where he had been. To anyone. Not even Madame. And when Maggie looked at Patrick, he looked back, his expression blank.

thirty-nine

Daniel
February 1916

Daniel woke to the scent of flowers and the voice of an angel. The ground beneath him was soft and warm. There was no thunder in the air, no shouting, no groaning. Only peace, at last. He had made it to heaven. But how could that be? He had taken lives and not repented.

He tried to open his eyes but they would not open. He tried to move but could not. With great effort, at last, he lifted a finger. Pain coursed through him. Could one feel pain in heaven?

'Are you all right, Sergeant Healy?'

Then he remembered. He was in the Number Four Canadian General Hospital in Salonika – far from heaven. And the angel voice was that of a nurse.

'Yes nurse,' he said as a reflex.

He wondered if he would ever see again. He struggled to remember his other injuries. He had shrapnel lodged in his back that they had failed to remove during surgery. They had saved his leg, though, had they not? Perhaps he was wrong. Perhaps he had dreamt all of this as he slipped in and out of consciousness. Perhaps he had confused his wounds with Michael's. They were almost identical. How Michael would laugh at that. He laughed thinking of Michael's laughter.

'Sergeant?' the nurse asked.

'Nurse... My face... Is it...disfigured?'

There was a pause. 'No, Sergeant. You were saved by the scarf you wore.'

Daniel did not understand why that made him cry or why he could not stop. He was shaking, his entire body, shaking.

A cool hand alighted on his. Nurse MacCormack, he remembered then. That was her name, the angel.

'It's all right, Sergeant.'

Shame swamped him. Out there, he had been a man. In here, with a little sympathy, he had become a baby. 'You must think me mad. Laughing one minute, crying the next.' Perhaps he *was* mad. Perhaps he had gone doolally after all.

'I make no judgments on men that have seen war,' she said. 'I'm going to dress your eyes, now, Sergeant. I'll fetch the morphine.'

'Thank you,' he said, remembering the pain that screamed through him whenever he was moved.

Minutes later, Nurse MacCormack returned with the morphine. She administered it into his mouth by syringe so that he would not have to lift his head.

'It will take a while to work. Then I'll be back to do your dressings.'

'Thank you.'

He heard the nurses tend to other patients. He heard coughs. He heard shoes squeaking on the floor. He heard... a bed being moved? He heard the unfamiliar accents of Australians and New Zealanders; the Anzacs, like the Irish, were infamous for their bravery.

As always, the morphine began to dull his senses, taking control from him, tempting him into sleep. He fought against it by trying to remember all that he could about what had happened in the hospital as the days slipped into one another and dreams merged with nightmares that merged with reality, until it was unclear as to which was which. He recalled that the operating theatre had been cold, the lighting poor. Medical staff had worn pullovers over their uniforms. Yes. That had all occurred. He was certain that he could remember the medical officer's voice. What had he said?

A specialist would be needed to remove the shrapnel. They had done all that they could for his leg. Yes, that was the story with the leg. He remembered now for certain.

Nurse MacCormack returned. After the harshness of trench life, everything about her was so painfully soft, gentle and motherly. It brought him close to tears sometimes. Distressingly.

'Will we give it a try now?' she asked.

'Please.'

Gently, she lifted his head and unwound the bandages. Then, slowly, she removed the dressing from his eyes. She placed a compress over them. The coolness of it brought relief.

'I'll leave that in position and return shortly. Rest now, awhile.'

He heard her faint rustle as she left. The pull into sleep was too strong to fight now. What harm would it do to give in?

'I'm going to swab your eyes now, Sergeant Healy.'

He started.

'I'm sorry,' she said. 'It's only me.'

He smiled to reassure her.

'I'm going to swab your eyes now.'

She did so in a slow and meticulous manner that he had grown accustomed to. It was strange the little things that brought comfort. Familiarity was one of them.

'Now, Sergeant, see if you can open your eyes,' she said brightly.

The compress had loosened the stickiness and Daniel forced his lids apart. For the first time, his eyes did not open to blindness. There was light. And though it was as if he were looking through oil, he could make out a figure in white.

'I see you! Well, the shape of you.' He blinked repeatedly to try to clear the oiliness. He saw black hair escape in wisps. He saw eyes dark like Maggie's. Then he began to doubt himself. 'Perhaps I'm imagining it.'

'What do you see?' she asked patiently.

He told her. As he did, he could make out a blurry smile.

'That is *indeed* good news!' She sounded so happy for him and yet she did not know him – or all that he had done in the name of war. He had killed and not repented. Even still, he could not find regret. And there she stood, smiling for him.

He looked up at the ceiling to distract himself. He squinted. 'Are we in a tent?'

'We are indeed! The great canvas tent of a hospital!'

He struggled to make out the detail. He squinted. He strained. His vision cleared. Then blurred again. But he would not give up, would not give in. He would fight for this one thing. And if he could master it, then he could take on a bigger fight. And all the time, he would use the same three words that he had got him this far. Missus Daniel Healy.

Daniel refused morphine in favour of his senses. With a clear head, he became aware of all that was being done for him. He was shaved. He was washed. To his mortification, he was given a bottle to urinate into. His only reassurance was that he had not looked into the eyes of the orderly who had been given the task of cleaning, delousing and shaving him when he had been admitted. A hunger grew within him to do all that he could for himself. This became a hunger to walk again, and, somehow, get home to Maggie. He forced his eyes to work, to focus in on the tiniest of insects, the legs, the eyes. He forced his body beyond pain, to rise from the bed, to walk with crutches borrowed from a jolly private from New South Wales.

'I *must* warn you against movement, Sergeant Healy, until you have seen a specialist,' the medical officer warned.

'When can I see one?'

'Well, we have no such specialist here. Once you regain your strength, we can transfer you to-'

'Are there such specialists in Dublin?' he asked with such hope that the doctor's face softened.

'Let me enquire.'

'Thank you.'

Outside, it snowed and froze. But there *was* an outside and Daniel had an image of it in his mind now, an image of a harbour, a ship and a sea that would carry him home.

forty

Maggie arrived at a small house off Harcourt Street. She delivered three quick knocks and two slow to the front door. After a moment, it opened. She entered with her bicycle into a dark hallway.

'You weren't followed?' Patrick asked, closing the door behind her.

'I'm not answering that,' she said, leaning the bicycle against a wall.

'Only making sure.'

'I'm doing you a favour, Patrick. I don't have to be here.' It wasn't a job for the Citizen Army; it was for a 'friend' of his. And she had her doubts about it.

She followed him upstairs.

In the smallest bedroom, there was a baby's cot, the blankets disturbed as though the child had only just been removed. Patrick began to move it aside.

'They haven't hidden guns under a *baby*?' she asked incredulously.

'What better place?' Already he was rolling back the carpet and lifting a floorboard. He took out two rifles and a handful of rounds. He passed the guns to Maggie.

They were Lee Enfields. She took a moment to admire them, then placed them on the floor. She took tape from her pocket.

'Turn your back,' she said.

As soon as he did, she lifted her skirt. She held it up with her chin while she taped one of the rifles to the outside of her right thigh. It was cold and hard against her skin but it would not be there long. She strapped the other rifle to her left leg and allowed the skirt to fall.

'All right,' she said.

He turned. 'That looks grand but we'd better check. Bend up a leg as if you're cycling.'

She held onto the cot as she did so.

'Either those are the pointiest knees I've ever seen or you're running guns. Strap them higher. An inch should do it.'

'Ah, shite.'

He laughed. 'That's the foulest mouth I've ever heard on a girl.'

'Who do you imagine I picked it up from?'

'Yes but I'm not a girl,' he said, turning around once more.

'Are you sure?'

He snorted with laughter. 'Oh, you wit.'

She smiled then pressed her lips together as she ripped the tape from her legs. She strapped the guns higher.

This time, she passed his scrutiny.

'Now put these in your wig.' He handed her the rounds.

She began to put them into her hair.

'Take it off, Maggie. It would be easier.'

'It's real hair, Patrick. It grows, you know.'

He blushed.

She smiled and replaced her hat. 'Right so, I'll be off.'

'Wait. It might look suspicious if you were to leave so soon.'

'I'll have a cup of tea so,' she said, giving him an expectant look.

'I don't know where anything is in this place.'

She walked with stiff legs to the staircase. Holding the bannister, she descended slowly.

267

In the kitchen, she pointed to a cupboard. 'Try that one.'

A quick check proved her right. 'Will I make you one, so?' he asked, reluctantly.

'Do.'

He presented her with a saucer-less cup.

The tea was good, though. 'You'll make a great wife.'

He choked on the mouthful he'd taken.

She laughed.

'What has you in such good form?' he asked.

'I had a letter from Daniel! Well, a nurse writing for Daniel! He's alive! And he's coming home!' She wanted to proclaim it to the world. 'He's to have an operation but he says it's not serious. He'll be at the King George V Hospital in Arbour Hill should you wish to visit.'

He grimaced. 'Look, I like Daniel but he's a British Army soldier now. That makes him the enemy.'

'He's fighting for Ireland, Patrick.'

He looked her in the eye. 'There's only one way to fight for Ireland.'

She bowed her head. On that, she could not argue.

'Give him my best.'

'I will,' she said quietly.

He gave her a look of intense scrutiny. 'I *can* trust you, can't I, Maggie? You wouldn't go telling him what we're up to, now, sure you wouldn't?'

She pushed the cup away. 'You can keep your tea.' She rose.

'I was only making sure.'

'It's not lemons I'm hiding up my skirt, Patrick Shanahan.' As she said it, she felt as though she was betraying Danny. She reminded herself that he was doing what he believed to be right for his country. She must do the same. 'Just tell me where to go.'

He gave her directions, out to Kimmage to a place called Larkfield House.

'What's there?' If he did not trust her enough to tell her, he could keep his guns.

'The estate of Count Plunkett.'

268

'Plunkett?'

'I *do* trust you, Maggie.'

'Then tell me,' she said calmly.

He shrugged as though he had no difficulty with that. 'The Plunketts harbour men who have travelled from Britain to avoid conscription to the Great War so that they can rise, instead, for Ireland.'

'I like the sound of *them*!'

He studied her with a curious expression. 'I never thought I'd say this but I may well prefer you as a girl.'

She sighed. 'Some day you'll see that not all girls are the same.'

'Don't I know that already?'

'Good. You're learning.' She winked at him and was gone.

Bicycling towards the canal, Maggie spotted a group of British Army soldiers, in conversation on the pavement. She was about to take a different route when one of them spied her. Holding his gaze, she kept her course and pace.

Closer now and they were all looking at her.

Lord God, she thought and produced a friendly smile.

They raised their caps.

She worried that somehow her knees were still pointy. She had to force herself not to look.

'Hello, boys!' she said to draw attention to her face. She brought sophistication to her smile.

They stuttered and spluttered and blushed.

Crossing the bridge, she closed her eyes and breathed out in relief.

At last, she reached her destination, a grand house on extensive grounds. She cycled up the driveway and then continued on to a shed at the rear that Patrick had described. She knocked, using the same code that she'd used in Harcourt Street. There was no reply.

She waited.

Nothing.

She glanced about.

The breeze bent the tall grass over in waves. A cow lowed in the near distance. She could feel her heart thunder. Had the person she was meant to meet been intercepted? Or was he not to be trusted? Perhaps this was a trap? And who *was* this friend of Patrick's anyway?

Instinct told her that it was not safe to stand about. She tried the door. It opened with a treacherous creak. She looked around again. But nothing had changed. She glanced into the shed. It seemed empty but for a mound of coal. She pushed the bicycle inside.

She'd wait ten minutes. Then she'd go. But where could she bring guns and ammunition? Not home. Never home. She would never put her family at risk.

After the slowest, most terrifying five minutes of her life, Maggie heard the sound of approaching footsteps. She froze. And looked about the shed in panic. Should she hide? Could she anyway behind a pathetic mound of coal?

The steps halted at the door.

She held her breath and stayed very still.

Time seemed to stop.

Then came a knock. It was the code that she had been instructed to use. Either Patrick had got it backwards or this person had. Slowly, she opened the door.

Standing before her was a giant of a man. His quick smile was warm and confident.

He entered without hesitation.

Maggie took a step back.

He closed the door behind him. 'Thank you for coming all the way out,' he said, looking at her bicycle. His lilting accent was from the country. He offered his hand. 'Michael Collins.'

She shook it. 'Maggie Gilligan.'

He rubbed his hands together. 'What have you got for me?'

'Two Lee Enfields and some rounds.'

He smiled, then looked at her as if to say, 'Where are they?'

'You'll need to turn around. I have them hidden.'

'Ah,' he said. He winked. Then he turned.

She moved quickly, ignoring the pain as she tore the tape from her legs. She held the guns in her arms.

'I have them now,' she said.

He turned back and, on seeing the weapons, chuckled. He took them from her, examining them as though works of art. Compared to Mausers, they were.

'Nothing like the sweet irony of fighting the British Army with its own weaponry,' he said.

She thought of Danny and wished that this would be all over before he got home.

forty-one

Daniel wished that he had never sent those telegrams to Maggie, Michael and his family to let them know that he had arrived back in Dublin. After his X-rays, he had been confined to bed and immobilised in a metal brace to restrict his movement. Now he looked up at the doctor standing over him and tried to take in his words.

'I would *like* to think that, with steady hands, I can remove the shrapnel successfully. However, you must understand that the operation brings with it the risk of paralysis.'

'And if you don't operate?' Daniel asked.

'There is a similar – if not worse – risk. As you move about, the shrapnel inches closer to your spine.'

He tried to nod but couldn't.

'I'll give you time to decide.' The doctor patted the bed awkwardly and left.

Daniel stared up at the ceiling. He had walked into that hospital. Now here he was again, flat on his back. It was as if all the progress he had made had been deemed a lie. About him, the familiar sounds of hospital life continued – hushed conversations, curtains being pulled around a bed, a nurse coaxing a patient to take another step. Daniel's next step would decide his future. He thought of Maggie and what she would do in his situation. And then he knew. It would be 'the steady hands' – or the promise of them. The alternative would be a life lived in fear. And he had enough of that.

He called the doctor before he changed his mind.

'Good!' was his one-word response. Suddenly, he was all business. 'If you'll excuse me, there is much to organise.'

The decision seemed to hurry away with him.

Daniel lay trapped, watching the hands of the clock advance another day.

He was slipping into a doze when a shadow fell across him. He opened his eyes. His father stood gazing down at him with the softest expression. He removed his top hat.

'My son,' was all he said but those two words seemed to hold all the love in the world. Daniel feared that he would cry in the face of a man who hated weakness.

'I'm sorry that I cannot sit up,' he said.

'The doctor has explained everything, Danny,' he said softly. He hadn't called him Danny in years.

To escape the emotion, Daniel glanced at the clock. His eyes returned to his father in surprise.

'Are the courts not in session today?'

'The courts can go a day without me. My son has returned from the war.' His hands circled the brim of the hat. He looked at Daniel desperately. 'Had I known that you would sign up I'd never have said what I did. I should never have said it, anyway. I have carried that regret with me like a weight since the day you left.' His eyes filled with tears.

Daniel's own eyes smarted. 'You didn't place the gun in my hand, Father.'

'I may as well have.'

Daniel tried to shake his head but the brace stopped him. 'There were other reasons.'

'What reasons?' he asked, disbelieving.

'A girl. Maggie. I am engaged to be married, Father.'

He laughed in surprise. 'Lord, but you're a fast mover.'

'War does that to a person.'

There was pain and regret in his father's eyes. He took a thin silver flask from his inside breast pocket. 'I suppose you're a drinking man now?'

Daniel smiled. 'War does that too.'

They were far from the trenches and yet his hand still shook. They pretended not to notice.

Whatever the drink, it tasted like honey compared to army grog. Daniel took another sip before passing it back.

His father lifted the flask in a salute. 'To my son! I am blessed to have you back, Danny.'

Danny speared a tear with his finger before it could go any further. 'I'm sorry.'

His father grabbed his hand and squeezed it. 'It is *I* who am sorry. I have changed, Danny,' he said urgently as though he feared that they would be interrupted or run out of time. 'When you left, I visited my properties. Till then, I'd had a man handle it all. Well, I was appalled by the conditions and instantly sacked the man. At first, I considered selling the premises, washing my hands of them but then I realised that, if I did that, nothing would change. So I invested in the buildings, improved conditions, indoors and out.' He stopped. 'What happened between us has brought some good, at least.'

'How that cheers me.'

'When you are well, perhaps we could visit the properties together and see how things have changed?' He seemed to be seeking Daniel's approval.

He smiled. 'I'd like that.'

'How I wish that you did not have to suffer for my eyes to open.'

'I'll be fine, Father.' *With steady hands.* 'Poor Michael did not fare so well.'

His father's eyes glistened. 'You were only boys. *Boys.*' He gathered himself. 'At least, you're home now.'

'Should the operation succeed, I'll have to return.'

His father pinched the bridge of his nose. 'I'll never forgive myself.' His voice broke.

'I need you to. I need for this to be behind us.'

Once more, he squeezed Daniel's hand. 'I prayed that we'd be given this opportunity. Every day, I prayed.'

Daniel smiled. 'You were not alone in that.' He looked at his father for the longest time, filling in the details of a face that had blurred in his mind, like all faces had – remarkably blurred, terrifyingly blurred. 'How are mother and Niall?'

'You can see for yourself! They are waiting outside in the corridor! I wanted to speak with you first. Will I call them in?'

Daniel hesitated. 'Will they be all right seeing me like this?'

'They are longing to see you, whatever way you are.'

But, on seeing Daniel, his mother burst into tears. 'They're tears of happiness,' she insisted. 'It is so good to see you, Danny.'

His own tears escaped again and he laughed to camouflage the emotion.

'You'll never guess what happened in school!' Niall exclaimed, saving the situation. His stories tumbled out, one over the other, each one reminding him of the next.

Daniel soaked up the normality, bathed in it. When, at last, Niall ran out of steam – it took half an hour – Daniel looked at his mother and smiled.

'I cannot think of any news whatsoever!' she said and laughed. It was as if her life between Daniel's leaving and returning was of absolutely no relevance.

How he loved her. How he loved them all.

'Your *son* has news of his own,' his father said. He looked at Daniel.

He was momentarily confused.

'He seems to have acquired a fiancée, somewhere along the line!' his father helped.

His mother's hands shot to her face. 'Good Lord! How did that happen?'

Daniel smiled. 'It's a long story, Mother. I'll tell you sometime.'

'I'll remind you.'

'I'm sure you will,' her husband said, grinning. 'You old romantic.'

Daniel looked at him in surprise and thought that maybe war did good things too, like dissolved the coldness between a father and his family.

Daniel's father launched himself at Daniel's next visitor, dragging him into an embrace and patting his back with almost brutal enthusiasm.

Michael laughed in surprise.

Mister Healy, fearing suddenly that he had overdone it, took a step back.

'It is wonderful to see you, Michael. But you and Danny will have much to discuss.' He nodded to himself. He looked at Daniel as if he had only said half of what he had intended to say. 'We'll call again, tomorrow.'

'They might be operating,' Daniel warned.

Worry crossed his mother's face, the worry of someone who knew the risks.

'I'm in good hands,' Daniel reassured. *Steady hands.*

'Are you all right in there?' she asked of the brace.

'Happy as Larry,' he lied. 'I can't tell you how good it is to see you.' Tears threatened once more.

'Tomorrow, I'll bring Humbugs,' Niall promised.

'I'll hold you to it.' Daniel winked.

But the final words were his father's. 'Let us leave our boy in peace.'

Michael approached the bed. 'What have they got on you?' he asked as if it was an instrument of torture.

'It's to stop me from moving.' Daniel explained about the shrapnel.

'But you'll be all right?'

'Grand.' Daniel looked up at his friend. Neither mask nor face was as bad as he'd imagined from the letters. He'd seen worse. 'You look well, Mick.'

'If only I could say the same for you.'

They laughed.

'I missed you,' Daniel said. The words did not feel strong enough. 'What happened to you, Mick? I watched that lighter take you away, not knowing if they'd get you onto a trawler...' He couldn't go on. Was this what happened when you left a war zone – you fell to pieces?

'Well, the story goes,' Michael cheerfully began. 'They got me onto a hospital ship, where I was operated on, then taken to a hospital in Malta where more surgery followed. Then it was off to England where the Countess of Carnarvon herself tended to me. After that, it was the *mask doctor*,' he said in the manner of "evil scientist". 'Do you wish to see my face?' It was a dare.

'Nothing would shock me, Mick. You know that.'

Michael closed his eyes and nodded. 'You're right. I use it to shock. It has become tired.'

'I missed you. Have I said that?' Daniel smiled.

'You'll have a smoke?'

They shared a slow cigarette and silence.

'How's school?' Daniel asked.

'I lasted a day.'

Daniel frowned.

Michael waved his concern away. 'My father has found me work in Dublin Castle. I begin tomorrow. It's only filing but it's a wage and a start and I won't end up in prison for the murder of a schoolboy.'

Daniel laughed. 'How I've missed your humour.'

'Maggie thinks it'll get me a girl some day.' He looked doubtful.

'How is she?' Daniel's heart swelled at the thought of her.

He longed to see her and yet he had a terrible feeling that on seeing him she would realise that she no longer loved him. How could she love him when she no longer knew him? He had changed so much. Everything had.

Michael sighed deeply.

'What is it?' he asked, panicking now.

'I could not write of this but...'

Fear gripped Daniel.

'She has joined the Irish Citizen Army.' Michael told him all that had happened. 'Perhaps you could talk her out of it, now that you're home.'

Daniel felt a tug at his heart. 'I would never try.' He smiled. 'She wouldn't listen anyway.'

'True enough. When she discovered that I was behind her dismissal from Na Fianna, I thought she'd kill me.'

Daniel smiled and his heart filled with sudden hope. Maggie, at least, had not changed.

And then there she was.

The light was fading and Michael had gone. Daniel stared up at her. She had changed entirely. Gone was the boy-girl he'd carried with him in his heart. Her hair had grown. It was nothing like the sad little clump he'd thumbed to death, the little clump he still had. The sight of her sent him into a blind panic. He had fixed his bayonet, he had climbed over the top, he had run into machine-gun fire and been shelled to kingdom come yet what he feared most was the girl he loved.

She slipped her hand into his and lifted it to her lips. But she was crying.

'Your scarf didn't make it home,' he tried.

'That hopeless tangle!'

'It saved my face, Maggie.'

She touched his cheek with the back of her fingers. It only reminded him of the gap between them. She was so soft, so gentle while he was hard, tainted, his heart compressed into a knot. He had taken lives and been glad. He would never be good enough, happy enough, *him* enough again.

'I'm a killer, Maggie.' There it was.

'You're a soldier. There's a difference.'

'I've done things, seen things...' he said with growing distress.

Her eyes held his. 'That doesn't change who you are.'

But it did, Daniel knew.

Maggie bent down and kissed his mouth, so softly, like a butterfly landing. 'We're here, now, together at last,' she whispered. 'That's all that matters.'

And there it was, suddenly, the scent that he had been chasing in a wad of hair. He closed his eyes. 'How I've missed you,' he whispered and heard the emotion in his own voice.

'I missed you more.'

'No.'

'Yes,' she insisted.

He could not believe that he was laughing. 'I love you.'

'Not as much as I love you.'

'You're so obstinate,' he said.

'Isn't that why you love me?'

He gazed at her face in wonder. 'You're a woman, Maggie.'

'Only pretending. As usual.'

'Michael told me about the Citizen Army,' he said to save her the admission.

She bowed her head. 'I'm sorry. I didn't want to tell you when you were overseas.' She frowned. 'How did Michael get in here before me anyway?'

He smiled. 'I assume you were in school. He was at home. Have you heard? He starts work in Dublin Castle tomorrow.'

'Dublin Castle of all places.' She shook her head.

'Can we put Ireland aside for a moment?' He had to say it.

'I'm sorry.' She looked at the brace. 'Will you be all right, Danny?'

'Of course I will. It's a tiny operation.'

'Then why this?'

'They're only showing off their equipment. Still, I'm glad of it. They had nothing at all in Salonika. Except the best nurses in the world.'

Then she smiled. 'Have you got my ring yet?'

He felt suddenly that they would survive this – The Healys. 'I've been a bit occupied,' he joked.

'No excuse.'

He laughed. 'Kiss me.'

'On one condition.'

'What's that?'

'You never leave me again.'

His eyes held hers. *If only eyes could keep people together*, he thought.

forty-two

Maggie

Maggie had longed for this day. She had dreamt of it, prayed for it. Imagined it. And, after Michael had returned as he had, she had prepared herself for it. But nothing could have prepared her for what she found. Seeing him lying there, so unsure of himself, so unsure of her and yet somehow a man, she began to cry – for him, for them. She wished to gather him up in her arms and hold him to her but she could not get near him because of the contraption. All she could do was kiss his hand. Then they were talking, each word bringing them closer, like rocks placed, one by one, across a stream linking two people on opposite sides. They were laughing and teasing one another again. And she began to hope.

Then, on her way out of the ward, she asked to see the doctor. And he told her the truth.

Her stomach plummeted. She should have known that Daniel would lie to protect her. Her heart ached for him.

That night, she tossed, turned and prayed. Just this one thing. His deliverance.

The following day, with permission from her mam, she headed for the hospital instead of school.

Daniel's bed was gone. She stood staring at the space left by it.

'He's having his surgery, love,' the man in the next bed told her.

'They took the entire bed?'

'Carried the whole lot out. Didn't want to move him.'

'Thank you,' she managed.

She paced up and down in the space where his bed had been, biting into her fist. And though she was sure the Lord was sick of her prayers she sent Him another.

'Don't worry, pet,' the man reassured. 'They have the best surgeons in the world here.'

She smiled and nodded.

The men in the other beds got involved. Every so often, one of them would appear beside her with the offer of a sweet, a newspaper, a chair, hope. In the end, she took the chair and the newspaper so that she could sit on one and hide behind the other.

At long last, Daniel was carried, bed and all, back into the room. Maggie stood aside, her eyes scanning his face. He was deeply asleep, turned on his side. There was no brace. She looked at the doctor questioningly.

He grinned. 'We got the little bugger! I'm sorry. I beg your pardon. The shrapnel. We got it all, every last bit.'

She began to cry tears of relief. 'Thank you. Thank you so very much.' She grabbed his hand and pumped it. 'I was so worried.' She should stop talking.

'He'll be right as rain in no time.'

She didn't want to hear that either. 'But his recuperation will take a while?' she confirmed.

'Oh yes. It will be weeks before he has to return.'

She smiled; he had read her mind.

She pulled the chair to the head of the bed. What she felt was joy. Absolute joy. Danny's face, relaxed by the anaesthetic, had become a boy's again, his eyelashes casting shadows on his pale, still cheeks. She did not care who was looking; she bent down and kissed him.

It was hours before he opened his eyes.

'They got the bugger, every last bit,' she said, delighting in repeating the doctor's words. 'You'll be right as rain in no time!' She laughed and cried.

He gripped her hand and fell back asleep.

Later, he awoke in pain and was given morphine.

'What time is it?' he asked her.

'Five in the afternoon.'

'You've been here all day. Have you eaten?'

'I have.' Hard-boiled sweets.

'How are you?'

'Relieved.'

'There was nothing to worry about.'

She raised an eyebrow at him. 'Doctors talk, Daniel. Anyway, the question is, how are *you*? You're the one who's had the surgery.'

He gave in with a smile. 'Relieved, too, I suppose.'

'I'm the *most* relieved, though.'

'Here we go again.'

But Maggie's face darkened.

'What is it?' he asked.

'Nothing.'

'Maggie?'

She looked at him. 'You'll have to go back.'

His eyes held hers. 'Not for a long time.' He lifted an arm. 'See, no muscle.'

'Keep it that way.' She bent down and kissed him.

He smiled. 'When you put it like that.'

Maggie sailed home on a sigh of relief. Not only would Daniel make a full recovery but also for the next few weeks he would be safe – and here – with her – while he recuperated. She would put everything on hold. Ireland. Her family. School. How bright the day seemed suddenly, how blue the sky. Spring had arrived in Dublin and she hadn't even noticed.

The song she was humming as she walked through the front door was not a rebel song. It was Daniel's favourite. She remembered calling him a romantic when he'd told her. But she had loved that he was. A year and a half had passed since their picnic in Kingstown. It was hard to believe. And yet it *did* feel that she had been aching for him for that long. Longer.

'It's lovely to see you smile, Maggie,' her mother said when they sat down to dinner.

'Don't I smile?' she asked in surprise.

'No,' Lily said, helpfully. 'Never.'

So she smiled. It was easy suddenly.

God but she was hungry. And there was so much to *talk* about. All of it Danny-related.

Smiling, it seemed, was infectious, as was conversation. Maggie had not enjoyed a meal so much in a very long time.

After dinner, when they were just settling in the drawing room, Michael called unexpectedly.

'Fetch your coat,' he said. 'We're going out.'

Her pulse raced. 'What is it?' she asked for something surely had happened.

'Just come, Maggie.'

'Is it Danny?'

'No. It's not Danny.'

'Thank God,' she said and hurried after him.

They were at the end of her street before he spoke and he did so in an urgent whisper. 'You must leave the Citizen Army at once. They have files on you in Dublin Castle. They have files on everyone: James Connolly, the Countess Markievicz...'

'But I'm nobody compared to them.'

'You know a Patrick Shanahan, who is somebody.'

'What do you mean?'

'He is high up in the IRB.'

'The IRB?' She had never heard of it.

'It's a secret organisation masterminding rebel activity.'

Maggie's mind raced. Suddenly, everything made sense, the way Patrick spoke, as if connected, the gunrunning job out to Kimmage, the best guns, and his certainty that James Connolly would return safely. And *he* spoke of trust!

'Whether or not you've heard of it, you've been spending a lot of time in the company of Shanahan and the spotlight of suspicion has fallen upon you. They have G-men watching every movement at Liberty Hall.'

'We know. They are as conspicuous as they are stupid.'

'Stupid people can make arrests. What then?'

She looked at him with genuine concern. 'Is there talk of arrests?'

'I haven't heard anything but, then, I'm not meant to. Think about it, though, if they have the names why wait for trouble?'

Maggie tried to stay calm. They would have to rise urgently. She'd have to tell Patrick, Mister Secret Organisation himself.

'I've mislaid your file, Maggie, removed all evidence of you from Dublin Castle. You are nobody again,' Michael said shyly.

'But what about you? What if they discover the file missing?'

He raised his eyebrow. 'Out of hundreds of files, one goes missing? I'm the son of a Dublin Metropolitan Policeman. I fought for the British Army. The only reason I'd mislay a file would be out of stupidity.' He smiled.

She touched his arm in appreciation. 'Thank you.'

'You're not out of the woods, Maggie. I've protected you as much as I can but they could storm Liberty Hall at any moment. You must give it up.'

'I cannot.'

'You must! It's coming to a head! I can feel it.'

'And when it does,' she said calmly, 'I'll remember, with gratitude, your warning. Now, I have a favour to ask. Don't tell Danny. Please, Michael. He'd only worry and there's nothing he can do.'

'Of course I won't bloody tell him. He'd go out of his mind. I'm going out of mine and I'm just your friend.'

She embraced him then. 'I'm sorry, Michael. I wish I could do as you ask.'

Maggie knew where to find Patrick. He worked by day as a hotel porter (keeping his eyes and ears open) and lived by night at Liberty Hall where he alternately slept and took turns on guard duty. The building was under twenty-four-hour guard now, given the stockpile of weapons it contained.

When she tracked him down, he was reshaping bullets.

She sat beside him.

'So I can trust you?' she whispered, raising a cynical eyebrow.

He looked at her in surprise. 'You know you can.'

'I know nothing of the sort, Patrick Shanahan.'

He glanced about the room. 'Let us take a walk outside.'

'As long as I get the truth.'

'I have never once lied to you, Maggie.'

'There are different ways of lying.'

He looked at her then. 'As only you know.'

She rolled her eyes.

They passed rebel guards on the stairs and again at one of the many hidden entrances. Just as they were about to go out onto the quay, he turned to her.

'It's swarming with G-men out there. Let's act as a couple so we'll be left alone.'

She nodded. He linked her arm and guided her out. Emerging from the shadows, she noticed three separate men turn to look at them. One busied himself lighting a cigarette. Another continued an apparent promenade. The third bent to tie his shoelace.

'You'd think they'd make a bigger effort to blend in,' Patrick muttered. 'At least be walking a dog or a woman or something. Laugh, now, Maggie, like I'm the funniest man alive.'

She tipped her head back and laughed and then leaned in to him as they walked past the smoking G-man.

'You're good at this,' Patrick whispered in her ear as though proclaiming undying love.

Soon they were crossing O'Connell Bridge.

Maggie glanced casually down the quay to make sure that they weren't being followed. Then she turned to him.

'So, you're in the IRB?'

He looked alarmed. 'Where did *you* hear of the IRB?'

'You're not the only one who knows people, Patrick.' She stopped walking. 'All that talk of trust….' She folded her arms.

'Maggie, there are times when the less you know, the safer you are. I was protecting you.'

'Well, you failed. I'm guilty by association, it seems.'

'What do you mean?'

'They have files on me – on all of us – in Dublin Castle.'

He looked thoughtful. 'It's as we suspected.'

She longed to know who the 'we' consisted of. Were there others she knew who were members of this secret organisation? It was as if the world had changed without her.

'Tell me this, Patrick Shanahan. If you're with the IRB, why are you also with the Citizen Army?'

'The IRB is not a fighting organisation and I, as you know, will not be sitting back when the time comes. But since you ask and since you believe that I *do not trust you*, let me tell you why the Citizen Army. I joined to keep an eye on Connolly.'

'You're a *spy*?'

He laughed. 'You make me sound more exciting than I am. We're all in this together, Maggie, all the rebel forces. Connolly, though, was a loose cannon, ready to go off half-cocked and rise without us. We needed to know what he was up to.'

'And there I was thinking that you'd joined because of me.'

'You gave me the idea but Ireland comes first for me. Before any organisation. Before any individual. Before even myself.'

That she understood.

They walked in silence for a while. Then she turned to him. 'Where was James Connolly when he went missing?'

'Ah!'

'Well?'

'If I tell you, you must swear to never tell another soul.'

'You know I won't.'

He looked at her for a long time and then glanced around to make sure they were not being watched. 'He was having a chat with the Military Council of the IRB. He was assuring them that he would not rise alone in return for helping them set a date for the rising.'

Her heart throbbed. Everything seemed to stop. '*Is* there a date?'

'There's a tentative date, yes.'

Dear God. 'When?'

'I cannot say.'

'Cannot or will not?'

'Cannot. We're awaiting a shipment of guns from Germany.'

'It had better come soon, Patrick. That's what I came to tell you; a friend of mine in Dublin Castle fears that arrests are imminent.'

His eyes narrowed. 'How imminent?'

'They could happen at any time. Liberty Hall could be stormed. And it will all be over....'

'Walk, Maggie, before we arouse suspicion.'

'We need to rise urgently,' she said as she did so. 'When are these guns coming?'

He looked at her. 'What I'm about to tell you must stay with you.'

She nodded, unable to breathe.

'We're hoping to go out at Easter.'

'Jesus!' she whispered. After all this time, this preparation, this dreaming, they would be rising up in *weeks*.

He stopped walking and raised a finger in warning. 'Not a word of this to Danny.'

She stared at him. It was hard enough being here, like this, on the day that Danny had been operated on. Before she knew it, she'd slapped Patrick, hard, across the face.

He laughed. 'Good. That was the reassurance I needed.'

'Feck off.'

'Who is your friend in Dublin Castle?'

'You're not the only one with secrets, Patrick.' Michael had done enough. She would have no more asked of him.

He nodded. 'I'll bring your news to the IRB.'

'Should I tell Danny you said hello?' It was a dare.

He looked at her and smiled. 'Do. And wish him a speedy recovery.'

A speedy recovery was the last thing she wished for. She wished Danny confined to hospital until they had risen for Ireland, until they had freed their country of British rule and until Irish soldiers were no longer obliged to fight for another country.

forty-three

Daniel and Maggie
April 1916

Daniel linked Maggie's arm as they strolled through the grounds of the hospital, as he had been encouraged to do by the doctor. Weeks had passed since his operation and every day he grew stronger. It was still incredible to be able to move around without fear of snipers, under a sun that was gentle and forgiving, to the sound of birdsong not artillery. Daniel had not known just how much he loved Ireland.

'I'm amazed that Mam is letting me miss so much school,' Maggie thought aloud.

He had to say it. 'She knows I'll be off soon.' He looked at her. 'I will, Maggie.'

Her face clouded over. 'Can you not slow down your recovery? Did you learn *nothing* from Hansel and Gretel? Starve yourself, Daniel Healy.'

He pulled her closer. 'When will you marry me?'

'The minute I turn eighteen. I've asked Mam.'

He smiled, encouraged. 'Was *I* not meant to do that?'

'Well, you hadn't and *someone* had to.'

He laughed heartily. How he loved her. 'Will you meet my family?'

'Even your scary father?' she teased.

'He has changed, Maggie. And he wants to meet you. They all do.'

'God.' Suddenly she was scared. She wanted them to like her. And she *never* cared who liked her. 'Then *you* will have to meet *my* family.'

'Tom will probably kill me.'

'Probably,' she smiled and leaned into him. 'I love you.'

And he wished with all his heart that she did not love Ireland more.

'Don't do it, Maggie! Don't rise! I've never asked you before. Now, I'm begging you.' He fumbled in his pocket. He pulled out an envelope that he brought with him everywhere. Then he thrust it into her hand before he could change his mind. 'Read it,' he said hoarsely. It was the letter with his last wishes, the one where he'd asked her to be somewhere else if it came to a fight.

She read in silence then looked up at him as though her heart had shattered.

'Grant me my last wish, Maggie.'

She closed her eyes. 'You're not dying,' she choked. Tears filled her eyes.

'I might, though.'

She'd rather die herself. Chances were she would anyway, given how outnumbered they'd be. She had come to terms with that a long time ago. It was Danny she feared for. They were getting closer to rising and his health was improving too fast. She didn't want him marching up a street where James Connolly and his men would be hiding. She didn't want him walking into an ambush. She didn't want him facing Patrick. Or Madame. Or Con Colbert. Every last one of them would shoot him, despite their shared past. She would rather him back at war than here in Dublin! She looked up at him as tears flooded her face. She could barely breathe.

'I just wish countries would leave each other *alone*,' she wailed.

He kissed away her tears. He thought of her father and what he'd asked of her, the pressure of that. 'I'm sorry, Maggie. But I had to try. Just once. For The Healys.'

'The Healys.' She pressed herself into him. 'I'm sorry too. You don't know how sorry.'

'I do.' He kissed the top of her head.

And her sigh was like all the combined sighs of the world.

Daniel did not think it possible to love Maggie any more than he already did and yet, watching her nervousness with his family, he felt his heart swell even further. He had never seen her so ill at ease, speaking only when spoken to and eating so quickly she finished her meal well before anyone else. Only when his father began to speak of his properties and improvements that he planned, did she forget her nerves.

'I wish other landlords took such care,' Maggie said.

'If I have anything to do with it, they will,' he said. 'At the club, I am busy persuading others that it is in their interests to invest in their properties.'

She nodded enthusiastically.

'Would you like to see the improvements I have begun with, Maggie?' he asked with sudden enthusiasm. 'I was planning on showing Daniel-'

'I would!'

He stood at once. As did Maggie.

'James! We are dining,' his wife exclaimed.

He looked down at the table. 'It seems as though we are finished, Elizabeth,' he said cheerfully.

Daniel got to his feet, amazed that the very thing he imagined would separate Maggie and his father seemed to be uniting them. For now, at least.

In the motorcar, Mister Healy chatted like a man starved of company. 'I have hired an overseer, a man unable to find work since the Lockout. He has sourced furniture, carpets, drapes, whatever I needed, at ridiculous prices. I have spent my life being diddled until now, it seems.' He smiled as though happy that he was no longer that man.

Arriving at the street, four properties, side by side, immediately stood out. They had been plastered and painted. New windows and doors had been installed.

Daniel's father was out of the motor in a flash, marching towards the first of the houses. They followed, running up the steps in time to witness him rap on the door of the first room on the ground floor.

After a short delay, it opened.

The woman standing before them smiled. 'Mister Healy.'

'I hope we're not disturbing you, Missus Murphy.'

'Not at all. Please, come in.'

They entered.

'Missus Murphy, this is my son, Daniel, home from war.'

Daniel was moved by the pride in his voice.

'And this is his future wife, Maggie.'

It was a shock to hear it spoken out like that, so definite. His heart filled with hope. Maybe it *was* possible for them to survive, to truly become The Healys. In Maggie's eyes, he saw the same. Their shared smile said it all.

'Come sit by the fire,' Missus Murphy said.

In the hearth, a fire blazed. Carpets, drapes and furniture added to the cosiness of the room. Daniel looked at his father. He could have sold the properties, washed his hands of them but he had done better.

'You'll join me for a cup of tea,' Missus Murphy said.

The man who would have once considered it beneath him accepted her offer with gratitude.

'I'm glad that you are having a break from the war,' Missus Murphy said to Daniel. 'Where were you posted?'

'Gallipoli.'

She nodded. 'I lost a brother in France, another in Ypres.' Her voice broke.

Maggie reached forward and squeezed her hand. It seemed the most natural thing in the world.

Missus Murphy smiled. Then she turned to Daniel. 'Your father was very kind to my mother when she was ill.'

'Alas, we could not save her,' he said.

'No but we did all that we could have for her and there's great comfort in that.'

His father bowed his head.

They visited two more tenants and had tea there too. In the automobile, on their way home, Mister Healy glanced in the mirror at Maggie. 'I hope that I have not drowned you in tea.'

She smiled. 'I love tea.'

Arriving back, Daniel and Maggie followed him into the house.

'He's lovely,' Maggie whispered.

'Despite the motorcar?'

She returned his smile. 'Despite the car, despite the servants but most especially despite being a landlord.'

On the Thursday before Easter, at Kingsbridge station, great plumes of steam collected under the glass ceiling and pigeons gathered in the rafters. Daniel, bound for the Curragh Camp, said his goodbyes. He cupped Maggie's face in his hands and looked deep into her eyes.

'Be safe,' he said as though his words could ensure it.

'You be safe.'

'I'm only building up my fitness.'

She threw her arms around him. At least he'd be out of Dublin for the rising and not well enough to fight.

A whistle blew and she pulled back. Conscious of his family waiting to say goodbye, she kissed her palm and pressed it to his cheek. 'Come back to me, Danny Healy.'

'Be there when I do.' He kissed her like it was their last.

They clung to each other, eyes closed. Then they forced themselves apart.

Michael was waiting with an embrace of his own.

'Watch out for her,' Daniel asked into his ear as he clapped his back.

'You know that I will,' Michael promised.

Niall, head down, was crying. His mother placed a hand on his shoulder but he shook it off.

Daniel squatted down to him. 'I'm only going to build myself up. We'll see each other again before I set sail.'

Niall shoved a crumpled pack of Humbugs into his hand. He half-smiled. 'Our tradition.'

'We could *not* forget our tradition.'

They held each other's eyes and, together, as though making a pact, they put a Humbug in their mouths. Daniel wondered how many times a person could safely return from war.

'I'll write to you when I arrive,' he promised.

Another whistle blew. One by one, train doors began to slam.

Daniel faced his father.

'You've turned into a fine man, Daniel. You make me proud every day.'

Daniel, overcome with emotion, thought of his goodbye letter; he'd have to change it now – and happily so. It occurred to him that he, too, was proud of his father. They embraced hurriedly.

'The train, Danny!' his mother said.

It had begun to pull away.

As Daniel hurried to it, his mother shoved a parcel into his hands. 'Cook wanted you to have some of her fruitcake and there are long johns and socks in there too in case you need them.'

Why this, of all things, this broke his heart, he did not understand. He threw his arms around her.

'Daniel the train!' Niall called.

He pulled himself away and ran.

In the carriage, he hurried to the window. Everyone he loved was on that platform. As the train began to steal him away from them, his father stood beside Maggie as if sending a message to his son. And though the lawman had changed, Daniel had no doubt that if he discovered her to be a rebel intent on rising he would take a very quick step away again. Daniel lowered the window, leaned out and waved. His heart soared as they all, in unison, waved back, Niall frantically. Slowly, though, their faces began to blur. It was starting all over again, the smudging of the people he loved. He could hardly bear it. He stared at Maggie until his eyes watered. And as she began to disappear from view, he prayed that something would happen to keep her safe – the arrest of the rebel leaders, Home Rule being granted early, something, anything, to keep her from fighting. He had done all he could. And failed.

forty-four

Maggie

Maggie arrived home from the train station to find Patrick waiting on the street outside her home. Her heart stopped, knowing that he would not come here if it were not urgent. Reaching him, she linked his arm and hurried him away.

'Is it on?' she whispered as they walked.

'This very Sunday! I came to tell you in person.' His face was alight. 'It's definite, Maggie.'

She stopped walking. Her hand touched her heart. Emotions swamped her – pride, excitement, fear – and relief that Daniel was out of Dublin.

'The arms shipment is due in the next twenty-four hours. Then it's set for Sunday. We'll all be out. The Volunteers. Na Fianna. The Citizen Army. Cumann na mBan. Thousands of us. Together we'll form the Irish Republican Army!'

'I can hardly believe it!'

'Don't tell a soul, Maggie, not even Tom. Only very few know the exact day. There'll be talk of a march of the Volunteers on Sunday. That'll be the signal.'

The symbolism hit Maggie; they would rise on Easter Sunday, the day that Jesus rose from the dead. 'What can I do?'

'Go home and rest for who knows how long we'll be out. But stand by for mobilisation. I'll try and bring the notice to you myself.'

'Do you not want me at Liberty Hall?'

He shook his head. 'There are too many there, already. Spend these last days with your family.'

They looked at each other, each of them knowing the significance of his words.

Walking through the front door, guilt poured into Maggie's heart like tar. These were most likely her last days with her family and she could give them no hint of that. She climbed the stairs. In their room, Lily slept. Maggie gazed at her and reminded herself of why she must put the fight before all else. Restless, she went back downstairs. She found her mother in the drawing room, at her desk, scribbling furiously. Maggie sat by the fire, watching her. She was everything to her– her mother, father, teacher and guide. How Maggie admired her, quietly raising them alone, quietly saving an orphan child, quietly accepting Maggie and Tom's will to fight for their country knowing she might lose them.

Frowning now at some miscalculation, she uttered her worst: 'Bloody, bloody.'

Maggie's heart swelled with love and sadness. And it occurred to her with sudden force that she had put her father's wishes before her mother's because he had died. There was no escaping it: she had let her mother down. For her father.

She went to her and wrapped her arms around her. 'You're the best mam in the world.' She kissed the top of her head and then, before the tears came, she said, 'I'll go up now. I'm tired.'

Her mother looked up and smiled. 'You have the right idea. I don't know why I insisted on dealing with this tonight. It's not as if the world is about to end.'

On Good Friday, Maggie went to Mass. She fasted and did

penance. She thought of heaven more than she would on a normal Good Friday. She treasured every moment with her family, noticed every little thing that Lily did or said. She laughed too loudly, tried too hard to be jolly and when she found her mother watching her, her stomach turned.

That evening, they had a backgammon tournament, the entire family. Maggie looked at Tom and realised that – somehow – he knew. Their eyes met. And in that gaze, they shared the words: 'How can we leave them?'

Saturday and Maggie was back at the church, this time to seek forgiveness for her sins and make her peace with God. The church was mobbed with men and boys also queuing for a clear conscience. If the British Army were to walk in now, they would surely suspect something.

Maggie took a seat at the edge of the last pew. One by one, she watched repenters, caps in hand, emerge from the confessional as though a weight had been lifted. They would not die sinners.

At last, her turn came but, as she rose, reality struck. She was about to take lives, break the worst commandment of all, intentionally, the following day. Forgiveness was impossible for sins yet to be committed. There would be no salvation here. She turned and stumbled from the church.

It was the slowest day of her life. With every passing minute, she grew more and more tense. She longed to say goodbye but could not. At last, as she was preparing for bed, she thought of a solution, a solution inspired by Danny. She sat at her desk.

Dearest Mam,

I have loved you with all my heart. I am sorry that I did not survive the insurrection but I have had the very best life. I would not change a day, a minute. Better a short and meaningful life than a long and miserable one. Go easy on yourself, Mam. You couldn't have stopped me if you'd tried. You did try! Always remember that. Even if you'd locked me up, I'd have got out!

You have been the best mother in the world. You have been more. You have been my father, my teacher and my heroine. And I am sorry that I could not stay alive for you.

Love Lily like two daughters in one. I hate, hate, hate to leave you both. I hate to leave you all.

I am sending you kisses from heaven. And always will.

All my love, Maggie

It was so hard to say goodbye forever. How had Danny done it? She wiped away her tears, placed the letter in an envelope and then took out a fresh sheet of notepaper.

My dear, sweet Lil,

I'm sorry for leaving you but I go knowing that you are a survivor. You are the strongest person I know. You have your whole life ahead of you. You can be whatever you want to be – a politician, an actress, anything. Make sure you study hard, though. I will not ask you to mind Mammy because I know that you have probably already begun! How lucky we were to have you come into our lives. How very lucky. Whenever you think of me, think of me with your mam beside me because that is where I'll be, looking down on you and blowing you kisses.

Goodbye dearest, dearest sister, all my love, Maggie

Lily sat bolt upright in bed.

'You're doing an awful lot of writing, Maggie.' She scratched her head and collapsed backwards, asleep again.

'Jesus,' Maggie whispered.

Dear David

How I have loved you. How you have lifted my soul, time and again. You are the silent, steady one of the family and I go so much easier knowing that you will be there for Mam and Lily – and Tom too, if he makes it. Though my choices were never yours, you have always trusted them and I am so grateful for that. I wish you a long and happy life, dearest brother.

Your loving sister, Maggie

Dear Tom

We put Ireland before our family. We had to. Now that you have survived you can make it up to them – for both of us. This is what I ask of you. I hope that our sacrifice has been worth it and that you are enjoying a new Irish Republic. How I would have loved to see it. Be happy, Tom. You've done enough now.

All my love, Maggie

And last, because it was the hardest, Danny.

Dearest Danny

Forgive me. But you of all people understand what it is to fight for what you believe in. I wish we could have been The Healys. I wanted it so badly and if there was any other way to make a difference, I would have taken it, believe me. I have loved you with all my heart. All. My. Heart. The hardest thing I have ever had to do is say goodbye to you. I pray that the war will be over soon and you will come home and find happiness and peace.

All my love always, Maggie

She knocked on David's door. He answered with his spectacles on and a finger stuck in a book, holding the page.

'Can I come in?' she whispered.

'Of course.' He glanced curiously at the letters in her hand as she entered.

She tapped at them awkwardly. 'I don't know how to say this, David, so I'll just say it. I have a letter for each of you – to be opened in the event of my death.'

His fist went to his mouth; he looked like he was in pain. 'It's happening.'

She nodded.

'When?'

'You can't tell a soul, David.'

'I know. Just tell me.'

She wrapped her arms around herself. 'Tomorrow.'

'Fuck.' It was the first curse of his life. 'Sorry,' he said quickly.

'Keep them out of the city, David.'

'I won't let them out of the house. I don't want you to spend one second worrying about any of us. Only watch your own back. All right?' Tears welled. 'They won't go anywhere.'

'Thank you,' she whispered.

A tear fell and he turned quickly to clear it.

'I'm sorry, David.'

He shook his head and then turned back. 'Had I the courage, I'd be fighting alongside you. I want you to know that.'

'And I want *you* to know that without you here with Mam and Lily I don't know how I *could* go out tomorrow.' She thrust the letters into his hands as tears of her own threatened. 'Now, don't go opening yours unless you have to – we don't want you getting a swelled head.'

But he did not smile. 'Promise me something. Promise me you won't do anything heroic.'

'If James Connolly has taught us anything, he has taught us that.'

'You have to come home to us, Maggie. After Father, it would kill Mam to lose you or Tom. I suppose he's in the same boat?'

She nodded.

He sighed deeply. 'Can I do anything at all to help?'

'You're already doing it.'

'I'll be praying like the pope.'

She smiled. 'Then pray for a miracle.'

Sleep escaped her. She thought of all the people she knew who faced death – Tom, Patrick, all the boys in Na Fianna, Madame, James Connolly, Con Colbert, Michael Collins. How many were saying goodbye to loved ones at that very moment? Maggie thought of men and women leaving children behind. It was they who would be making the greatest sacrifice. She thought of Danny and prayed that he would not be called up. She would never forgive herself.

She gazed across at Lily, who was more than a sister; she was a symbol. A moonbeam fell across her delicate features and she looked to Maggie like an angel that had come to show her the way.

She was doing the right thing. She knew it so strongly in her heart.

On Easter Sunday, she rose early, her stomach tight, her heart already beating too fast. She knelt by the side of the bed.

'Dear Lord, You know what I am about to do. Forgive me. Amen.'

She chose civilian clothes, a dress and coat that were dark and respectable. In the pocket of the coat, she placed the armband of the Red Cross. She checked her reflection. She did not look like a rebel. It was how it should be. She stood tall. The day of her dreams had finally come. She would *not* fear it.

She turned and went downstairs.

Tom, in full military uniform, was standing by the breakfast table with the newspaper up to his nose, frowning as he read. Behind him, his mother stole a worried glance at him. Then she looked at Maggie as if to say, 'What's going on?'

Tom dropped the newspaper onto the table, grabbed a slice of toast and left.

Maggie lunged for the paper. Her eyes scanned the front page. Then there it was, the source of her brother's rapid departure – an announcement by Eoin MacNeill, the leader of the Volunteers, calling off the march.

'What is it?' her mother asked in concern.

'I don't know.' Maggie did not understand. Was it just the Volunteers that would not be rising or was the entire insurrection being called off? If so, why? And would the Citizen Army go out alone anyway, as James Connolly had always insisted they would? Maggie remembered the oath she had taken. If called upon, she would rise – to certain annihilation. She had meant it then. She meant it now. If they did not rise now they never would.

And yet she could do nothing but wait to hear from Patrick.

To put her mother's mind at ease, she laid aside the newspaper, sat at the table and, as calmly as she could, ate breakfast.

David arrived down, pale and silent. He kept stealing glances at Maggie.

'What is wrong with everyone today?' their mother asked.

'Where's Tom?' David asked.

'Shot off like a hare after reading the newspaper,' their mother said.

David reached for it.

'Not at the table.'

He got up from the table and read. He looked at Maggie as if to say, 'What am I looking for?'

She shrugged.

'Maggie what's going on?' her mother demanded.

'I honestly don't know, Mam.' It wasn't a lie.

Lily arrived down, singing. Maggie wanted to hug her.

An hour later, David, Lily and their mother readied themselves for Mass. Lily looked at Maggie expectantly.

'Hurry up, Maggie. You'll be late.'

'I'll go later,' she said. She could not miss Patrick – if Patrick was indeed coming. Why had Tom not said a word to her? Was he as confused as she was?

'I'll wait with you,' Lily said cheerfully.

'No, Lily.'

Maggie's mother looked at her questioningly.

David put his hand out to Lily. 'Come on, Lil,' he said brightly. 'Maggie will go later.'

Lily looked at Maggie. 'Will you be all right without me?'

Maggie smiled. 'Give me a hug and I'll be grand.'

Maggie held her tightly, closing her eyes and inhaling deeply. At last, she let Lily go. She smiled widely and pressed her sister's nose. 'Say a prayer for me.'

'I always do, Maggie.'

'I love you, Lil. You're the best sister in the whole wide world and you have changed my life.'

Maggie remembered her mother and glanced up. Her hand was covering her mouth.

'I'm sorry,' Maggie said with her eyes. She got up and threw her arms around her, not knowing if she would see her in an hour or never again.

Her mother clung to her and when she let her go, there were tears in her eyes. 'There's nothing I can say, is there?'

'No, Mam,' Maggie whispered.

She embraced her fiercely then. 'I love you, Maggie Mae.'

'I love you too, Mam.' Maggie pressed herself into her, fighting a surge of tears.

She stood at the door, watching them go. At the gate, they turned and waved.

'It's Easter Sunday, Maggie,' Lily called. 'You should be wearing something happier.'

Maggie pressed her lips together and waved ferociously. Then she ran inside before they could see her cry. In the drawing room, she watched from the window till they were out of sight. A country could ask an awful lot of a person.

Half an hour later, Maggie was pacing the empty house when there was an urgent banging at the door. She ran to it.

It was Patrick.

She pulled him inside. 'What's happening? Is it off?'

'No one knows. The arms shipment was intercepted and that damned fool MacNeill got cold feet.'

'Will the Citizen Army rise alone?'

'I can't imagine Connolly sitting on his hands, can you? Here's your mobilisation paper.' He handed it to her. 'We're all to be at Liberty Hall by three o'clock today.'

'To rise?'

'Only to be there, for now. It's chaos, Maggie. I'd better go. I've a pile of these to deliver. I don't know how I'll get back in to Liberty Hall by three.'

'Give some to me. I'll deliver them.'

'Would you?' he asked in relief.

'Rather that than stay here going out of my mind.'

'Be careful. If they get a whiff of what we're up to, we're doomed.'

And then he was gone.

Maggie left a note for her mother saying that she would be back shortly. Outside, she leapt onto her bicycle and was off.

It was a glorious day. Church bells called people to prayer while she tore around the city she knew and loved so well, standing at doors that opened to confused, enquiring faces. She left them no less confused. It was the same message for everyone: be at Liberty Hall by three.

Maggie arrived home at one.

'Did you get Mass?' Lily asked.

She grimaced. 'I've been busy, Lil. I'll say a prayer.'

Lily looked at her like she was committing sacrilege. 'Mind that you do.'

Despite everything, Maggie laughed.

'I'm serious,' Lily said wagging a finger.

'You are seriously wonderful. That's what you are.' She lifted her up and swirled her around.

Lily's smile could have lit up Dublin Castle.

Cycling to Liberty Hall for three, the warm sun on Maggie's back felt like an omen. Approaching the quays, her heart soared at the banner across its facade, proclaiming, 'We Serve Neither King Nor Kaiser'.

Inside, the place was alive. At last, she found Patrick.

'Well?' she demanded.

'We're to march.'

'You mean fight?'

'No. March. But if it comes to a fight, we'll fight.'

They hurried to arm themselves.

Shortly after, a bugle sounded and they were off.

Heads high, they marched the streets of Dublin, men and women who shared a dream. Nearing Dublin Castle, tension rose. It was as if the world was holding its breath to see if a fight would break out. Maggie imagined rifles pointed at their heads. It would not make much of a statement to be cut down here in the briefest of battles. She put one foot in front of the other and reminded herself to breathe. That was all she could do. Keep going. Her shoulders felt like they would snap with tension. Her whole body was ready to spring into action. Her heart was a runaway train. And she was perspiring like a man.

Then, magically, they were beyond immediate danger, out of sight and shot of the Castle. Maggie's shoulders fell in relief – not that there wouldn't be a fight but that there would be a better one.

Returning to Liberty Hall, guards were posted at every window, door, stairway and corridor. Such was their readiness for battle that, should the British Army attempt a search, the fight would begin. A large unit of men, Patrick included, was ordered to remain at Liberty Hall, in readiness. Maggie was instructed to go home and return at eight the following morning.

forty-five

Maggie

Maggie stole from the house before anyone was up – anyone except Tom, who she had not seen since he stormed out the previous day. She wondered where he was and if it meant that the Volunteers would be rising after all.

The streets were deserted as she made her way to Liberty Hall, the citizens of Dublin taking advantage of the bank holiday. Nearing the quays, she saw men converging on the rebel base from all directions and her heart soared with pride.

Inside, they were ordered to attention and their numbers counted. Then, as their names were called out, they fell into line behind their assigned captains. Patrick was under Seán Connolly, who would be leading the march on Dublin Castle. Maggie was assigned to the St Stephen's Green garrison, under Michael Mallin. She looked at Patrick with regret; she had always believed that they would fight side by side. He winked as if they were preparing for a day at the races. And still Maggie worried that the Citizen Army would be rising alone. If so, they would be annihilated.

As they awaited orders, unfamiliar men with an air of authority began to arrive at Liberty Hall. They were immediately ushered upstairs to meet with James Connolly.

Patrick looked at Maggie with fire in his eyes. 'We may not be rising alone, after all.'

'Who are they?' she whispered.

'The Military Council of the IRB. Pádraic Pearse, the teacher. The poet, Joseph Plunkett. The shopkeeper, Tom Clarke.'

She squinted at him. '*These* are rebel leaders?'

'Don't let appearances fool you, Maggie.'

'You said Plunkett. Is it the same Plunkett who was harbouring rebels?'

He nodded. 'It's the count's son.'

'Is he unwell?' Despite his flamboyant dress, he looked incredibly thin and pale and had had to be helped up the stairs by Michael Collins.

'He was operated on last week for consumption. Discharged himself. He was due to be married this week but has put it off for the insurrection.'

Duty asked so much of a person, Maggie was thinking when Madame burst into Liberty Hall in a khaki shirt and breeches. She took the steps two at a time, an automatic hanging from one side of her cartridge belt, a Mauser the other. On her head was a black hat with a heavy plume of feathers.

'Good day for a Rising!' she called.

At last, the leaders emerged together in great spirits. A united force would rise, after all!

James Connolly began to distribute weapons. Maggie noticed in horror that he was giving revolvers to women to be used as a 'last resort'.

When he presented her with a revolver, she raised her chin. 'I'll take a Lee Enfield, too, Commandant Connolly, seeing as we're all equal and I'm one of the best shots you've got.'

A smile crept across his face. Then he called on the quartermaster to bring a Lee Enfield. Presenting it to her, though, Connolly frowned. 'Remember all that I said about cover.'

'I would never forget it.' Neither would she forget him – whatever lay ahead.

She stepped out of the line and began to examine her gun.

'Take a look at this,' Patrick said, holding out a sheet of paper.

'What is it?' she asked impatiently. It was time to fight, not read.

'The Proclamation of the new republic, printed by the hundreds to be distributed to the citizens of our fine nation so that they know what we're about.'

Maggie took it eagerly. She read of a new republic with equal rights for all, where happiness and prosperity would be pursued for the entire nation. She looked up at Patrick, her eyes glassy. 'Here's an ideal worth dying for.'

'We're making history, Maggie,' he said more reverently than she had ever heard him speak.

When the fall-in was finally sounded, Maggie and Patrick looked at each other. He surprised her, then, with a sudden, clumsy embrace. He pulled back, holding on to her arms and looking into her eyes.

'Mind yourself,' he said.

She felt a sudden rush of affection for him. 'You be careful, Patrick Shanahan.'

'Now *why* would I be careful when I can be dangerous?' He grinned.

She frowned. 'Heroics will get you killed. You know that.'

He put a hand on her shoulder. He looked as if he was going to say something important. Then he simply winked at her. 'See you on the other side.'

At the order, they fell into their separate battalions. And as Maggie began to march out into the sun, from the mouth of James Connolly, she heard the muttered words, 'We are going out to be slaughtered.'

forty-six

Maggie
Easter Monday, 1916

The bugle sounded. Maggie's heart leapt with excitement and nerves. So many times she had marched in preparation for this day. Taking her first step, now, arms swinging, she filled her lungs with air. This was it.

Reaching O'Connell Bridge, a large unit, including rebel leaders, Connolly, Pearse and Plunkett, turned right onto Sackville Street, headed for the headquarters of the new Irish Republican Army, the General Post Office.

Maggie's unit was ordered over the sparkling Liffey and up Grafton Street. The few people who were out took no notice, well used to the sight of parading rebels. The odd child stopped and waved. And still, Volunteers continued to arrive and join the ranks.

'Go home and stop playing soldiers,' one policeman shouted, while barefooted newsboys distributed the Proclamation.

On St Stephen's Green, Dubliners were enjoying the lazy sunshine. Couples strolled in quiet conversation while nannies and their little charges fed the ducks.

'Clear the park,' Commandant Mallin ordered.

But when the rebels asked the people to leave, they would not believe that a revolution was taking place. Weapons had to be produced.

A cacophony of shots rang out from the direction of Dublin Castle. Maggie turned automatically to the sound, thinking of Patrick. She prayed, not just for him but also for his mother; the woman had suffered enough.

Cleared of civilians at last, the park was locked. Orders went out for trenches to be dug inside the railings. Maggie's thoughts turned to Gallipoli. And Daniel. But such thoughts were for another day. She was ordered to stand guard at one of the entrances to the Green. As she was marching to take up her position, Madame arrived by motorcar, waving in a state of high excitement.

'The City Hall has been taken by Seán Connolly and his men!'

Maggie touched her heart in relief as a great cheer went up.

Madame leapt from the car and hurried into the Green as though late for a garden party.

Maggie took up her post opposite a rebel she did not know.

'Do you want to get yourself shot?' he warned onlookers, who were peering in through the railings.

They turned and, without urgency, began to leave.

One looked back. 'Go on off and fight the Germans. Make yourselves useful.'

Maggie's colleague grinned at her. 'You wouldn't want to be looking for respect.'

Maggie smiled but her stomach was churning, reminded of all that Danny had gone through in the name of Home Rule – Danny and so many thousands of others. But Home Rule was a pup being sold by the British. They needed nothing short of a republic. And that was the truth of it.

Outside the Green, rebel units were setting up barricades using carts, bicycles, furniture, whatever they could get their hands on. They halted motorcars and then drove them into the barricades. They stopped a tram, ordered the passengers to disembark and then turned the vehicle into a barricade. Maggie wondered how long they could hold off the British Army.

'Halt,' barked her companion.

She turned to see a constable trying to gain entry.

'Halt, I say.'

He rattled at the lock.

The sentry lifted his gun and took aim. Still, the policeman did not retreat.

'I *will* shoot. So help me I *will* shoot.'

Maggie, fearing that his gun might accidentally discharge, raised hers too in the hope that it would intimidate the policeman into a retreat.

He stood his ground.

'You there!'

Maggie turned and breathed out in relief. Madame was approaching at a clip. If anyone could make the constable see sense it was she. Maggie was turning back to face the policeman when three shots rang out. He crumpled to the ground. Maggie swiveled around to see who had fired.

'I got him!' Madame exclaimed, as though talking of a fox.

Someone was shaking her hand. Had she *really* fired?

Maggie turned back to see the young man lying in his own blood on the other side of the gate. Her first instinct was to help. Then she heard running and looked up. A group of civilians was rushing to his aid. The shine on his shoes seemed so particularly sad. Had he polished them that morning before going on duty? Had his wife done it for him? A sister, mother? He was a policeman but he was also Irish, unarmed, and only doing his job.

'You ought to be ashamed of yourself.'

Maggie looked up into the eyes of a young civilian glaring at her as if she had pulled the trigger. She was filled with a sudden, overwhelming shame. This was not how she had imagined revolution.

forty-seven

Daniel
Easter Monday 1916

As darkness fell, Daniel waited with hundreds of soldiers to board trains that would steam their way to Dublin from the Curragh Camp. All afternoon, it had been organised chaos as troops, weapons and ammunition were prepared for battle. Not believing that the day had come, he was silent.

His fellow officers were not.

'I'll enjoy putting down every last one of those fools.'

'What have we been doing in France, only risking our lives for this country?'

'They may be fools but they picked their day well. With half the army on leave, Lord knows how long it will take to call everyone back to barracks from all around the country, assemble them into battalions and get them up to Dublin.'

Daniel envied them the simplicity of their thoughts. To him, the rebels were boys he'd drilled with, sang with, laughed with, cursed with, grown up with. He understood the honour of their cause. How easily they would fire on British Army soldiers, knowing them only as the enemy, not as men they had shared trenches with in Gallipoli and Salonika, those God-forsaken places where Irishmen fought alongside Englishmen for the same reason.

Sweet Jesus, how had it come to this? How could he fire

blindly at a sniper that he might have learned to shoot alongside, a sniper that might only be a boy of twelve or thirteen, fired up with a passion that had been stoked up within him in the Dublin mountains? How could he fire into a building (for they would be in buildings; that is how they would fight) knowing that they could be women, children, friends, *Maggie*?

He stubbed out his cigarette. He could not fight his own people. And yet if he did not, he would be shot for treason. Everything was smudged, ridiculous almost. Here he was, expected to fight with the British against the Irish, who were armed with weapons from Germany, their mutual enemy in the Great War. One by one, he looked at the men, *his* men. Who could he trust to do their duty? And what did it matter when he could not trust himself? Only one thing mattered. Maggie. He did not know how he would find her, let alone protect her, but he would die trying.

forty-eight

Maggie
Easter Monday Night, 1916

As night fell, Maggie climbed down into one of the trenches that had been dug at the perimeter of the Green. Being female, she had had to argue herself into that position. Luckily, Madame had seen her shoot. Now, she stored her Lee Enfield and settled down on a bed of earth. She inhaled the smell of freshly dug soil and wondered if Daniel had smelt the same in the trenches of Gallipoli. It was cold and a light mist lingered. She curled up and rubbed her arms. The lad beside her took off his jacket and offered it to her. She looked at him in his shirtsleeves.

'I'm grand,' she lied.

'Sure, take it anyways.'

'No. Honestly, I'm grand.'

He held it out to her. 'Go on. You're doing me a favour. I'm too warm, altogether.'

She smiled and took it with thanks.

'It's great, isn't it?' he said, wistfully looking around him.

She smiled back. 'It is.'

And then, like a lark, he burst into song. *Wrap the Green Flag Around Me, Boys* carried Maggie back to starry nights in the mountains and dreams of freedom. In the darkness, voices rose from all around the Green. If she lived, she would remember this moment forever.

She jolted awake in the thick of night to the sound of machine-gun fire. Bits of clay were falling in on her.

'Stand to! Stand to!' came shouted orders from across the Green.

The trench came alive with curses and fumbling. Maggie got to her knees and felt for her Lee Enfield. Bullets sprayed the soil in front of the trench, showering them with earth. Beside her, her friend was up, aiming at The Shelbourne Hotel. A great plume of fire shot from the barrel of his Mauser, illuminating him.

'Drop down!' Maggie called.

But it was too late. Already, bullets were tearing into him, flinging him back. Maggie scrambled to his aid. But when she reached him, lifeless eyes stared up at her as if in surprise. Anger ripped through her but she did not stand up to fire. She waited. Only when the machine-gun fire had moved to the far end of the trench did she raise her head. Peering up at the windows of the Shelbourne to locate the shooter, she took aim, fired and dropped down. The rat-a-tat-tat halted. But seconds later, it took up again as the gunner was replaced. From positions all over the Green, shots were being returned. Then came a scream.

It was *so hard* to stay down. Only by reminding herself of David's words about what her death would do to their mother, did she manage it. As soon as the bullets had passed, she was up again, picking her man and firing. The soil in front of her exploded as a second machine gun started up. She dived to the bottom of the trench, chest rising and falling, breath ragged. One thing was clear, ducking about in holes, they proved no match for machine-gun fire from a height.

A whistle blew ordering a retreat. Maggie crawled to her dead comrade, closed his eyes, joined his hands and prayed for his soul. Then she took his gun and ammunition to prevent them from falling into enemy hands.

Crouched but ready, she waited for a break in fire, then she was up and running, others too.

Firing resumed in a sudden burst and she ducked behind a tree. She pressed herself against it as bullets tore at the bark. Flashes of light over to the right revealed another British Army unit that had taken up position in the United Services Club. It was Daniel's father's club and a reminder that the rich would always see themselves as part of the British Empire.

She waited what seemed like an age for the next lull. The minute it came, she raced to the bridge that crossed the pond. Halfway across, the firing began again and she dived to the ground as bullets whizzed past, chipping off pieces of masonry above her head.

At last, she reached the statue of Lord Ardilaun, which was providing cover for a large group of rebels attempting to leave the Green. At every break in fire, two or three would dash out across the road, down York Street and in through the side entrance of the Royal College of Surgeons. Rebels had taken up position on the roof of the college to draw fire from the soldiers in the United Services Club so that their comrades could make the three-hundred-yard dash safely.

A fresh three men ran out onto the road. Almost immediately, they came under fire. One fell. He lay motionless as the others kept going. Bullets sprayed the ground and the facade of the college. Finally, the firing ceased. The young man sprang to his feet and raced to safety.

'Jesus, Mary and Joseph,' Maggie said in relief.

Commandant Mallin barked a brief laugh, then pointed at Maggie and two other rebels. 'Make ready.' He looked out onto the street. 'Go!'

Maggie shot out, legs and arms pumping, fearing a bullet at any moment. She raced onto York Street and came to an immediate halt. An angry mob stood facing them.

'Get off of our streets,' one ordered, slapping an iron bar into his palm.

One of Maggie's comrades stepped forward. 'Go on home, now,' he said with calm authority. 'This is not your fight.'

'Our boys are over in France risking their lives for this country. So it *is* our fight.'

'And look at *you*,' a woman spat at Maggie, 'with your head uncovered, you floozy. You should be ashamed of yourself.'

She ran at Maggie, who reacted by reflex, raising the butt of her weapon and bringing it down on the woman's shoulder. She fell to the ground with a surprised yelp. The crowd surged.

'Run!' someone called from the door of the college, opening it wide.

They raced to it and through. It was immediately slammed shut and barricaded behind them. A pounding followed.

'Such fury!' one man said.

'What has them so exercised?' someone asked.

'They're going to lose their separation allowance due to the rising.'

'Separation allowance?'

'The money they get from the British Army for their boys being overseas.'

'Ah.'

Maggie looked towards the door. She felt as though she had butted Danny himself with that gun. Their anger was about more than the allowance. It was about betrayal.

Maggie was amongst those instructed to rest. But she could not rest. She wandered from room to room of the college where Daniel would have been studying medicine were it not for the war. It was cold and dark and the rooms smelled of formaldehyde. Floating human eyes stared out from jars. There were other organs – stomachs, hearts, all of them coldly, methodically labelled. How many rooms would it take to hold all of the organs that could have been collected from Gallipoli? How many people would die in the rising? And why did anyone, at all, have to die for the basic right to freedom?

forty-nine

Daniel
Easter Tuesday Morning, 1916

It was the early hours of Tuesday morning. At Kingsbridge Station, train after train coughed up its military load. Hundreds of men shifted nervously, awaiting orders. At the entrance to the station, a horse whinnied and pawed the ground, picking up on the tension. Daniel wondered how he might slip away. Given the situation, they would be watching for deserters. If he were caught he would be arrested and no good to her then.

At last, they began to march along the quays on the opposite side of the river to where Daniel had set out on with the Pals, a year earlier, almost to the day. The sound of sniper fire from all across the city jolted him back to Gallipoli. His senses heightened, his shoulders rose. He felt that he could even smell the place but that was madness.

As they advanced, they came under sniper fire from a building across the river. A man fell.

'Return fire,' their Commanding Officer ordered.

They turned, lowered themselves onto one knee and opened fire. Daniel trained his field glasses on the windows of the building but he could not see her. He could not see anyone. They were too smart for that.

Rebel fire had ceased.

Ordered up side streets and alleyways to avoid further attack, they finally approached the rear of Dublin Castle, which was now back in the hands of the British Army. After a brief officers' meeting, it was decided to support troops already advancing on the City Hall.

As they fell in, Daniel glanced up at the copper dome of that splendid building. Flashes of light from the rooftop preceded echoing sound. Daniel prayed that she was not there. The rebels did not stand a chance against so many troops. And she would never surrender.

A whistle blew. Daniel took a deep breath and advanced. At the gates of Dublin Castle, they came under fire from snipers in nearby buildings. They were ordered forward at a trot. Quickly, they joined forces with the troops on the ground and stormed the City Hall, pouring in through the enormous windows, glass already broken by the rebels, shattering underfoot as they landed.

Female screams filled the air.

'Hold fire,' Daniel shouted. 'Hold fire.'

'Drop your weapons!' his CO ordered as the room was plunged into light.

Arms were raised, rebels surrendering without a fight. Daniel scanned faces for Maggie's. But he did not find her amongst the unarmed women who had been tending to the wounded. Neither did he find her amongst the wounded. But he recognised a face. It was one of the girls that he had spent a happy afternoon with, peeling potatoes. He approached. Though he guessed her to be a rebel, he asked aloud as though she were a prisoner of the rebels, 'Have you been harmed?' Under his breath, he added, 'Maggie Gilligan, where is she?'

The girl's eyes showed, at first, surprise, then recognition. 'Not here. But Patrick Shanahan is upstairs and he'll know.'

'Thank you.' Then, under his breath, he added, 'Take care.'

The ground floor had been taken without a fight. Already, the CO was preparing his men to advance on two spiral staircases that led to the next level. With Patrick upstairs, there would be no surrender. How could Daniel get up to him before the columns of already advancing men? How could he find her? What could he do?

Terrific fire showered down on the men advancing on the stairwells. Casualties were heavy. The CO ordered an immediate retreat. He ran a hand over his mouth.

'I have an idea, sir,' Daniel said.

'I'd like to hear it, Healy,' he said doubtfully.

'Let me advance alone. I might be able to negotiate them down.'

He raised a cynical eyebrow. 'And *how* might you do that, Sergeant?'

'I would advance, unarmed, speaking in Irish, advising them that they're surrounded and outnumbered and that the only reasonable option is surrender.'

'These are not reasonable men.'

'They gave up easily enough down here, sir.'

'Because they had women prisoners.'

'How many men will we lose storming the stairwells?'

The CO surveyed the staircases once more. Moments passed. At length, he looked at Daniel. His eyes narrowed. 'How is it that you speak the Irish language?' he asked with suspicion.

'The Gaelic League, sir. It's a cultural organisation.'

He eyed Daniel closely. 'I can trust you, Healy, can't I?'

'Yes, sir.'

'At the first shot, we'll be up behind you.'

'Yes sir.' He handed over his weapons, cap and jacket, then advanced with arms raised. Approaching the staircase, a shot pinged off the metal bannister. Behind him he heard the order, 'Shoulder to arms.'

He called up, in Irish. 'Don't shoot! I'm unarmed! I'm searching for my wife, Maggie Gilligan. She's with the Citizen Army.' He hoped to God that Patrick was up there, that none of the soldiers behind him could speak Irish or, that if they could, they would be sympathetic. He awaited a shot from above. And behind. He took another step.

'Cease fire!' a voice ordered in Irish. Daniel recognised it as Patrick's.

Relieved, he looked up but the place was in darkness.

'Allow him up but watch that stairway behind him,' Patrick continued in Irish.

Daniel did not trust him. But he had no other option. Reaching the top of the steps, he halted, squinting into the darkness. He could feel rifles trained upon him. A shot rang out and he ducked. He heard laughter.

'It's only the Brits firing in through the window and missing as usual,' Patrick said.

More shots followed, hitting off the ceiling, shattering chandeliers but injuring no one because of the angle of fire.

'Your *wife*?' Patrick asked.

'I was being concise, under the circumstances.' Daniel turned to Patrick's voice and saw the silhouette of a man, a soldier. How they'd changed. 'It's good to see you, Patrick.'

'Surrender or join us, that's your choice.' Patrick's voice was cold.

'Where is she?'

After a long pause, he said, as though for old times' sake. 'At the Stephen's Green garrison.'

Daniel turned and began to walk towards the stairs.

'Halt!' Patrick shouted. 'Or I'll shoot. And trust me, Danny, I will.'

Daniel turned to face him. 'I must find her, Patrick; she's all that matters to me.'

'She's where she wants to be, doing what she wants to do, fighting for her country – as you ought to be.'

'I'll join you as soon as I find her.' He did not, in truth, know what he would do when he found her – if he made it to Stephen's Green without getting his head blown off – by either side.

'Why should I trust a British Army soldier?' Patrick asked.

'I joined for one reason only – to get Home Rule so that she wouldn't have to fight.'

After a pause, he said, 'If she knew that, she'd kill you herself.'

'I don't doubt it.' Daniel looked at him, appealing to the friend he once was. 'Patrick, if I'm to die today, let me die alongside her, fighting for Ireland. Let me go to her now.'

'How will you get past your friends, down there?'

'Leave that to me.'

In the darkness, he heard a sigh. 'I'm a fool.'

'I'm the fool.'

'Take care of her, won't you? Who would have guessed that first day we met how fond of her I would grow?'

Daniel heard in those words the affection Patrick had for her, perhaps more than affection. If so, how could Daniel blame him? 'Patrick, the place is surrounded.'

'Don't I know it?' He smiled.

'You should surrender.'

He gave Daniel a look. 'Go on now before I change my mind.'

Daniel stepped forward and offered his hand. They shook. Then Daniel made for the stairs. Reaching it, he turned. 'Godspeed.'

'And you.'

Hearing footsteps on the stairs, Daniel looked down. Advancing troops had their rifles drawn, ready to shoot. Daniel was in their direct line of fire. Patrick threw him a revolver. On reflex, he caught it. His eyes met those of his commanding officer who, seeing the gun in Daniel's hand, took aim and fired. Daniel was reeling back before he heard the shot. Light and sound erupted all around him. He thought of Patrick. He thought of Maggie. Then he thought no more.

fifty

Maggie was ordered to rebel headquarters with a dispatch. Having hidden it in her boot, she covered her dress (muddied and torn from the trench) with a Red Cross apron. She left her coat open and donned the armband.

She approached the exit at the rear of the college, praying that British Army rifles were not, at that very moment, trained upon it. She took a deep breath, then opened the door and instantly raised both arms. To her relief, the street was empty. She took off, staying in close to the buildings, alert for signs of danger and careful to avoid broken glass and debris that littered the streets.

Soon, she reached Dame Street. Looking to her right, she saw a sandbagged, heavily defended Trinity College where a year ago the Pals had received that tremendous send-off. Turning to her left, she gasped. Her hand went to her mouth. British Army troops were herding rebels out of the City Hall at gunpoint. It had fallen!

Stunned, she stared, straining to see Patrick. It occurred to her then that she would not see him. He would never have surrendered. She prayed that he was wounded. It was the only way he could still be alive.

'Halt!' a voice barked behind her.

Already halted, she slowly turned. Two British Army soldiers had their rifles trained upon her. They looked young and nervous, a dangerous combination. She felt for her revolver, cold inside her hand muff. She thought of the dispatch in her boot and how valuable it would be to the enemy. She would not let them get it.

'Where are you headed and what is your business?' the smaller of the two demanded.

'I have been ordered to the Rotunda Hospital for medical supplies.' She indicated her armband and, with a flick of her coat, the apron.

The men exchanged a glance. The taller of the two looked like Daniel.

'You're with the Royal Dublin Fusiliers!' she exclaimed. 'My fiancé, Daniel Healy, is with the Pals. He served in Gallipoli and Salonika. He's at the Curragh Camp now.' She felt a stab of guilt, using him to get out of this situation. At the same time, she knew that he would want her safe.

'I doubt that he is at The Curragh or any camp,' the short one said.

Her eyes widened. 'What do you mean?'

'Everyone has been called up,' he said.

'Not the wounded, though? He's not yet fully recovered!'

'If he can stand on two legs and hold a gun, he'll be here in Dublin. I can guarantee you that.'

Maggie swayed.

The other lad gripped her arm. 'Don't be worrying,' he said, glaring at his colleague. 'The rebels are entirely outnumbered. Our men are pouring into the city in their thousands. More are on their way from England. Very soon there won't be a rebel left standing in this city. Your fiancé will be grand altogether.'

'I must get to the Rotunda,' she uttered.

'It's far too dangerous for a young woman to be out on the streets.'

'I have my orders.'

'Well, whoever gave them to you ought to be shot. Do your business and refuse to go back out. Your life depends upon it.'

She nodded. 'I will. Thank you.'

The other Private softened. 'And I wouldn't be going down Sackville Street or anywhere near the General Post Office.' He looked at his colleague. 'Perhaps we ought to escort her.'

'No, no,' Maggie rushed. 'You, too, have your orders. I know a back way. My aunt lives down around there.'

'All right but once you reach the Rotunda stay put. It'll get worse before it gets better.'

'I will. Thank you.'

She hurried across Dame Street and immediately down one of the cobblestoned alleyways that led to the river.

Reaching the quay, she made for the Ha'penny Bridge only to see a crossing civilian come under fire. She looked right to O'Connell Bridge. It was even more exposed. Removing her coat to ensure her Red Cross apron was on full display, she took a deep breath and left the protection of the shadows. She walked smartly towards the Ha'penny Bridge where she had once witnessed a slaughter so appalling that she had become a rebel.

She had almost crossed without incident when she was startled by the sound of smashing glass. Up ahead, on the quay, a hoard of women and children had broken a shop window. Now, they swarmed in through the resulting hole. In under a minute, they began to pour out again, their arms laden with looted goods. Two children fought over something too small for Maggie to see. Then flames came lapping out through the shattered glass.

Reaching the quay, Maggie disappeared up back streets she knew like old friends. A woman scuttled past, a bunch of bananas poking out from under a rough shawl. Two men pushed a piano along the pavement. It was as though she had stepped into a nightmare.

At last, she arrived at the back of the General Post Office. There, suddenly, was James Connolly. Despite his lectures on street fighting, he was out in full view not taking cover but rallying his troops as though unafraid of bullet or enemy.

He spied her then and hurried her inside rebel headquarters.

She rooted for the dispatch but her hands were shaking. 'I'm sorry,' she said.

'Take your time, Maggie. Catch your breath. How is it out there?'

She looked up, breathless. 'The City Hall has been taken!'

He nodded. 'We heard.'

'On the quays, people are looting! It's as if the city has gone mad.'

He looked sad. 'They're looting on Sackville Street too. There's no stopping them. We tried.'

She found the dispatch and handed it to him without delay. 'From Commandant Mallin.'

He read in haste, frowning in concentration. He tucked the note into a pocket of his uniform.

'Thank you, Maggie. You've done well.' He ushered her into a great room at the front of the building. Rebels manned windows barricaded by piles of weighty ledgers. One had threaded rosary beads through fingers that held his weapon. Commandant Pearse was walking about, reading words of encouragement to the men. Maggie imagined him at the head of a classroom. She wondered if he had taught Tom or David. Then she scanned the room urgently for Tom. Behind Pearse, Michael Collins was rolling his eyes as if to say, 'Ireland would be better served by bullets than words'.

James Connolly turned to Maggie. 'Go on upstairs to the canteen and have yourself some food and rest. I'll have another dispatch ready for you shortly.'

'Yes, sir.'

Upstairs, a chef was preparing food with the help of British Army soldiers being held captive. Maggie's eyes fell upon a whole salmon, laid out like a work of art. She remembered Lily's favourite story – and her own. On a whim, she touched the edge of the fish with a thumb, then slipped it into her mouth. She glanced up to find the chef looking at her.

'You got there before me,' he said with a smile.

She smiled back. They were ordinary people. They were all just ordinary people who wanted fairness.

Maggie scanned the canteen for Tom but there was no sign of him. Two men in Volunteer uniforms were dining at a table. Maggie approached them with her tray.

'Would you mind if I joined you?' she asked.

They looked up in surprise. 'We'd be delighted,' they said together.

'Are you with Cumann na mBan?' one asked.

'Citizen Army,' she said.

They raised their eyebrows. 'Fair dues.'

'Would either of you boys know a Tom Gilligan by any chance?'

They looked at each other.

'Would we *know* a Tom Gilligan?' one asked the other.

Then they laughed again like a comedy duo.

'*Anyone* in the Volunteers would know Tom Gilligan. He's one of our best.'

'Where is he garrisoned?' she rushed.

Two hands fell heavy on her shoulders. She jumped and swiveled around.

'Tom!' She leapt up and threw herself at him.

He laughed, looking more alive and happy than she had ever seen him. And bigger too. Gigantic.

'I'm so glad to see you!' she said with such relief.

'And you. How are you, Maggie?'

'Better now. I was hoping I'd get to see you and say a proper goodbye.'

'We won't be needing goodbyes, Maggie Mae.' He winked.

'Another of your women, Gilligan?' one of two comedians asked.

It occurred to Maggie that there was so much she did not know about her brother.

'This is my sister, McCarthy. Show some respect.'

'*Women*, no less?' Maggie teased him.

'Dreamers, those two. Here let me get some food and I'll join you.'

Less than a minute later, he was back with a tray of food. He looked down at his salmon then up at Maggie. 'I'm hoping it'll give me some brains.'

'God knows you need them, Gilligan,' one of the duo said.

Maggie marvelled at how normal everything seemed right in the middle of a revolution.

'Where are you garrisoned, Maggie?' Tom asked.

'Stephen's Green but now the College of Surgeons.'

'How is it up there?'

'Quiet now but we're low on food and ammunition. Commandant Mallin sent me down with a dispatch.'

He nodded. 'And how was everyone at home when you left? How's Mam?' he asked with uncharacteristic softness.

'I couldn't tell her, Tom.'

'I was the same. Couldn't do it to her, like.'

'So I told David and warned him not to let her or Lily near the city.'

'Good girl.' He looked thoughtful. 'I've always been a bit distant. I didn't want ye to feel attached, you know, in case...'

Maggie wished they had spent more time together. 'You should write letters.'

'Ah, I'm not a man for notes. You tell them... if the worst comes to the worst.'

'It won't,' she said but they both knew the numbers.

He stood. 'I had better get back.'

She stood with him. 'Mind yourself, Tom.'

He tugged a holy medal out from under his shirt. 'Sure, haven't I my lucky charm?'

'I thought you *hated* the church!'

'I've never been one for the middleman. That doesn't mean I've a problem with the main man. Come here.' He put his arms around her and then ruffled her hair before pulling back. 'Be safe.'

'*You* be safe.'

He winked, then turned and strode towards his destiny.

'We're lucky to have him,' said one of the pair.

'That's the truth,' said the other.

Then they rose together as though synchronised.

'Best of luck, Tom Gilligan's sister.'

'And the best of luck to you too.'

James Connolly's dispatch was taking an age. Maggie rose and returned her tray. Then she approached the chef.

'Would you like a hand until I have to go?'

He looked surprised. 'Only if you want to lend one.'

She smiled. 'I'm restless.'

'Ah.' He smiled back. 'Aren't we all?'

But she was more than restless. She was desperate to talk to the prisoners. They were Royal Dublin Fusiliers. Perhaps they were up from the Curragh.

The chef handed her an apron and grimaced. 'How good are you at peeling potatoes?'

'I'll give it a try,' she said, recalling the time she had asked the same of Danny. Where was he? She longed to know. Not leading his men into an ambush, she prayed. How could she fire upon any British Army soldier now, knowing that Danny was one of them?

The prisoners, struggling with the vegetables, were glad to see her.

'Hard luck on getting caught,' she said quietly, to get on their side.

'Rather in here with these potatoes than out there firing upon our own people,' one of them said.

'I have a fiancé with the Royal Dublin Fusiliers.'

They looked automatically at her finger.

'Still waiting for the ring.' She smiled. 'Daniel Healy. Do you know him?'

'No, Miss.'

'He was in the Curragh, training to go back to the front.

Would you have any idea where in the city he might be?'

'Ah, he could be anywhere, Miss. I'm sorry. We're only just back from France ourselves on leave.'

'Some leave,' the other grumbled.

'Hopefully, you'll all see the wisdom of your ways and surrender. You haven't a hope in all fairness. It's not a country you're up against but an empire.'

On that sobering note, she heard her name being called. The dispatch was ready.

'Good luck,' she found herself wishing the enemy. This revolution was becoming stranger than she had ever imagined.

'And to you, Miss. I hope you find your man and happiness.'

Maggie tucked the tiny note into her boot, hurried into her coat and heaved a bag of food and medical supplies over her shoulder. She stood at the back entrance while James Connolly checked the street outside.

'Go, Maggie,' he ordered.

She shot out, walking fast. The further away she got, the safer she would be. Turning down a back street, she heard footsteps behind her. Heart racing, she darted into an alleyway. Still the footsteps. She glanced behind. It was a group of women in shawls, every one of them looking at her – and her bag. She did not know which she feared most, the British Army or the people she had risen for.

Head down, she took an immediate left onto a street leading to the quay. She quickened her step.

'Get her!' one of them called.

Hearing them break into a run, she reached for her revolver to warn them off but, before she could produce it, a section of British Army soldiers appeared around a corner, a hundred yards ahead.

She heard a woman's voice startlingly close behind her now.

'Hand me the bag and I won't shop you to the Brits,' she whispered.

Maggie knew that she would do it. So she turned and held out the bag.

A small, rat-like woman snatched it. Quickly, they all scurried away.

'Halt!' a soldier ordered.

They scurried faster.

A shot was fired.

They stopped and raised their arms. The bag fell to the ground.

The soldiers reached Maggie.

'Were these women harassing you, Miss?' an officer asked.

'Miss, me arse!' one of the women shouted. 'That slip of a thing is no more Red Cross than we are. In and out of the GPO with dispatches, she is. She's just come from there now.' She spat on the ground. 'Dishonouring our boys overseas, the lot of them!'

'You, there! Bring that bag here,' the officer ordered.

She looked at her partners in crime. They nodded. Grudgingly, she obeyed.

The officer snatched the bag from her. 'Now clear the street this minute or I shall order my men to open fire,' he said in an English accent.

The women looked at each other. Admitting defeat, finally, they turned and scurried away.

The officer approached Maggie. 'What is your business on the streets of Dublin?'

'I'm returning to Red Cross headquarters with supplies from the Rotunda.'

'Who would send a woman out on the streets in the middle of a revolution?'

'We did not imagine it was as bad as it is. And I insisted.'

He raised a dubious eyebrow. 'Tell me, why would those women lie?'

'They wanted my bag.'

He peered inside it. Maggie thanked the Lord that James Connolly had no ammunition to spare.

'Why does it contain food?' the officer demanded.

'Supplies are running low,' she said simply.

He squinted at her. 'You wouldn't be the first rebel to hide behind a Red Cross uniform.'

'I'm not a rebel and the longer you delay me here the more wounded soldiers who will suffer. We are understaffed-'

'Then let us accompany you to Dublin Castle where you can introduce us to your colleagues at the Red Cross. I'm sure they will be *delighted* to confirm your identity.'

'I don't need to be accompanied.'

'Oh, I think that you do,' he said. 'Guard her, men.'

Two soldiers flanked her.

'Are you *arresting* me?' she demanded.

He smiled. Then he turned to one of his unit. 'If she proves *not* to be Red Cross – as I suspect she shall – I want her searched. Is that clear?'

'Yes, Lieutenant.'

He ordered the unit to march.

How would she get rid of the note and revolver?

fifty-one

Daniel woke to the sound of distant gunfire. He was lying in a hospital bed, his shoulder bandaged. He thought only of Maggie. He had to get out, get to her. More shots in the distance and he was calling for a nurse.

'What is the time, nurse?' he asked when she came.

'Four in the afternoon.' She pressed a note into his hand. 'I'm Nurse Joyce,' she said loudly as though she wanted others to hear. 'You'll be having surgery shortly on your shoulder.' As she settled his blanket, she whispered, 'Don't open it now. Ask to go to the lavatory.' Aloud, she said, 'Let me fetch you some water. You must be parched.'

His eyes followed her to the door. Guarding it were two soldiers. Neither was particularly huge but both were armed and looking at him. He closed his eyes as if unable to do otherwise. From the bed beside him came the heavy breathing of sleep. Another man groaned. Daniel was sharing a ward with rebel prisoners.

Nurse Joyce returned with the water. Daniel drank with genuine thirst. He refused pain relief in favour of his senses and asked to use the lavatory. The nurse turned to the guards. One stood and left his post, arriving beside Daniel.

'Be quick about it,' he snapped as though irritated by having to get up.

Daniel moved slowly, exaggerating his disability. Leaving the room, he looked right and left as though crossing the road. In reality, he was searching for an escape route.

'Straight ahead,' the guard ordered.

Daniel shuffled forward.

'You're worse than the lot of them back there. Turncoat!'

Daniel kept walking.

'In a matter of days, my friend, you'll meet your maker. If I were you, I'd be working on what to tell Him.'

It was true – and also ironic – when Daniel was well enough, he would be tried for treason and inevitably shot.

At last, the lavatory door shut behind him, Daniel hurried to open the note. It had been wrapped around a key. He smiled as he read.

Healy, you old fool, you're a magnet for the bullets! This is a key for the door at the end of the corridor. It'll get you into the courtyard outside where I'll be waiting for you. Look out for a distraction. But be patient. It may take a while. Your old pal.

Daniel ate the note, slipped the key into his pocket, then remembered to piss.

'What took you so long?' the guard barked.

'Shoulder,' Daniel said.

'That is the *last* of your worries.'

They made their way back in silence, Daniel watching out for the door to the courtyard.

He heard her before he saw her.

'People are in need of my help! This is time-wasting!'

Then there she was, rounding a corner, under guard. She was alive, unharmed and as feisty as ever! He had an urge to laugh. Then their eyes met and her face was like an explosion of emotion – joy, relief, love. He could read it all. He wanted to run to her and take her in his arms. But they were both prisoners.

'Sergeant Healy!' she called out in an exasperated voice. 'This officer does not believe that I work here! Can you credit it?'

'I cannot.'

Nurse Joyce emerged from the ward. Only she could save Maggie.

'Nurse Joyce,' Daniel called. 'Please reassure this officer that Nurse Gilligan works here. There seems to be some misunderstanding.'

Nurse Joyce looked from person to person. At last, she turned her very beautiful face to the officer.

'Officer…?'

'Smyth.'

She smiled delightfully. 'Officer Smyth, Nurse Gilligan is one of our best nurses.'

'Oh. Well. Good,' he stumbled. 'Then I am returning her safely to you. Best not to send her – or anyone else – out on the streets again. It is a war zone out there.'

'Indeed. We were desperate, I'm afraid.'

The officer turned on his heels and marched up the corridor as if aware that female eyes were on him.

The guard turned to Nurse Joyce.

'What's going on? I've never seen this person before.'

'Lord God, O'Neill, but you're the height of suspicion. Nurse Gilligan has been working different shifts to you,' she said, laying a hand on his arm.

He seemed to float a little.

'We had better get you ready for surgery, Sergeant Healy,' Nurse Joyce said cheerfully. 'We must have you right as rain for your court martial.'

The colour drained from Maggie's face.

fifty-two

Maggie
Tuesday

She had to get him out, get him to safety. It was all Maggie could think of.

'Come,' Nurse Joyce said to her. 'Let me give you a full report on our patients.'

'Prisoners, Sabha, prisoners,' O'Neill corrected.

'Of course, Gregory. You're right, as always.' She produced another of her magical smiles.

'Gregory' escorted Daniel back to bed.

In the tiny nurses' station, Maggie whispered her thanks to Nurse Joyce. 'Why did you save me?'

She smiled. 'I saw the way you and Daniel looked at one another and knew immediately that you must be Maggie.'

'But how do you *know* us?'

'Through my good friend, Michael Hegarty.'

'Michael is *here*?'

'Michael is here. Keeping his head low.'

'I need to speak with him! I need his help to get Danny out!'

'Maggie, he is already planning an escape – but we need Danny as strong as he can be. Getting him through the castle gates is only the beginning. So we're waiting until after his surgery.'

'But the court martial!'

'They'll want him better for it.' She smiled. 'The great wisdom of the British Army.'

Maggie looked at her. 'Why are you doing this for us? Why are you risking your own safety?'

'Two good reasons, Maggie. Ireland and friendship.'

Maggie gripped her hand. 'Thank you.'

'Let's not get ahead of ourselves with the thanking,' smiled the calmest person Maggie had ever met. 'Let's get you both out of here and away. Then there'll be plenty of time for thanks.'

Daniel woke in a sweat. Maggie went to him and placed a cool hand on his.

'It's all right, Sergeant,' she said, professionally. 'You were having a nightmare. It often happens after an anaesthetic.'

He smiled. 'And then there you were. Nurse Gilligan,' he said quietly.

'Tomorrow, when you're stronger, we'll get you out of here,' she whispered.

He looked at her and shook his head.

She frowned.

'You'll only go back fighting,' he whispered. 'And I want you here. Safe.'

'And I want *you* alive.'

'What's going on over there?' One of the night guards was already on his way over.

Maggie turned to him. 'I've seen this before in men who have seen duty. It's a reliving. I'm helping to bring this patient back to the present.'

He nodded seriously as though he was a medical professional and they were conferring over a patient. His respect for her shone clear in his eyes. She would need that, she knew, when the time came. She watched him return to his post. Then she looked into Danny's eyes.

'I won't go back. I promise. When I saw you here, facing court martial, I knew: *you* come first, Danny, before all else.'

'Even Ireland?'

'Even Ireland.'

He closed his eyes as if in relief. When he opened them, he said, 'I have a key to the courtyard.'

'Why didn't you *say*?'

He smiled. 'You've been too busy talking.'

She wanted so badly to kiss him. 'Be ready. Tomorrow night we go. Now get some sleep. Do you want morphine?'

'I'm grand.'

'A small bit will help you sleep. And you need sleep, Danny, for what's ahead.'

He nodded then.

She rested her hand on his and he closed his eyes as though to better feel it.

Then she left.

Passing the guards, she stopped. 'I'm making this patient a cup of tea to settle him down. You'll have a cup?'

'Go on, so, twist my arm,' one said.

'Ah, well, if he's having one...' the other guard said.

And, just like that, she had bewitched them.

The following day, Maggie grew more and more tense. At any moment, they could come for Danny. And that would be it. There would be no escape.

'We have to get him out now,' she whispered to Sabha in the nurses' station.

'Tonight, under cover of darkness. Trust me, Maggie. Just tend to the wounded and put it from your mind.'

'How can I?'

'You're too jumpy. The guards will notice.'

Maggie nodded. She had never imagined that calm and patience would be necessary qualities for a revolution. And so she worked hard, used her first aid skills on new patients, prepared others for surgery under Sabha's instruction, and tended to the needs of others as they arose. And, as more and more men crammed into the Red Cross base, she feared for her comrades facing the full force of the British Army. She prayed for them all. She prayed especially for Tom and Patrick. She had hoped to find Patrick here, wounded and under arrest but there was no sign of him.

In the afternoon, she was changing the sheets of a man who had bled, when there was an almighty explosion. She looked automatically to the window. The ward had gone eerily silent.

'They wouldn't use artillery in the centre of a *city*, would they?' one man asked.

''Tis the Germans coming to our rescue!' a boy exclaimed, throwing back his covers.

'Pipe down,' one of the guards shouted. 'Anyone leaving his bed will be shot.'

The bombardment continued all afternoon, coming closer and closer. Even the guards began to look nervous.

Then wounded began to arrive.

'They're shelling Sackville Street! A gunboat has come up the Liffey and is firing on the GPO.'

'Ah, Jaysus,' whispered the boy who had hoped that the Germans had come.

Maggie feared for Tom, for James Connolly, for the lovely chef, for Pádraic Pearse reading to the men, for Michael Collins and for poor unmarried James Plunkett. She feared for the man with the rosary beads standing guard by the window and she feared for the comedy duo she had broken bread with. They would surely abandon the building. They would take to the streets, down back alleys. They would move through the houses, breaking through walls. They would not stay to be shelled. Surely.

'It's as if Ypres has come to Dublin.'

The wounded could not stop talking. It was the shock, Maggie knew, but it wasn't helping. She longed to be out there doing her bit for Ireland but her duty was here, now, with the man she loved. It had always been. How blind she had been. She looked at Daniel, his eyes on the window, as distressed for the people of Dublin as she was. How would they get him out? The challenge seemed suddenly overwhelming. She knew a way to get past the guards and out into the courtyard but what then? They would still be in the very heart of British military headquarters, surrounded by walls and gates and God knew how many – highly exercised – soldiers.

And then it was upon her, the time to act. She made two cups of tea. Into them she was pouring morphine when she heard someone approach from behind. She hurried the drug into her pocket, praying that she had not been seen.

'Jesus. Go easy on the morphine,' Sabha whispered. 'Or you'll do more than knock them out.'

Maggie closed her eyes in relief. Then she began to pile sugar into the tea to hide the taste.

'Cover for me while I go and get Michael,' Sabha added.

'Where is he anyway?'

She smiled. 'Camping out in the filing room pretending to work.' There was a fondness in her voice when she spoke of Michael.

Maggie watched her carefully when she asked, 'How do you two know each other?'

'Oh, he wandered down here when I was incredibly busy and made me laugh.'

'I knew it!' Maggie grinned.

'It wasn't the laughing, Maggie, that did it. It was the fact that he'd come into the heart of the city in the middle of a revolution to look for you and Daniel. Arrested or injured, he'd hoped you'd turn up here.' She smiled. 'But the laughing *did* help.'

'I'm so happy for you both.'

'It's far too soon for happiness, Maggie. Things are about to get dangerous.'

Maggie smiled. 'I can still be happy for you.'

The wait seemed to take forever. Then came the beautiful sound of a thud. Followed by another. Maggie and Sabha hurried into the ward. Already Daniel was up, helping himself to the guards' guns. Sabha ran to get Michael.

There were no embraces. Nothing was said. Michael hurried them to the door at the end of the corridor. Daniel produced the key. Outside, in a shadowy arch, Michael presented them with two British Army uniforms. Then he helped Daniel into his.

Inspecting them carefully, he straightened Maggie's hat.

'Go,' he urged.

'What about you and Sabha?' Maggie asked.

'If Sabha leaves her post, she'll fall under suspicion. She'll take a little morphine and become an innocent victim of treachery. I'll return to the filing room. We'll be grand. Go! Hurry! No! Wait! I almost forgot. The city is under curfew. Any civilians on the streets during darkness will be shot. If you get outside the Castle, remain as British Army soldiers. I know that it makes you rebel targets but it is the lesser of two evils.'

Maggie and Daniel quickly embraced him then turned. Maggie inhaled deeply. If any girl could be a soldier, it was she.

'Ready?' Daniel whispered.

'Ready,' she said firmly. Her heart had never beaten so fast.

Sounds of war echoed as they marched across the courtyard, arms swinging, backs erect. Two words got them through the most southerly gates. 'Reconnaissance Patrol.'

As they marched out onto Ship Street, Maggie imagined the guards waking or someone finding them asleep. She waited for the sounds of running, barked orders, shots. If only they could make it to the corner and out of sight.

It seemed an age away.

'Now we know how Red Hugh O'Donnell felt, escaping Dublin Castle,' Maggie whispered of her favourite rebel hero.

'Let's try to avoid amputation,' he whispered back.

She smiled. 'How can we be joking when, at any moment, we might be shot in the back – or the front, too, for that matter?'

'That, Maggie, is how you know an Irishman on the front-line.'

At last, they turned the corner. The street before them looked deserted but who knew what it hid? Anyone out now would be either a rebel or a British Army soldier; both constituted the enemy.

They kept in close to the houses, slipping into doorways at the slightest sound, standing backs to walls at every crossroads and peering up streets before dashing across, guns at the ready. And yet, despite shots that rang out all over the city, not a soul did they come across.

The sun was rising as they approached the canal. They stopped and looked at one another. Crossing it would take them away from military action. The act of doing so, however, would expose them terribly. For a few hundred yards there would be no cover whatsoever. And the canal lock itself was not one that warranted running across. And yet they had no choice. They could not remain out in the open for long.

Leaving the cobbled street leading onto the canal, they heard the sound of running. Daniel grabbed Maggie's hand and pulled her back into the nearest doorway. They heard the hurried footsteps of people giving chase, then a 'halt' followed by rifle fire. Their eyes found each other in the shadows.

They stayed put until long after silence had returned, then, cautiously, peered out. All was still. They could see no bodies, no blood, no sign of what they had heard. And they didn't go looking for it. Revolvers drawn, they raced on tiptoe to the canal. The water was like glass. No movement in the reeds. A pair of swans slept, their heads tucked under their wings. On the other side of the lock, the water fell smoothly like glossy hair.

They began to cross back-to-back, Maggie first, Daniel covering the rear. They were almost halfway across when, out of the silence, came the sound of horses' hooves clattering on cobblestones. Maggie and Daniel exchanged a glance. It was too far to run. And there was nowhere to hide. With a nod, they each lowered themselves onto a knee. Guns trained on the end of the street they'd just left, they faced what was to come.

Bursting from the shadows raced, a lone, galloping horse. Riderless, its eyes were rolled back in its head. The swans flew up and Maggie, startled, toppled backwards. She grabbed a rusty railing and stopped her fall.

'My heart!' she said.

'Are you all right?'

'No.'

He smiled. Then they helped each other up.

Across at last, they ran for cover.

fifty-three

Daniel
Thursday

Now that the sun was up, they discarded their military uniforms and weapons, hiding them deep in bushes.

'Where can we go?' Maggie asked. 'We can't put our families at risk. And they'll come looking for you at your home.'

Maggie was safe now. That was all that mattered. 'I'll ask my father to represent us in court.' Maggie would get a small sentence. He'd take his punishment.

She looked at him as though he had lost his mind. 'You want to *surrender*? Daniel, you face *execution*.'

'But with my father representing me...'

'What influence do you think an Irish civilian would have in a British military court? Why do you think the army shoots deserters? To deter others. You know better than anyone, rules are rules. I'm responsible for your desertion. I will *not* let you die for it. We're leaving Ireland together, this very day.'

He squinted at her. 'You would leave the country that you were prepared to die for?'

'For us I would. For The Healys.'

He held her to him. He inhaled the scent of her hair, the most beautiful scent in the world. When, at last, he pulled back, (and it pained him to do so), it was to admit the truth. 'I can't desert.'

'You would rather *die*?'

'I'll take my punishment.'

She raged suddenly. 'You have given the British enough of yourself. You owe them no more, not one more drop of sweat, not one more ounce of blood.'

How could she understand? He was not just deserting the army but the friends, the *brothers*, he had left behind on that hill in Gallipoli, MacDonald, Wilkin, Walkey...

'I have given up my fight, my dreams of a better Ireland, for us,' Maggie pleaded. 'I'm asking the same of you.'

He looked at her, standing there as fiery and passionate as the day he first saw her. The irony was, he had never *been* fighting for Ireland. It had all been for her.

She grew desperate. 'If you surrender, you're giving up on us. I'll do the same, Danny. I'll go back to fight.'

Her words jolted him. He could not let that happen. Everything he had done had been to avoid it. He thought of MacDonald, Wilkin, Walkey, Lecane. In his mind, he returned to the trenches. None of them had ever understood what they were doing over there in Gallipoli. If the roles were reversed, now, he would want them safe. And they would want the same for him. He did not doubt it. He closed his eyes and wished them well, every last one. And when he looked at Maggie, it was to say, 'You're right. It's time to put The Healys first.'

She flung herself at him.

'I love you, Maggie Gilligan.'

'Not as much as I love you.'

He wiped her tears away with a caress of thumbs. He kissed her forehead.

She took a deep breath. 'We'll sail to America where the British Army has no power.'

'America? But your family! You'd never see them again!'

'I want you alive, Daniel Healy. If it means going to America, we'll go to America.' She smiled. 'Anyway, you know what a great letter writer I am.'

But he did not smile. 'Even if I could ask that of you, I don't have enough for the passage.'

She frowned in concentration and then, finally, looked up. 'Perhaps your father....'

His hand went to his forehead. 'The law is his life, Maggie. I couldn't ask him to break it.'

'But British Military Law does not apply to him!'

'I couldn't ask him to break *any* law.'

'Then ask him for a loan! You don't have to tell him why! When we reach America we can work night and day to pay him back!'

He wracked his mind for another solution. But there was no other solution. No one else could help. And so, for Maggie, for The Healys, he nodded. He would – somehow – look into his father's eyes, as a deserter, and ask for a loan. He would lose that relationship again, this time forever.

Daniel did not know which of the servants he could trust, if any, should the British Army come to his home asking questions. Whatever happened, he did not want his father implicated. So he waited in the shade of a sycamore outside the house in the hope that his father would take his usual morning stroll.

At eight, the front door opened and he emerged in top hat and frock coat. He did not look up at the sky as usual. He looked down. He did not swing his cane, only planted it firmly as though poking the ground in anger. Daniel took a deep breath and emerged from the shadows.

'Father,' he said quietly.

'Daniel! Thank the Lord!'

Daniel looked about. 'Let us talk in the gazebo.'

A look of concern crossed his father's face. He said nothing, only hurried his son down the garden at the rear of the house.

Maggie stood as they entered the gazebo.

'Maggie?' he asked in surprise. He looked at Daniel for an explanation.

'I have left the British Army, Father.'

'You have *deserted*?'

'Only to come to my aid!' Maggie defended him.

Daniel widened his eyes at her in warning, willing her to say no more.

His father looked at her with concern. 'You got caught up in the insurrection?'

She lowered her gaze.

And, sharp as he was, his father knew. 'You are a *rebel*?' He spat the words.

'An idealist, Father.'

He turned to his son in rage. 'Have you not *seen* what idealists get up to when they are exercised? They have placed you in danger, Daniel, your men in danger, civilians in danger! Innocent bystanders have been killed, children...' He was growing puce. 'This, this... *madness*, will do *nothing* for Ireland except upset the apple cart and prevent us from getting Home Rule.'

Daniel looked at him in surprise. He had never imagined him a Home Ruler.

Mister Healy turned from Maggie. In a controlled voice, he asked, 'How can I help you, Daniel?'

Daniel bowed his head in shame. 'You think I should surrender,' he said quietly.

'No, in fact.'

Daniel looked up. 'No?'

His father sighed. 'Once, I might have. But I have learnt much in one and a half years. I have learnt that there *is* no good reason to die and that there *is* a limit to what a man should be expected to give for his country. You, Daniel, have given enough. You are a good person and I will continue to love you whatever you do, wherever you go. But I would suggest America.'

Daniel and Maggie exchanged a surprised glance.

Mister Healy removed his wallet from his inside pocket. 'I do not have enough on me for your passage but I do have enough for you to lie low until I can get to a bank. As you know, the city has shut down.'

'Thank you, Father,' Daniel said. 'I'll pay back every penny.' But it was not the money as much as his love that Daniel truly appreciated.

'Don't thank me, Daniel. This is my chance to put things right, though I can never truly make up for what I did to you.' He stood suddenly. 'Now! You'll need false papers! I take it you are travelling together?' he asked without looking at Maggie.

'Yes, Father,' Daniel said.

'You should stay at a hotel,' he thought aloud as he paced the gazebo. 'Away from the city.' He stopped walking and tapped his stick against his shoe. Suddenly, he pointed it at Daniel, his face alight. 'The Royal Marine in Kingstown! From there you could catch the mailboat to England, then on to America.'

Daniel looked at Maggie. She smiled through tears of relief.

'Let us go at once!' his father continued. 'The minute this rising is put down, arrests will be made. And trust me, they will show no leniency.'

Neither would they show *him* leniency if he were to be found harbouring a rebel and a deserter. He would be stripped of his beloved job and possibly jailed. 'Thank you, Father – for all you have done – but we'll make our own way to Kingstown.'

'You will do nothing of the sort. For a year and a half, I have searched for a way to make it up to you. Finally I have found one. By God, I'm going to see it through.'

They lay on the floor of the motorcar, behind the two front seats, under a rug. Daniel's father drove at his usual smooth pace. The humming, though, was new and Daniel wondered if it was nerves or excitement – his father loved a crisis. Daniel felt no such excitement. If his father were to lose his job, how would he feed the family? How would he face his friends? His life would be ruined.

Too soon to have reached their destination, the car drew to a silent halt.

'Can I help you, Sergeant?' Daniel's father asked in a cheerful tone.

'We're in search of rebels, sir.'

'My dear man, do I look like a rebel to you?' His laughter was hearty.

'Nevertheless, I must ask – where are you off to at this hour?'

'Well, my workplace has been overrun by insurrectionists. My routine has been disturbed. I am leaving this *wretched* city to take some air at Kingstown.'

'And you are traveling alone?'

Daniel lay very still, imagining a pair of eyes peering into the car.

'Let me ask you this, Sergeant. Do you know what it is like to have a wife that talks incessantly? And by incessantly, I mean, *non-stop*.'

'Can I see your papers, sir?'

'Certainly.'

There was rustling.

Daniel wondered how Maggie was faring.

'I wish that you had said that you were a lawman, Mister Healy.' The sergeant spoke apologetically. 'Lord knows what state the rebels will leave the Four Courts in,' he said as though they were suddenly on the same side.

'I'd rather not dwell upon it.'

Daniel had no doubt that his father had spoken the truth.

There was a pause, then the sound of his papers being returned.

'I'm sorry for detaining you, sir. I do hope you enjoy your breath of fresh air.'

Daniel expected his father to take off immediately.

'Any news on when this wretched uprising will end?' he heard him ask instead. The man had nerves of steel.

'Very soon, I suspect. They say that the rebel headquarters will fall imminently.'

'That is, *indeed*, good news. Thank you, Sergeant. I bid you good day.'

'Good day, sir. Drive with care. But stop for no one.'

The engine revved up and they were gliding forward, once more.

Under the rug, Daniel found Maggie's hand. Her dreams of a new Ireland were fading fast.

'I haven't lost my touch!' his father called jubilantly from the front. Then his voice changed as he warned them. 'Once in your hotel rooms, do not leave for any reason. I will find you the minute I have your papers and tickets.'

'Thank you, Father.'

'You will have to be patient. God knows how long it will take with the city as it is.'

fifty-four

Maggie

The soft piano music, the chatter and polite laughter in the hotel lobby all belied the fact that there was a revolution taking place only miles away. Lives were being lost for the greater good and no one cared. But Maggie was no one to talk. She herself had deserted the fight. Patrick had been right, after all. When the time had come to choose, she had not chosen her country.

The bellboy showed them to their separate rooms. As soon as he had left them, Daniel walked through the interconnecting door and took her in his arms.

'I love you,' he said.

She leant into him, surprised at how desperately she needed to hear it. She had done the right thing. Of course she had. A great tiredness came over her.

'I might lie down,' she said.

He looked deep into her eyes. 'Did you get any sleep, at all, over the last few days?'

She shook her head, unable to speak now, to think even.

'Come.' He helped her into bed and kissed her forehead. Then he locked the door to the corridor. 'I'll just be through here.' He showed her the interconnecting door one more time.

'Stay with me, Danny.' She did not want to part from him. Rather, she wanted to curl up in his arms and listen to the slow beating of his heart, her favourite heart in the world.

And so he stayed.

Maggie woke to a rising sun and no sign of Daniel. She leapt from the bed and hurried to his room. He was standing at an open window.

'Thank God,' she said.

He turned, smiled and came to her. He took her hands in his. 'How are you feeling?'

'How long have I slept? Is there any news of the insurrection?'

'It's Friday now, Maggie. And no. No news. I ordered a newspaper but there are none. It has affected everything, it seems.'

'Not this hotel,' she said bitterly.

He brought her to the window. 'The sea is still there. The sea that will carry us to safety.'

She closed her eyes and inhaled the briny air blowing in through the window. It smelled of hope and freedom. *Soon*, she told herself. *Soon, he will be out of danger.*

Looking down, she saw a mother arrive with a little girl. Maggie thought of her family. She longed to let them know that she was safe. She longed to say goodbye. But she could not trust a telegram and could not leave the room.

By Sunday afternoon, she was going out of her mind, pacing both rooms. She had just marched into Daniel's again when there was a sharp rap on his door. They looked at each other.

'Go to your room,' he whispered. 'Stay there until I come for you.'

She hurried inside and closed the door. She put her ear to it but could hear nothing. Moments passed and still no sound. She inched the door open. Then she was bursting through it.

'Michael!'

He looked grave. 'It's over! The rebels have ordered an unconditional ceasefire.'

She stopped in her tracks. 'No. It can't be. They wouldn't-'

'And yet they have.'

Daniel hurried to her with a chair. She sank into it as her legs gave way.

'You must leave on the first ship!' Michael urged. 'People are being rounded up in their thousands, not alone revolutionaries but those whose homes were commandeered by them, members of Sinn Fein, anyone at all that looks at a soldier sideways. They're arresting first, asking questions after. They've all but taken out the hounds. I saw them stop a priest! No one is safe. You must get away at once.'

'We're awaiting false identity papers,' Daniel said, looking at Maggie.

'You don't have that luxury. For all we know, they could already be going door-to-door in every hotel in Dublin. Take my papers. Use my mask.'

'What about you?' Daniel asked him. 'What will you use?'

He smiled. 'My face. They won't ask for papers once they see it.'

'We still need papers for Maggie.'

'No, Danny,' she said. 'You go. I'll follow when my papers are ready.' She wondered if Mister Healy would bother with her documentation once his son was safe. He might even turn her in. Well, it was a risk she was prepared to take.

But Daniel stood firm. 'I'm not going without you.'

'You face execution! I want you on the first boat.'

'I'm waiting.'

Michael surprised her then. 'You're better together. You can provide each other with alibis. And I've given those alibis some thought. I think that you, Maggie, should be a governess travelling to England to take up a position with a good Catholic family. You, Michael Benjamin Hegarty, should be her cousin, escorting her there to ensure her safe passage during these troubled times.'

Daniel looked at Maggie.

'It's good,' she said.

Michael turned to Danny. 'I called to your home and spoke with your father. He said that you're bound for America.'

'Does he agree that we should leave immediately?'

'We spoke before news broke of the surrender. I'll return and tell him we only need papers for Maggie now. It might speed things up.'

'Thank you, Michael,' they said together.

'Would you do me the greatest favour, Mick?' Maggie asked. 'Would you visit my mother and let her know that I'm safe and where I am? I'd love, more than anything, to say goodbye.'

He nodded, a softness in his eyes. 'Of course.'

'Make sure that you're not followed!' she added.

He smiled. 'You underestimate me.'

'I would never. Who got us out of Dublin Castle? I will never forget that as long as I live.' She regarded him with such fondness and admiration. 'How we'll miss you.'

He raised his eyebrows. 'You may not have to. If Sabha is as keen on adventure as she seems to be, we may follow you out.' He looked so happy that the mask seemed to melt away.

'I told you that you'd make someone laugh!' Maggie said, delighted.

'And I didn't believe you. As usual, I was wrong.' He winked. 'Now, I'd better go.'

'Thank you, Mick, for everything,' Daniel said.

'Thank me when we're all in New York.'

And there it was suddenly, a dream for Maggie to cling to. She threw her arms around him and wished him Godspeed. But as she pulled back, her face darkened. 'Is the city very bad?'

'Ah,' he said with regret. 'It's as though the Great War itself has passed through Sackville Street. Entire buildings have been turned to rubble. The GPO is a blackened shell, smoking still.'

'Is there any news of James Connolly, the countess, Patrick Shanahan, Michael Mallin, any of the leaders?' she asked, knowing that it was only they that would be spoken about, not the ordinary men, women and children who had risked everything for their country. But, then, the leaders were ordinary people too.

'I don't know. It's chaos out there.'

She longed for news of her brother and friend. If they were alive – and she *prayed* that they were – they would be raging at the thought of a ceasefire. They would have wanted to fight to the death. Not give up. Never give up. She was surprised that James Connolly had. But then she did not know the circumstances. She sighed deeply.

'All for nothing,' she whispered. The cycle of poverty would continue. Life in the tenements would go unchanged. Working conditions would remain poor and workers underpaid. There was no one to change it now. They had given it their all and failed.

'I will bring as much news as I can when I return,' Michael promised. 'I'm sorry, Maggie, that it has ended like this.'

She forced a smile, not trusting herself to speak.

Michael hurried away.

Then, with Daniel's arms about her, Maggie cried for dreams that would never be realised and guilt that she had not, after all, done her bit.

Then, they were there, her little family standing in the corridor – everyone except for Tom. Emotion flooded Maggie. She hurried them inside where all four fell into one embrace. Maggie's heart ached with a loneliness that had already begun.

'Any news of Tom?' she and her mother asked at the same time, each as desperate as the other.

Both shook their heads.

''Tis a lovely room,' Lily said from the window. 'Look at the pretty lamps all down the pier. 'Tis like a fairytale.'

Maggie smiled at her.

'You must move quickly to get away,' David urged.

Their mother fetched her purse.

'No, Mam, we're grand,' Maggie insisted.

'It's not much, Maggie, but you don't know how happy I am to be able to give it to you. I feared that we'd lost you.'

'I'm sorry for the worry.'

'Aren't you here?' she said brightly. 'Now how are you fixed to get away?'

'Danny's father is arranging false papers and our passage to America.'

'America!' Lily exclaimed.

The word had the opposite effect on their mother who looked at Maggie sadly.

'How long will that take?' David asked urgently.

'That's the problem,' Maggie said. 'Danny can use Michael's papers but we have to wait for ones for me.'

Lily turned from the window. 'Use mine!' she said simply.

'You were *listening,* over there?' their mother exclaimed.

'I'm forever listening, Mammy.' She looked at Maggie. 'Use my papers.'

Maggie went to her sister and lifted her up. She kissed her cheek. 'If we were the same age, I'd take you up on it, Lil.'

'There's ten years between us, Maggie, that only means slipping in a one in front of the seven.'

Everyone stared at her.

She shrugged. "Tis simple.'

Maggie, David and their mother exchanged a glance. Then a smile.

Maggie swirled Lily around. 'Where did we get you?'

'At the food kitchen,' she said simply.

'Wasn't that the luckiest day of my life?' Maggie said.

There was a rap at the door.

Eyes wide, Maggie looked at her mother.

'It's only the trunks,' she reassured. 'I asked them to be sent up.'

'Trunks?'

'You don't think I'd let you away without your things?' She turned and went to answer the door.

'Is America very far away?' Lily asked, doubtful for the first time.

'It's not forever, Lil,' she said and felt guilty for the lie. If they got away they could never return home. This was Maggie's last time with her family. She pulled Lily close, trying not to cry.

'Now, let's hope I've not forgotten anything,' their mother said looking up from the trunk she had begun to open. 'Ah, there it is!' she exclaimed, reaching for a small box. From it, she lifted a gold locket and chain, which she presented to Maggie.

Maggie assumed that it would contain a picture of the family she was leaving behind. But when she opened it, it was her father's face that she saw. Her eyes welled.

'It's you I'd like the picture of,' Maggie said to her mother. It was she, after all, who had raised them, who had taken Lily in, and who had let Maggie chase dreams that might have killed her. Maggie's father had left her with a legacy that had demanded too much – of all of them.

Her mother touched her heart. 'I'll send you one to New York.'

'And send me news of Tom.'

Her mother nodded, her eyes glistening with unshed tears.

'First, we must get you onto that boat,' David said.

fifty-five

Daniel
Wednesday, 3rd May, 1916

'What's your name?' Daniel asked Maggie.

'Lily Murphy.'

'Date of birth?'

She knew it all – the date and place of birth, the name of the family she was to work for in England, the address. She grilled Daniel in return, though it was no challenge for him; he knew everything there was to know about Michael Benjamin Hegarty.

They embraced, took deep breaths and opened the door.

Out on the corridor, Daniel linked Maggie's arm. They would walk out of the hotel and board the boat at the nearby pier. Daniel's father had taken care of the hotel bill in advance. There was no reason to stop. No reason to get involved with anyone. Only go to the boat and leave.

At the top of the stairs, two gentlemen were engaged in an animated conversation. Their words floated down the corridor.

'I know they were fools to rise but executing men who have surrendered is an outrage!' one said.

Maggie stopped. She turned to Daniel, eyes wide. She stared at the men.

'No stopping,' Daniel quietly urged. 'Let us get to the boat.'

She slipped her arm from his and was gone. He strode after her, his heart racing.

'Pardon me. I could not help but overhear. *Who* is being executed?' She sounded shrill.

The gentlemen looked at her, then at the mask on Daniel's face. They seemed at a loss for words. Daniel lifted his hat, his calm belying his concern for Maggie, who was now repeating the question.

The men looked at her uncomfortably. 'I'm sorry but this is no talk for the ears of a lady.'

'Please. I must insist.'

They hesitated.

'Please,' she said gently.

One of the men gave in. 'Three of the rebel leaders. Pádraic Pearse, Tomás MacDonagh and Thomas Clarke have been sentenced to death for their part in the rising.'

Maggie's face blanched.

'Let us return to the room a moment,' Daniel said, linking her arm once more. 'We have time.'

She smiled at him. 'I am quite well, Daniel.'

'Perhaps a chair,' one of the men suggested.

'Not at all,' Maggie said brightly. 'Daniel, we have a boat to catch.'

And as she propelled him towards the stairs, Daniel sensed with growing alarm that this shock could unravel them. If they were to be stopped and questioned while boarding the ship – as they more than likely would be – how would Maggie bear up? She had already slipped up by calling him Daniel.

The boy who had offered to carry their luggage made a valiant effort not to gawk at the mask. He failed. And when Daniel smiled reassurance, he dropped the trunks and made off as though he'd been bitten. Daniel feared that the mask, too, had been a mistake, drawing attention to them.

An older boy with knowing eyes approached. Without a

word, he lifted the trunks and began to stride with them towards the Carlisle Pier. His confidence boosted Daniel's. He followed, limping as Michael did, eyes scanning for trouble. Ahead of them, the RMS Leinster loomed into view. They kept their eyes on it, looking neither right nor left, engaging with no one, simply doing all that they had planned.

Soon the ship was no more than a hundred feet away and, to Daniel's great relief, there were no uniformed men checking papers.

They were almost there! Almost away!

'Halt!' A G-man stepped in front of the chap walking ahead of them, blocking his path.

On his arm, Daniel felt Maggie tense. Then he himself almost collapsed. Arriving beside the G-man was a uniformed officer of the Dublin Metropolitan Police, not any officer but Michael's father. Daniel tried to steer Maggie around the three men but Michael's father glanced his way. The glance became a stare.

'Michael? *Daniel?*' he asked in confusion.

'Daniel,' he replied quietly so as not to alert the G-man.

'Papers,' Michael's father demanded coldly, eyeing him with suspicion.

As he handed over the papers, Daniel looked into the man's eyes imploring his help or, at least, his understanding that he was in trouble. For a moment, they stood looking at each other, the lawbreaker and the lawman. Then Michael's father looked down at the papers.

Suddenly, the chap under original suspicion bolted off like a fox. The G-man pulled a gun but such was the crowd he did not shoot. He took off in pursuit. Michael's father looked at Daniel for the longest moment, then shoved the papers back at him and raced after the G-man.

Daniel urged Maggie forward. Boarding in haste, they did not look back. At length, they reached their cabin. The boy who had carried their luggage looked at Daniel for a tip. His face brightened when he saw the size of it.

'Good luck,' he said, as though he knew.

'And to you,' Daniel replied.

Inside the cabin, Daniel locked the door and leaned against it. He closed his eyes. 'Jesus.'

'I thought we were done for,' Maggie said, sinking onto one of the tiny beds. 'Why do you think he let us away?'

Daniel breathed deeply as his body recovered. 'I don't know. Perhaps he, too, has had enough of fighting. Or maybe it's that he's known me all my life. Or perhaps he had two seconds to decide and went after the rebel before the deserter. Thankfully, we'll never know.'

'I can't stop thinking about poor Pádraic Pearse, the gentlest of men. You should have seen him in the GPO, Danny, encouraging the men, thanking everyone for doing their duty. I don't think he even picked up a gun.' Her eyes watered.

Daniel went to her but already she was up, pacing the tiny cabin.

'What of the other leaders – James Connolly, Michael Mallin, Madame? Are they all done for? What of poor, failing Joseph Plunkett? Will they execute him, too, with his consumption? Will he never get to marry now?' She looked at him, eyes wide. 'What of Patrick, Tom, Con Colbert? They didn't sign the Proclamation but they were important. Dear God, Danny.'

There was nothing he could say.

And still she paced. 'If they'd died *fighting* and we had *won*, it would be different now. But *this*?'

A sudden pounding shook the cabin door.

They exchanged a panicked glance. Daniel had always known that he faced death. He had never imagined it for Maggie.

'Stay here,' he said and went to the door.

The air left his lungs when he saw whom it was. Michael's father seemed taller than ever. Daniel had forgotten that the policeman had time on his side, time to get the rebel and come back for the deserter. He would give himself up quickly before suspicion fell on Maggie. He nodded and extended his arms, wrists together. But the policeman only took a hold of one hand.

He shook it firmly. Daniel stared in surprise. The giant of a man from the country had tears in his eyes.

'I never got a chance to thank you for saving my son's life, for bringing him home to us.'

Emotion swamped Daniel as he remembered all that had happened, how close to death he and Michael had come, so many times. And how, in truth, they had saved each other.

The policeman looked past Daniel to Maggie.

Daniel closed his eyes and prayed.

'And I never thanked you, either, Maggie Gilligan, for being a friend to Michael when he most needed one. He was very low. We worried....' His voice trailed off.

Maggie hurried over and took his hands warmly in hers. 'He has found love now and he is happy.'

His smile was like a sunrise. 'Go with God, the pair of you. And may He be good to you.'

Maggie threw her arms around him.

He laughed in surprise. 'I had better go or I'll end up in England.'

'Thank you, Mister Hegarty,' Daniel said. And when Maggie finally let the man go, he closed the door.

This time, they both leaned against it.

Epilogue

Two months later

Maggie looked at the envelope in her hand and wondered. When she had seen the stationery and handwriting she had assumed that the letter was for Daniel. Then she noticed that it had been addressed to her. What could Daniel's father want? With a sense of dread, she opened the envelope.

Dear Maggie

I would like to offer a sincere apology for the way I addressed you, the last time we met. At the time, I saw only the destruction and danger that the insurrection had plunged Daniel and others into. Since then, I have been appalled, no, outraged by the fate of your leaders. Their execution following surrender was the very worst violation of human rights. It has opened my eyes as to why you rose against a regime as oppressive as this. I was so cosy in Ireland's present that I let myself forget her past. The rising has forced me – and others – to remember who we are at the core: Irish.

The tide of opinion has turned. Your leaders have become martyrs. Ireland is changing. I am confident that, one day, you and Daniel shall return freely to a new republic. I understand, now, that my son is a lucky man to have you. You stood by your beliefs in the face of certain death.

I hope that you receive this letter before your wedding day for I have a proposition. If you are in agreement, it would be my honour, as a wedding gift, to fund you to attend university. It strikes me that you are a person who might wish to be afforded this opportunity in the new land you find yourself in. I hope I am not being presumptuous.

I have met with your wonderful mother and sweetest *sister. Your brother, David, is a very impressive young man. We are going to have a little celebration for you, here in Ireland, on your big day.*

Please forgive an argumentative and explosive old man.

With the greatest respect, your future father-in-law,

James Healy

Maggie, hand on heart, glanced up at the sound of approaching footsteps. When she saw Daniel she began to wave frantically.

'Get out! Get out! You're not meant to see me on our wedding day!'

He smiled. 'Then how can I marry you?'

She laughed. '*Go*! No! *Wait*! Come back! Read this letter. It's from your father.'

'And you opened it?' he asked in surprise.

'Seeing as it was addressed to me, I did.' She handed it to him.

As he read, a smile began to form. At last, he looked up and reached for her. He enfolded her in his arms. 'I am a lucky man to have you, it seems.'

'It does.'

And as she laid her head against his chest, she thought of James Connolly, Michael Mallin, Con Colbert, Pádraic Pearse and Joseph Plunkett who had been amongst the sixteen rebels executed.

'It wasn't for nothing,' she said, with both sorrow and hope. 'We have changed the mindset of the people. It is not the end but the beginning. A beginning for others, though.' She smiled at Danny.

She had cried enough tears. She had cried for Patrick who had died fighting for his country. It was a noble way to go but the fact remained: he was no more. She had cried for James Connolly who had been executed strapped to a chair, unable to stand due to bullet wounds he had received over a week earlier. It was like losing her father all over again. She had cried for Joseph Plunkett who had married his love the night before he was executed. That, in particular, had broken Maggie's heart. She had cried in relief for Tom who had been wounded, captured and interned in a prison in England. Madame didn't need her tears, having escaped execution by pleading leniency on account of being a woman. Madame aside, there had been a lot of tears.

'Will you take him up on his offer?' Danny asked.

Maggie looked at him. His father was putting him through medical school. She knew how happy that made him. And so she smiled. 'Well, I *am* curious to learn more about this wonderful thing called democracy.'

She would leave the fighting to others now. She had given enough of herself. She had caused enough worry. She would make a difference the way her mother did – by doing the best for those she loved. One day, she and Daniel might return home but for now her life was here with him. If his dreams came true, he would become a plastic surgeon specialising in war wounds; he already had his first patient lined up.

'Now you truly *must* go,' Maggie insisted. 'Sabha is coming to help me get ready.'

He stole a quick kiss and ran.

The sound of her own laughter still surprised her. There would be more of it, she promised.

Outside the church, Sabha made some last minute adjustments to Maggie's dress, a dress that could not have been more precious to Maggie, given that her mam and sister had crafted it, with 'every stitch filled with love', as Lily had written.

'You look beautiful,' Sabha said.

'No, you do,' Maggie argued.

She smiled. 'We can both look beautiful, Maggie.'

'That is true.' How grateful she was for their friendship, she who had once imagined herself incapable of friendship.

'Better not keep them waiting,' Sabha said.

Maggie took a deep breath. She could not explain her nerves. She had never been more certain of anything.

Sabha hugged her. 'Good luck, my dear.'

Walking into the shadow of the church, a thought struck Maggie. How strange it was that she who had never planned to marry was about to walk up the aisle before any of the girls at school.

And then there he was, Daniel Healy, standing waiting at the top of the church in his new and adorable suit, the boy who had become a man in countries she had never known, the boy who had once told her that she did not have a monopoly on caring, the boy who had stayed when she had tried to make him leave. The boy she loved with all her heart.

His smile was like honey pouring into her heart. She hoped that her smile had the same effect on him. She walked towards him, incredulous that this day had truly come, that she and Danny would make it to the altar. Even now, she half-expected a thunderbolt to crash through the roof of the church and strike them dead, yes, both of them, a forked thunderbolt that selected only them. She had to cover her mouth to keep her laughter in. How giddy she felt suddenly.

She had waited so long for this and now she couldn't wait, couldn't wait, couldn't wait to be his wife, to have the ring on her finger and his mouth on hers.

Unbelievably, there was no thunderbolt – just words following words and finally a dream come true. And then, somehow, they were holding hands and running down the steps of the church.

They turned to each other.

He grinned. 'Hello, Missus Daniel Healy.'

'Hello, Mister Daniel Healy.' She jumped up into his arms, wrapping her legs around his waist – wedding dress, veil and all.

Michael and Sabha covered them in confetti. And laughter.

Today was about The Healys. Not about Ireland. Ireland's stories were forever sad. And there was no room for sadness on this day. Only new beginnings.

THE END

acknowledgements

Special thanks to the wonderful (and fellow Corkonian) Philip Lecane, my go-to man for all things military. Thanks also to Mike Lee, Jonathan Maguire and Paul O'Brien who were invaluable sources of historical information.

Thank you to Katie Green for amazing editing and Rachel Lawston for the gorgeous cover.

So grateful for the wise counsel of: Maruja Bogaard, Ellen Barnes, Amanda Byrne, Nikki Concannon, Maria Duffy, Roisin Duffy, Eoin Duffy, Eleanor Fitzsimons, Valerie Judge, Claire Hennessy, Catherine Ryan Howard, Marieke Nijkamp, Claire Rudd, Dana Sadan, Barbara Scully, Jane Travers and Laura Tyrrell. There is nothing better than honest friends!

Grateful thanks for authorly support to Kate Beaufoy, Eleanor Fitzsimons, Hazel Gaynor and Kate Kerrigan. Huge respect, ladies. Huge.

Muchas gracias to Emily Lyons for delicious cover photography and the very gorgeous Aimee Concannon for modelling.

Heartfelt gratitude to my readers, especially those who take time to share their love of my books. So appreciated. A very big thank you to reviewers and bloggers, in particular Book Connectors, who play such a major role in supporting authors. Love you.

Huge love and gratitude, as always, to Joe, Aimee and Alex for being there and being great.

66625374R00224

Made in the USA
Charleston, SC
25 January 2017